Kids

'By the way,' he said, 'they're not delinquents.'

'Who? The kids?'

'Yes. Most of them aren't anyhow.'

'So what – who, rather, are they, then?'

'Well there's no short answer to that. They come in all sizes and flavours. They're with us for all sorts of reasons. Their own safety, protection, and—'

'Child battering?'

'Sometimes. Too often. But often just bereavement – orphans with no living next of kin. Illegitimate kids, whose one parent's given up on them. Illegitimate kids who didn't get aborted in time and whose mother's decided she doesn't want to know. Not surprising as she's most likely fifteen – although later she may change her mind and cause all kinds of static for half a Social Services Department and a couple of utterly admirable foster parents . . . In most of our cases we're a sort of wayside pull-in *en route* to fostering.'

'Doesn't that mean you end up as a sort of bumbledom wastebin?'

'Bull's-eye. You've got it in one. My biggest grouse. If a kid's in trouble send the poor blighter along to Kingston House. "They'll know how to cope." '

ANNE DAVID

Kids

MAGNUM BOOKS
Methuen Paperbacks Ltd

A Magnum Book

KIDS

ISBN 0 417 03100 9

First published in Great Britain 1979
by Magnum Books

Copyright © 1978 by Anthony Fowles

Magnum Books are published
by Methuen Paperbacks Ltd
11 New Fetter Lane, London EC4P 4EE

Made and printed in Great Britain
by Hazell Watson & Viney Ltd
Aylesbury, Bucks

Chapter One

EARLY EVENING SUNSHINE slanted gently down through the well-leafed trees that, mature and frequent, gave Albany Road much of its summer character of a grander, more spacious, more gracious era. And more cruel, Chris Langley thought. He looked at the handsome, four-square Victorian houses – most with three or four bells on their front doors now – and thought not of the strawberry teas and parasols on the lawn but of the tweeny struggling upstairs from the cellar at six-thirty in the morning with a bucket of coal too heavy for her to carry, three grates to clear out, three fires to make and light and no noise to be heard in the doing thereof. And after a night suffering the young master, as like as not!

He grinned at his exaggeration. He was, he recognised, in a bad mood. As always, he brought his sense of professional discipline to bear on dealing with it. The four teenage boys jiving and cross-talking their loose-limbed way along the pavement with him must be given no idea that he was not the Rock of Gibraltar twenty-four hours a day. But, oh God, just once to have the luxury of blowing his stack again!

It was not so much anger as a bitter, resigned frustration that was on him. Like so much it had arisen from one of those 'little things' that involve so depthless much. It being Saturday and all quiet on the Kingston front, he had taken four of the eldest lads around the corner to watch the Wanderers for a couple of hours. A top-class London club side with a very pretty tree-lined, Victorian-pavilioned ground, they always managed to capture an older, romantic spirit of cricket for him, an age of run-stealers flickering to and fro across the background of a golden past. For all the plethora of trendy modern bats designed to advertise themselves in television close-ups, he could still lose himself remembering how it had felt pulling on the wicket-keeper's gloves at college and standing up to Bryant who bowled leg-breaks bloody close to medium . . . But not today. Today he'd come away with this metallically distinct and quite literal nasty taste still in his mouth.

It hadn't just been pleasure today. He'd slipped away from the four boys for a while to have a word with the Club Secretary, beer-faced and ex-military to a clichéd fault behind the inevitable red and gold diagonally striped tie; to have a word on behalf of Gary. Gary was the tallest of the four cross-talking teenagers walking homewards up the dusty street. Big for his age at fifteen, gangling, you would have said he was unco-ordinated until you saw him swoop down low to cut a ball off in the covers. All the same the energy and speed of his bowling run up was still too raw, too blurred in the final delivery stride to do his effort justice. He needed more expert coaching than Chris could deliver. Perhaps the club. . . .

The Secretary had been sympathetic, enthusiastic even. Yes, they ran a Colt side that was not faring too well of late: a bit of pace was what their bowling could do with. Which one was he? Chris had pointed across to where Gary, still for once, was sitting intently watching the game close to the sight-screen. In that moment the hope had died. Beaumont had seen the jeans, the garish sweater, the black skin and at once been warily, so utterly, polite. It was too late, of course, to disturb the side this season, not fair on the others; it was a Committee decision, naturally, membership; they would be meeting again in about a month. . . . Smiling, not betraying the smallest negative emotion, Chris had thanked him for his time and interest. But the muted rage had been smouldering inside him. The possibility that, with the galaxy of famous West Indian pacebowlers there to inspire him, Gary could have worked towards acquiring a level of excellence, a literal control of himself, to balance the rootless resentments festering inside him, had been postponed. Perhaps forever. No, not forever. There were other clubs. Other coaching schemes. But as he'd made his own way back to the sight-screen, Chris had felt the tiredness of a man trying to paint the Forth Bridge single-handedly weigh upon his shoulders, seep into the back of his mind.

He still felt tired as in the dusty, colour-fading sunlight they turned into the entrance of Kingston House. An old tennis ball lay near the edge of the balding, gravelled driveway. Predictably Gary had pounced upon it and, a scrum half suddenly, flipped a reverse pass accurately at David.

'Wing it! Wing it!' Kevin yelled.

David flicked the ball across to him and catching it he jinked his way past imaginary tacklers out on to the beat-up patch of lawn in front of the house.

'On the ground!'

The three converted to soccer. Only Howard, shackled by the presence of iron braces the length of his lower right leg continued up the path. His already adult face had abruptly become studiously unaware, it seemed, of his surroundings. Then came the moment that rescued Chris Langley's afternoon. Without warning Kevin had flicked the ball up with his toe and caught it in his hand to throw it hard but unerringly straight at Howard. The huge hands had no difficulty in swallowing up the ball, the powerful arms in lobbing it high, high, into the air. A year ago Howard would have thrown it away in fury at being patronised, Chris thought, but Kevin had had a sense that time had gone. And the class to involve him. Without fuss, without making a big deal out of it all.

The ball was hurtling down. Gary, an out-fielder now, was underneath it. A split-second before the ball was in his long, slim hands Kevin had tackled him hard and low and to the ground. The ball smacked hard on Kevin's back as both of them went over but Chris had eyes only for the sudden flash of white in Gary's eye, the flailing out of his unpinned arm.

'Hey, you two!' Chris called. 'Knock it off! At once! Kevin! What did you do that for?'

The two boys had scrambled sullenly to their feet.

'Don't know, sir.'

Chris did. The sight of Gary poised like that must have

7

been irresistible. Once upon a student time, he would have probably pulled the same stunt.

'I didn't mean to hurt him, sir. It was just a joke.'

'A dangerous one. This isn't the rugby season. He wasn't expecting it. When you get hit and you're not expecting it, that's when you get hurt.'

'I'm not hurt, sir. But he bloody well will be when—'

'That's enough, Gary! Now don't spoil a pleasant afternoon away from the funny farm, here. Either of you!'

He looked hard at Kevin. Then so that the boy would not feel too pushed around, stooped to pick up the ball.

'Sorry, sir,' Kevin said. 'Sorry, Gary. Was a bit bleeding stupid.'

Swearing had helped him save face while apologising. Chris let it ride. And the earlier gesture of involving Howard had earned him an advance reprieve.

'O.K. We'll forget it,' he said. 'Now get on it and get cleaned up for supper. You, too, David. The last thing I need now is Mrs Hughes moaning on at me about her lost weekends. Howard!'

He tossed the ball casually to Howard again but as he did so gave him a quick look. Somehow without changing his expression, the seventeen-year-old conveyed the message had been received and understood. He'd keep an eye on them.

'Off you go, then.'

Three of the boys ran, and one limped, up towards the house. Chris Langley stayed behind a moment. No doubt it was the sunlight, he thought, invitingly warm and mellow on the old grey-yellow London brick, but this was the first time in a long time he'd taken a moment to step back and, monarch of all he surveyed, look at his empire. It's not much, he joked to himself, but we call it home. . . .

It was austere rather than handsome most of the time. Early Victorian with bits built on later on, Kingston House possessed four storeys in all and, if you took the wide front door as the central line, tended to divide itself into two visual halves. To the left as he looked at it there was an imposing run of bay windows up from the sub-basement to the second floor. They weren't curved – hence a loss of style – but evolved by two angled projections being joined straight across. Still, they made the Common Room and the two bedrooms above, the most pleasantly proportioned rooms in the whole house. To the right of the front door, the house's facade was dead straight. The big sash windows were as undeviatingly rectangular as if the first owners of the house – tea merchants, he had been told – could have brooked nothing devious. The ground floor on the right had once been a great single salon running thirty paces from the front into a back conservatory. But it had long since been sub-divided. It was in one resulting semi-cubbyhole that he had his office. And it was on one sub-divided floor that he had his private dwelling. He, Pat and Robert lived 'over the shop' in the three-bedroomed apartment spread the length of the top floor.

It doesn't look bad in this light, he thought musingly as once again his thoughts turned to idyllic Victorian house-parties, but I must try and finally get down to doing something about those flower-beds. Alert, capable, never quite relaxed, he stood enjoying the rare luxury of a few moments alone.

He was thirty-six. At first glance anyone staring back at him from the house would have thought him younger. His medium build was broad-shouldered and lean-bellied and his jeans and blue American work shirt enhanced the impression this gave of youthfulness. So did his open, rather fine-boned, clean-shaven face, his light brown, long but straight and parted hair. Seen quickly he had a sort of classic Battle of Britain Englishness to his neat looks. Closer acquaintanceship, however, must needs have qualified that hint and revealed him as too old to fly a combat plane. His light-coloured hair, for instance, naturally concealed its forerunner contingent of grey as yet but it was beginning to recede from where his parting met his forehead with a greater obviousness. That high, rounded forehead showed three faint but constant horizontal furrows. The green-blue eyes needed as yet no glasses but a fine mesh of lines around them were waiting to leap out to sharper

9

definition whenever he smiled or frowned. If the nose was classical public school (he'd attended Raynes Park Grammar but appearances lie), two permanent creases running in a diagonal curve down from it to either side of his wide mouth suggested that he must have done a little growing-up out in the world. A man glancing at Chris Langley might have thought him a bit anonymous, a bit of a lightweight. A woman would have let her eyes rest on him longer and felt chagrin, possibly, at her certain intuition he'd be married. Otherwise she would have found the hint of determination implicit in his good looks as sexually interesting as the sense he gave of a slight permanent sadness, a sense of always being on the point of sighing.

Quietly, unconsciously, he sighed now. The warm evening breeze had stiffened, chilly for a moment, and recalled him to himself. His brief island in time was over. He must step back into the on-duty flow of his workaday life. More specifically, round to the back of the house.

Like the front it wasn't out of *Homes and Gardens*. It could still boast a beautifully mellow rear brick wall but the lawn where the tea merchant might once have genteelly purveyed his own wares to his family was a trampled flat, more-earth-than-grass, play area. Where his gardener might once have planted neat vegetable rows now stood the bare bones of an adventure playground – a climbing frame, a double swing, a concrete crawl-through tube heaped high with earth and turf. One last recalcitrant tiny – Peggy, wasn't it – was hiding in it now half-wetting herself with glee as Bill Hutton shepherded the other young ones in through the french windows. Chris frowned – he must try to keep Mrs Hughes; shouldn't have run her down like that in front of the boys – and started to go forward to the hide-and-seeking little girl. But Bill had eyes in the back of his old, wise head. He waved at Chris to show it was all right and, the last tiny having entered the house, doubled back to round up the stray. Chris was left free to cross toward the sand-pit and Wendy Raeburn. She was lingering there with two young boys. As he approached, Chris had time to feel again the two negative feelings that the first renewed sight of his newly arrived and as yet untested housemother consistently conjured up for him. Neither, of course, were her fault. At twenty-two she was inexperienced and only one thing could cure that. The trick was going to be to see she didn't learn at other people's expense. But at twenty-two she was very, very pretty. No, dammit, no point in being mealy-mouthed, she was very sexy and if he'd caught himself casting a too lingering look at the curve of her breasts, the thrust of leg against her skirt, God alone knew what that did for the likes of the Garys and Kevins. He must get Pat to drop more of a hint to her. . . .

'Hello, Wendy,' he said now. 'All O.K.?'

'Fine,' she said smiling. 'We're just waiting to let Peter finish his last sandcastle. Aren't we, Peter?'

'Yes,' Peter said with an iron preoccupation. He was four years old. Using a classic seaside bucket he had all but created a circle of lop-sided, crumbling, Martello towers. Chris watched as he scooped sand into the bucket for the last. It was a good decision on Wendy's part. Peter was only with them while his mother had her second baby and there was no justification for allowing his brief stay to bulk in his later life as an ogre-haunted nightmare.

Wendy had made no mention of what the second little boy, Dean, was still doing out. There was no need. And Chris had been careful to halt a good ten paces away from the sandpit. The adult men at Kingston House had all found that to go close to Dean was to reduce him to a bloodchilling state of uncontrollably screaming fear. Dean was five. Before his fourth birthday his still teenage father had broken six of his ribs and his right thigh when hurling him the length of a one-room bed-sit apartment. Since then Dean had had three foster homes. Two short-term while his father was being held and the family's future decided on and a long-term one when, the father having been placed on probation on condition he attend a psychiatric clinic, the local social services department had applied for a Care Order under Section One of the 1969 Act. But the best laid plans fail. After eight gruelling months the foster mother, as was her legal right, had upped and quit. The strain of a guaranteed wet bed each morning, of not being able to leave the room

11

for half a second without hearing a wail, of not being able to do more than nod in passing to her older natural daughter, had all worn her down to a grey defeat. Dean had come to Kingston House while the powers that were cast around for another foster home. Gibbering with terror he had been deposited in the hall by a harassed social worker. His trousers had been soiled and soaked through. When Chris had approached him his screams had tripled in volume and pitch. It had been Wendy who on the point of going out had approached him and managed to lift him up. Slowly the whimpers had died and as Chris had watched his latest staff-member hold him tight against her, quite careless of the ugly smears befouling her grey coat, he had known that, his own guidance willing, she must prove herself a godsend.

Since that evening Dean, in his waking hours, had not strayed more than two yards from her. At night he slept in her own room and each morning the first thing Wendy did was strip the sodden clothes from off his bed and remake it with clean sheets. He was clinging to her left hand now with his right as, peak-faced and white, undersized for his age, he sucked his other thumb.

Peter removed the bucket from the most crumbly castle of all. It all but collapsed. But his need for completion had been appeased.

'Finished,' he said. 'Go in now.'

He looked up at Chris.

'Have I got a brother yet?' he said.

'It might be a sister,' Chris said.

'Yes,' Peter said without enthusiasm.

Wendy looked enquiringly at Chris. She had very dark hair, light blue eyes and the palest of complexions.

'Any news?' she said.

'I asked Pat to call this afternoon,' he said. 'But it's only just due. Today was the actual guesstimate day.'

They were wandering back towards the french windows.

Chris cast a quick eye round the scruffy fringes of the garden.

'Just Jamie to account for now?' he said.

'I think so.'

12

She must have sensed him stiffen.

'Yes,' she said.

'Ah well. He'll be in as soon as he's convinced himself his camouflage has fooled us once again.'

He checked his stride to let her cross the threshold first.

'Aren't you running a bit late for your great day of days?' Wendy asked as she went in. 'An actual Saturday night out away from the reservation?'

He looked at his watch.

'No,' he said, 'tons of time. It's only dinner. With friends. They only live the other side of the Common.'

'Long-lost friends, Pat was saying.'

'Yes. Mine. Went to school with him. Now out of the blue he's turned up in the area.'

'Were you close friends?'

'Er. No. Well, up to a point. Same year. Look, Wendy, I am sorry if our going out is screwing up your love-life tonight.'

'Hardly the happiest way of putting it, kind sir!'

'All right, then. Not screwing it up – no that's not right either, is it?'

She laughed. When she did that she looked sixteen herself.

'It's no problem,' she said. 'Ronnie's coming over later to see how the other half live. I dare say I'll immensely enjoy my heaven-sent chance to watch *Match of the Day*.'

'You'll have a job. Or a long wait. This is the cricket season.'

'Well highlights of the Test or something?'

'Sure it's O.K.?'

'Of course. My pleasure. You make sure you have a good time.'

They were in the rear portion of the house's wide straight-through hallway. Even as he'd been talking he'd remembered how since coming here he had managed to eliminate the once ever-present smell of Dettol. But the cooking, of course, would never go. She turned away from him now in the direction of the sub-basement kitchens and dining room.

'They also wait who only stand to supervise,' she said.

'Oh yes,' he remembered, 'try and be nice to Mrs Hughes.

13

She's been going on about weekend work and if she gives up on us, we'll never find a replacement.'

Wendy smiled.

'Not easy with her,' she said. 'But I'll try.' She disappeared down the old service stairs to the sub-basement.

A little wearily, Chris began to climb the right-angled flight of stairs to the second floor. Acting on a decision that had not been easy he had had the bars on the upper storey windows of the home removed. It was still something that brought him out in a cold sweat but his reasoning at the time had been better to risk the possibility of physical injury to a child than impose the certainty of institutional trauma by leaving them. But the wire mesh between the stair-rails he had left. That didn't have the same associations and large marble tiles still made up the floor of the hall at the bottom of the stairwell. He saw now that part of the mesh on the first landing was coming away and made yet another mental note. As it happened he saw no children scurrying about but their sounds came at him from all sides as they made ready for their supper. A transistor played. A toilet flushed. Taps ran and water gurgled. And of course the endless taunts and giggles, challenges and put-downs came to him from all sides through original solid doors and recent thin partitioning alike. It's like climbing inside of the Tower of Babel, he thought, or being inside a giant loudspeaker. But he knew these were the sounds he listened out for all day. When they stopped a crisis of some sort was being tacitly announced.

He reached the green baize door that closed off the far narrower flight of steps that once had led the tired-out tweeny to her cramped, low-ceilinged garret. He drew a breath and consciously squared his shoulders. He always went through the motions, at least, of leaving the work behind. It never lasted, of course; constant availability was the name of his game but as a gesture to wife and son he could try not to drag himself up that last flight into their presence with a tread like a condemned man and all the troubles of the welfare state there to read upon his brow.

He pushed the door open – it was never locked – but even

14

as he did so heard a different creaking on the stairs below. He moved swiftly across the landing to the bannister. Just in time! He had caught a glimpse of Jamie McEvoy's military knapsack disappearing into the boys' section of the house. It was smiling genuinely that he went up the stairs and, through a second door, into his home within a home.

The main all-purpose-except-sleeping room looked, as ever, uncomfortably lived in. More so than usual, actually – the late rays of the slanting sun were highlighting the motes of dust spinning in the air, the obdurate coffee stain on the Habitat two-seater. He would have liked to have had just one corner of his life where order and precision reigned, but given Pat's job (and his income!) the eighteenth century would have to wait for the future. Then, perhaps, their servants would take care of the sprawled stacks of books, the usual cup on the coffee table, the hazard about the floor of indented cushions, the displaced dining chair four-leggedly confronting with open-mouthed back a television it had forlornly learned saw the world only in terms of black and white. Of course if in that never-never land they did run to servants, he and Pat might just as well curl up and die. If servants were doing the living for them, what other occupation would there be? He was not so sure, though, that in Robert's case, that would apply.

His son had looked up on his entry and matter-of-factly smiled. He was sitting at the dining work table on one of the two chairs that matched the one in front of the television. A cup of something was in front of him and he was reading a thick book. In the split but familiar second before he had looked up, Chris had been impressed for the thousandth time by the aloof, contained and, yes, ordered front his son presented to the world. As only child, he had long ago developed a quality of self-possession that seemed to allow him to ghost through life inviolate from the chaos of living above a human Battersea Dogs' Home. It had been his hallmark so long that it seemed he had been born with it. But in his more thinking moments Chris judged it had been a trait instinctively acquired in self-defence. Find yourself an only child and going to the same comprehensive as half a dozen of the 'in care' kids your father has temporary, near-total, power over and you're bloody well likely to turn into a kid with strong tendencies to eyes-down academic application. Well, could be a lot worse. If Robert at times bordered on the swot and at others could be something of a smart-arse pain in the neck, his ability to stay apart from the madding crowd often allowed him to be touchingly considerate. He could often volunteer to help in circumstances he alone had had the time and sense to see were coming. All the same, his name was already Robert. He'd have nobody call him Bob.

'Hello,' Chris now said. 'If it makes you feel justified in your decision, you picked a good couple of hours to miss.'

Robert looked up from the book.

'Not much cop the Wanderers this year,' he said. 'They keep setting these limited over fields but their bowlers aren't accurate enough to keep their line right.'

'That was true enough today. The opposition had one really good bat and he kept nudging ones and twos away through gully. Do it often enough, you don't need the boundaries. . . .'

Already Robert's eyes were turning back down to the book. He had a face studiously symmetrical, his father's colouring and build.

'What are you reading?'

'*War and Peace.*'

Bloody hell, that was going it a bit at thirteen.

'Oh yes. I think I was just about your age when I first started reading it myself . . . finished it last week.'

'Thought it might make a good film.'

'Smart-mouth.'

'It's good, though. The Russians are just having the living shit knocked out of them at Austerlitz.'

'You let your mother hear you using language like that you'll suffer the same fate.'

A hint of a blush acknowledged that Robert conceded he had presumed too far.

'Anyway,' Chris said in forgiveness, 'wait 'til the return home-leg on their Borodino ground. See how it stands then.'

'That's right, ruin the end.'

'It's not the end and that much history even you know. Where is she, by the way?'

Instantly understanding, Robert jerked his head towards the far trio of doors.

'In there getting tart – getting ready. She had a bath.'

'Damn. Water'll be half cold.'

'Or half hot.'

'Sophist . . . you eaten? I mean as we're going out—'

'I had a breakfast, thanks.'

'Breakfast?'

'A fry-up. 'S fine, thanks. I'm O.K.'

'O.K. I'd better go and make myself incredibly beautiful as well.'

'Take your time.'

All a bit too self-conscious, Chris thought, as he pushed through the two-way hinged door into the passage to the bedrooms and bathroom. Still, it was their respective ages and, thank God, it was thoroughly amiable. He pushed open the main bedroom door and came upon his wife.

Disappointingly she was not totally undressed. Despite a marriage that had lasted fifteen years (thus outlasting better than a quarter of their contemporaries'), the sight of his wife naked still never failed to provoke in Chris a heady combination of erotic stimulus, aesthetic pleasure and awe at his good fortune. At thirty-five she still had the same weight and figure she'd shown him at twenty. And if her body was not on unconscious display now, it might yet be coaxed forth. Wearing the short kimono-style wrap he had brought her in a panic fit of orientalism one Christmas and whose geometric patterning she had unguardedly let slip a couple of years later she detested, she was sitting legs elegantly, sexily, crossed in front of the pedestal desk he had converted into a sort of dressing table.

'Hello,' she said. 'Cutting it a bit fine, aren't we?'

The hair brush had not missed a single beat in its swift, even rhythm as she spoke.

Comme d'habitude.

He moved around the bed and coming up behind her

17

slipped his hand inside the loosely hanging front of the kimono. She smiled, laughed and stretched her head back and up the better to kiss him glancingly, the better to allow his hand to cup her breast. Ah! He had rather thought she'd already be wearing bra and pants. But she was not. Good! He squeezed gently and caressed, indulging himself for a minute in the sense of feminine softness, ripeness, fullness against his harder skin. Her breasts had always been no larger than your choice 34B's but the aggressive, sharply self-defining nipples had always been something she could feel, well, proud about. He felt this one now hardening between his fingers and even as its firmness began planting the inevitable thought in his mind, she was slipping sideways and out from his clasp. Her reflection smiled at him.

'Not what this particular doctor's ordering at this precise moment,' she said.

He knew what had been going on. She had suffered (and enjoyed) the caress for the minimum moments required by diplomacy. This, she had decided, would be the smoothest way of avoiding a complete cold shouldering on the one hand, a more protracted hold-up on the other. But enough, she was saying, at this hour was enough. Straight, dark-haired, brown-eyed, her sharp-chinned face projected an amused urgency at him from out of the mirror.

'Come on,' she said, 'if this is paint-the-town-red night, I want to see you getting your half of the show on the road.'

Seeing her at a party another woman might have found her nondescript. Most men would have correctly detected that the hint of severity in her straight-nosed, wide-mouthed, cleanly chiselled face was the first line of defence for a woman aware to what extremes her senses could take her when given free rein. The severity went with her everyday professional manner. It could function socially as well. It was in a double sense that it could be called her bedside manner.

'Two more minutes,' Chris Langley said. This time on the outside of the kimono, he put his arm back around her.

'After all,' he went on, 'you're pretty lucky I haven't forgotten all about it.'

18

'It was just crossing my mind to wonder when you came in. Did you get Gary fixed up at all, by the way?'

'No, damn it. The old fart.'

'Why? What happened?'

'I'll tell you later. Don't want to spoil the evening. I'm actually, I find, quite looking forward to it.'

'Charm of novelty, I suppose.'

She was trying to choose a lipstick.

'Incidentally, unless he's changed radically – pun intended – I should think red is the last colour David Newman wants to paint anything.'

'Oh, how disappointing! Boo!'

'Politically speaking.'

'Hurray!'

He straightened up, began to unbutton his work-shirt.

'What does he look like these days, anyway?' he said.

'Well, I only saw him for a second, you realise. While she was getting—'

'Bald? Fat?'

'Oh no. He looks pretty good.'

'No fallen arches? Haemorrhoids?'

She turned, grinning, to face him as he loosened his belt.

'How long is it since you've seen him?' she said.

'About twelve years.'

'Actually, he's devastatingly handsome and, for your school contemporary, just as incredibly young-looking.'

'Thanks a bunch. No compensations, then?'

'How do you mean?'

'For me.' He paused mock dramatically. 'He married money, you know.'

Had it all been a mock reaction?

'That was your first mistake,' Pat said.

Left arm raised, Chris Langley stood in his underwear sniffing dubiously at his own armpit as if he suspected his ability to register smells might have been impaired.

'I was wondering if I might get away without having a bath,' he said.

Pat sniffed with the maximum possible exaggeration.

'Not from downwind where I'm sitting,' she said. 'And as

19

I put the immersion on for you regardless of all expense,
I'm blowed if I'm going to let you waste it now.'

❦❦❦

As well as colours, the children at Kingston House came in
all shapes and sizes. No two of them ever did anything quite
identically. And this universal and so important law – you
ignored it at your peril – extended even, perhaps particularly, to the way they ate. The tinies had to be helped.
Wendy Raeburn on this Saturday night, for instance, had
taken care to sit with four of the smallest around her at one
end of the long refectory table. She had cut their sausages
into small pieces, coaxed, helped Peter Jackson build a dam
with his mashed potato to keep out the floods of the raging
baked bean juice. With Dean, the problem was more subtle.
He was quite able to handle his knife and fork but the bang
of a plate or tray set carelessly down on the scrubbed wooden
table would set him wincing, flinching, ducking his head
down between his shoulders to avoid the blows he was
conditioned to expect invariably followed sudden, violent
noises. Consequently he ate next to nothing. Life had given
him very little stomach for his food. Wendy was determined
not to force him to eat up like a good little boy. Good little
boys arrive at that state of felicity without their fathers
having made fairly thorough-going attempts to murder
them. It was not too much, Wendy reasoned, to subject
them to the passing stress of being required to eat their
cabbage. But Dean already had enough stress indelibly
stamped upon his psyche to last a lifetime and in one corner
of her divided attention she was particularly furious that
Mrs Hughes was self-centredly proclaiming her wrath at
having to work Saturday night when Bruce Forsyth was on
by making as much noise as possible in her every indignant
passage from the tables to the big cooking range where Mrs
Wilson endlessly ladled and stirred and served like one
o'clock. Staff problems or not, Wendy was deciding, she'd
have to have words about – or with – Mrs Hughes before
the next evening. She held out some sausage on the end of
her own fork.

20

'Another bite, Dean?' she said smiling.

His grey eyes like an old man's, the little boy finally dared to shake his head.

'All right, then Dean, you don't have to, love, we'll say you've finished, shall we?'

Slowly he nodded. Perhaps for a moment the cloud at the back of those eyes that had seen the greatest betrayal known on earth – a parent's of a child – lightened. But the dawn was false. The instincts telling Dean to fear the worst were, as always, totally correct.

Hissing like a goose, Mrs Hughes had pounced at once to clear his plate. Wendy all but went for her then and there. The orange-lipsticked bitch's look of outrage that good food should be wasted had been thrown from behind Dean so he was, at least, spared that. But, as it whipped the plate from right under his nose, the vehement sweep of the great blotchy red, adult, forearm had caused him to start back and then freeze like a terrified rabbit.

'It's all right, Dean, love,' Wendy said. 'Mrs Hughes only wanted to take your plate away.'

She smiled gently. Blast the bitch, she thought, a day's patient, tiring kindness wiped out in a second. Bitch! Bitch! Bitch! But she must on no account open her mouth to tell the bitch. Dean knew what shouting grown-ups ended up meaning for him.

'You did very well, Dean,' she said, 'for a boy who wasn't really very hungry.'

She had a bar of chocolate in their room and she would give it to him to eat while she told him a story. She had the idea he liked the stories and behind the white staring face something was listening. If Ronnie fancied her so much, he could amuse himself with the older kids for a while. After all—

'Wendy, miss! You're not looking at my pond!'

She sighed. Peter Jackson was feeling resentful because it seemed she had neglected him. Well, she had been but she only had one pair of eyes.

'Peter,' she said breathlessly, 'how absolutely splendid!'

Across the low-ceilinged but fluorescently bright room,

Bill Hutton nodded mental approval of the way Wendy had coped. He had a very good idea of what was going on. There was not much he missed at any time but, in this instance, Chris had asked him to keep a special eye on Wendy. The need, though, seemed to be diminishing. She was going to be all right.

His job at dinner was usually much easier. He sat with the bigger kids at one of the two folding tables put up for just the actual serving of meals. There was seldom any need to get kids to eat up here. Although down to the last one they all complained about the quality of the food, the kids nearly always bolted it like locusts. After the complaints on quality came the next grouch.

'Sir! Mr Hutton, sir! I never had enough!'

The only trick necessary at the big kid's table was to keep their chatter good naturedly down to some kind of a bearable level and in the case of old stagers like Gary make sure he wasn't creating some kind of diversion with his left hand while he nicked the kid on his right's rasher of bacon. As so often, he was pushing up the decibels right now.

'What do you mean, Lillee's better'n Holding,' he was challenging Kevin with. 'Lillee you see him run up and bowl he's trying like stink, you can see.'

'Well, what's Holding do then?' Kevin reasonably wanted to know.

'Holding he comes in as smooth as cream and when he lets go it don't look like he's hardly tried at all.'

'He ain't as fast, that's why.'

' 'is! Every time he bowls at Greig it's like a train going through a tunnel.'

Bill Hutton smiled in private agreement. Wonder whether Chris got a word in round the corner? he thought.

'Mr Hutton, sir. May I leave please, sir?'

It was Jamie McEvoy. Bill was mildly surprised. It was usually Gary or Howard who finished first. But Gary had been talking sixteen to the dozen about his passion and Jamie, come to think of it, had been putting it away like there'd be no tomorrow. He'd hardly even had a word for Donnie, his room-mate.

'You in a hurry to watch tele, Jamie?' Bill Hutton said.

'Er . . . yes, sir. In a minute, sir. Yes, sir,' Jamie said.

Bill Hutton's lifetime of experience noted the confusion . . . might be nothing, of course. Still, better run a little check in a while or so.

'O.K., then Jamie. Clear yours away and off you go.'

Because of the difference in the times it took the various children to finish or not finish their food, there was no ironclad rule about waiting for an *en masse* dismissal. The one rule was that if you sat on the big kids' tables you cleared your own scraps away in the bin and stacked your plates on the dirty pile.

Trying not to seem in a hurry, Jamie did this now. He walked slowly as he left the cream-walled, warm-smelling dining room but the instant he was on the narrow twist of stairs up to the hall he ordered himself to advance on the double. He darted across the hall and up two flights of the main stairs. He flung the door to the boys' half of the home open and crashed into the room he shared with Donnie. When it had first been shown him he had been amazed at how big and comfortable and cosy it was compared to his cold room at home. Just when he had been secretly so scared about what kind of a prison he was going to. But he had no thoughts like that on this occasion. There wasn't time. He had remembered while he was washing the camouflage mud off his face just before dinner that he hadn't kept his promise to himself that day. There hadn't been time before dinner and Donnie might come back at any moment now if he didn't go much on that apple crumble. And he'd kill himself as a traitor if Donnie should ever discover the secret despatches he'd been trusted with – Barry's letter. In a soft leatherette frame on the inelegant but capacious cabinet beside Jamie's bed was a large eight by ten photograph of a youth whom it would not have been difficult to imagine as living in Kingston House – he looked so young – if he had not been wearing the Number One blue uniform of a Marine Commando. Bill Hutton, carefully looking at the obviously treasured possession when it had first been unpacked, had seen the uniform and registered 'soldier' and then felt a terrible pang of anger and pity pierce through him as he was struck anew by how young, how unknowing they took them these days. He had thought, for an instant, of all the kids he'd known for whom the Army had seemed the way out of the closed-circuit of misery; of how many of them had gone to their otherwise unmourned deaths in France and Belgium, Burma and Italy. Slowly, he had sworn, he must wean Jamie away from his fixation on the forces. Let him have his fill of it for now, but later ask him to wonder what good had ever come from killing.

But that was for the future, possibly, and so far unknown to a Jamie, who now, in his shared room, breathless, eyes turning to the door, was slipping a paper of some kind out from behind the photograph of the solemn, self-conscious youth in uniform.

The paper was a Forces Air-letter, creased as is the way with letters from loved ones read over and over again, half come apart along one of its original folds. And Jamie's promise to himself was that he would read this letter at least once every day. It made no matter that by now he knew it by heart and could recite it much more fluently than, say, the Lord's Prayer. Making himself take care now so his haste would not further fray the thin tattered paper, he sat on the edge of the bed and, his lips moving childishly in step with his mind, began to read.

The photograph was inscribed in one corner in an awkwardly over-careful hand unused, you would guess, to using a pen.

'*To Jamie,*' ran the wording, '*Best of British, Barry.*'

The letter was in the same awkward hand. Jamie did not know it but his eyes were not really following the words on the paper now. It was his memory that voiced them in his head:

'. . . *then every four months we get a five day pass – "R and R" they call it. Rest and Recuperation. It seems a bit short for a break after all that time on the job but it'll give me a chance to get back to Blighty (good old England that is) and for you and me to have some more chats. Otherwise not much is new, not much to write home about. There's lots of rain and lots of patrols out in it but I*

24

told you already that I can't write to tell you about them. I'm glad you say you like the belt. I'll try and bring you another badge for it when I come. . . .'

The boy's lips moved on. He could almost have been praying. People do shed tears when they pray. Quite frequently, in fact. Or again, quite frequently it has been known for people, having read a letter, to let their hands holding it drop to their lap while their tears flow. . . .

There was a sound of light feet running up the stairs. Jamie's head snapped up like a deer's. He had folded the letter, was sliding it back behind the photograph whose subject's pose was like his handwriting. There! It was done! The frame was back in place. Jamie cuffed at his moist cheeks with his sleeves.

'Not going to cry!' he exclaimed belatedly.

He realised that the footsteps had gone off in the direction of the girls' half. He realised too that today, for the first time, he had almost forgotten his self-imposed obligation. He did not cry every time. Perhaps, unknown as yet to himself he had cried on this occasion because a deep part of his mind had already acknowledged that a day would sooner or later dawn, the first of many more, on which he would forget.

But now he sprang suddenly up. Old Bill had sussed something was up. He'd be in the tele-room pretty soon doing a check. Better get down there.

Before he left his room, Jamie had strapped around his waist the army belt decorated at regular intervals by a dozen or so badges of British Army line regiments.

❖❖❖❖

'Will I do?'

Chris Langley swung round from contemplating his head-to-one-side image in the mirror and looked at his wife instead. Fully dressed now, she was also fully aware as she posed in the bedroom doorway that she looked terrific.

'Not bad,' Chris said, 'you'll do at a pinch.'

'Beast! I don't look too virginal?'

'Hardly. You look gorgeous. No, not gorgeous that's too

lush. You look like a Cleopatra who means business – who's out to chuck the Romans out of Sinai.'

It wasn't a bad description.

He had returned to the tie but either the collar of his shirt had shrunk or he'd put on half an inch around the neck. It would be a murder going through the evening like this. He'd disgrace himself with a thrombosis in the middle of the *osso bucco*.

'Hell!' he said. 'Do you think I have to wear a tie.'

'I shouldn't think so for a minute. This is the twentieth century and you're in the Social Services.'

'You've rather set the tone. New dress is it?'

As he said the words he became aware of his error but they were on the wing.

'Just a joke,' he added hastily.

'It wasn't and you know it. Rosemary's twenty-first.'

'Oh my God, yes.'

'Won't get so smashed tonight, I hope.'

'Lucky you weren't raped that night.'

'If you did but remember, I was.'

He gave a self-satisfied grin of remembrance.

'Hang it!' he said. 'They're not royalty. If it's all right with you I'll wear my sports jacket and leave the shirt open.'

'All right with me. It's in a damn sight better condition than your suit in any case.'

Two minutes later they were passing through the living room on their way out. Robert had forsaken Tolstoy for an Airfix model. His tiny pots of paint were spread methodically out on the newspaper he'd laid across the table. Middle-aged again and a mum, Pat pretended to search for something in her purse.

'You'll be all right on your own, love, won't you?' she said.

His face as he looked up was studiously dead-pan.

'You must be bloody joking,' he said.

'Christ, Robert! What kind of language is that?'

'Your kind, mum.'

Game, set and match.

'No excuse at all,' Chris said. 'Come on, love. I expect

26

we'll be quite late, Robert. The number's by the phone. Just in case. But please only if it's an emergency emergency.'

'Roger and out,' Robert said.

They slipped quickly, self-consciously, down the stairs. They were out of place in these clothes, over-dressed. But not unobserved. Karen and Tracey, two of the older girls were climbing the stairs and their eyes visibly opened at this passing apparition of Mrs Langley all dolled up and looking sexy. Their badly stifled giggles came bursting down from the flight above.

'Probably just worked out we still do it from time to time,' Chris murmured to his wife.

'Do we? I can't remember.'

'And got you figured for the *Sun*'s page three.'

They went out of the stained-glass panelled front door, down the steps and round to the right of the house where the beat-up VW bus was parked. The sun was set but it was still more light than dark. The air was still soft and warm and romantic. Thank God it's the summer, Pat was thinking and I don't have to wait twenty minutes for the heating to work its way through. Should start O.K., this time of year, Chris thought, be dry as a bone.

Pat actually had the door open before it struck her.

'Chris,' she said, 'Robert. When he said we must be joking asking if he'd be all right by himself – what way do you think he meant it?'

Chris Langley paused in the act of searching for the ignition keys. The evening seemed perhaps a little darker, the air a little more chill.

'I see what you mean,' he said. 'He was more serious than not, wasn't he? But now you mention it, I don't know which way he meant it either. Hmmn.'

They climbed into the bus. The third time of asking, it fired.

Chapter Two

'CHRIST, MAN,' FERGUSON said, 'there isn't room enough in here to swing another tit.'

Manton winked.

'Oh, if one came to hand, I'd probably manage to squeeze it in,' he said and was drunkenly aware at the back of his mind he had laughed rather more loudly than the Scot. But it was hard to tell. The small service-flat he'd fetched up in after his divorce was incredibly noisy. It was splitting at the seams with the nine or ten blokes he'd pub-crawled his way back from the Dealer Conference with and the four or five birds they'd picked up along the way. Any minute now he'd have the bloody neighbours on to him and no mistake. But who the hell cared? It wasn't often, was it?

'Christ, man,' Ferguson said, 'it's hot in here. Can't you open the windows for us now and get us some fresh air?'

He was sprawled back in the room's one armchair, his old-fashioned parted fair hair lank and straight above his slack and sweaty young man's face. The tiny part of Manton's mind still sober had registered how thickly he'd spoken.

'Er, well,' that same part made him reply, 'it's pretty late and the neighbours might reckon—'

'Oh, for Christ's sake! The neighbours! Who the hell cares what they think! It's like an oven in here, I'm telling you. And I'll tell you this as well – if you don't open that bloody window over there I'm going to do it myself from here with your TV.'

For an instant Manton hesitated. He was nearly twice as old as Ferguson but Ferguson's father happened to be head of Vehicle Supply. And the sod made you remember it every time he opened his mouth. Manton made himself smile.

'It's not for you, mate,' he lied, 'it's just to preserve my cheap thrill every night when Angela Rippon comes on.'

Short and paunchy at forty-five, his dark hair receded to the point of baldness, he pushed his way past the confused lines of the giggling tarts, the groping blokes going through the motions of pass the orange all the better to feel you up with, my dear. He felt vaguely it had been a mistake coming on back here. It wasn't as if it was very impressive, even. Not like his last place, his home. Thanks to the running sore of the alimony he coughed up, that bitch still kept that immaculate, no doubt. As he sidled around one right old bag who'd split her sleeve under an armpit, and reached the window, he was feeling sorry for himself. 'Would you buy a second-hand car from a bloke who looks like me?' he had used to tiredly joke. But lately it had been too near the bloody truth to be a laughing matter, second-hand or new.

The window was sticking. He banged on the handle thing with the heel of his hand and the whole thing juddered open. The shouts and coarse knees-up laughs, the Forty Golden Greats rushed past him and into the night, but the fresh air came streaming in. He rested his elbows on the sill a moment feeling it cool upon his face. Well, what the hell! They deserved a few jars, a bit of slap and the old how's your father after a bummer of a Conference like that.

There'd been no new model launched. Well, you could tell that even if you didn't know it from the grapevine by the fact that this year they'd been relegated to that morgue of a hotel the wrong side of Croydon. Once it was somewhere with a bit of go in it like Majorca or Monte Carlo but, I ask you, bloody Purley. The Managing Director and the Sales Director had stood up on their hind legs and read out a lot of empty threats and emptier promises from their supposed-to-be-invisible tele-prompters and all the slides had clicked away trying to make a silk purse out of a sow's ear. But the reality was they didn't have an entry in the hatchback market to give them volume or a really de-luxe saloon to give them a flagship vehicle and high profit-margins. In their different ways Datsun and Fiat and BMW had been cutting their balls off for years. That was how it was and after that banquet only fit for pigs or the bloody strikers up at the factory, you couldn't blame the blokes from Scotland

and the North-East – the ones stuck in the hotel overnight on account of distance – you couldn't blame them coming up and asking him, a local dealer, where it was all happening. Christ, those strikers! Supply on the new models now was – oh, yeah, if he was going to keep an eye on the main chance he'd better get back to him. He pushed his way back through the scrum of panting, heaving couples – Christ, look at her boobs! – and back to Ferguson.

The bloody young know-all seemed more cut than ever. He was slumped down in the armchair, his eyes glazed and motionless. But seeing, staring at something. Manton turned his own head to follow the line of vision. Bloody hell! One of the younger tarts, the one in the black skirt that showed off her bum and the white scoop-necked sweater that did the same for her tits was paired off with the big bloke from Berwick. She had the orange under her chin and he was going through the motions of getting it off her. But in the meantime he had both hands full and kneading on her breasts. And she was pressing hard at him, squirming, getting her jollies for all to see while she enjoyed every moment of it. The orange fell and bumped down to the floor but no-one paid a blind bit of notice. Instead, the bloke was grabbing her to him and pushing a hand against her backside to push her harder in to him as his tongue went halfway down her throat.

'What about the other girl?' Ferguson said.

Manton turned his head back to look down on him. He hadn't moved a muscle, wasn't blinking an eyelid as he looked at the clinch in the room's centre. Manton turned his head further around. The other girl, the halfways pretty one, well you wouldn't kick it out of bed, was standing in the kitchen doorway. Her round jaw was moving rhythmically from side to side. Bloody marvellous, Manton thought, scrubber of the month!

He jerked his head.

'She's over there,' he said.

'Tell her she's on.'

Manton began to move to her but with no more than the tone of his voice Ferguson stopped him.

'What did we say?' he said.

'Sixty.'

'Ask her if she wants to make it up to an even hundred,' Ferguson said.

'Doing what?' Manton asked.

Ferguson just looked at him.

'Ask her.'

'Well . . . I . . . I mean I don't know as. . . .'

Manton's voice trailed ineffectively away and he felt himself wanting to shuffle his feet as Ferguson kept looking at him with those glazed unblinking eyes.

'How many silver 1250's did you want me to have a word to my old man about?' Ferguson said.

He smiled the nasty smile of a weak man in a powerful position.

'Three,' Manton said thickly. Without more words he turned towards the kitchen. His main chance was there as well as the girl. He moved up to her.

'Time to shake it around darling, and earn that fast forty,' he said.

She turned eyes to him as black, shiny and two dimensional as buttons.

'Sixty, we said,' she said.

'You don't even have the gear to start with,' he said.

'I got it underneath and that's where it bloody counts, mate.'

'Fifty.' He wondered what she looked like without the false eyelashes, the acres of eye-shadow. Prettier, really, but not right for this.

'Sixty.'

'I've only your word for what you come equipped with. Fifty.'

'You're old and fat and sweaty,' she said. She was reaching for the buttons on her blouse. His eyes followed her fingers.

'Not too old,' he said mechanically. 'Not too old for what I might be thinking.'

'Good enough?' she said. Without seeming to give it a second thought she was shoving her almost totally exposed

31

breasts under his nose. One nipple was well clear of her minimal bra.

'How old are you?' he said.

'Old enough to earn sixty quid. Sixty quid.'

'I've a daughter older than you.'

'Then go ask her to do it!'

She was buttoning her blouse. He wanted to smash her hard across the mouth for suggesting that about Deidre but he could feel Ferguson watching him. She was reaching for the cheap and nasty handbag at her feet.

'All right,' he said quickly. 'Sixty.'

'In advance.'

Oh no, she wasn't catching him like that.

'No way,' he said. 'Deliver the goods and after due inspection you'll get paid. No business in the world that don't go on like that.'

She looked at him a long hard time. Her jaw muscles were tightening, relaxing, tightening, relaxing without a break as she worked on her gum and he did not know that she was thinking that if he tried ripping her off she would scare him shitless by letting on how old she was. But a bird in the hand.

'Forget it then,' she said. 'I do it, I got no guarantee I'll ever see a penny. But if you cough up and I try copping out – well a bunch like you – you can always bleeding rape me, can't you.'

Was that a hint? It sounded as if Ferguson was in. He tried to get a smile across his face but he felt too much like one of his own salesmen.

'Fair enough, love,' he said.

She watched with her jet beady eyes and he fished a roll of notes from his pocket and counted a dozen fivers openly out for her.

'Put some music on then,' she said. 'Something better than this muck.'

He pretended to move off to do this and then to have had a second thought.

'Fancy making it an even hundred?' he said.

Her chewing missed two beats. She looked at him as if he

was some kind of animal and even as he made up his mind he hated her he felt himself feel old.

'Not me,' he muttered. He jerked his head. 'Him.'

She looked at Ferguson.

'Not interested,' she said. 'Looking – all right. That's as far as it goes.'

Well, sod her. And Ferguson. He could do his own pimping!

Glumly, realising he really wanted to go the bog and lose some of that gin, he pushed back through the crowd and pushed the stop button on his cassette player. That brought the couple of dancing couples, the bunch of grapplers to a puzzled standstill. They looked towards him and he was on show. He put on a happy face and a cabaret voice.

'Don't be alarmed, one and all,' he said, 'it is not chucking out time, it is not a raid from the Vice Squad. On the contrary it's cabaret time here at the Wilf Manton Hilton and here by popular request is the Gypsy Rose Lee of the South Circular, the Fiona Richmond of Norwood, Croydon and places thereabouts, the one and only—'

He did not know her name.

'—Miss Juicy Fruits!'

'Wahay!' Boozy and leering his houseguests licked their chops and whistled noisily in anticipation, unaware of what he'd thought had been a brilliant bit of improvisation name-wise. He waved his arm and, stumbling back gigglingly, they made a pocket handkerchief of space appear in the middle of the floor. He actually had a cassette with *The Stripper* on it and as he'd talked he'd slipped it home in the machine. He could see her stuffing the notes in her bag as, jerking his head to tell her to move it over, he pushed the 'Play' button down more forcefully than there was need.

He made for Ferguson and to reach the bit of space she had to push right past him. As she did so he saw that she was still chewing.

'For Christ's sake! Lose the bloody gum!' he said.

She glared, then spat it out. Before he knew what she was about she had rammed it smearingly against the shoulder and chest of his shirt.

'Why you little—'

The music blaringly cut him short and to cheers, jeers and whistles, she was in to the bumps and grinds of her performance.

She didn't give too bad an imitation of the real McCoy. Her clothes – a blouse, a denim skirt – were dead against her. They were too commonplace and not designed to zip and rip provocatively away. There was an unpleasantly unprofessional hint of hair under her armpits and, when she got down to it, though her bra was skimpily close to a club stripper's, her pants were more like sensible knickers than bikini briefs. But in between she gyrated, shimmied and thrust with something approaching provocativeness. The breasts when they swung free and clear were full, firm and high and deserved all the whistling applause that seemed to make no difference to her.

'Off! Off! All off!' one of the men chanted.

Manton looked that way. None of the men were troubling to try appearing cool at that late drunken hour and their sweating, grinning, do-it-with-their-boots-on lust was nakedly blatant on their coarse faces. The women's looks were more ambiguous. Their grins seemed more forcedly pasted on and the threat of comparison, of competition, hovered uneasily but clearly in their eyes. They must have been glad at seeing the distinct roll of almost puppyfat around the girl's hips and belly.

'Off! Off!'

She was removing the too large pants now. A bit unsteadily. If she'd had more room to work in she could have hung it out more, Manton thought. His need to pee had quite gone from him. Her triangle of hair was a bit unkempt and as she pirouetted her waggling bum had one clearly visible yellowhead dead centre on her left cheek. But all the same—

'She want to earn her little bonus then?' Ferguson said abruptly. He caught Manton off guard.

'Er. Playing hard to get. I – er – think it'll be all right but – er – she said she'd like to hear it from you in person. . . .'

34

He heard Ferguson click his teeth in disapproval and annoyance.

'Dear me,' the little sod was saying, 'And I was counting on your help. And I've been hearing you've been discounting new models all on your own q.t. up to as much as fifteen per cent. I don't think the old man is going to go for that. But maybe he won't find out and your franchise won't be in danger . . . Why don't you have another word with the little lady, Wilf? I'm sure you can get her to change her mind if you set yours to it.'

Manton let his breath out noisily. He could feel fresh sweat breaking out all over him beneath and through the old. The sod! The bastard! Who'd told him about that? Oh, Christ! There had been something about the girl that told him that she wouldn't do a thing like going all the way for ten times the money.

The track had finished, the cassette progressed but throwing her shoulders back and forward, sweeping her hair up over her head with her upraised arms, she was now continuing her now stark naked performance. The men stared hard but she seemed oblivious. The display of nudity was now fulfilling some obscure need of her own. He sort of recognised that even as it occurred to him that if he stalled for a while and could manage to spike the snot-nosed little cheapskate's drinks, he might be able to make him incapable of serious action.

'I'll talk to her again,' he said. 'Here, your glass is empty.'

Chapter Three

THE POOL'S UNDERWATER lights seemed to lift it into the air. A block of translucent turquoise subtly marbled and framed all around in white, it hung in magical limbo on the velvet darkness of the night. Occasionally a ripple shimmered across its surface and it became a magic harp on which invisible fingers plucked chords beyond the coarse powers of human ears to hear.

Chris Langley perceived he was a little drunk. He paused for a second to sip some brandy from the balloon he carried. No point in spilling any of the stuff the frequency it came his way. A purist would have fumed and pointed out that the glass was way over-filled but Newman had said it would save a trip back to the house for a second bash. So who was complaining? He followed his host towards his floating representation of a Hockney painting.

Newman was standing halfway down one of the longer sides stock still and staring down into the water. If it had not been for the equally over-full glass he clutched to his chest, he might have been someone on the verge of suicide trying a last time to read his destiny upon the water's surface. Infuriatingly, he had opened the door to them wearing jeans and a University of Southern California sweat shirt. Now a faint, redundant, drunken logic made Chris go and stand exactly opposite him sixteen feet away across the pool. He raised his glass.

'To his Majesty over the water,' he said. 'So this is how the other half lives.'

David Newman's leading man face broke into a grin that for all its man-of-the-world ease was not without an apologetic undertow.

'Not bad is it,' he said briskly. 'Six grand. Six grand cash, that is. No receipts, no invoices. No VAT and, nudge, nudge, no tax. Would've come out nearer ten doing it by the book. But I suppose you think that's all pretty reprehensible.'

Chris shrugged. He had actually been thinking how marvellous it would be if they had one back at Kingston for the kids. Properly fenced and guarded, the professional in him insisted immediately. He jerked his head.

'I've been getting the home's bus out there in your drive serviced on that principle – or lack of one – for years,' he said.

'Certainly. If it's in a good cause, like your home or me, why not? Judging by the noise it was making when you arrived, mind you, you still may have been coming away short-changed.'

'As long as it runs. You've been spoiled, you see, listening all these years to the sweet nothings of your Lancia.'

'True. How very true.'

Solemnly, Chris drank. Near the pool's edge, he swayed suddenly and a tiny drop of the Martell V.S.O.P. rained down from his glass into the pool. He stared down past the ripple it made. For a second there was a sense of amber integrity in the midst of the turquoise waters infested with the brandy-eating piranha chlorine. For a second he had a sense of the interface of the two liquid surfaces as the wrapped around brandy stayed whole. Then the dissolution had taken place. The chlorine gobbled the brandy up. Christ, he thought, I must be drunk.

'So I can take it you're tolerably successful these days,' he said. It came out a trifle thickly and, as he said it, he hoped not too aggressively.

Newman smiled with no hint of apology at all.

'Doing well enough to subsidise guests purifying my pool with brandy,' he said. 'Turnover last year was four point three five.'

'I seem to remember that's good. It sounds it, anyway.'

'On our capital and in the electronics game it's bloody fantastic.'

'Ah, the electronic light fantastic.'

'Ha! Mind you don't trip, now.'

'Ha!'

37

The two stood facing each other still as if about to enter upon some formal aquatic duel. Newman gestured largely with his free hand.

'Let us to yonder canopied divan,' he said, 'and get the weight from off our plates.'

'Good thinking.'

They both walked to the swing seat that presided over the cluster of *Good Housekeeping* garden furniture by the far corner of the pool. With some unsteadiness they both sat down on its slightly swaying, squishy seat.

'Have a dip if you feel like it,' Newman said.

Chris shook his head.

'No thanks all the same,' he said, 'I've lost the art of taking exercise these days.'

'No cricket any more, then?'

'Nope. Not for some years. Reduced to watching – when I can.'

'Likewise. I miss a lot going abroad, though. I do get in my squash, though, twice a week most of the time.'

He looked it. Newman was not only literally tall, dark and handsome but, damn it, just as slim as he had been opening the batting for the Old Boys.

'You don't see any of the old bunch nowadays, then?' he was asking.

'Not really. I went to a dinner a few years back but it was a bit like going to a youth club.'

'I know the feeling.'

'Bit of a busman's holiday, in fact, for me. I very occasionally see Peter Goddard who lives near the home as it just happens. But no-one else. I don't commute or anything, you see, so my chances of running into people are pretty non-existent.'

'Probably better that way.'

'I mean, we wouldn't have crossed paths again if Jenny hadn't walked into Pat's surgery.'

'True. Must seem funny in a way.'

'Well, you've sort of got it turned round. She goes out to work. You stay in to. Exchange of conventions.'

'That's seditious talk these days. They'll have your balls

off right away. Anyway, as it happens, Pat out-earns me by a fairly useful whack.'

He always found himself obliged to proffer this fact of life for conversational inspection and, ridiculously, it always made him feel embarrassed. It must be rather like being a conscientious homosexual. Ridiculous!

But Newman was reacting admirably.

'Yes,' he said, 'how did a nice boy like you get to end up in a place full of delinquents?'

He made the stock joke.

'By degrees,' he said.

'But after Reading you went into Marketing, as I recall, with Fords.'

'Right.'

'So what went wrong?'

'Or right . . . I did, I suppose. Couldn't take it. I got tired of looking at the world through a rose-coloured newspaper, I suppose.'

'That's better. That is actually funny. I'll use that next week.'

'Please do.'

'And you opted out.'

'Yes.'

'Regrets?'

'Well, of course, a dozen times a day.'

'Really?'

'No. Not really.'

'Yes . . . I know what you mean,' David Newman said. 'I can make out a very good case defending the capitalist system but, I don't know, I sometimes wonder if any of us ever really gets the chance to make a real choice . . . Know what I'd like to do?'

'What?'

'Take three years off and read. Read, read, read, read, read. Read all the books I've always meant to and never got around to. Rotten to think you're going to die one day and half the books on your mental list still won't be ticked off.'

'. . . yes.'

For a few moments the two contemporaries lapsed into a

39

not unmaudlin silence. Both were intelligent enough to know what was occupying the other's thoughts: envy of himself. For Langley in the brandy, the pool, the five bedrooms of the 'Swedish modern' house that Pat was now inspecting, there were, all round, examples of the glittering material prizes he was just drunk enough to think might have been his if he had nailed his colours more permanently to the Industrial-Commercial mast. Nor in his foolish, do-gooding pursuits had he acquired the poise, assurance, the hard cutting edge of his host. For Newman his guest's presence seemed an unspoken condemnation of the – face it old man – single-mindedness with which he'd always sought out Mammon and amassed gains selfishly ill-gotten. It had been a life of voting left with his heart, right with his wallet. It made no matter that his interest in his business was now not that of a Scrooge pursuing money for its own dear golden sake but that of a skilled player of real-life Monopoly seeking still better coups. He'd been blindly doing his own thing and not seeking himself, his perfect freedom, in the service of others. Of course, the same might be no less true of old Langley, when you really looked at it. Kingston House might be his little hobby, empire, variation on Monopoly and, at the end of the day, the kids might be no more than the counters that he moved around the board. . . .

He flexed his right leg in the merest rhythm and the canopied swing swayed gently back and forth in the soft night. Bound to each other by a mutual affection, a mutual sense that in the other's life style was a standing rebuke to their own, the two men sat side by side in an unstrained silence. Then Chris Langley suddenly recalled he had one ground for complaint.

'By the way,' he said, 'they're not delinquents.'

'Who? The kids?'

'Yes. Most of them aren't anyhow.'

'So what – who, rather, are they, then?'

'Well there's no short answer to that. They come in all sizes and flavours. They're with us for all sorts of reasons. Their own safety, protection, and—'

'Child battering?'

'Sometimes. Too often. But often just bereavement – orphans with no living next of kin. Illegitimate kids, whose one parent's given up on them. Illegitimate kids who didn't get aborted in time and whose mother's decided she doesn't want to know. Not surprising as she's most likely fifteen – although later she may change her mind and cause all kinds of static for half a Social Services Department and a couple of utterly admirable foster parents. . . . In most of our cases we're a sort of wayside pull-in *en route* to fostering.'

'Doesn't that mean you end up as a sort of bumbledom wastebin.'

'Bull's-eye. You've got it in one. My biggest grouse. If a kid's in trouble send the poor blighter along to Kingston House. "They'll know how to cope." '

He paused.

'We don't always,' he said.

'Win a little. . . .'

'We've no margin for error. It's a bastard when we screw up.'

'I imagine.'

His reply had been too facile. The edge in Langley's tone had been unmistakable. David Newman hastened to correct his glibness.

'Really,' he said. 'Especially if you're running Battersea Dogs' Home rather than a mini Scrubs.'

'Well we do have some who've offended against the Law of the Land. Got one thirteen-year-old in at the moment who set fire to a shop.'

'Good Lord! Why?'

'Can't get it out of him. But we will. Did a thorough bloody good job of it, I must say. Planned it all like a military operation.'

'He's got initiative, then.'

'Jamie's got that, all right . . . along with his problems. But give him the time, Roger'll get to the bottom of it.'

'Roger?'

'Roger Benton. He's our consultant psychiatrist. Come in from Abbotsfield General. Good bloke, actually. He assesses the kids to see whether they're suitable for fostering or not and—'

'If they're not—'

'There are longer term homes.'

'I bet.'

'We get most of ours fostered. He furnishes official reports for the courts too, of course. And, of course, wherever a child ends up being sent, we've got to send reports on with him on his mental and physical health, recommendations on how it seems to us—'

He broke off. The two women were at last coming to join them. It was an eerie approach. Jenny's blouse was as light in tone as Pat's dress and the light spilled upward from the glowing pool rendered them both ghosts against the night. For an uncanny instant Chris had the feeling that they were about to glide towards their menfolk straight across the mirroring pool – beautifully sinister spirits conjured from a lake by the low full moon Newman had enough clout to have laid on as decor. But instead, palpably human as they came nearer and the drinks they carried on their own behalf became apparent, they merely skirted the pool's edge in an approach less sensational but ultimately, Chris could not but think, rather more acceptable.

'You two been doing the "whatever happened to old Ginger Bates?" routine?' Pat called out while still alongside the pool.

'Not much,' Chris called back. 'I seem to be faintly aware I've just been bending David's ear with a Reith Lecture on the theory and practice of contemporary social service institutions and procedures.'

'I don't believe a word of either explanation,' Jenny Newman said. 'What it's all been has been "whatever happened to that dark girl with the absolutely enormous knockers? What was her name, now?" '

'Quite right,' David said. 'Chris and I once shared a mistress, you know, Pat. Oh Christ! He has told you about little Mimi, hasn't he?'

'Big Mimi, by all accounts,' Pat said.

'Well, on two anyway,' Jenny said.

With liberated latterday politesse neither man had risen to his slightly befuddled feet. There happened to be precisely two single patio chairs hard by the swing and that was surely good enough. Neither of the two svelte ladies seemed to take umbrage. With an equal grace both sank into the respectively nearer chair. Jenny was dressed with a more off-handed expensiveness than her husband. Her jeans had plainly been tailored to embrace her legs-up-to-the-armpit slimness and her plain white blouse was plain pure silk. It had been reasonably transparently obvious to Chris during dinner – *paupiette de veau clementine* and not *osso bucco* but none the less delicious for that – that she wore no bra beneath the silk. It had been as transparent that he was to notice this intentional absence but he had not let him put it off his food. It had tended, in fact, to sharpen his appetite. The breasts might be decidedly on the boyish side but, what flesh was discernible seemed, like the veal, choice. And yet she'd just made two pretty heavy-handed references to breasts. With her very pale blonde hair cut short and slantingly tight to her skull, the straight narrow nose and high cheek-bones in the just saved from roundness face, Jenny had genuine claims to thoroughbred beauty. But like many thoroughbreds she seemed skittish, insecure. He wondered if a rather obvious sense of inadequacy lay behind the extreme competence of her cuisine.

'Darling,' Pat was saying, 'the house! I'll tell you later in the car to spare these livers of the good life their blushes but, I'll tell you, Chris, you're in the wrong business all right.'

There was a barely perceptible pause.

'Well as a matter of fact,' David said, 'that's more or less what we were talking about and as a further matter of fact I'm not by any means so sure.'

There was an edge of sadness to his voice he made no attempt to hide. It was lost on none of the other three. He sighed. It was hard to know quite with what topic to pick up the conversation but he rescued it himself.

'Two different worlds, eh?' he said. 'Well as a further matter of fact, our pool is scandalously under-used during the week – eh, my pet? I was wondering – would it be any use for you and your mob, Chris? You know, bring the kids over, sort of thing.'

Chris' heart leapt up at the suggestion, but, as so often, Pat beat him to the verbal punch.

'How fantastic!' she said.

'It'd be a bloody godsend,' Chris said. 'Quick, let me take you up on it before you change your mind.'

'I have spoken,' David announced with stage Navajo pomposity. 'It'll be my pleasure,' he added as himself, 'I'll get a bang out of it, I promise.'

'We'll see the kids are supervised and all that, of course,' Chris thought it just as well to still say rapidly. 'And, show us how, we'll bung in chlorine by the bucket load.'

David Newman laughed.

'Not necessary,' he said.

'Anyone fancy a dip now?' his wife abruptly asked. 'The water will be really warm after all today's sun. The air's still quite warm out here even now.'

'Oh I couldn't,' Chris said, 'not after that gorgeous – pun intended – dinner.'

'Well I might risk it in that case,' David said. 'Some of the old professional mouth-to-mouth from Pat would be well worth risking a coronary for.'

Chris smiled. He tried to gauge whether the gusto might have gone a little way past routine gallantry.

'What about costumes, though?' Pat said.

'Oh that's the point,' Jenny took up quickly. 'We're not at all overlooked here, you know. I mean since we're all obviously in good shape – let's flaunt it. Naked as nature intended and devil take the hindquarter.'

Chris looked at Pat and found her smiling rather pertly. So that was how the land lay, was it. And pool. And hostess too it seemed. Well he could be flattered and he was but there had been something in Jenny's slightly brittle tones that earned her his saddened sympathy even as he went on his male guard. Her voice had been skirting the edge of emptiness. It flicked his mind that if ever there might be a *prima facie* case for fostering. . . .

'Well, I don't know,' he was meanwhile saying, 'but I think it's a case of "thanks but no thanks".' He was trying to pick up a signal from Pat but silently laughing at him, he knew, she was deliberately maintaining her Mona Lisa act. There was this sense that on this one night out together after so long and in the company of such civilised people all rules might be broken. It hung in the air between the four of them.

'I don't think we can,' he nevertheless said. 'If we all go skinnydipping – well, it could very well be then that, for whatever combination of circumstances – or people, the two of us would end up wanting to spend the rest of the night *chez vous*. Sorry. No can do. Got to be on crack of dawn duty tomorrow morning.'

Even as he said it he was becoming poignantly aware how much a part of him would have liked to welcome Jenny's cool, slim beauty to his bed and gentled her to a quiet calming. It was her he looked at most as he spoke.

'Oh come on,' David Newman had said, 'there's no need to see an orgy lurking behind every bush – pun intended.'

Chris wondered uneasily if he had been rather vulgarly prim and the suggestion continued to float between the four of them on the pool-lit softness of the night.

⚜⚜⚜

The shirt was one hundred per cent synthetic and the stripe in it was made by a slightly raised thread. Tacky little bits of the gum had got themselves bleeding embedded in this sort of embossed bit of the stripes. The fingers of Wilf Manton's right hand fretted away at the sticky grey patch on his shirt the way they might have kept returning to press a bruise, play with a ripening boil. He was half aware of their action. A sullen, wiped-out fatigue, penetrating far the other side of drunkenness, had left him morosely bloody-minded. It was his best bleeding shirt! He'd bought it specially to impress at that wash-out of a bloody conference. Now look! He hated himself, everyone in sight, his pigsty of a bloody flat, Ferguson, the girl, the whole of his bloody cocked-up life.

The flat was a disaster area by now. It would take a hard day to get it anywhere near to rights. Stubs from about two million cigarettes had long ago spilled out of the ashtrays to end up any old where – trampled into the carpet, dowsed in glasses, crushed on the tiled mantlepiece – you name it. They stank the place out and the ash they had generated had trailed a sordid lace over every surface in sight. Half-gnawed spare-ribs from the slant-eye take-away up the road had ended up stickily scattered on every flat surface in sight. Sweet and sour sauce had leaked its way through one of the cardboard boxes and was doubtless corroding its way through the so-called polish on the miserable apology for a table at this minute. There were splinters underfoot from at least two broken glasses. And worse than that in the hall from the bathroom where one bastard, not making it in time, had up-chucked his Chinese input reekingly straight back out again against the wall, over the floor. Well, sod it! There was sod all he was going to do about it now.

The squalid mess had become increasingly more apparent as the sodding bunch of freeloaders had thinned out. Four or five of the northern sods had sloped away when the tarts had finally got around to making up their minds who were the lucky lads they'd give a dose to tonight. That was after all the bedroom coming and going, mind you. That sod from Berwick had done his best to get them all in it. Scarpering with the white one with the tits, he'd opened the door to find one of the relays of complaining neighbours standing right there, her fist raised to knock. If it had been a bloke, it would have been a punch-up and no mistake. As it was, there'd been enough shoving going with the language to make it all very nasty for a minute or two. Of course to hope that Ferguson would be one of those buggering off was asking too much of life. He was laid out like lino on, natch, the only halfways decent bed in the place. He'd hung on, no doubt, hoping he'd still have a chance of working his hots off on the girl.

Manton scowled. His hand worked at the tiny, intractable gobbets of gum. It was the girl who was pissing him off more than anything else. She'd insisted on her bleeding sixty quid before she'd shifted a stitch. Then, O.K., she'd done it. Not so bloody well either, if you really wanted to know. Then she'd slipped a raincoat on and sort of disappeared. But then! Then, she'd only bleeding come back from out the bedroom or somewhere and done a bloody encore all for nothing! Just to get her own cheap thrills. She was doing it all over again now, spot on her bum and all, flashing it around for the benefit of three or four hard core – ha! – sods who hadn't got off and hadn't passed out. Sixty quid! If they'd just bloody waited Ferguson could've seen her let it all hang out for absolutely bloody free.

Manton had spent a good fifteen sweaty minutes looking for that cheap handbag but the little bitch had hidden it too well. . . .

He levered himself paunchily to his feet. Talking of that little runt Ferguson, he'd better check on the Vehicle Supply Manager's bastard. The state he was in he could already have sucked some bit of under-cooked, re-heated pork down the wrong hole and choked to death on his own bleeding vomit. Manton staggered wearily to the bedroom door and opened it. Oh Christ! Bedclothes half off him a patently stark-naked Ferguson was breathing with the drunken stertorousness of a steam-engine in labour. It would take a stretcher team to remove him before mid-day. Shit! There'd be no sleeping in that bed for anyone else – least of all its poor bleeding rightful owner. Mind you – looking at the twist of sheeting on the floor and that stained pillow, nobody with an ounce of hygienic sense in his skull would want to.

Pulling a face with a disgust that started with himself and went outward to embrace the world (or was it the other way round? – he was too tired to tell), Manton also pulled shut the bedroom door. As he did so, he heard knocking once again on the flat's front door. His heart jumped and began to pump ice-water the length of his rapidly de-alcoholising veins. There was an official weight about that knocking which bore in upon him instant awareness that a foetid slush of vomit in his passage had suddenly become the least of his problems.

Without the Newmans pushing, the VW bus had fired on the fourth time of asking. Now, five minutes later, Chris cut the engine and they coasted up the driveway to the home. The tinies, once asleep, would not wake to the clatter of its tappets but there were older kids whose daytime restlessness was mirrored in an endlessly turning shallowness of sleep. He pulled on the handbrake, helped his wife step down.

'A model of circumspect driving considering what you knocked back tonight,' she said.

'It was because of what I knocked back that it was circumspect.'

He was fumbling for his door key. The central hall-light in Kingston House was always kept on but this night the moon shone with such a white brilliance there was no need for it. Yet Pat, for one, was glad of the burning bulb. The moonlight bathing the house silvered it over with the leprous sheen of a Gothic horror story. She preferred the universal nightlight her sensible husband insisted be kept on for the comforting of any night straying child.

'Oh dear,' she sighed.

'What, love?'

'All my life, one thing I've really wanted – a bathroom with a bidet.'

'And the Newmans have a bathroom with a bidet.'

'Two bathrooms with a bidet.'

'Well you've only got one pair of cheeks.'

'Not true, actually. And I haven't got one bidet.'

'Ah well. That's the old social worker game for you. . . . I suppose on a clear day you can see right across the kitchen.'

'That's it.'

'Well at least she knows how to put the acreage to use – food was delicious.'

'I could cook like that if I had the money to buy those kind of raw materials.'

'Ah well, they're rich, successful, happily married and adjusted to each other – but we both know there's more to real life than that don't we?' He hugged her

'He's all right, actually, young David,' he said. 'Considering.'

'You'll hold him to his promise about the pool?'

'You bet.'

He pushed the key home and opened the front door. They tiptoed inside and as softly he shut the door after them again.

'You don't think—'

'Sssh!'

Sharpened by his years of work, his ears had picked up a change in rhythm to what should have been the home's night norm. He put his hand on Pat's arm to hold her back a moment. Yes – overhead quite perceptibly now they could hear the uneven noise of step-lift-step that Howard made whenever he walked but which the careless clatter and scufflings and steps of normal feet drowned maskingly out for him the best part of his day. Howard had a problem. He was enuretic. At seventeen he still wet the bed one night in three or thereabouts. God alone knew what the God who made him had permitted one of his other creatures to do to him as a small child, but the legacy was the piddling – yet, in his eyes, so gigantically shaming – curse that every night he still must fearingly anticipate and try and wrestle with. His pride would have no truck with chamber pots. If he could catch himself in time he would stamp to the toilet with the grim doggedness he brought to everything. If he failed, he would fetch fresh linen and make the bed he must lie in the next night himself.

'If only he'd relax,' Pat whispered. 'He's so uptight. If he could relax he'd have it beaten. Fighting it head on is the wrong way!'

'Sssh! . . . That'll come soon. He's nearly got it whipped. It used to be every night, remember.'

They waited another long minute to make sure they were sparing his blushes, then crept carefully upstairs. At this hour there seemed an extra flight. They could pick their way across the crowded living room by the moonlight streaming into it. At such a height, they rarely drew the curtains in this room.

49

Pat disappeared to check on Robert. It was a superfluous gesture, she knew. He was best part of the way to adult. But her heart turned over with affection each time she looked down on his sleeping, darling face and she knew that if she still persisted in the habit, it was probably because she was acknowledging that the times when she might yet do this were starting to dwindle down.

When she returned to their own bedroom, her husband was adjusting the wind-up alarm clock they still used.

'Might as well try for another hour,' he yawned. 'Sunday, lovely Sunday, after all.'

She started to undress. Annoyingly, the dress zipped at the side.

'You looked lovely tonight,' he said suddenly. 'Really.'

Well, she would do it with words, then.

'Are you sure?' she said. 'I could see what an effort it cost you to turn down that nude bathing offer. I mean, it was a prelude to wife-swapping wasn't it?'

'Oh, I shouldn't think so for a minute.'

'Wouldn't you? You never took your eyes off her after that.'

'Or before, actually, if you'd thought to look. She is rather glam . . . Would you, if I hadn't spoken up?'

'Certainly.'

'You would!'

'Of course. I've got a better figure than her.'

'Oh I don't know. Not for us leg men, necessarily.'

But by this time his wife was totally undressed and the pleasure and awe the sight gave him was producing in him the effect for which she'd aimed.

'Stop yawning,' she said as she came to him, 'and start thinking about making love.'

Chapter Four

'Brring, brring. Brring, brring.'

He had been dreaming of a happy time, he thought. Perhaps of when between school and university he had hitchhiked down to Provence and found a magic land where myth and history had seemed to swirl invisibly about him from the harsh rocks and, the world before him, he had romantically wondered what he might be, writer, teacher, politician. . . . But the dream had been instantly erased by the shaft of sound piercing sharp into his brain. All that he retained as his consciousness rose sluggishly upwards was a sense of lost happiness. Then light searing whitely in upon his eyes completed the shock treatment. He was returned to the necessary meanness of everyday reality.

'Doctor Langley,' Pat was saying. 'Just a moment.'

It was every night reality. As he took the receiver he looked at his watch. It was two-thirty. They had been asleep less than an hour and a half. The knowledge drenched him through with conscious fatigue. He covered up the mouthpiece.

'Who is it?' he said thickly.

'The Duty Officer.'

'Oh. . . .'

He sighed, ordered his mind to attention.

'Chris Langley,' he said.

Pat Langley watched as, not blinking now, his voice awake, her husband listened to a short harsh burst of information at the police end of the line. She knew that she was lucky. Their respective professions made small hour calls all part of the day's work but since her time as a hospital junior she had always had the inestimable gift of total awareness the second she awoke. Chris rose from sleep like a dog emerging from water, paddling shorewards with painful effort, shaking himself to shed the lingering effects.

And always succeeding. It was in such prosaic acts of will that she found him most heroic and most loveable.

He handed back the receiver.

'Customer?' she said.

He nodded.

'Yes,' he said. 'Teenage girl. "Place of Safety" order.'

He settled squarely back a moment gathering himself.

'O.K. chaps,' he said in a clipped British parody, 'we're going in. It's the big push.'

And throwing the bedclothes aside he was swinging himself up out of bed. He found his pyjama trousers and pulled them on, put jeans on over them and blundered his way into his baggy Aran sweater.

'How long is this likely to take?' Pat said.

'Oh, half an hour at most. She's already on her way.'

'You want me to get a room ready for this girl? I mean, as I'm already awake.'

Chris stopped brushing his hair back with his hands to shake his head.

'Wendy's job,' he said. 'Good for her soul to be reminded what she's signed on for. I'll go give her a knock.'

Pat grinned at him with affectionate malevolence.

'Just make it her door,' she said.

He grinned at her as rudely.

'Ah, insecure about me in the face of nubile youth, eh?' he said. 'How flattering!'

He came a step nearer the bed.

'Actually, when it comes to it,' he said. 'You've had my all for tonight. And all of next week too, I shouldn't wonder.'

He shook his head slightly as he momentarily recalled how tired he felt.

'First night out in months,' he said. 'I'm getting too old for this game.'

He went out. Half an hour. Pat reached for a paperback.

⚜ ⚜ ⚜ ⚜

Coffee might stop him getting back to sleep. He made cocoa while he waited. He heated enough milk to include Wendy but did not pour hers out. All the time he kept his ears open for the bell: no virtue in having the whole house woken up. Now that his body had had time to register and communicate the fact, he was realising that the brandy seemed to have dehydrated his entire alimentary canal and the muffled drums of hangover were being beaten in a queasy rhythm just behind his itchy eyes.

The bell sounded. He went upstairs to the hall, and opened the front door. Three people confronted him in a symmetrical line astern. At the front was a W.P. Sergeant. Next was a defiantly stone-faced girl. At the rear was the P.C. who would be driver of the Panda car.

' 'Morning, Mr Langley,' the W.P. Sergeant said.

'Not too hearty, please, if you don't mind, sergeant,' he said. 'Come on in.'

He backed away and the trio regrouped in the vestibule. Their formation was informal in appearance but the girl could have had no illusions that she was free to come and go just as she pleased.

'Feeling fragile, are we?' the W.P. Sergeant said.

Chris knew her quite well as Millie Andrews but mateyness would undercut her authority. Tall, she was by no means the butch wrestler of popular legend. There was a hint of light blonde curls at the edge of her cap. Definitely a better class of girl in the force these days, Chris thought.

'A late night,' he said. 'Business was slack so I thought I'd guarantee a sudden surge by actually trying to enjoy myself.'

For the first time he looked directly at the girl.

'What have we got, then?' he said and not unpleasantly.

'A 401. Possible care proceedings. Name's Lucy. She says it's Lucy. Up to now that's all she's said.'

'And the story?'

'A party over in Westmount flats. We had complaints, saw a couple of girls no better than they ought to be come out with fellows who didn't seem worried by the prospect of penicillin treatment. No abatement in noise. We thought it might be a touch of your disorderly houses. It wasn't but when we went in Madam here was up on a table with

53

nothing on except the cassette player and a soppy grin across her face.'

Again he looked at the girl.

'How old are you?' he said.

She jerked her head sullenly away in a gesture that whipped her dark hair about her face. It was a reaction that, had she but known it, softened some part of his heart toward her. It had been so predictable. So cliché. Derived from countless films and television shows, countless fan magazines, countless fellow girls at school showing how tough they were, it showed immediately that in her whole life she had never found a moment to live as her own self. The gesture had been like everything else about her – derived and hence cheap.

The silver lurex blouse was cheap – cheap in its flashily synthetic material and in the obviousness of its doubly crude styling. As cheap and obvious was the lightweight trenchcoat she had draped over her shoulders. Stone-coloured but grubby it held no suggestion of either Hollywood or Bond Street swagger. It cut only a mean, suburban, dash. It said, quite simply, that she did not know – no-one had ever told her – where or how to shop. Or dress. Or to make up: Under the lurid and now greasily messed make-up there was quite a pretty face struggling to get out. A little too heavy about the chin, maybe for his taste, but, given a wash and half a chance, well able to turn the heads of men other than those looking for a quick jump. Colouring apart, in fact, she could well have passed as W.P. Sergeant Millie Andrews' kid sister.

She was staring at him now with all the ill-tempered, unblinking insecurity of a barrack-room lawyer.

'Come on,' he said, 'it's three o'clock in the morning. Make life a little easier on all of us and yourself most of all.'

Again the toss of the head. He had long learnt better than to show any reaction himself. He flicked his eyes ignoringly away.

'What would you say, Sergeant?' he said.

'About fifteen. We started at twenty-two but we had trouble working out what year we were born. Then we shut

54

up. I've got my own money on fifteen. We've put a request in to the Missing Girls Index.'

The sudden blurt of distorted South London voice over the P.C.'s transceiver rescued both of them from acknowledging with their looks that the Index, this early in the proceedings, was well the wrong side of a hundred to one shot. The constable muttered something back into the gadget, then, with a quick look at Millie made for the door and, presumably, his car. At the same time a soft footfall on the stairs made known that Wendy had joined them.

Neither coming or going made any difference to the girl. She was working hard still at seeming bored.

'Hello, Miss Andrews,' Wendy said.

'Hello. Sorry to be ruining your beauty sleep.'

'Far too late for that, I'm afraid.'

It was the first time Chris had heard her lie.

'Wendy,' he said, 'this is Lucy. We think it's Lucy. She doesn't want to talk to us at the moment. See if you can make her feel at home.'

'O.K.,' Wendy said. 'Good. I've put her in the single next to the twins. Come on, Lucy, I'll show you where. Do you want anything to eat or drink?'

With the ungraciousness that was the last weapon remaining to her, the girl shook her head. An improvement, Chris thought: that is direct communication.

'Easily satisfied,' Wendy said. 'O.K., follow me.'

The girl held herself still for three don't-tell-me-what-to-do seconds then, expressionlessly, docilely, she moved toward Wendy and with her up the stairs. Chris watched them to the first turn. In his sleep and drink befuddled state, with the night-time silence outside the house echoing strangely inside his head, he found himself thinking in a way that had no definition of the workings of a life that could take two girls and put them side by side and yet whole worlds apart. It was W.P. Sergeant Andrews who bumped him back to earth.

'She's got sixty quid in her purse,' she said.

'Damn sight more than me.'

'Or me.'

'Apart from the strip show any sign of sex?'

'Not obviously. Doubt if she's exactly still in the chaste white grip of virginity, though.'

'Well, the sixty quid argues otherwise.'

'She could well be from up West,' Millie said. 'Not from our patch at all. Special import for the lads.'

'Yes. Well, we'll soon know.'

The front door opened as the constable re-appeared. He looked less than happy in the exaggerated way of most young men.

'How we doing?' he said.

'Just about finished. Why?'

'Car down the road abandoned and vandalised,' he said. 'Three guesses who's nearest.'

'I was just going to offer you some cocoa,' Chris said.

For a moment the temptation less of cocoa than of routine work postponed showed in the faces of the police team. But it was a night for duty all round.

'Thanks but we're not allowed to touch the hard stuff while on duty,' Millie said. 'Quicker we get this done, quicker we get back to the station and real drink.'

'Aha!'

'Besides you need some beauty sleep as well as Wendy.'

Chris showed them out. He went silently upstairs. No screams or thuds came from the direction of the room that now was Lucy's – if that was her name. Quietly, so as not to disturb Robert, he threaded his way through his moon-lit sitting room and down the corridor to Pat. The light still on, she was sitting up in bed reading.

She looked up.

'What's she like?' she said.

'Her name's Lucy.'

He kicked off his shoes.

'We think it's Lucy. She's fifteen. We think she's fifteen.'

'Oh. The strong silent type.'

He nodded.

'I don't know how you can,' he said. 'Read like that at this hour.'

'Better than being woken up twice.'

'What is it?' He was pulling his sweater off.

'That thing *The Deal*.'

'The one about Hollywood?'

'Yes.'

'Whatever made you buy that?'

'Didn't. Someone left it in the waiting room weeks ago. Surprisingly good, actually.'

'Oh?'

'Trouble is someone's ripped out what was obviously the big sex scene.'

'Ah,' he said, 'well, tomorrow's Sunday. We'll nip over to the vicar and get it back.'

He got into bed and, a second time that morning, snapped off the light.

But awake and thoughtful her voice came on at him out of the darkness.

'You know,' she said, 'Robert's French accent.'

'. . . yes?'

'It's tolerably atrocious. We really ought to do something about getting him over—'

'Oh, for Christ's sake!' he said.

Chapter Five

SUNDAY. MORNING. BREAKFAST. Sleep still coiled at the centre of her power to think straight, Wendy dabbed with a paper towel at the milk which Rebecca Roberts had just cascaded across the tinies' table with all the exuberance of her five-year-old arm. Far from crying over what she had brought about, she had seen it as cause for dissolving into a fit of guiltily awed giggling almost as shapeless and, Wendy feared, as fluid, as the mess she had caused.

'Rebecca!' Wendy had snapped. 'It isn't funny! It's a waste and it means more work for whoever is nice enough to clean up after you!'

There was a bad-tempered edge to the voice. It had come from the weight of tiredness, not genuine anger, but it had none the less proved very effective. Rebecca had shut up at once. Perhaps, her guilt otherwise directed, she had blushed. But, granted her Deptford-Jamaican complexion, it was hard to judge. Wendy looked swiftly down at Dean. Her waspishness did not seem to have rattled him. Perhaps it was because, purely by luck, she had begun by calling Rebecca by name. Certainly he was as hunched and in-drawn as ever as he sat beside her but the too rigid concentration was at the moment all upon his bowl of corn-flakes.

'Silly girl's stuff!' Peter Jackson called out from Dean's other side across at the now contrite Rebecca.

'That's enough, Peter,' Wendy said as mentally she cursed their ability to go from zero to a hundred within five seconds of waking. 'Especially from a young gentleman who may have a brand new baby sister before the day is over.'

'But we don't know yet,' Chris Langley said. He had made his first appearance of the morning looking as washed out as Wendy felt.

'I've just been talking to your Daddy on the telephone,

58

Peter,' he said. 'He sends his love. But he says your Mummy hasn't started to have her baby yet. So we still don't know if it's going to be a boy or a girl. Exciting, isn't it?'

Enthusiasm was rather conspicuously lacking from Peter's token nod.

'Shall we have a bet on it?' Chris said. 'Bet you two p it's a boy.'

Peter gravely considered.

'No,' he said at last, 'I don't think we'll do that.'

'Won't we? Oh, all right, then.'

Chris turned to Wendy.

'How are you this morning?' he said.

'Marginally better after seeing what you look like.'

He nodded as he grimaced.

'That's all right,' he said. 'I find I can't face the snap, crackle and pop this morning. Too loud. By the way, I never asked – how did Ronnie take to the *dolce vita* of a Saturday night in Kingston House? Or don't I ask?'

'Oh you can ask. But I've no lurid confessions. Bit of a non-event, if you really want to know. He pushed off as soon as it wasn't absolutely indecently early. I don't think he found us up to *Annabel*'s.'

'How's our newcomer, in that case?'

'Laid out like lino snoring her head off when I looked in twenty minutes ago.'

'All right for some, isn't it. Still, hardly surprising. How are we on the clothes front?'

'Front's the operative word. But I dug some things out of the linen cupboard. Any further word from the police?'

'No. I had a quick word just now. But no.'

'Won't go to court, will it?'

'Shouldn't think so. I'll pop into the Court Section tomorrow when I'm in town. If you can get her talking in the meantime. . . .'

'Yes. Will do. Will try to do, that is.'

'Who she is. Why she left home.'

'Where home is.'

'Right. You might do worse than try using Mrs Wilson as your under-cover agent. Oops – excuse me.'

Very, very slowly Chris leaned across Wendy with his arm stretched out towards Dean's cornflake bowl. His empty spoon half-way down from his mouth, the thin, large-headed child froze into a statue. A statue that began visibly to tremble.

'It's all right, Dean, no-one is going to hurt you,' Chris said with a gentle slowness. 'Just let me have your spoon a minute, please, Dean.'

He tugged the spoon free from a hand that did not resist but, once empty, did not move.

'Look,' Chris said.

As all the children watched he delved with the spoon in the bottom of the cornflake bowl and scooped up something a bright, shiny green.

'Look,' he said, 'a badge. Dean's the lucky one today.'

He was wiping it clean on the sleeve of his shirt.

'A frog,' he said. 'But we couldn't have you eating a frog, Dean. Not when he's a smart one like this and you're supposed to wear him on your pullover. Here.'

Slowly, again, he pushed the spoon back into Dean's small, clenched fist. The trembling had stopped. To Wendy's surprise, the head that had stared at the table throughout twisted on its thin neck and the wide grey eyes looked up. Wendy could see the man they now looked at reflected in their enormous irises. It was as if a pet animal had just conceived there were beings in the world it might be possible to trust. But Chris did not push his luck. He slowly handed the cheap plastic promotional gimmick to Wendy.

'I'll give this to Wendy,' he said, 'and when you've finished eating she can help you put it on. You sit and think whereabouts on your pullover he should go. And perhaps if you're very clever you can think of a name for him.'

'Kermit!' Rebecca shouted.

'That's another frog,' Wendy said quickly. 'Not Dean's frog.'

Chris winked at her. Good girl, he thought.

'Going after some real coffee,' he said. 'Upstairs. Let me know how it goes with Lucy.'

He made for the door but as he did so Bill Hutton had risen from the senior table to intercept him.

'Yes, Bill?' Chris said.

Unobtrusively Bill Hutton paced with him to the doorway out of anyone's earshot amid that clattering degree of hubbub.

'While I think of it, Chris,' he said. Unlike his famous namesake he had nothing of Yorkshire in his voice. Rather he had the flat, matt-finish accent of sub-Cockney. He was pushing sixty. There was a coarse-pored, unfinished look about his features that suggested a lower-class poverty in his past and an upright stance, a short back and sideness to the cut of his iron grey hair suggesting the military or, perhaps, the police.

'It may be nothing,' he was going to say, 'but last night, it being Saturday, the older ones were staying up a bit later to watch the tele.'

'Yes?'

'Well, I was actually outside the room, just passing, when Howard called me in. He came to the door to do it, too.'

'Why?'

'That was the funny thing. The news was on. There was some report from Northern Ireland about the army patrols doing a sweep operation in South Armagh after this last bomb outrage. . . . Well, you know how all that means nothing to most of the kids. It's just another war film. I mean, they don't associate what they see with murder and people getting blown to pieces who won't be put back together just by counting to a hundred in fives.'

Chris possessed himself with patience. When Bill was setting a context you didn't rush him.

'Well, there was one kid sitting there with his eyes screwed as tight as he could manage and his hands squeezed ditto over his ears. I mean he just didn't want to know.'

'Who was it?'

'That's it. Of all kids it was Jamie McEvoy.'

'Good Lord!'

'Exactly. Our little "I can't wait to join the army"

61

merchant. I mean, a John Wayne film and he's glued to the set. He's halfway down the tube.'

'. . . yes. What happened next?'

'Nothing. The item changed to something else and, I suppose he could still hear a bit because he opened his eyes, took his hands down when he saw it was all right and slowly relaxed. He was as pale as if he'd seen a ghost, though. I was trying to remember . . . McEvoy. Are his people from Ireland? Belfast. What's left of them.'

Chris shook his head.

'No,' he said. 'Not for the last couple of generations, anyway. They come from down the Milfield Road actually.'

'I thought so.'

Chris paused a moment lost in immediately pointless thought.

'I don't have any instant explanation either, Bill,' he said, 'but I'm sure you're right to bring it up. I'm sure it's significant. . . . No fire bombs on the screen, were there?'

'Not that I saw, Chris. I thought I'd mention it now. By the time I'm back from church I'll most likely have forgotten it.'

'No-one believes that, Bill. You say Howard picked this up first? That's nice to know, isn't it?'

Bill Hutton looked past Chris Langley toward the home's thick-set unofficial Head Boy.

'I thought so,' he said.

⚜⚜⚜⚜

Surfacing toward a consciousness of strange sounds, strange plays of light across her face, but, for the moment, still asleep, Lucille Wyatt stretched in bed with a natural animal pleasure. Something about the ease, the luxury, the sense of space with which she did this completed her coming awake. She opened her eyes upon a strange ceiling. And remembered! God! If her Dad found out!

Shaken, terrified, she sat bolt upright in the strange bed in the strange new room. Get away! Get home! She must get away! Before they found out her name and all about her. School. She must – no, wait! What day was it! No, she must think straight. Be smart. Outsmart them. . . . A curtain with a cheerful, pretty yellow pattern was flapping against a slightly opened window. Even as she tried to get some grip on herself the thought came to her how much nicer, brighter, larger this room was than her own cramped, partitioned excuse for a place to sleep in at home. Why there was even a wash basin and mirror in the corner. You could sleep and get washed all in the same room!

Money! Her money! The rotten bastards would have taken it all away! She sprang sideways out of bed and snatched her scuffed, once shiny, always cheap evening bag up from where she'd let it fall the night before. She fumbled it open. The sleeves on this God awful night thing they'd given her were a mile wide. The sods! She'd just known they would – oh no! Thank God! It was still there. Now – where to hide it? No. Get ready first then stuff – Christ! Someone coming! She dropped the bag and scooted back into bed. She was still and breathing slowly through her open mouth a split second before she heard the door handle turn. Steps, a woman's, she reckoned, came into the room. She could feel, really feel, the hot sort of feeling of someone looking at her. She moved slowly in the bed and groaned slightly to show she was still asleep. It worked. The footsteps went away. The door handle went again. The door closed. Lucy Wyatt opened her eyes and sat up.

And found herself staring straight at the cow who'd shown her up here the night before. The rotten bitch had conned her. She hadn't left the room at all! She was even bloody smiling. Lucy glared straight back at her. Stuck up bitch, you could bloody tell.

'If you want breakfast, it's now or never,' she was going on about. 'You'll find something to wear on that chair. You'll have to make do with your own undies, I'm afraid. Breakfast is all the way downstairs. Just keep on going.'

Another phoney smile and this time the cow had really gone and left the room. Her steps faded away. Lucy stuck her tongue out at the fast shut door. It didn't help that at the back of her mind, the part that couldn't lie was telling the rest, be honest, the stuck up cow was rather pretty. If

63

you liked that sort of thing. Not that she'd be frightened of any comparison. . . .

Less than fully aware why she did so, she once more got out of bed, and went towards the mirror. Now she had time to think about it, it was a nice feeling having carpet under your feet when you got out of bed even if it was a bit patchy.

Oh my Gawd! Not even the most dishonest part of her brain could get away with telling her she was a pretty sight this morning. She looked a right bleeding mess.

The diagnosis was correct. The overkill make-up of the night before might have served its tarty turn in the dim lighting of 'The Crown' and Manton's flat, but the cold light of dawn showed it as cracked, smudged and run. No face cream here, of course but soap, at least. Least she could do was have a sluice and clear this muck right off her chops. . . . Not naturally, hesitating at the novelty of doing such a thing in a bedroom, she slowly turned on the hot tap. Real live hot water came out and she nearly bloody scalded her finger off getting the stopper in before she wasted half of it. Fancy! She stared almost as if mesmerised as the basin began to fill. Her left hand scratched unconsciously at her scalp. Then consciously. Christ, her hair was as greasy as all get out. And it didn't look no better. . . .

Twelve minutes later she was following her nose downstairs. A partial transformation had taken place. The working estimate set on her age of fifteen now seemed, if anything, almost pitching it too high. The scrubbed clean face, the white blouse and navy blue skirt Wendy had found for her had reduced her to the school girl ranks to a degree that would have brought a cold sweat forth on Manton's brow. The knowledge on which part of her person she currently carried sixty pounds might well have given him a cardiac arrest.

Yet for the duration of her descent of the staircase, it was Lucy who was nervous. She did not mind the sound from down below of little nippers singing nursery rhymes. That was square and corny but still nice. The thing was she didn't know this place. Any of them might jump out on her anytime. And there were some kids about. About her own age. They could be bloody anything. Real criminals. Nutters Sex maniacs. There was one long thin streak of nig-nog in the hallway who definitely gave her a dirty grin as she came down the last few steps and did his best to look right up her skirt.

'Things are looking up, man,' he told his mates, 'and I sure wish I was too.'

They all laughed, the rotten piss-takers, and she had to look hard at him to make sure he kept his black hands to himself as she went round them. She was glad when she got down to the basement sort of room and found this kitchen thing empty except for a fattish woman who looked like Mrs Earnshaw down her road going at a great wad of dough like one o'clock. Lucy quite liked Mrs Earnshaw. Sometimes she let her mind her little girl. Perhaps this woman would be nice as well. She'd be better than a nig-nog with wandering hands, at any rate.

The woman had stopped pounding at the dough.

'Yes?' she said.

'They said there'd be breakfast,' Lucy said.

'Who did?'

'I don't know. Her.'

'Her? . . . You new here?'

'Must be, mustn't I?'

The woman nodded at a large old-fashioned clock up on the wall as she went back to her kneading.

'Nearly half past ten,' she said. 'What you think this is – the Ritz?'

Sod her then. Lucy turned to go.

'As you're new and you don't know better I can do you tea and toast. Suit you?'

Lucy turned again. The woman had paused again.

'Well,' she said, 'yes or no? I got work to do.'

'Great,' Lucy said. The way it came out it sounded quite nasty. It was really quite nice of the woman but she didn't want to seem too grateful.

'Sit down, then,' the woman was saying. 'Try and keep your elbows out of the flour.'

She was rubbing and smacking flour from her own hands

65

as she moved up to a big gas cooker like they had in the school kitchens. Lucy sat down at the unused end of the long, scrubbed wooden table the dough was sitting on. There was a nice feel to the room. It felt all clean. It was partly the way a clear bright light was coming through the window high up in the wall facing her. You looked up through the window and you could see the ground. Some kids must be playing. Their outlines kept running backwards and forwards against the light and there were shouts. The woman was reaching for a loaf. With a "pow" she lit the oven grill.

'Ever made pastry?' she asked.

Lucy had. At school domestic science was the one thing she liked. The lessons were always too short. But she didn't want to give too much away.'

'No,' she said.

The woman shook her head and Lucy wished she'd told the truth. She could feel the money stuck in her drawers now that she'd sat down. The woman was pouring water into a tea pot.

'Always warm the pot,' she muttered half to herself. 'How long you in for, then?'

'Don't know,' Lucy said. 'Don't know anything about it. Don't care either.'

'You'll like it, you know,' the woman said.

'Oh, yeah?'

'If you don't, it's your fault. Jam or marmalade?'

'Jam.'

The woman looked sharply at her and Lucy knew at once what she was getting at.

'Please,' she said.

The woman nodded. She went to a wall cupboard and fetched down a jar of dark red jam. Plum or strawberry, most like. She had a nice face, Lucy suddenly decided. It was round and rough looking, a bit like her. It looked as though it wouldn't put up with any cheek but there was something nice about it all the same.

'What's your name?' the woman said.

'Lucy,' Lucy said.

66

'Lucy who? Lucy Lockett?'

'Lucy mind your own business.'

They'd probably told the old cow to pump her.

'That's no trouble dearie.'

'I don't like being spied on.'

'Don't flatter yourself, love. I couldn't give a monkey's who you are. Only names that mean anything to me are Heinz and Sainsbury's. And Wilson.'

'Wilson?'

'That's right. That's my name.'

Lucy nodded. She decided to try and say nothing. She sat and watched moodily as the woman – Mrs Wilson – flipped the toast over, put tea-pot, cup and milk on the same tray as the jam. Now she could smell the toast she realised that she was ruddy starving. It seemed like ages before Mrs Wilson was satisfied the toast's second side was done enough. Finally, she was bringing the tray across.

'There you are,' she said. 'Nothing like toast done under gas. Crisp on the outside, all soft in.'

'Thank you,' Lucy remembered to say.

She made no effort to be ladylike or anything as she tore into the first slice. She knew it was her speed that had brought a slight smile for the first time to Mrs Wilson's face as she went back to shaking the table with her going at the dough, but to hell with that! She was too hungry to care. She reached for the jam again for the second slice – plum it was – and so, for all her sharpness, missed the quick shake of the head that Mrs Wilson gave to Wendy Raeburn on her entrance.

'Okay, Lucy?' Wendy asked.

Startled, Lucy looked up suddenly. Not this time from surliness, she nodded. Her chewing mouth was full. Wendy nodded back the once.

'Good,' she said. 'Leave you to it, then.'

As Lucy swallowed her way clear to speak, she began to go. Lucy was taken by surprise. She had expected a long, serious grilling this time. Bossy boots had almost got to the door before she remembered the way to get people's attention.

'Excuse me, miss,' she said.

Because of the initiative, because of the formality with which it was expressed, it was now Wendy's turn to be surprised.

'Don't call me "miss",' she said. 'My name's Wendy, remember. Wendy Raeburn.'

She waited but the response to her cue was not what she had hoped.

'Is there a place somewhere I can wash my hair?' Lucy asked.

'Yes. There's a telephone shower thingummy in the bathroom.'

Something, Wendy was thinking. She must try to build on it.

'I'll let you have some of my shampoo,' she said. 'And I've got a drier you can borrow.'

'Thanks.'

'And then perhaps we can have a chat.'

No answer. Wendy almost saw the portcullis crash defensively down. But she'd put the cards back down on the table.

'You don't want to stay here, do you?' she said.

No answer.

'Sooner you can start talking, sooner we can help you.'

No answer still came as the sullen reply.

⚜⚜⚜

The shower thing had been lovely. She had got the water just right. Almost too hot to stand but not quite. The shampoo had seemed so much nicer than the stuff her Dad got for them all at the Cash and Carry. Her hair had never felt cleaner, fresher.

And now this dryer. Her Mum had said they were a try on. A rip-off, she meant. But they weren't. They were terrific. She was going to get one for her next birthday if it killed her. It was lovely feeling the dry heat get right down to the roots.

Sitting on the edge of the bed far nicer than her own bed in the room far nicer than her own, Lucy Wyatt closed her

68

eyes the better to enjoy the sheer sensuous feel of the hot air drying her clean hair. She had not put her blouse back on after the shampooing and the minimal but cleavage-thrusting bra, the crossing of her legs, the overtones of old film glamour associated with girls brushing their hair all conspired to push her age upwards again. As her longish hair swayed and swung as she tossed her head about, parted and reformed as the air currents passed through it, no distinct style but hints of a dozen framed her face. She was schoolgirl and housewife, secretary and whore within seconds. She was thirteen and thirty.

At last she was satisfied. She turned off the dryer and stood up. She bent forward and, hair streaming forward, shook her head wildly from side to side. So clean! It felt so good! She straightened, tossed the hair back again. Fluffing it up with her hands back-combing fashion, she walked over to the mirror.

This time she liked what she saw. Even like this her hair looked good. Sort of Afro, sort of punk. Now she'd slick it back. She raised her hands and, as so often, found herself looking at her breasts. As always, they excited her. They were good ones, she knew. Just what men liked. Some girls she knew at school were embarrassed by having big tits and boys saying dirty things about them. But, fancy! Fancy being all flat as a boy yourself like Sonia Lewison who hated games and changing. Not much fun in life for her or many easy sixty quids! But boobs like these – you could be a star, maybe, one day. She stared hard at herself until the reflection staring back went all hard at the same time the room behind it went all soft. It seemed then to be almost someone else staring back at her. Someone pleased with herself. As Lucy watched she reached her hands up and cupping her breasts pushed them higher and more forward. She began to sway and twist to the very same music Lucy had stripped to the night before. Lucy heard her humming it. Of course, it was really all herself.

Humming louder she moved from the mirror and began to make her movements, her turns and looks over the shoulder broader. She was pretending she was in some night club or something now, like in Soho or Las Vegas or somewhere famous like that. She didn't actually take off her clothes – that would have been a bit pointless considering – but mimed unpeeling an outer skirt, mimed unhooking the bra and being ever so slow in letting her hands let it slip down her front. It was only pretend but she was feeling the warm, soft, sweet and sexy feeling she always got at the thought of lots of men all looking at her when she had nothing on. Looking never done no-one no harm. There were special daring briefs they advertised in the papers. If she could just think of an address to have them sent to – Christ! She had to start thinking about getting home! Before her Dad found out all about what she'd gone and done!

She stopped her imitative little routine. She stopped her fantasy. She moved to put on her blouse. She'd told her parents that she was going to spend the weekend at Jackie's. Her Dad didn't go much on that but when she'd done it before, really done it and behaved herself that is, it had all gone off all right. Jackie would make something up for her. Saying she was there gave her a whole weekend without having to account for all her comings and goings. . . . She'd said she'd go straight on to school from there on Monday. That was tomorrow. If she could go on getting away with not letting on who she was for one more day. . . .

⚘⚘⚘

Clouds were beginning to nudge their way into the afternoon sky. For the moment, the first time in weeks, it seemed, one had actually covered the sun. It was still warm. It must have been the sudden unaccustomed change in the quality of the light that had made her shiver. Yes, that was it. Satisfied by her explanation, Wendy Raeburn brought her hand down from shading her eyes and, lowering her head, resumed her careful watch upon Dean.

There was good need. As had been agreed by Dr Benton, as was their defined legal right, Dean was being visited by his parents.

They had been obliged not to take him out of the grounds of Kingston House. He sat now on one of the child's scale

70

benches to one side of the play area. Awkward, hunched on account of its lowness, his mother sat next to him. His father and erstwhile bone-breaker uneasily stood obliquely facing them. On Dean's tee shirt where Wendy had pinned it was the bright green blob of his plastic frog. It didn't move. There was something compellingly horrifying in the way that all the time, trying to attract his attention, his mother talked at him, he sat holding himself quite rigid, his grave eyes not leaving your face for more than three seconds at a time. Wendy wondered if it had been the change in the light.

The mother was squat, round, a mediaeval peasant. The teenage coupling that had been the instant of Dean's unwanted conception had not been on her part the turned-on going-all-the-way of some sadly false-precocious school-girl sex kitten. A look at the broad, round face spoke instantly of a thick, animal desire stupidly, not quite comprehendingly gratified.

And for the father – the husband trapped for what must now seem to him forever to this, well, stupid cow? Wendy could only guess with any certainty at his feelings that time he had been engendering Dean's life. Here was an easy mark. Do anything to get it. Let you do anything. You didn't have to look at it when you were inside and on top. And afterwards – a life sentence. She'd probably been too stupid and dismayed to tell him anything before it was too late, thank God, to try the things he would have tried to make her try. They had been married two months before Dean's quite normal birth. Now, almost certainly, there would be other conventionally sexy girls and the first dim awareness of divorce possibilities would be coming together behind that pale, blank face.

In appearance Dean's father was an enigma. Just into his twenties, he was short – so short that you could almost have taken him to be a jockey at first glance. He had something of a jockey's sharp-faced wariness, a jockey's disproportion-ately prominent hands. But he was a touch taller than most jockeys and certainly a deal stockier. There was a distinct impression of street-corner tough-kid strength in the thick-ness of muscle across his shoulders. What gave him over-

71

tones of a surly inscrutability above all this was his colouring. He was pale to a point close to albino. And two-thirds bald. His very fine hair had almost entirely receded from the centre and top of his skull. The barest thinned-out residue remained to sketch in what once had been the limits of the full head of hair.

Again Wendy felt unnaturally cold. The overall effect of this boy-father was less than prepossessing. The hint of pent-up violence in him was too strong for comfort. It promised to be a violence against the whole world. That was the chief cause for disquiet. Given the world as a potential target, the white, tight-lipped face gave no clue in which particular direction that violence might explode. So far only history had provided clear, dreadful indication of what might most easily prove the violence's whipping boy.

Unsure of quite how to stand, where to put his hands as his wife talked, his son ignored, the father was now reaching a tube of Smarties out from the breast pocket of his denim jacket. He held them out. With an intense seriousness Dean took the tube as if to do so were a necessary, dangerous chore. He made no attempt to open it but immediately turned his eyes to look for Wendy once again.

⚜⚜⚜

'Jamie! . . . Jamie!'

There was still no answer. Chris Langley looked round the wide expanse of low but densely growing gorse and bracken that made up the Common on both sides of the horse path. He felt his irritation swelling to a real anger. Careful, he warned himself, no indulging your own feelings. Why not? the other side of him objected. Why not just this once. It's no help having little Angus on your shoulders like a ton of lead now, is it? Go on! Let yourself go!

'Jamie! Come on now! We've got to get back for supper! It's not fair on the others.'

Still nothing. He could tell that some of the other lads were still finding it funny but for most the joke was over for them too. Angus shivered and he felt the chilly vibration run across his own shoulders. It had been a mistake bringing

72

Angus. He was just a bit too young and small to keep up with the others. And the ramble, the game of 'Tin Can Copper' had gone on just that bit too long perhaps. Well, too long certainly if Jamie was going to bugger them about like this. He was out there somewhere, of course, watching them right now, camouflaged up to the nines somewhere between a Royal Marine Commando and the last of the Mohicans.

'Please, sir, you want us to spread out and look for him?'

'No, Billy, we won't do that. That's just what he wants us to do. If he's going to spoil our supper, we'll spoil his fun.'

The cluster of boys looked at him uncertainly. Whatever happened to my Muggsy Spannier L.P., he inconsequentially thought.

'Jamie, this is the last time! You report here at once! And that's an order!'

The paramilitary ploy utterly failed to work. No figure abruptly stood up in the flat sea of green to right or left. The Common didn't look anything much when you zipped by on the A road it ran up to border. But stop your car, wander along one of the sandy tracks across it, and you'd soon see that finding one determined thirteen-year-old, his mind set on hiding, made searching for a needle in a haystack marginally the softer option.

'Donnie!'

As best Angus' straddling presence would allow, Chris jerked his head at Jamie's room-mate. He led him slightly apart.

'What do you think, Donnie?' he said.

'Don't know, Mr Langley.'

'Come on, Donnie. Is he lost?'

'Him, Mr Langley. You must be joking.'

'I think I must. All right.'

He looked round a last time. The flat greenness. Nothing. He felt Angus shiver once again. The day had seen the end of the long run of soft halcyon summer days. Not quite a heat wave, the weather had flowed on for weeks with one day to fall in love on followed by another. But that afternoon a chill wind had sprung up. Pewter-coloured clouds had built up from the West to cover the whole sky. As the Kingston House party had roamed across the Common, the light green of the gorse had visibly been darkened as the blue sky was effaced. Rain, and a lot of it, was not long away.

'O.K., gentlemen,' Chris called out, 'back to the V.W. We'll make him follow us. This time Mahommet can come to the mini-bus.'

Pleased to be done with hanging about, the boys filed by. Chris tilted his head up as far as he could.

'Soon have you in the warm, Angus,' he said. 'Tell you what – I'll let you down and you'll be out of the breeze more. You and I can have a little run to get warmed up.'

He crouched down and, with difficulty, Angus got himself dismounted. Chris took his hand. In awkward step they began to jog together after the others up the yielding, dusty, horse-shoe printed track.

Flat on his stomach on a slight rise in the sweep of bracken, Jamie McEvoy watched them moving off. He was rather less than pleased. He was pleased they had not located him but annoyed no party had set out to hunt him down properly. His plan had been to slip through the advancing cordon and then spring out on the general, Mr Langley, to kidnap him. Now he would have to think of something else. That was it! The bus could be a machine-gun nest. He'd make a wide sweep and come at it using the ditch alongside the main road. They'd not be expecting him from that direction. The thing was to keep low and right out of sight all the way up to the road.

His grand manoeuvre took him twenty-five minutes. Not once during that time did it occur to him they might drive off and leave him.

It did to Chris. The knowledge that their now inevitably way-overdue arrival back at Kingston House would push his luck with Mrs Hughes right up to the limit had nagged him seriously into considering the idea. For five seconds. That was the one kind of betrayal, desertion, he could never inflict on any of his charges. Then, as time crept coldly along and the remaining boys began to moan and grumble and

74

complain of being starving hungry a much profounder worry started to gnaw into his thinking. Bill Hutton had reported that Jamie had been made excruciatingly uptight by that actuality news-footage from Armagh. You never, never could be sure of what exactly, what pained, mistaken, proud, neglected, misunderstood and fearful feelings were going on inside their heads. They all came deprived and abused in some way or another. Perhaps beyond repair. Could Jamie have taken it into his head to abscond? Was he making a run for it? Was he bolting desperately, despairingly toward some magic, over-the-rainbow land that existed for him alone and only in his mind? In his mind because the pain of the real world caused that mind – obliged it – to picture an escape that, yes, if you really did try really hard, you could make-believe was really real.

Cradling Angus on his lap and in his anorak, Chris looked at his watch. If Jamie was not back in the next seven minutes, he might leave one of the responsible boys here, whip the others back, come straight back here himself and. . . . A quarter of an hour later, pacing up and down outside the bus, he had otherwise made no movement. He was doing that when out of nowhere Jamie at last broke cover. There was a swagger in his walk which visibly diminished in proportion to the distance between the two of them across the stony car-park area. Chris noticed that. For the moment, he decided, that would be enough. A serious talk later. Time for that later but not now.

'Just get in,' he said deliberately tersely.

He slid the side door of the bus open for Jamie, slammed it shut after. Irrelevantly, by no means for the first time, the note-taking part of his mind chose this moment to notice the boy's pudding-basin hair-cut. It had 'institution' written all over it. And Jamie was not alone. Being denied a bit of well-cut flair in their hair-styles was such a social handicap for the Kingston teenagers. Old Mr Witherspoon really wasn't up to anything beyond short back and sides and the girls had even less chance of a hint of professional class. Perhaps Wendy might have ideas on that front. Talk to her later, too. He climbed in through the driver's door and slid behind the wheel. Behind, the rear of the bus was as silent as a tomb! It was a silence that compelled Jamie to counter-attack.

'Couldn't find me, could you, anyone!' he said. There was a central emptiness to his would-be triumphant tone that correctly anticipated the response he was in for. Nothing. Pissed off, the other boys had decided to repay him in a sort of kind. They were sending him to Coventry. Good, thought Chris vindictively, that'll get the message home to him better than anything. He reached out and turned on the ignition.

The engine coughed, rattled and groaningly died away. He tried again. This time there was a sustainedly hollow moan, quite loud for a moment, that faded to a dying whisper. He pulled out the choke and asked the engine the question for a third time. The answer this time sounded strangled at birth and the heavy, sweet smell of petrol flooded through the inside of the microbus.

Ten further minutes later his hands and the anorak cuffs he had neglected to roll back both soiled with grease, Chris was kneeling at the rear of the bus staring in disconsolate defeat into its crammed engine compartment. A movement at the corner of his vision caused him to turn his head. It was Jamie, his face still caked with the dust he'd camouflagingly smeared across it.

'Forty minutes waiting for you,' Chris now found it necessary to say. The engine break-down had not brought any fresh sweetness and light to his voice.

'Didn't you hear me, for God's sake?' he added.

Unconvincingly, Jamie shook his head. Knowing he had made him lie did nothing to improve Chris' temper.

'Anyway, that didn't make the motor go wrong, did it?' Jamie said.

Chris spun round on him.

'Believe it or not,' he said fiercely, 'but at this precise moment I find that particular piece of useless information absolutely no bloody consolation whatsoever.'

'But, sir, I was only—'

'For God's sake, Jamie! Don't you know the first requirement of any soldier who's going to be taken seriously is being able to obey orders? If this had been some military operation we were all involved with here we'd probably all be bloody blown to bits by now!'

The boy gulped in a great swallow of air. Under the smeared dirt his face had paled. Chris cursed himself. He wanted to reach out an arm and touch Jamie on the shoulder and say something nice. But it seemed dramatically wrong. It seemed as if it would be too abrupt a change of mood. The gesture remained unperformed.

ෂෂෂ

'There they are at last! Thank God!'

Standing at the top of the short flight of steps up to the main entrance of Kingston House, Wendy Raeburn let her breath out in a heartfelt sigh. At least part of her could relax now. It wasn't being involved in some ghastly accident that had made them late. She had found herself making up dreadful headlines while she waited but the good old bus was all in one lovely piece. It had been quite irrational, of course, to think that hanging about outside would make it come any quicker, but, well, maybe it had.

'Howard,' she said, 'go down to the kitchen, please, and tell Mrs Wilson they've finally arrived.'

He must be miles away. He was staring straight at her but he hadn't taken in a word. She hadn't said 'run' now, had she? No. He had said he'd keep her company. She stared straight back at him and, seeming to come to, he blinked.

'Howard,' she tried again, 'go and say they're here, please.'

He nodded and, swinging round, limped back inside the door. His leg was such a cruel impairment. He was a strong, good-looking boy in every other way. And seventeen. You could just tell what crippled adolescence must be doing to him. She would have to work at a more businesslike relationship between them in future.

The bus rocked to a stand-still. Unusually, Chris had brought it right up to the front door. Plainly starved out of

77

their minds, the boys jumped down from it like . . . like Howard would never do. They came bounding, scrambling past her as she came down the steps to Chris.

'This once you needn't wash your hands,' Chris was calling after them. They seemed all present and correct.

'Except you,' he added quickly. The one boy in no hurry to scuttle away was Jamie McEvoy. He was closer to creeping and subdued to the point of totally crestfallen.

'If you think anybody wants to sit and eat looking at you in that state, you've got another think coming,' Chris was going on. 'That's if there's anything left us to eat!'

Jamie McEvoy came up the steps past Wendy and she could tell the whiteness of his face was part of his effort not to cry. He'd obviously been on the receiving end of a lot of stick from Chris.

'Whatever kept you?' Wendy asked.

Chris slammed the driver's door violently to.

'Bloody thing wouldn't start again,' he said. 'Ended up phoning all over the place to get hold of Ted Campbell. Public bloody call box. All the palaver of finding enough two p's. Got him in the end and he came out and managed to jump start the damned thing. Good bloke, really. Says he'll swing by tomorrow and take her in for a lookover. Whether it's a one hundred pound lookover or a three hundred pound lookover we shall doubtless discover in due course.'

'Oh, come on, Chris, we thought you'd spilled their blood all over the road.'

'Well . . . damned thing.'

'It looks as though you spilt some of Jamie's anyway.'

'Yes. Well, you're beginning to know how it goes. When things break down it's always a kid who gets blamed.'

Wendy looked sideways at him. There was something in his voice she hadn't heard before and didn't know could be there. As they climbed the front steps together she gathered herself. He was far from being in the best of moods but he might as well have all the bad news at once.

'Chris,' she began, 'I think I'd—'

78

'Sorry, love,' he interrupted her with, 'but let it wait five minutes. I'm absolutely dying for a pee.'

Necessity proving stronger than good manners he dashed forward up the steps and abruptly in through the front door. Wendy reached out to stop it closing on the rebound and felt the first drops of the evening rain upon her arm.

When, five minutes later, Chris Langley descended the stairs to the kitchen-dining room he was beginning to be more like his usual self. The negative ecstasy of no longer having a burstingly distended bladder almost made the near endless wait to relieve it worthwhile. It was warm inside. The bus was at least home. The clatter from below declared that, better late than never, the boys were getting stuck into their grub. Not such a bad idea, his own stomach reminded him. He came through the doorway to the dining room and the first person he saw was his own wife. She was carrying a tray of dirty plates.

'Pat!' he said, 'for heaven's sake! What are you doing here?'

It was their ironclad rule that Pat had her own work and that she should stay with it in a water-tight compartment. But now she was shrugging and smiling with amused resignation. It was Wendy Raeburn who came quickly forward with the explanation.

'I'm afraid it's all my fault, Chris,' she was saying. 'I tried to have a word with Mrs Hughes about being especially careful around Dean and, well, I'm afraid she took it personally. She didn't say much at first but after a while she just upped and took her apron off and said she was leaving. I tried to put it tactfully but—'

'Weren't that at all! Well, not much.' Mrs Wilson felt sufficiently involved to forsake her range and sink and push into the knot of adults by the door. Token of her domain, she still carried a somewhat threatening spatula.

'What it was was you getting back late. Cutting into her tele time, you see. Said it was against her religious conscience to miss *Stars on Sunday*. I ask you. More like against her conscience to put off her first Mackeson too late into the evening, if you ask me.'

79

Pat grinned broadly at the crack but Chris knew it was no laughing matter. It was a menial job, the hours and wages rotten. It would take a minor miracle to discover a replacement.

'You're telling me she's gone for good,' he said. It wasn't really a question.

' 'Fraid it looks like it,' Wendy contritely said.

All he bloody needed. His worst fears realised. Sundays were supposed to be days of rest and he'd been knackered since he got up. And yet . . . Wendy had been far more wrong than right.

'Well – worry about it, tomorrow,' he said. 'I was probably over-valuing her services too much, anyhow. Any adult whose nose gets out of joint on being told that the kids come first here we're certainly better off doing without. Not to worry. A large scotch I owe you, Pat.'

And myself, he thought, as Wendy flashed him the same grateful smile she had just bestowed on the protective Mrs Wilson.

'Come on,' he said, 'I'm eating here tonight. Whatever you've got Mrs W. – I don't care if it's raw kippers – it's what I want!'

As he spoke, a shadow squeezed glidingly by between him and the door – a scrubbed and shiny Jamie McEvoy. Hunched, knowing he'd been seen, he sidled on towards a vacant place on the senior table bench.

'Jamie!' Chris called out. The boy stopped dead, not quite turning to look in the direction of the voice.

'Sir?' he said.

Chris went up to him. As always he was wearing his soldier's belt of regimental badges. The other boys had lowered the volume of their eating – all the better to hear you bawl him out, sir, Mr Langley, sir. Chris motioned him further up the room.

'Jamie,' he said, 'I'm sorry if I yelled at you a bit. You see that it was a bit of a nuisance, though, don't you?'

'Yes, sir.'

'You get the point about obeying orders – sensible orders?'

'Yes, sir.'

'No repeat performances?'

'No, sir.'

'We'll forget it then, eh, private. No court martial or firing squad.'

'Yes, sir. Thank you, sir.'

The reward was instant. The basic urchin liveliness of Jamie's face was restored immediately by his relief. Chris hoped it wasn't relief at a punishment escaped but a friendship proved undamaged.

'Everything else O.K.?' he asked as casually as he could. 'No problems?'

'No, sir.'

'. . . O.K. Better get some nosh before the others bag it all.'

With the sketch of a nod of thanks for his reprieve, Jamie scuttled over to the one in-use table. Chris was slower following. Days you feel like Vesuvius, he was thinking, days you feel like a giant melting blancmange: and all they let you behave like is the Rock of ruddy Gibraltar. Well, I just bloody hope that bloody bus starts first thing tomorrow.

Chapter Six

MONDAY. EARLY MORNING. Pat Langley was the first of her family to emerge from behind the green baize door at the top of Kingston House and descend through the waking-up sounds to right and left, the rising smells of breakfast under preparation. The overnight rain had stopped but the morning would be cool. She lowered her well-packed and heavy flight-bag to the floor as she passed inside the front door. Monday. Early surgery. A full house after the weekend and then some. Malingerers, O.A.P.'s, worried girls, men not worried who would be if her initial diagnosis was confirmed by a biopsy. . . . Oh, God, aaaah! The weight of fatigue still on her, tiredness still behind her eyes, she yawned. As if in merry rebuke, there was an answering yap of car horn from outside and the white Fiat belonging to Neil Inman, one of her partners, was sweeping up the driveway. She pushed the collar of her raincoat up around her neck and, stooping, gathered up her bag. Did she have money now! Yes. She must remember to get sprouts and peas before she came back and some more coffee beans might not be a bad idea either. Neil was completing putting the Mirafiori through a U-turn. She pushed open the door and went out.

A cup of coffee was what Chris Langley carried in his hand as within five minutes he too came down the staircase. Real coffee was his one running luxury, his one indulgence. To hell with the cost. He wasn't bankrupting the household as he smoked himself into an early, lung-less decline and the instant, apart from working out more expensive, had the other noticeable disadvantage of being undrinkable. Several good cups of dark-brown French-style coffee were sovereign for setting him up in the morning. The last he always took down with him into his ground floor office. And here he was again. Outside its green, weary-looking door at the beginning of another working week. Monday. Get a good two hours in first thing and it could set up the whole week. Fail to do so, you spent the next days never quite catching up. There were confidential files in the office. This was one door they kept locked. He balanced the cup carefully in one hand as he juggled the keys out of his pocket with the other. For a moment as his spirit sensed the sea of details waiting for him on the door's far side, he hesitated before turning the lock. His shoulders sagged. Well, once he got going it wouldn't be too bad. He straightened his back and twisted his wrist round. The lock clicked back. He pushed the door open and went in.

Robert Langley was as close on his father's heels as he had been on his wife's. There was a defensive, in-drawn something about his manner of making this descent. Of all the moments in the day this was the one he positively disliked the most – the first coming down stairs each morning. He never made it without seeing them, being seen. Breakfast was in full swing down below. The stairs were always busy with early-risers, late-starters coming and going. Them, of course, were the kids in care. Kids not lucky enough – if you called it luck and at the end of the day I suppose you did – to live in a 'normal' home and set-up with their own parents. Well you could make out a pretty good case for saying the way things were he didn't have that sort of home either and, in fact, a fair sprinkling of the kids in at any given time went to his school but, what bugged him, no, be honest, embarrassed him, on the stairs was not the way they nearly all ignored him even as they looked sideways at him, it was the sense he always had that he was lucky, privileged, and they were not and that he didn't deserve to be so. There was reproach in the way they largely ignored him and he almost felt his unasked for superiority made that deserved. There were two now on the landing. Kevin's nod was just a get-it-over flick and Gary managed to avoid his eye completely. Of course there was the black thing with him as well. And, of course, passing the girls, the older girls, on the stairs was harder still. It was best, all things considered, to keep yourself pretty much to yourself. It was almost right, almost O.K., that the normal kids at school tended to lump him in with the 'cons' so that he fell between two stools . . . He must pick up that stuff. He reached the bottom of the stairs and went into his father's office.

'. . . well as far as I can tell it's electrical. I mean you had a chance to judge for yourself and—'

His father was on the phone. About the Wolfsburg Wreck no doubt. Well, good riddance as far as he was concerned but it was obviously not the best start to his father's week.

'You know we can't do without it,' he was saying, 'don't you? The home revolves around it.'

False move, Dad. Tipped your hand. Losing wicket. Robert moved towards the notes he had left in the typewriter on the side table.

'If we're into that kind of expense I'd rather take a chance and soldier on.'

Better, Dad. Hard to get is how to play it.

'I haven't got the pounds to be foolish with in the first place, of course I'm going to be penny-wise.'

Aha! Tough guy talk.

'How can that possibly affect the M.O.T.?'

Just wait, Dad.

'Oh. Yes, well, I see . . . Well, you'd better come out when you can then, after all . . . Yes, O.K. fine . . . well, how should I sound? . . . All right, fine. Right . . . O.K., we'll see you then.'

The force with which Chris Langley cradled the phone belied the cordiality he had just about managed to get back into his voice at the conversation's end.

'Tsk, tsk, tsk!' Robert shook his head reprovingly.

'What do you want? The man wants to rip us off a hundred and fifty plus for a new con. rod and you expect me to be all sweetness and light?'

Robert smiled as he shuffled the pages of his notes together. He knew better than to finger his father's current bruise further.

'I'm off,' he announced.

'You haven't fouled up the typewriter?'

Bloody cheek!

84

'No, of course not!'

'What was it?'

'Just some notes.'

He saw interest raise his father's head a fraction higher.

'Oh, what on?'

'Nothing much. History.'

Well, that was true and, without a lot of explaining for which there wasn't time, they were boring in themselves. Out of context, as old Lloyd would say.

'O.K., suit yourself,' his father was saying.

But he hadn't meant to sound rude. He tried to make amends.

'Mum was saying something about me going to France,' he said.

'How's it grab you?'

'Can we afford it?'

'Don't be so bloody penny-pinching. Of course we can afford it!'

At a penny-pinch, they just might.

'All right, then, no need to shout. Great, then, super, marvellous. The clear-cut opportunity of a lifetime.'

'Really?'

'Well, 's not bad.'

'You don't have to overdo the enthusiasm.'

'How should I sound?'

'Er – keen?'

'O.K. I'm keen.'

Snotty little smart-mouth. Time to inject a touch of Monday morning reality.

'Done your prep?' Chris asked.

'I keep telling you we call it homework. The private sector does prep. We do—'

'Homework. Yes, thank you. Got it. Have a nice day.'

'See you.'

'Getting a lift with Mum?'

'No, it's early surgery today, isn't it? Monday. Right?'

Oh yes, of course.

'Oh yes, of course.'

'I'll walk.'

85

'Don't laugh,' Chris said, 'but assuming after all that it will start for Bill, why not the mini-bus drop off?'

'Er . . . giving it a miss for a bit.'

'Why?'

'Well . . . you know, Dad.'

'No, I don't know.'

'You don't know what they call this place at school?'

'Why don't you just tell me?'

'The Scrubs.'

'Really? We're considered that good, are we?'

Chris found he was amused.

'Why don't you tell them different?' he nevertheless heard himself go on to say.

His son was then looking at him with an expression in which sympathy only just had the better of reproach for his ignorance of how things really were.

'Oh, Dad!' his son said.

'Yes. Well. Right. If you're going to walk, you'd better go.'

'Yes. See you.'

His son went out. Feeling less than at ease with himself, Chris Langley sighed vaguely. The coffee suddenly seemed acid in his stomach. The perfunctory hardboard partitioning that gave his claustrophobic office separation from the other small cells to which the generous proportions of the old drawing room had been sacrificed pressed even more oppressively on him than usual. The two metal filing cabinets, an annoying miss-match in green and khaki; the cheap, prone-to-splinter standard-issue desk, seemed to be leaking a faint aroma of institutional, local government, defeat. Should've stayed in the private sector, they were saying, and had a big office with a thick carpet on the floor and a bank balance to match.

A metallic cough came from outside the window. At least he had the window. He stood up, went to it and looked out. As Gary feinted to exclude a late arriving Kevin from the VW by holding fast the side door from inside, Bill Hutton tried starting the engine a second time. Don't flood it, Chris was mentally enjoining him. No need. The engine caught and roared with a surprising vigour. Bill turned and snapped out something. Kevin was given a last-second reprieve. He dived aboard and the bus moved off. As it accelerated down the drive it overtook Robert looking strangely small, round-shouldered even. And alone.

Well, he would do something about that. And the kid was tough enough when it came down to it. He had his strength, his self-containment. He wouldn't welcome help he didn't think he needed. Yes, he would see. . . . He was a good kid, Robert, and it helped a lot he already understood so much.

Chris Langley turned back to the desk. The pinched office had not grown any the more magnificent while his back was turned but suddenly he was reminded that he utterly preferred it to any company executive-suite you could imagine and – let's get on with it – he had his work to do and standing thinking wouldn't do it for him.

⚜ ⚜ ⚜

'Wendy – could you come in and join us for a while? Perhaps Mrs Wilson can keep an eye on Dean, eh?'

Chris Langley, poking his head out of his office, had found the very person he was after right outside his door. Her inevitable companion was with her. The first thing she had been required to do that morning was take the green frog off his tee shirt and pin it to the grey pullover which, a little too large for him, he now wore.

Wendy nodded. She knew there was the best of reasons why Dean could not accompany her into the office.

'Be right with you,' she said.

She bent down and carried Dean down to the kitchen.

'A big biscuit, Mrs Wilson, for our friend, Dean,' she said loudly as she sat him on the stool nearest to the cook.

'I won't be very long, Dean,' she told him. 'Our friend Mrs Wilson is going to look after you for a few moments. Look, she's given you this nice biscuit all for yourself. If you want to perhaps she'll show you how she cooks. Now you wait here. I'll be back quite soon, I promise, and you know I always keep my promises.'

The little boy nodded. It was a serious nod but she almost

87

could dare to believe there was something of matter-of-fact acceptance in it. With an answered nod of her own to Mrs Wilson, she went back up the stairs.

She had to push hard to open the door to Chris Langley's office. Then it gave suddenly and, had she been the least bit concerned about maintaining an image of unruffled poise, her abrupt entrance into the room would rather have let her down. As would her obvious expression of surprise. The small office seemed to be bursting at the seams with people. With men. Wendy Raeburn was sufficiently concerned about her image to know when she was a lone woman in a room with four men.

'Goodness!' she had exclaimed. 'Pay day, is it?'

'An even more auspicious occasion,' Chris Langley said, 'one of a nature you are not like to look upon again. Three professional men all involved in the same 'in care' case all in my office at one and the same time. Guinness Book of Records' day beyond a doubt. John and Roger you do know but you don't know Graham Cunningham. Graham — Wendy Raeburn.'

'How do you do?'

'How do you do?'

'Graham is appearing on our behalf in Dean's case.'

'Ah! Yes, I had heard, of course. Hello, again.'

She looked with additional interest at the stripe-suited young solicitor who was stretched rather precariously back in a chair at the corner of Chris' desk. Quite properly in the informal circumstances he had avoided leaping to his feet in a flurry of good manners. The friendly smile on his rather broad face would do quite nicely, thank you. John Graydon, on the other hand, had sprung to his feet almost before her precipitate entrance was complete.

'Wendy, sit here,' he was saying now. With athleticism impressive to the point of alarming, he braced himself and with a mid-air about-face had vaulted into a sitting position on top of the khaki filing cabinet. Wendy smiled and took the chair. She didn't want to make the social worker look a complete idiot by insisting on standing on her own Women's Lib two feet. She liked John a good deal. She liked him for the fact that though his Zapata moustache made him look even younger than his mid-twenty age, she had never seen him wearing anything but the most recently polished shoes or boots. Noticing that she had been almost as impressed as by the observation that he was obviously prepared to like her a very great amount indeed.

'Graham was kind enough to run John out here because they actually had it together enough to be together and I'm stuck waiting for Campbell to come over and see the bus,' Chris was saying. 'And by a miracle, when I phoned, Roger was able to make it too.'

Wendy smiled at Roger Benton. Now that she was seated (she crossed ankles rather than legs, she had opted for a longer length skirt for work after that look from Howard) she could see the consultant psychiatrist more readily. It was typical of him, she thought, that in absent-minded professor manner he should have been the one blocking the door. Even in this cupboard of an office his inability to sit still for two minutes on end, his need to roam about and pace, had kept him on his feet. Very tall, thin, a shock of wiry hair tumbling sideways above a sharp-beaked face exactly right for his angular and all-elbows Don Quixote body. A youngish Don Quixote. The oldest person in the room, he was probably no more than forty-two or three. It was he who now conversationally prodded the meeting more formally forward.

'There's no need to tell you what's brought us all together like this, Wendy,' he said. 'Sorry. That came out like a bit of a joke but of course it's serious. Very serious. We're discussing Dean.'

'Yes, of course.'

'Graham is trying to pull together all aspects of his case history for when we go before the magistrate on Thursday. I think he would find it very useful if you could simply tell us what your current impressions on Dean are, how you find him on a day-to-day basis. I know it would be a considerable help to me.'

For the first time Wendy noticed the strange contrast between Benton's boney, whirling movements and his relaxed, deep voice. She took a deep breath. The thing was to be accurate. Not to invent.

'Well,' she said, 'there's no doubt he's still terribly shell-shocked – walking wounded, if you like. He's been badly hurt in the past and, well, you can see he's expecting it to happen again sometime. When he least expects it. So he's always expecting it. Especially from a man. He's hunched into himself all the time, watches everything. Never makes a movement or takes an initiative. Never speaks. At night when he's sleeping he whimpers and cries out. And of course he wets the bed every night absolutely without fail.'

'He's still sleeping in Wendy's room,' Chris Langley explained to Cunningham.

'And he still clings on to you like grim death? Still follows you everywhere?' Benton asked Wendy. He was perfectly still, watching her intently as he waited for her answer.

'Yes, I was coming to that,' Wendy went on. She found herself very conscious of the solicitor's jotting down notes at the other end of the desk. 'The basic answer to that is, "yes he does". But I have been able to leave him for slightly longer moments of time lately, without him showing any outward distress. I've just left him with Mrs Wilson downstairs, for instance and he knows by now, I think, that I'll keep my promise and come back for him soon. I think he's got it into his head that when somebody helps him on with his coat it doesn't automatically mean he's going to be dragged off to some different home. Yesterday Chris offered him this silly little badge thing out of a cornflake packet and he actually took it and wore it and today he came up to me and showed me he wanted it pinned on what he was wearing today.'

'So,' Benton resumed, 'such changes as you think you may be able to detect are for the better. He seems possibly more stable, re-assured, than when he first arrived? Even if it's only by the slightest degree?'

'Oh, it's infinitesimal. Of course when he arrived he was anything but passive. He was sobbing, incontinent. Almost uncontrollable. But of course he was hysterical from not knowing where in the world he was ending up this time.'

'So what would you say he needs from life, then, Wendy?' Chris asked suddenly.

'Time,' she said at once. 'Time to find out it isn't all made up of terrible horrors. Time to find out there are kindnesses, too, and good things. People you can trust.'

'But time spent where, Wendy? Who with? Us?'

'Well no, not us. Not for ever. We don't have that kind of time. He's making it very hard for me as it is, of course, following me everywhere. I'd say what he needs, if you're asking me, is—'

'Yes, we're asking you.'

'—is a really solid, gentle foster home where possibly there are no other children. Or even an adoptive home.'

'But you wouldn't think the natural parent's home?' Graham Cunningham said quietly.

'Good God, no!' Wendy said on reflex. It sounded unconsidered. 'Well,' she went on, 'I don't want to sound, well, ungenerous, but they were here yesterday visiting and, well, he was like a condemned man sitting between two executioners—'

'Yes, I think I get the picture,' Cunningham said. He had a lazy, cultured, drawling way of speaking which coming out of his rather wide face seemed rather supercilious. Wendy wondered whether she liked him. But he was turning his bland gaze away from her.

'Dr Benton,' he was saying, 'would you consider that it is in fact an accurately drawn picture?'

'Absolutely,' the psychiatrist said at once. 'I'm sure long-term fostering is the one chance Dean has of achieving a normal life. And indeed – if he's given an undisturbed run now – there's no reason why he shouldn't sooner or later have all the damage to his personality permanently mended. The one area that does concern me somewhat is his obvious dependence on Wendy, here. What she's doing on his behalf now is the stuff of ministering angels. I think at this precise moment in time it's best for him but the danger is, of course, too much dependence too long sustained will precipitate more trauma on separation.'

'That worries me too from my point of view,' Cunningham

said to the room in general but perhaps particularly to Chris.

He seemed to be hinting at something.

'Yes, Wendy,' Chris said, 'we've played something of a mean trick on you. Graham was keenly interested in hearing what you had to say about Dean with a view, possibly, to asking you to appear as a witness on behalf of the authority this Thursday. How do you feel about that? I rather think you've just landed yourself in the box and—'

'Hold on a second,' Cunningham said with some sharpness. 'Not to be mealy-mouthed, I'm in some doubt in my own mind on that one at the moment. Of course everything Wendy has said is grist to the case-history mill. But we can establish all that through Dr Benton. I'm doubting the wisdom of putting someone in the box who because of her age and, obviously, her sex, might strike the magistrates as a direct competitor to the natural mother. A personal competitor aiming to alienate the child's affection permanently.'

'But it's not like that!' Wendy exclaimed at once.

'No, of course not. And I know that. I'm utterly convinced. But the magistrates aren't. And their every instinct – the law's every tendency – is to equate the well-being of a child with his natural parental environment.'

'But, surely,' Wendy burst out again, 'it's an open and shut case. The facts are simple. Dean was brutalised. He's in a sub-normal condition on account of it. The parents may have asked for the 'in care' order to be revoked and all that, but who on earth is going to restore their rights to them after what they've done.'

Graham Cunningham drew in a deep breath and looked momentarily out of the window. He was stretched right back in his chair almost foppishly. He hitched up the waistband of his trousers as he looked back at Wendy and let the breath out in a long sigh.

'Mrs Ingrams and her fellow magistrates on Thursday, unless I'm very much mistaken,' he said.

'You can't be serious!'

'Graham!'

Wendy and, opening his mouth for the first time, John Graydon had both spoken simultaneously. Cunningham sighed again. He brought the chair forward on to its front legs again and sat leaning forward himself.

'Never more serious,' he said. 'I wish to God I wasn't. Look – let me make a little speech. You know I'm utterly on your side. You know that because if I wanted my brain pickled in gin at the age of forty I could be earning three times as much fleecing the public on conveyancing or whatever rather than appearing for a local authority in these kinds of cases . . . In fact what this father did to this child makes my – well, it doesn't make my blood boil, it makes it go into some kind of ice-cold fury in my veins and I pray now I'm wrong. But, looking at it from a devil's advocate point of view, the case is arguably inarguable.'

'Graham! For Christ's sake! Come on, now,' John Graydon said. There was a youthfully undisguised anger in his voice. 'You've read the file! There's the sheer medical history for a start.'

'Which I'll make the most of. But they'll concede that and claim it's ancient history. That everything has—'

'But how can—'

'Look. Put yourselves in the magistrates' position. They come on the scene with open minds. What do they find? Well, first – incomplete documentation. You said I'd read the file. But I haven't. Parts of it are literally illegible – faded pencil scrawl and so on – and two bloody great chunks are missing. About six months ago in 1976 because some bright-eyed and bushy-tailed Webb's wonder didn't lock it away the night some villain turned over the Social Services offices. And the best part of last year is lost for reasons that no-one seems to have the slightest idea of.'

'Well, we are still looking.'

'Yes, John. Thanks a lot.'

'. . . Yes, well. That's obviously unfortunate. But is it such a vital consideration when set against a fractured skull?'

'Don't you see – from the magistrates' viewpoint it's going to be symptomatic of the main count against us.'

93

'Which is?'

'John – you may only have just inherited Dean's case but you know the answer to that as well as I do. In fact, your newness on the scene is all part and parcel of it too. The big strike against us is the historical record – what's happened to Dean in the last two years. At your end his case has been assigned to no fewer than four social workers in turn who between them clocked up precisely – or rather, imprecisely, because we can't reach two – eleven visits to the—'

'O.K. So there's been a high turnover in personnel over the last two or three years.'

'I'll say! One so dedicated to social work she's now on a kibbutz in Israel. And one who as far as I can make out just disappeared into thin air. She just never turned up one Monday – right?'

'We all assume Jenny must have had some sort of a breakdown. She was finding the going tough . . . and . . . well—'

'She's probably wandering lost at this minute in the town hall corridors. She's probably the one with the missing bloody files!'

Indignation on Dean's behalf, at professional incompetence, had taken from Cunningham's speech all trace of lazy superiority. Wendy had decided she liked him a lot.

'But all the coming and going by your lot is going to appear almost insignificant in the face of what was happening in the meantime to Dean. How many times has he been moved from pillar to post since he was placed "in care"?'

'Four homes, counting here. Five moves.'

In two years. Hardly what any magistrate is going to construe as tending towards stability.'

'Well it was always understood that the Jacksons were only a temporary measure. They would have Dean while we assessed—'

'Excuses! Excuses!'

'No, reasons! Good reasons!'

'All right! Yes. I know. From your point of view and as I began by saying I'm on your side. But in court on Thursday, Mrs Ingrams and Co. may well decide that in the interest of

94

stabilizing Dean's environment, his parents – his reformed parents – represent the least of all evils.'

'But they can't! They can't!' This time it was Wendy who was unable to credit that a bureaucratic system could make possible such an enormity.

'I'm afraid we have good reason to believe Graham is right,' Chris Langley said. 'May be right. The magistrates know quite well we're only basically an assessment way-station – that sooner or later Dean will have to be found somewhere else yet again. And knowing how Mrs Ingrams feels on the subject of the ratepayers' hard-earned tax money she may well rationalise that a return to the parents and the consequent saving of fifty quid a week really is in the quote paramount best interests of the child unquote.'

'There's no way any objectively-minded person could come to that decision,' John Graydon said. A measure of disblief in his own assertion was discernible, however, in his voice.

'It's not an objective situation,' Graham Cunningham said. 'Assessing what are the "best interests" of any child is a very subjective activity. And the magistrates are going to be influenced very much by what they conceive as a need to take into account the natural parents' feelings.'

'Feelings. Them. Unnatural swine!'

'Wendy!' Chris Langley cut in disapprovingly. 'The argument is going to be that they're older now and wiser: that he's got a good job now and means – he has. He's driving a pork-pie delivery van, makes more than I do, I'm sure: that they've a home of their own now, a whole house: that he's led a blameless, exemplary life while on probation and has grown up. And that on the face of it is true. Graham says he's religiously reported to his officer – never missed – and you yourself know the two of them have shown up here on a regular basis to see Dean.'

'Yes. Don't I!'

'They've a strong case, you know,' Chris said, 'on paper. The very fact that they've asked for the order to be revoked has the effect of suggesting somehow they've turned over a new leaf.'

'But I've watched them with Dean,' Wendy said. 'There's no rapport, no feeling. The mother rabbits on at him in a mindless, non-stop way, but there's no feeling, you can tell.'

'Court room impressions are like distorting mirrors,' Chris said.

'I don't understand, though, why they should think of wanting him back anyway,' Wendy said. 'I don't really believe they do. Not looking at them.'

Graham Cunningham looked enquiringly at Chris who passed on the look to Roger Benton. The psychiatrist extricated his arms from their convoluted folding across his chest.

'You're probably right,' he said. 'I doubt if in their heart of hearts they do. I doubt if they've given it a moment's thought that goes beyond the point when he's returned to them. But social pressures – a feeling the neighbours know they're not "doing their duty" by their child. Family pressures – the "to think I should live to see the day when a grandson of mine should be brought up in an institution" sort of thing. Sheer possessiveness. He's ours. No-one's got the right to take what's ours away.'

'He's ours to do with as we like. It's our right,' John Graydon said savagely.

'John!' Chris snapped. 'That's less than objective!'

But Wendy felt the blackness of a terrible shadow chill the last seeds of hope the meeting had left her with. As if reading it in her face Benton seemed to hurry on with his catalogue as a deliberate diversion.

'On her part, I'm sure,' he said, 'there'll be a strong factor of playing at "Mothers and Fathers". Dean, in other words, is not a human being but a pet, a toy. And, no doubt, somewhere in all this, mixed all around, is a genuine human desire to be given a second chance, to put the record right by showing that the first time was all a mistake.'

He paused a moment.

'If Graham's pessimism proves justified and it does go against us, we'll have to hope that proves a stronger factor on their part than I perhaps give them credit for.'

'If it does turn out for the worst,' Chris said, 'at least we know that in John, here, the assigned social worker is somebody who really will be round there every other day keeping tabs on the situation. All the same. . . .'

'All the same,' John agreed, 'nice of you as it is to say that, it runs a terribly, terribly, far-off second best to what Wendy is doing for Dean nearly every hour of the day and night. I mean – consider. I've got over seventy cases on my personal list now, geriatrics, remedial – well, you know the scene . . . Honestly, Graham, we can't afford to lose this one.'

'You know I'll do my damndest to see we don't,' Cunningham said. 'Wendy – can I have a little think about whether or not I ask you to get up on your hind legs in the box for us?'

'Yes, of course. Whatever's best I'll do or not do.'

He smiled.

'Your being so pretty may prove counter-productive,' he said. 'But if it's a "yes" I'll get in touch with you before, of course, and brief you pretty thoroughly on the chapter and verse of how we'll make it go.'

In her mild confusion at the compliment – more at its unexpectedness, really, as compliments she was used to – Wendy had looked away from Cunningham. Her eye therefore caught John Graydon's and in his complex and far more confused reaction, she could easily pick out his male annoyance at what he obviously considered the solicitor's presumption. Well, that was nice to know as well. Two compliments at once.

'You know,' Chris was saying, 'even allowing for all the Department of Stealth and Total Obscurity's bureaucracy at its worst, all the left hands not knowing what the right are doing and so on, I still refuse to believe that some mixture of commonsense and compassion won't win the day for us on Thursday. And you know, Roger, regarding long-term fostering, we managed to bend the rules with Howard and keep him here on account of his old association with me at Mannerly. Perhaps we might contrive something on those lines for Dean.'

He was looking at Wendy as he concluded and the chill

97

lifted from her hope as she realised how much she would enjoy the long on-going difficulty of bringing Dean back to something approaching a normal life. Roger Benton, she saw, was nodding provisional agreement back to Chris. Graham Cunningham was looking seriously worried, however, as he slid papers back into his briefcase. Wendy stood up.

'If that's it for the time being,' she said, 'I'd better be getting back to the topic of all this talk.'

'Yes, of course,' Chris said. 'Thanks very much, Wendy, for going on trial for Graham here.'

'Don't phone us, we'll phone you,' Cunningham said, looking less worried as he did so.

John Graydon had jumped lithely down from his filing cabinet perch to do the door thing, but this time Roger Benton was perfectly positioned to unconsciously beat him to it. There was a chorus of goodbyes.

'Gents – while I've got you,' Wendy heard Chris saying behind her, 'we had this girl thrust on us on Saturday night. Teenage stripper, would you—'

The door was closed after her. And on her thoughts about Lucy. They can't return him, she was thinking, they mustn't. It would be like putting a baby rabbit in with a snake.

As she went down the old servants' stairs to the kitchen she made sure she had an extra bright smile on her face to show him as she walked in. It was something of an effort.

Chapter Seven

LUCILLE WYATT, CORRECTLY supposing that she would be the object of discussion and speculation that morning, had decided her best bet was to lie low for the day. These clothes they'd given her made her look like a rotten schoolgirl. You stood out hanging about the streets, nipping into cafés and libraries in gear like this. She couldn't ask for her mac back without giving the whole bleeding game away. Her mum would be in if she tried going back home and want to know why the hell she wasn't at school. No, best bet definitely was to hang about and not let on to anybody who she was. When it suited her she'd do a bunk. She'd keep her head down for a while and they'd soon get tired of trying to track her down. They were all understaffed. Everyone knew that.

She was right in two respects. A hundred and one daily routines obtruding and the Missing Girls Index not having produced any mention of her, Lucille Wyatt was semi-out-of-sight-and-out-of-mind that morning. The shadow over-hanging Dean's future had given the office discussion mention of her something of an afterthought low priority. And she did look like the schoolgirl that technically, perhaps fundamentally, she was. Schoolgirl not show-girl. Her scrubbed-clean face, her pulled back hair and change of clothes had completely obliterated the sad, amateur preten-sions to Las Vegas of her night-time self. Where she erred was in supposing that she had it in her to keep to her room all morning and half the afternoon. Neither at home or at school had she ever had opportunity to acquire that kind of self-discipline.

The room was larger, brighter, airier than where she slept at home. But it had no transistor. It had running water, a basin and mirror. It had no record player. It had a far nicer carpet, a much better bed. It had no cassette player. She lay on the bed, her mind a thin association of film and pop stars and dreams of the day when, discovered in a way she never could quite see in detail, she too would be on the cover of the 'TV Times'. When she checked the time, minutes not hours had passed. For all its airiness the room began to press its walls upon her. As she aimlessly paced round it looking at the underside of this chair, following that thread of pattern in the carpet, she seemed actually to see it shrinking. She felt dizzy. By late morning, it never occuring to her to pick up and open one of the half-dozen books upon the mantlepiece, she felt like climbing up one of those walls. And she was hungry. Well, there must be something to eat down in that kitchen.

Mrs Wilson saw her come in through the door and instantly more than half-knew to what she owed the honour of this unexpected visit. She applied fast, expert common-sense to the situation.

'Big ones who are in to lunch have to help serve the little ones. If they want feeding themselves, that is,' she said.

Lucille considered. Mustn't get involved, she told herself. But don't make yourself stand out, either.

'Not many for lunch,' Mrs Wilson was saying. 'Just the little 'uns. But it's a real big meal for them. This time of day they're hungry. Dinner time they're tired.'

Lucille had decided. She nodded. Mrs Wilson nodded cursorily back.

'You can put these knives and forks out for me for a start,' she said.

So, short-term, Mrs Wilson solved the problem of a deserting Mrs Hughes. And with visible improvement. As the youngest children came in from their volunteer-taught nursery school morning, Lucy, fetched and carried with a largely silent but wholly noticeable efficiency. She helped Reuben and Sally by lifting them easily, unfrighteningly onto their places on the bench. She cut up their food for them. She actually sat down at one time next to Louise and, picking up the little girl's discarded fork succeeded in getting her to eat several more mouthfuls of beefburger. And she talked. To the children, gradually at first, then with a more natural to and fro-ness, she talked. Wendy Raeburn, observing all, thought to herself that whatever, whoever else she was, this girl quite certainly had younger brothers or sisters., It seemed incredible that she should ever want to take her clothes off in front of a pack of leering men or, indeed, that they should be concerned to drool over somebody so, well, immature and everyday. Look – she was actually getting Louise to giggle! Wendy glanced across at Mrs Wilson who, noticing too, gave back a quick nod of approval. This might be the moment to get Lucy, if that was her name, to open—

'Miss – can you come to the phone? It's the comprehensive. Something about Gary. I think it's important and I can't find Mr Langley.'

It was Howard from the doorway. Wendy nodded.

'I have to go to the telephone, Dean,' she said, 'but I'll be back very soon. You wait here with Mrs Wilson and I'll come back.'

Again the grave sketch of a nod. She got to her feet and, although she glanced at Lucille as she did so, the telephone had first priority. So the moment for a talk had passed.

Later, Lucille wandered into the shout-filled garden. The tinies were out playing on a dry afternoon that had the sun trying to break through thin clouds. Lucille was a bit past caring. No-one had much seemed to take any particular notice of her when she'd shown her face and anything was better than that room. Even the washing up. She'd quite enjoyed helping with that. The old battleaxe had had the sense not to try and pump her so that had been all right. And it felt a lot better having some food inside you. By the time she'd finished plonking it down under those kids' noses she'd been bloody starving. All right now, though. Pity there was only some schools rubbish on the tele.

Half unconsciously, because there was movement there, she walked towards the swings and climbing frame of the playground area. There were three swings. On the nearest a boy with thin arms and legs was churning about like one o'clock as he tried furiously to get going. Next to him two girls were flying up higher and higher with each swing, their screams of delight and the creaks of the chains growing louder all the while. Lucy could guess how choked the boy must be to be stuck all helpless and unmoving. Though maybe that was better. She frowned as she approached. Bloody dangerous swings could be: split your head right open. She remembered that kid down the rec that time. You'd think they'd have sense enough here to look after them better.

'Want a push?' she said.

Peter Jackson looked round. He nodded. Lucy straightened his swing.

'Hold tight, then,' she said.

She gently set him in motion. Oh, someone had fixed bits of old tyres around the seats. All the same, though.

'More?' she said.

His back to her the kid nodded again.

'Say "whoa" if you want to stop,' Lucy said.

He didn't. She kept pushing.

'What's your name?' she said.

'Peter,' he said quite easily.

'Peter who?'

'No, silly. Peter Jackson. My mum's having a baby.'

'Oh, yes. What hospital's she in, then?'

'Not in a hospital. In home. That's why I'm here.'

'Oh. Someone for you to play football with.'

'Might be a girl.'

'Girls don't play football.'

'Don't.'

'Do and all. Better than boys.'

'Don't! . . . Do you play football?'

Mustn't open her mouth too much. She gave the swing an extra hard push.

'Try and swing your legs up and then back,' she said. 'Yes. That's it. Keeps you going all by yourself like that.'

'You a new teacher here, miss?' Peter Jackson said.

⚓⚓⚓⚓

He'd parked in the street. Now as he walked up the driveway it sort of felt as if the whole house was watching him. And the VW bus parked at the side. It didn't help a bit he'd put

102

on his best suit. It was all the windows made you feel like that. She could easily be behind any one of them looking out. Christ alone knew what sort of stories she was making up. He would swing for that bloody Ferguson yet.

He rang the bell. No one came. There were kids' noises coming from round the back. He reached forward to ring again and a coloured shadow was wavering behind the glass and getting larger. The door opened. A real cracker of a darling was looking enquiringly at him.

'Yes?' she said.

He must forget the old how's your father stuff for a while. It had got him deep enough in it as it was.

'Oh . . . good afternoon,' he said.

'Good afternoon,' Wendy Raeburn replied. She was puzzled. There was something very unlikeable about this character, something very shifty.

'I was, er, hoping it might be possible to find Mr Langley,' Wilf Manton said. 'It is Mr Langley, isn't it?'

'You don't have an appointment, then?'

'Er, no. Not as such, no. It is rather urgent, though.'

'Could you give me some idea what it's about? I'm one of Mr Langley's assistants.'

Lucky bastard.

'Well. er, it's about the girl who was brought here the other night.'

'You're not her father by any chance?'

'No. Not as . . . No. Nothing like that. I was at the party . . . there was a party you see . . . it was at my place, actually, and—'

'You know her name, then!'

'No. No, I don't, actually. All I know—'

'Whatever you know, I suggest you contact the police. I can assure you Mr Langley won't discuss it off the record.'

'Can't we ask him that for ourselves?' Wilf Manton tried with. In an effort to clinch it he had put on his best salesman's smile. The low-key, not too pushy one. It worked its usual charm.

'I'm sorry,' Wendy Raeburn said. 'If you like to try calling him to—'.

Stuck-up bitch. He turned and walked away in her mid-sentence. If that was her toffee-nosed attitude she could take it and stuff it she knew where.

As he stomped off down the driveway, he heard the door close after him at just short of slam level. The noise cut across the shouts and twitterings from behind the house. Hey – wait a minute! He stopped in his podgy tracks. Why not? He'd tipped his hand by calling. Might as well be hung for a sheep as a lamb . . . He doubled back towards the house but this time bearing to the right cut across the lawn towards the corner.

Oh, not much joy there. A bunch of toddlers and some older kid messing around on the swings. Gormless like as not. No point in asking there. Christ! The nerve of that bitch on the door! . . . Obscurely he was acknowledging that it was his failure to charm a bit so eminently worth the charming that had got up his nose. It was awareness that at his age and weight, with his appearance, the girls no longer looked at you that irked him. Sad anger replaced apprehension. While he was here he might as well do a circuit of the house. Ignored by the kids on the swings, he went on and around to the back of the house. Large rooms that seemed deserted. A T.V., though. They did all right. He turned to the other side and there crouched by the back of the VW bus was some long-haired cowboy of a mechanic. You knew the sort, going around saying they could fix it for half the price and taking the business out of his authorised service bays. Still, an adult.

'Er, excuse me . . .' Manton said.

The mechanic looked up. You could tell he didn't know what he was at. He seemed a bit put out to be caught with so many bits and pieces round his knees.

'Can I help you?' he said all posh-like.

'I'm not sure. I'm looking for Mr Langley.'

'Then I can. That's me.'

Christ! Types they put in charge of kids these days! Still, you read about those cases.

'Oh,' Manton said. 'Er, can we talk?'

Chris Langley held up his oiled and greasy hands.

'If you don't mind it being here,' he said.

'No. Fine.'

Better do a bit of the old softening up stuff first, maybe. Wilf Manton nodded at the bus.

'Good old all purpose war-horse in its day, eh?' he said.

'I've got a feeling its day is what it's had.'

'Well, power-unit's getting a bit long in the tooth these days.'

'. . . . Possibly.'

Wilf Manton saw a glint of some kind of annoyance appear in this Langley character's eye. He was putting down the knackered set of points and getting up.

'What was it you wanted to talk about, Mr—?'

'Manton,' Manton said. He was suddenly at a total loss for words. This whatever he was was looking hard at him but offering him no help.

'It's all a bit embarrassing,' Manton finally got out gruffly.

'Well . . . just you and me. Take your time.'

'You've got a teenager here, I think – a girl. Brought in the other night from a party.'

'You know who she is?'

'No. Not as such. Not exactly.'

'Mr Manton – why don't you start at the beginning?'

'Well, I know of her.'

'How do you mean?'

'I was at the party.'

'I see – well, did you speak to her?'

'. . . Yes.'

'Then you must've called her something.'

'. . . er, "Juicy Fruits", if you really want to know. The chewing gum.'

'Really.'

Manton shifted his paunchy weight from foot to foot. It seemed close all of a sudden. He wished he hadn't put on his brown suit. It was too heavy for a day like this. He seemed always to be sweating these days.

'I feel somewhat responsible,' he said.

'Oh? Was she your . . . er, date?'

'No! Nothing like that!'

'Well it must have been something like that. Whose date was she?'

'Well . . . being honest, I've really no idea. She sort of turned up with the booze and the night – know what I mean?'

Chris Langley did. About the time I was fancying Jenny Newman a part of his mind was conceding. Listen to the confessional whine making this right nasty piece of work's voice grow cheaper and nastier with each squirm another part was pressing his conversational advantage.

'Perhaps she popped up out of a cake,' he said.

A mistake. The fat-gutted bookmaker or cigarette salesman or whatever he really was had twitched with anger at that as much as with embarrassment. Careful, now, Chris Langley told himself. Don't let your personal distaste overrun your professional cool.

'How did you know she was here?' he asked with as much sharpness as he could combine with low-profile authority. Manton again shifted his weight from leg to leg. It was like being a prefect and grilling a fourth-form bully. And Lord – that suit!

'A friend on the force, actually,' he was saying.

'Really? I find that—'

'You see, I'm a car dealer and we, er, supply and, er, service some of the local station's fleet, er, demands . . . So, I, well, I know quite a lot of the lads in blue. So I picked up the old phone, you know and, er, cut out the old red tape like.'

So that explained the lead-in to a salespitch that the creep had led off with.

'Well, whoever it was,' Chris Langley said, 'it was very indiscreet of him.'

'You wouldn't quote me!'

Manton's face fell as he realised he had wandered into one game that was not crooked.

'You wouldn't, would you?' he repeated.

'Probably.'

'Oh, God . . . look, what happens to her now?'

'I'm not prepared to say,' Chris Langley said. 'But anything you say or have said I shall report to the police. Even if you do lose a few customers.'

Manton's hand was sliding in between his brown jacket lapel and blue-striped, convex shirt.

'I appreciate you have your, er, professional, er, parameters to consider,' he said. 'Perhaps it would be possible to make some sort of contribution. . . .'

'You do. It's called Income Tax.'

This time Chris had failed utterly to keep the contempt out of his voice. Manton squirmed the more.

'Yes . . . of course,' he said. The hand came out empty.

'Er . . . tell me,' he went on, 'do you give these people some kind—'

'I don't think I quite understand. "These people" did you say?'

'Like the girl. Do you give them some form of medical?'

'Why should you ask?'

It was obvious why but let him flounder.

'. . . this really is most embarrassing.'

'I'm not embarrassed.'

'Well, you see, one of my, er head office bosses . . . the er, Vehicle Supply bloke, actually . . . his son thinks, well, you know. . . .'

'Suppose I say I don't know.'

'Oh for Christ's sake! I'm only here because he hasn't got the bleeding nerve to show up himself!'

'And because of what his Dad can do for you. Or not do for you.'

'If you like.'

'You wouldn't possibly be here out of concern for the girl.'

'If you really want to know she looked more than capable of looking after her bleeding self.'

'That's one type we get, Mr Manton, who when it comes right down to it are among the least able to do that.'

Angry yet abject, Manton doggedly insisted on slinking back to the topic which had inspired his grubby mission.

'. . . it's only a case of might, you understand,' he said.

'He was too drunk to remember.'

'Yes.'

'And in the cold light of hung-over dawn he's shit-scared he's picked up a dose.'

'If you must put it like that.'

'Why not? Clap is clap, however you tart it up.'

'It could have been one of the other girls, you see. If we could just find—'

'Well you can't. Not from me. Not from her. All the same your answer's simple.'

'Yes?' For the first time the thick jowly features expressed hope.

'If he did . . . and if she is . . . then he might be.'

The worm in Manton turned. His thick, blubbery under-lip managed to stretch itself quite thin as it twisted with frustration.

'And sod you, too!' he said. A second time that afternoon he was turning on his heel to walk away.

'Oh, Mr Manton!'

Chris Langley's voice contained enough command to bring the car dealer to a halt and twist him round.

'What's your boss's son's name?'

That he had not let ill sufficiently alone visibly dawned on Manton's face.

'What's it to you,' he tried to bluff with. 'What's it matter?'

'It'll matter to the police,' Chris Langley said. 'And, don't worry, they'll soon enough find it out. You see, there is one bit of news you can carry back to this super stud. If it was her and he did, then it was with a girl we've every reason to believe is under age. Age of consent. You can tell him she's fifteen and what he did is a criminal offence.'

Manton no longer floundered. But as if hit by some kind of wet fish he positively staggered. It was by some grotesque continuation of that movement he whitefacedly turned to walk finally away.

Chris Langley watched him out of sight. His own feelings were complex. Underneath the indignation and scorn he felt towards the coarseness embodied in Manton, he could feel, as always, the swell of pity for the mean, wasted life locked in the sad man's corpulence. What richness of spirit could a man like that have known, expect to know? To look at him was to think 'why bother to start out?' Chris basically felt glad he hadn't gone for him tooth and nail as part of him had wanted to. The poor sod was obviously terrified he'd get the sack or whatever it was they did to all the losers like him. He'd got himself onto a hiding to nothing from the word go.

Chris got back down upon knees he realised were beginning to ache quite noticeably. Careful, he told himself, you know cheap pity's your besetting professional sin. Think of the girl. His jaw clenched with anger at himself. On the professional front he was a lot less than blameless. Because Dr Hartley was coming in the next day for her weekly check on Diana, their fifteen-year-old alcoholic, he had done no more than leave a message with her that there would be an additional medical on a new arrival to perform, one that would include a venereological check-up. But if what Manton feared was true . . . given the circumstances of sex and the cheap, would-be orgy that had attended the girl's being picked up, he should have had her looked at right away. He could have asked Pat to do it.

'Damn!'

Annoyance at his own remissness had caused him to yank too much and too awkwardly on the spanner. It had slipped suddenly off the nut and the continuing force had smashed his knuckles up against the edge of the hatch. Damn! Apart from the little matter of the agony, he had broken the skin. Globules of blood were oozing up from underneath the grease. He should never have started to mess with it. If Campbell had kept his word and come early, of course, the temptation would never have arisen. Blast Campbell!

Doucement, he told himself.

He would have a talk with the girl that evening. A long and serious talk. As long and serious a talk as necessary.

✣✣✣✣

The girl, Lucille Wyatt, had passed an afternoon not half such a drag as that last-forever morning. In fact, tell the truth, she'd had quite a nice time. Still no-one had pestered her. She'd been left all alone to do what she liked with the kids. Nearest she'd got to being nicked for questioning was the old bloke being there to keep an eye on things. For a while she thought he was going to come over any time and do her for speeding or whatever but he hadn't. Just sat and watched. She'd ended up ignoring him. She'd been more scared by the sight she'd caught out the corner of her eye of some other bloke in a brown suit paddling round the back of the house. But he couldn't have been police or anything much. He'd disappeared and left her to enjoy herself as well.

After the one called Peter had got tired of the swing, she'd had to give umpteen others a go. Before Peter got off she'd stopped the swing completely and told him to start it going by himself. This time, after a few false starts, he got the hang of it.

'It's like riding a bicycle,' she told him. 'You'll never forget it now.'

'I can't ride a bike,' he'd seriously told her.

'Well, one day someone'll teach you that as well, I expect,' she'd told him.

He'd gone off to the sandpit. After a while she'd gone over there herself. There were quite a bunch of them all down in it and it was pretty messy – full of crumbling castles that kept being trodden on anyway.

'I know,' she said, 'let's all build a village. We'll have a big street up the middle here and everyone can build a special building. Reuben – you can do the Post Office just there. Peter, you do the fire station there . . . What's your name?'

'Sally, miss.'

'Sally, you do the baker's . . . .'

They'd all got on with it. It had got quite elaborate. The old geezer had come over and taken a look but gone away again without saying anything.

'Yoo hoo! Biscuit time everyone!'

Lucy had looked up and been quite sorry to see what's her face, yes, Wendy, calling the kids into the house from the french windows. They had sixteen buildings done by now and the lay-out looked quite good. They'd made a second street to get a cross-roads in and in a minute she'd find a stick or something to put up as a sign outside the pub she'd made. Oh – she must give that girl back her hairdryer.

'Aren't you coming in, miss?'

'Er, no. In a minute. I'll just finish my bit, Sally.'

Better not. If she went in she might not get out again. Anytime now would be a good time to leave. She'd leave the bag and tell her Dad she'd lent it to Jackie if he ever noticed it was gone. There was nothing in it with her name on it. Shame, really, she wasn't going to be able to give the dryer back in person, it had been nice enough of her to give her a lend of it. Perhaps she'd get one herself just like it. She had the money for it now – right where she'd notice most if anyone tried taking it.

It felt a bit lonely now the kids were all gone in. Without the childish giants the sand village looked properly deserted and, looked at again, not much like any village she'd seen pictures of . . . Still . . . Feeling watched she wandered back to the swings and used one to sit down on. If she just walked out down the main path she'd probably get spotted even though they did seem so short-handed . . . Perhaps if a delivery lorry or something came it would block the view. Not much chance of that at this hour, though.

But someone was coming. Kicking a football and showing off like they all did, this lanky kid was coming across the lawn. He was coming right over. Well she'd just ignore him until he gave up on whatever he had in mind – three guesses on what that was. Oh, he wasn't exactly coming right over. He'd stopped at the climbing frame thing. Oh yes, he was going to show off first.

Across from where Lucille Wyatt sat three-quarters turned away from him, Gary began to chin himself on the top bar of the climbing frame. Bit of form on that, he was thinking, if you stop to look for it. Making out she's cool but she'd get over that. Better not say anything about niggers, though, or I'll split her mouth up to her ears for her.

He'd done twelve and it was getting to him a bit. He'd stop before she heard him getting out of breath.

'What you in for, then?' he said.

She turned her head to look full at him a moment, then turned away again.

'Not minding my own business,' she said.

Knowing she couldn't see him, he allowed himself a grin. Not bad that answer. She'd been around a bit. Things would be looking up if she was in to say a while.

'What you doing, then?' he said.

'Sitting on Concorde flying to New York.'

'Wrong way round. Or don't you like facing the engine?'

Ha! Fancied himself no end. They all did. He was good looking, though, in a browny sort of way. He didn't have their usual sort of ugly nose. His was quite nice and straight like a proper nose. Her mum said they all smelt. Had this different smell. Mind you, her mum was nearly always wrong on everything. Her dad couldn't stand them either. Down the labour all the time. He'd gone and voted for old Mrs Whatsit on the strength of it even though his own dad, he'd said, would've turned over in his grave to think his son had ended up a thingummy.

'Why aren't you at school, then?' Harry Belafonte was asking.

'Too old, ain't I.'

After those fat pigs Saturday night handling him was kid's stuff. He might fancy his black self but he hadn't copped sixty quid last night now, had he? Who'd want to look at him. Actually he was quite well built, though, all the same. Flat stomach. She liked men to have flat stomachs. They said you couldn't tell how big it was from how big or small the bloke was. She'd never seen her dad's. Couldn't be no harm in talking to him.

'Why aren't you at school yourself, then, anyway?' she said.

'Was, wasn't I? Walked out then, didn't I? Started bugging me. Something starts bugging me, I ain't around no more.'

'Walk out did you?'

'Yeah.'

'They'll have you for that.'

'See if I care.'

'Live here do you, then?'

'Temporary, like. Hostel before that.'

'Like it here, do you?'

' 'S all right.'

'That all?'

'Better'n some places. Better than the hostel. Bugs me sometimes though.'

'Run away, then.'

'Mug's game, that is. Try it and they come after you. No papers, have I? You got to work, ain't you? Got to eat. I mean. Nowhere to go, have I?'

I have, mate, she thought. He'd moved across to face her now. She wished she had something better than these rotten schoolgirl clothes on. And a bit of make-up. Not that she'd be around much longer if she could help it at all.

'Got no home?' she said.

His very even face came all over sulky. He looked at the ground and shook his head.

'No mum?'

'Dead,' he said.

'No dad, either?'

'In prison.'

'Oooo! What'd he do?'

'Killed her, didn't he.'

'Christ! How?'

'Mind your own fucking business!'

She couldn't really blame him saying that, considering. But she mustn't get him off the point. She crossed her legs to stop him getting angry.

'Bet you'd run away if you knew how,' she said. 'Bet you just don't know how to get out of here without them seeing you.'

'What you talking about?' he said. 'Easy, ain't it, if you wanted to. Just make like you're going to school and go straight on out down the path there and just keep on going. Get a whole day's start that way.'

'What if you don't go to school?'

'Go anyway. They're all too busy here to notice half the

113

time where anybody's at. Or you can go over the wall in the corner there. There, see, where the dustbin thing is for the leaves and stuff. Big house on the other side — there ain't nobody there 'til late at night. Know that for a fact. You can get in there and go right on out up the side path. Mate of mine did. Kevin.'

'Go on. What happened?'

'Caught him, then, didn't they? Mug's game.'

But she had somewhere to go. She mustn't go on about it, though, and let him suss her out.

'Saw you playing football,' she said. 'What team you stick up for, then?'

⚜⚜⚜⚜

As, his briefcase ominously heavy with homework, he came up the driveway to Kingston House, Robert Langley was still striving to be philosophic. The week before he had made thirty-seven not out. It was probably no more than the law of averages that going in Number One today he'd been out first ball of the innings. It had been a fantastic catch, after all. And a bad ball. He'd done the correct text-book thing in trying to punish it. You didn't expect a half-volley hit like that to be picked up on reflex action so close to the bat. Still, if the law of averages dominated every game, what point in playing. Perhaps the thing was not to try to force things too soon however tempting. . . .

He filed the thought away in his mind and so was able to sensibly shrug off the duck. Surprised to see Gary home from school ahead of him and Lucille Wyatt there at all, he went in to the house. At least getting out early you were changed and off home quickly and didn't have to run the edgy gauntlet of the stairs. He had them to himself as he climbed up to the flat. By the time he was pushing the green baize door open he was thinking about Charles II.

To his further surprise his father dressed only in vest and pants was standing in the middle of the floor strenuously towelling his hair. He broke off and looked up with his own dishevelled, Wild Man of Borneo surprise.

'Hello,' he said, 'you're home early.'

114

'Special privilege for getting out first ball.'

'Oh dear. Not bowled, I trust.'

'Brilliant catch. Felt four all the way.'

'Well, then. Will be next time.'

'Lunch was rotten too.'

'Macaroni cheese?'

'Right.'

Chris Langley had resumed towelling. When he next spoke his voice came in a muffled vibrato.

'There you are, then,' he said, 'indigestion affected your optic nerve causing error of timing in your stroke. Want a cup of tea?'

'Please.'

'You put the kettle on. I'll make it.'

Robert went through to the kitchen and, filling the kettle, switched it on. He dug out a couple of biscuits and munching one came back to the general purpose living room.

'What's so special about today, then?' he asked.

Chris was smoothing his hair back with his hands.

'How do you mean?' he said.

'You having a bath.'

'Oh. Like an idiot I tried having a go at the VW myself. Covered myself with grease. Didn't think Campbell would show up. I failed utterly to do a thing to it and just as I came in he put the cap on it by ringing up to say he'd come this evening.'

Robert had wandered over to the bookcase by the window.

'Dad,' he said, 'you know Charles II.'

'Not personally.'

'You know what I mean. Would you say he was a sharp operator? You know, under the Nell Gwynn bit.'

'As I dimly recall very much so. Why?'

'I reckon Mr Bannister's selling him a bit short.'

'What he wanted wasn't it? I seem to remember him doing a pretty good con job on Louis IV. Have you done the Popish Plot yet?'

'Not yet. No.'

Robert had moved to the window and as he crunched his second biscuit was staring out.

'What's she doing here?' he said.

'Who?'

'Lucille Wyatt.'

'Who?'

Suddenly his father had joined him at the window. Robert knew from the urgency the move communicated that business had climbed the stairs to the flat once again.

'Her,' he said, 'by the swings. Down there by herself.'

'You know her?'

'Lucille Wyatt. Goes to our school.'

'You sure?'

'Course I'm sure. Aren't many with as much in the balcony as her.'

Chris Langley shot a quick glance at his son.

'Whatever happened to English? Stacked, you mean,' he said. But Robert knew that the main part of his father's mind was absorbing new and important information.

'Whatever happened to the tea?' he said.

⚜⚜⚜

A half-hour later, feeling a lot the better for his bath and a clean shirt on his back, Chris Langley was sitting at his office desk again and speaking into the telephone. His right hand made quick notes on a sheet of D.H.S.S. paper. There was the quickening tone to his voice of someone who believes he's getting somewhere.

'Thirty-seven Lindsay,' he was saying. 'Right. Where's that? Up by the new estate? . . . yes, got you . . . great . . . What else can you tell me about her? . . . well, yes, I'm afraid that usually it does mean "anything bad" . . . ah, well that's good news . . . and how much longer does she have at school . . . fifteen – that's what we thought . . . indeed. As I said I don't think it's as serious as at first sight. . . .'

He looked up as the door opened and Wendy Raeburn came in. She stood just inside it waiting for him to finish.

'Right . . . And thank you too very much Miss Ames for your help . . . Yes. Indeed. Goodbye now.'

He replaced the receiver with a decisiveness matching his tone of voice.

'It is Lucy!' he said. 'We've got her. Lucille Wyatt, thirty-seven Lindsay Road, S.E.—'

'Hold on, Chris,' Wendy said. 'Don't get too excited. I've got some quite bad news and I've got some maybe really bad news.'

'Oh. Well, I'm sitting down.'

'The lesser evil is Gary. I've had two phone calls from his school today. Seems he deliberately pushed one of those expensive scientific-type balances on to the floor.'

'Glass case and all?'

'Apparently.'

'Hell. He's such a . . . All right, go on.'

'Physics master sent him to the Head. Apparently never reported to him. Didn't show up.'

'He's not absconded?'

'No. Came straight back here. He's down in the kitchen right now cadging a "little something" off Mrs Wilson.'

Chris Langley audibly sighed out his relief.

'O.K.,' he said, 'could be worse.'

'Well – perhaps this is. Talking of absconding . . . I finally found half an hour free to get to grips with our new girl. I decided she'd had enough rope . . .'

'And?'

'Can't find her anywhere. I think it's very likely she has done a bunk.'

Wendy Raeburn saw a sudden tensing of cheek muscles impart to Chris Langley's face the stoniness that always signified his effort to contain an inner fury.

'I'm sorry,' she said.

He brought his face back to life by shaking his head.

'Not your fault,' he said. 'Mine. I should've followed up on her a lot harder. There was a man here this afternoon . . . it could be a lot worse than I just let Miss Ames believe.'

He reached for the phone.

'In any case, if we don't get her back fast she's made it a lot worse for herself. Might end up in court after all. She's not bad at school, it seems. Under-achiever but bright.'

He was dialling.

'Who're you phoning?'

'John Graydon. If I can reach him. If he can get on it right away, we may have her back before we have to let the world know she's gone.'

'But she could be anywhere.'

Chris Langley shook his head again.

'Uh-huh,' he said. 'It may have been more luck than judgement but she doesn't know yet we know who she is and where she lives. She'll go home. Aim to keep her head down . . . Damn, bloody thing's engaged! Well, don't you worry, Wendy, I'll get on to it. And I'll see Gary first thing in the morning. Tell him he's not to go off to school with the others, please. O.K.?'

'O.K., Chris.'

He nodded. She smiled a little dubiously and went out. He sat there tensely at his desk forcing himself to not pick up the phone until the line had had a chance to clear. Within the wrapping of the whole house's routine sounds, the room's inner silence buzzed in his ears as he tried to steady his thinking so that his professional judgement would not be affected by his intense annoyance with himself any more than by his pity or, it had been known, by his happiness.

Chapter Eight

STANDING IN THE queue waiting for a bus – any bus – to come and take her away somewhere had been pretty awful. Lucy kept feeling everyone was looking at her. It was like one of those dreams where you're out in the street with no clothes on. The bus wouldn't come. Waiting was even worse than going down the side of the old house. That had been like a nightmare. What if that black kid was just talking big, she'd thought, and there were people there or no way out. But there had been a way out and no-one had jumped out to grab her and though it had been just like a nightmare or a horror film at least by rushing down the side path she'd got it over quickly. Waiting was different. There was a little parade of shops opposite and mums with prams and cars spinning by on the road and they were all making her feel dizzy. After her couple of nights away from it all, there seemed to be too much going on for her eyes to take in. She felt all exposed and everything seemed much too busy. A million times she almost decided to walk up to the next stop but she had the feeling that would make her stand out more. . . .

When the bus finally came it was the best one possible. She had a hell of a row with the conductor because she only had a five pound note, but it dropped her right at the top of Middleton Road. Then all she had to do was walk a couple of minutes just like she would coming home from school anyhow. She had no key, of course, but still. She rang the bell. Her mother opened the door.

'Where's your bloody key, then?' her mother said.

'Left me bag in me locker,' she said. 'Sorry, mum.'

'Get it stole, you will. Won't be there tomorrow.'

'Be all right.'

She'd have to leave a window open round the back tomorrow, get a key cut somehow, say her bag had got stole. Something. Her dad's bike was cluttering it all up in the hall, so he was back.

'Got better things to do than traipse to the door on your account,' her mother was saying. She would.

Lucy followed the stream of grumbling down the hall to the kitchenette. Her dad looked up as she came in. He could only have just got in. He was still smoothing the creases out of his *Mirror*. He always folded it up in a neat little, fat square to put in his haversack. His thermos and lunch box were on the kitchen table and he was scrunched into the corner next to the fridge. Daren was at the other end of the tiny table. He'd spread goo all over the tray of his high chair.

' 'Lo, dad,' Lucy said.

'You're late, aren't you?' he said. But not unfriendly.

'Stayed on to get me homework out the way,' she said. 'Maths. Done it with Denise.'

'Necking at the bus stop more like,' her dad said.

It was funny. He'd've beat the living daylights out of her if he'd thought she had been doing that – let alone for what she had been doing – but so long as he thought she hadn't, he could make a joke about it. He'd always liked his bit of a joke with her. He was a short man, very dark, with hair slicked straight back all old-fashioned. He was thin but ever so strong. Wiry. She wished he wouldn't do his hair like that just as she didn't like the way he always took sandwiches to work. Made him more common than he was. Not that it mattered much at his age any more – nearly forty.

'Hey!' he was saying, 'where'd you get them?'

He was talking about the blouse and skirt. Her mother hadn't noticed but he had straight off.

'Popped over to Paris in lunch break, didn't I then,' she said.

'Muck up your dress, did you?' her mother said. Old cow.

'It's old stuff of Jackie's,' she said. 'She said I could have it.'

'I should think so. Old stuff's right. Don't even fit you.'

120

'All right for school.'

'Didn't give her your dress, I hope.'

'Course not.'

'Make sure you get it back.'

'Yes, mum.'

'What was the film like?' her dad said. 'All right, was it?'

Quick – which one was it she'd said they were going to. She couldn't remember! He'd only been trying to help her. She'd have to bluff it.

'Bit of a waste, actually,' she said. 'Not much cop after all.'

It seemed more believable to say it hadn't been up to much.

'All publicity, ain't it, these days,' he dad said. Her mother just sniffed. She was trying to scrape up the goo from in front of Daren. He kept sploshing his hand in it. Lucy could see that any minute now he'd be getting a smack.

'I'll do that if you like, mum,' she said.

'Manage all right myself, thank you very much.'

'Any ironing or anything you want doing, then?'

'Done it, haven't I?'

Sod her then if that was how she felt. Like she always did these days.

'What's Jackie doing now these days?' her dad asked.

'Same job. Still got it.'

She might as well go upstairs a bit or something. Put some make-up on and a decent dress and make herself feel human. Supper would be hours by the look of it. She gave Daren a big smile to try and cheer him up and he gave her a big smile back and jerked his arms about.

'Sit still, for God's sake,' his mother snapped at him. His face went all sad.

'And you,' her mother said, 'if you're going to put that bloody cassette thing on, keep it down. He's teething again.'

'Oh, not again, poor little blighter,' Lucy said.

For some reason that got right up her mother's nose. She turned round like she'd said he was a bastard.

'Doesn't upset you, does it,' her mother was yelling. 'Not your sleep gets ruined. You don't have to do his bloody nappies.'

'For God's sake—'

'Try thinking of someone else for a change!'

There was no reason in it, no arguing with her in that mood. And Daren had started to cry. Sod her again. Let her get on with it. Lucy went out.

Her father tried to let it all go by him. His head always ached in here. A good player who can count, the *Mirror* said, will always beat a great player who can't.

'They're all the same today,' she was saying. 'Self. Self. Self.'

The kid was wailing away. Years before he could take him down the rec, start teaching him football, take him down Charlton. For the umpteenth million time he cursed that bloody funeral that had made him get drunk and saddle them with him. It was useless but he wouldn't be allowed to sit and have a read in peace and quiet now. He might as well say something.

'She did offer to help,' he said.

'Only 'cause you're here. 'S all different when you're not around.'

Well, how could you argue against that?

'Bit hard on her, though, weren't you?' he tried.

'Just what you would say! I knew you'd say that! You always take her bloody side.'

The baby was still bawling. He sighed inwardly and sliding out from the chair sideways like you had to so as not to bang your head on the shelf, he got to his feet. He looked at his wife as if she were a bit of furniture he had always had around and, for some reason he couldn't quite explain, always would be lumbered with.

'Think I'll make a pot of tea,' he said.

He moved to the sink. Thank God it was Monday. He'd get down to *The Fox* a good bit before the game tonight.

He always played better on two light and bitters. *The Tuns*
had that funny bloke who always worked the nineteens.

⚜ ⚜ ⚜ ⚜

At Kingston House it would soon be supper. In the small
room they shared, Jamie and Donnie were both killing
time in ways that came naturally to them. Donnie was
spread out on his bed beneath a poster picture of Barry
Sheene. Skimming rather than reading, he was turning
over the dog-eared pages of a magazine devoted to the life
and times of Bruce Lee.

Jamie was on his knees on the floor. A sheet of newspaper
was on the floor in front of him. He held one of his shoes
in one hand, a rag in the other. A tin of polish was at his
side. Spitting onto the rag from time to time, dabbing it in
the polish, he was working it over the shoe in small, hard
pressing circular movements in a perfect imitation of a
soldier bulling his boots.

The room displayed the same split of personalities.
Everything on Jamie's side was squared and stowed away
in apple-pie order. Donnie's was an amiable clutter of socks
on the floor, open drawers, an old dismembered radio. The
Barry Sheene poster curled down at one corner. Whatever
qualities Donnie possessed, a methodical turn of mind was
not one of them. Or single-mindedness. He tossed Bruce
Lee on to the floor now and absently began to pick his
nose. He swung into a sitting position.

'I still reckon he done it,' he said.

'Was all bull,' Jamie replied fiercely and at once. This
was an old battleground and the lines already drawn.

'It was in the film!' Donnie insisted.

'So what? It's rubbish!'

'You're so bloody sure.'

'Course I'm sure. You can't pull the pin out like that.
Not with your teeth.'

'Who told you?'

'None of your business.'

'There you are! You don't know!'

'I do.'

123

There was a more persuasive element of confidence in Jamie's quieter tone of voice. Donnie was obliged to become more strident.

'He did it!' he insisted. 'We saw him!'

'See all sorts of things in films, bird brain. Ghosts. Monsters. Fairies. They fake it, don't they?'

'That's science fiction and stuff. This was a real story. They were copying how it's really done – right? Someone had to do it for real first.'

'You know something,' Jamie said, 'you're real thick. Believe anything. I bet you'll tell me next Bruce Lee is still alive.'

'How would you know anyway? All you know about is fairies.'

Jamie was balling up the rag in his hand before Donnie had finished speaking. He threw it fast and furiously. It missed its aim but the gesture was provocation enough. Donnie dived off the bed at him. Violently but, because they quite liked each other, because each knew he was already in enough trouble, not viciously, they began clumsily to wrestle.

🕆🕆🕆🕆

The huge sprawl of the council estate was on the extreme south-east of his patch, but John Graydon knew it quite well. Hastily built right after the war to absorb several thousand bombed-out East-enders, its addresses figured quite heavily on his case-work. Its claustrophobic ill-planning guaranteed that people underprivileged to begin with and uprooted from their old deep comforts should continue to be on the receiving end of life. There was nowhere for kids to do their homework in peace as televisions blared the same programme through ninety-nine per cent of the paper-thin walls. Teenagers were stuck cheek by jowl with their edgy parents. It was better to fling out of the house each night for a bit of fun round the cafés with your mates. Or up Pringle Woods with your girl. During the winter the places froze. The joinery after the war had been sub-apprentice standard and in any case the seasoned wood had all been used up in the war effort. This had all been green and had warped something rotten years ago. The open fires smoked out the place, sent most of their heat straight up the chimney. There was no way the council were going to put in central heating, mate, and who the hell was going to have it installed themselves when they didn't own the place? Money down the drain. Not a garage to be seen, of course. No-one ever reckoned the people living here would so far get above their station to presume to own a car. Consequence was, of course, the too narrow roads were parked solid nights with the Datsuns and Skodas and Reliants and the second-hand Cortinas. No point in owning something a bit classier even if you could afford it. Between the rust and the kids nicking radios, bending aerials, envy-striping your paintwork, it wasn't bleeding worth it. In the winter, of course, scraping the ice off, getting the cow to start, was a right bastard and a half.

The awareness that everything pleasant or worthwhile came three times harder here, that the quality of life was here beset by a thousand daily irritating cheapnesses, was well in John Graydon's consciousness as, stepping out from behind a Lada Fiat, waiting for a glum kid on a skateboard to scowl by, he crossed Lindsay Avenue on a diagonal and made for number 37. He'd been brought up on an estate just like this on the edge of Sutton.

As he'd travelled back there by train and bus from college each evening, he had been able to see the faces of the people – all snobbery aside – grow meaner, more pinched, uglier, the nearer he got to home. Those faces were the reasons he had chosen this career.

The gate was on its hinge, the pocket handkerchief of a garden unkempt and dried up. The bell worked. Mechanical type, then, no green fingers. As far as you could tell, though, there didn't seem to be a car outside to go with the house. He hoped she was in: that she'd see reason. He was supposed to be at the Otuluski's already by now.

The door was being opened. Oh good, it was the girl. Her. Had to be.

'Yes?' she said.

'Hello,' he said. 'My name's John Graydon. I'm a Social Worker from the Department—'

'Oh my Gawd!'

It was her all right. Her face had fallen a mile. She was stepping out onto the joke of a front step and, obviously shattered, pulling the door shut after her. She'd gone much too heavy on the make-up but you could see why she would turn on quite a lot of men. You had an idea why she'd gone out and met trouble more than halfway. But underneath the Boots-bought Mary Quant you could see the fifteen year old. The schoolgirl. He tried to pitch it low key. Christ, when he came to think of it he was feeling tired. He could've done without this today.

'You didn't think you'd get away that easily, did you?' he said gently.

She'd gone pale. She was shaking her head.

'Can't just walk off, you know, pretend it never happened.'

'Who is it?' a shrill voice called. It'd be the mother, the wife from the kitchen. That really brought out the schoolgirl in her.

'Er . . . someone for me,' she called out, her voice loud but uncertain.

'They'll kill me,' she whispered at him frantically. 'I haven't told them, you see.'

Easy, he told himself, don't alarm her further.

'It's my dad. I don't care about her, old cow. It's him. I don't want him to think I've let him down. I've been too ashamed to tell him because I know he'll feel let down.'

'It's not so bad. Not the end of the world. Would you like me to talk to him?'

'No!'

'I won't drop you in it. I'll just explain—'

'No! He's not here. He's round his allotment.'

'Is that that Frank come back to pester you?'

Abruptly in a way that irresistibly reminded John of a Punch and Judy entrance, a thin, sharp, weary-faced woman had poked herself out from behind the door. It was the baby she carried that gave you that impression.

'Oh!' she said suspiciously. She really did have beady eyes. She'd know him again when she saw him next.

'It's Mr Grayman,' the girl got in quickly and inaccurately. 'He's a Social Worker.'

'Oh yes?'

The first reaction of the badly educated: closed-mind hostility.

'It's, er, about one of the kids at school,' the girl was madly inventing. 'That Eunice. Not been in for a month, she hasn't.'

He should have stopped it there. But the tiredness of his endless day was on him. His feet ached, his eyes ached. And he was trying to give the girl a break, still, win her confidence. If the woman had not been so obviously a shrew and stupid with it he might have played it differently. As he should.

'Typical,' he instead let the mother say. 'Don't stand out here on the step talking all hours.' She sniffed and, not looking at him further, went back into the house. He looked at the even more scared girl.

'They'll have to know sometime,' he said. 'He will.'

'I'll tell him,' she said. 'Honest. I'll go and tell him right now. Myself. I'll hate it but I'd rather I told him than someone else – than he heard it from someone else.'

He looked at his watch.

'I don't have the time to let you do that now,' he said.

'I must tell him first! He mustn't hear from her.'

'I've got another call to make. Sorry but you'll—'

'Let me tell him! Please! By myself. I'll go back. Honest! I didn't know you knew who I was, you see but now you do I got no chance except to do it right, have I?'

She'd grasped that point, then. Chris Langley had said she was supposed to bright. She had started to cry. She was trying not to but the tears were there all right. Her mascara had run. It brought out the clown in her, made her look thirteen.

'You realise it's in your own interest,' he said.

127

'I realise that now. I wasn't going to fool around again. I just didn't want my dad to be ashamed on account of hearing what I've done.'

'If you don't show—'

'I will! I will! Honest! I'll go back. I'll be there by half-past seven. At the latest! God's truth! . . . Please!'

She'd learned her lesson. It would help her case if she went back of her own free will.

'All right,' he said. 'But, if not, it's the police and no holds barred. They'll throw the book at you. Maybe the station, too. Your dad'll like that lot even less!'

'Honest! You can count on it!'

'I am.'

He nodded sternly, turned and went back down the garden path. He crossed back to where he'd parked his fourth-hand mini-van. It was in gear, he was pulling away, before it came into his mind that a bloke who kept a garden as untended as that was not your first choice as a bloke to spend his evenings working on some allotment. The discrepancy flicked his mind but in that split-second he was having to brake like a bastard to avoid going into the kid on the skateboard. Now the sullen, wised-up before its time face was grinning at him derisively. The little sod had been playing chicken with him! Well, another three years, he'd no doubt have him as a case. If either of them lasted that long.

'Gone then, has he?' Mrs Wyatt was meanwhile calling. She had heard the front door shut.

'Yes, mum,' Lucy called back as nicely as she could.

Her father was coming down the stairs as she started to go up.

'Let's get down, then,' he said. 'Unlucky to cross on the stairs.'

He reached the bottom, gave her a kiss on the cheek.

'Cost me the game,' he said.

She smiled, went up to her apology for a room. Stuffed in the dancing shoes in the box at the back of the wardrobe top she had exactly one hundred and seventy two pounds. She'd miss her dad but she would write once she was sorted out. Her heart was beating like the clappers and she found it hard to breath. She seemed to make oceans of noise dragging the chair over to the wardrobe so she could reach the box.

The main thing was to scarper. To get while the getting was still good.

Chapter Nine

TUESDAY MORNING. BACK on the firing line. The coffee for all its pungency only just beginning to send its fumes up to dispel the old sleep still applying its dull ache to the back of his eyes, Chris Langley sat behind his desk endeavouring to seem official. In sullen, passively insolent posture opposite him slouched the boy who if he'd sacrifice a fraction of pace for an increase in control of line and length had it in him, surely, to play cricket up to county level: whom two-and-a-half days earlier he had tried to place with a good side and, for his pains, been snubbed. It's as well, thought Chris I'm not facing up to him out in the middle now myself. If looks mean anything it would be six bouncers on the trot. Right, time for play to start.

'How about it, then, Gary?' he said.

'How about what, then?'

'What happened?'

'Where?'

'Don't get smart with me this morning, Gary. I've got bad news all around me today. Which could be bad for you. The Physics Lab, that's where.'

'It bust, didn't it.'

Yet again, as from each one of them, the surly defiance of the caught red-handed and defenceless guilty. If they'd just see. Lucille had been like that when she'd come in. Oh, damn Lucille! And Graydon too!

'How?' was all he said.

Just shrugging, Gary said even less.

'Did it fall or was it pushed?'

'Don't know, do I?'

Chris pushed his chair back a further six inches from the desk. Without affectation or conscious striving for effect he gave the black teenager a long, level look. For all the poise his symmetrical good looks gave him, for all his attempt at defiant nonchalance, the boy shifted uneasily under the stare.

'I do. I know,' Chris said at considered last. 'You blew your cool, didn't you? Like when you wrecked that hostel room. Right?'

Now a look of not so buried triumph quivered on the edge of full expression across Gary's features. Chris was not going to allow him the luxury of that misconception. He drove on quickly.

'You're a phoney, aren't you, Gary,' he said, 'a fraud?'

'What!'

The boy had not liked that. Good. Chris shook his head.

'All this talk about Gary and his big bad temper that's going to be the death of him. You and—'

'All got to die some day.'

'You don't ever really do your pieces, do you, Gary? It's all a blind, a cover. "Old Gary's blown his stack again," they say, don't they? What they should be saying is Gary's gone chicken again. Right? That's the truth, isn't it?'

'Bull shit!'

'You know better than that, Gary. You only sound off when you can't cut it, don't you? What was it this time — you couldn't quite figure how to work something that takes a little thinking out? Or was it that you screwed up on what you were supposed to be weighing?'

His secret, his inadequacy, correctly exposed the boy stared at the man with all the insecure hatred of the defeated. He kept up the pretence.

'It was whatever you say it is, whitey,' he said.

'Don't hide behind that one either, Gary . . . Look, you're supposed to be here another three weeks. If we kick you out with a big thumbs down you'll end up in some community school, somewhere like that.'

Gary shrugged.

'Don't you care?'

'Nothing to bust a gut about. Easier'n my old man's got.'

Chris spoke with a real cutting edge.

'I already told you, Gary,' he said, 'where he is, what he did — it's all irrelevant to what you are and what you do.'

It wasn't, of course, but what basis for a life did the boy have except believing otherwise?

'You don't hide there, either,' Chris said. 'Not from me.'

'So what you going to do?' Gary asked at last.

Chris ignored the question. He had not made up his mind.

'You're a fool, Gary,' he said. 'You can't afford to blow your chances. You're a black boy in a white world. To get ahead, get yourself a decent job, a decent life, you've got to be as good as the white boy and then twenty per cent better. I know that. You know that. But you aren't going to make it.'

'What do you mean?'

Indignation was better than nothing, Chris decided.

'You're scared of competition,' he said.

'No!'

'You chicken out.'

'No!'

'Yes. Oh, I'm not talking about back alley fights or going into a tackle with all you've got. That comes easy to you. That doesn't count. What counts, where you show your class, is dealing with all the stuff that isn't easy. There's usually a hell of a sight more of that.'

'So what you going to do?'

'The question is – what are you going to do? Me – I'm going to phone your Headmaster and tell him that you're sorry and on the way back into school. Are you sorry?'

'Guess so.'

'Don't guess. Be. Then I'm going to recommend he throws the book at you. And I expect you to start showing your class by taking whatever he decides that is right in your stride.'

'Suppose I don't.'

'You walk away a loser. Now – and for the rest of your life.'

'What if I don't care?'

'Then you're an idiot and none of this matters because idiots aren't worth wasting time on.'

The boy drew himself up to his full thin height at the prospect of yet another desertion from an adult.

'That all?' he said.

'That's all. Get off to school. I'll phone to say why you're arriving late.'

It was a moment before Gary moved. He had expected some token reconciliation, a softening word. Neither were forthcoming. In Gary's case, Chris had decided, seeming indifference was the better part of charity. He would not speak as Gary reached the doorway and send him out of the room with a kind afterthought as in a mediocre play. He watched the boy walk out and the door close in silence. Then, reaching for the phone, he sighed. How were you supposed to talk to a kid whose father had killed the mother by soaking her clothes in petrol and, eventually, burning her to death? They hadn't taught him that at Goldsmiths College. . . . Well, if no better, feigned indifference was probably no worse than any other way.

He made the call. The scales were just repairable: just about worth repairing at the price. There wouldn't be much change out of fifty. As he heard the details, made all the right noises, the weight of his entire job bore down on his awareness like an inverted pyramid. The point of the pyramid was needle sharp and ground on the knowledge Lucille Wyatt had left home. It dug that deeper when, as he put down the receiver a knock came at his door and, tentatively, as he had good reason to, Christ knew, John Graydon came in. Chris motioned him to a chair. The young social worker set down a battered, old-fashioned briefcase that seemed long ago to have lost the battle of the bulge and then sat down himself. Contrite, he seemed even less happy than the defiant Gary.

The two men looked at each other without saying good morning or hello.

'What can I say?' John Graydon said at last.

'Sod all that I can think of.'

'I'm the conventional sort. Suppose I tell you I'm sorry.'

'Sorry's not good enough, is it?'

133

'Probably not . . . Look, all right. I was a fool. I should—'

'Don't tell me about you. It's not you I'm worried about. It's her! The damage you've done to her!'

John Graydon's handsome, conventionally casual features whitened in the face of vehemence from this source. This was a whole new Chris Langley. His hand came up to his mouth and he ran thumb and index-finger out and apart from each other down the line of his moustache.

'Yes,' he said and nodded sickly.

'It starts out as a simple misdemeanour – not really a court case at all – now where the hell's it going to end?'

'I . . . I don't know.'

'Nor do I! She's on the run. God knows where! Doing God knows what! Yesterday evening we knew exactly where she was.'

'I – I just believed her. It seemed—'

'You said you'd phone.'

'Only if I couldn't find her! I had to move on. I thought she'd—'

'You thought! It seemed! She's fifteen. She's into stripping. Where's that lead? Leader of the Conservative Party? What do they call it? The Meat Rack? Have you walked round the back of Piccadilly recently? Seen all those sad faced old slags?'

'Yes, I have, as a matter of fact,' John Graydon said. A less worked up listener might have detected a certain ominous something of resentment in his voice.

'On pleasure, then! It couldn't have been on business!'

This time the young man's pallor came from anger. Framed by his long black hair his face seemed very white indeed.

'I'll go and talk to the mother,' he said stiffly.

But Chris Langley was too much enjoying having before him in his office someone who was not one of nature's victims, someone on whom he could legitimately vent his spleen.

'What for?' he said tersely. 'What good'll that do? Or did

you have in mind a couple of choruses of *Auld Lang Syne* over the family album?'

'There's a chance I might turn something—'

'Oh, give it a rest! There's not and you know it. You had that kid in the palm of your hand. All you had—'

'Look, Chris,' John Graydon said on a rising inflection, 'I think you're the one who'd better give it a rest.'

'What do you mean?'

'You never made a mistake?'

'I—'

'I blew it. O.K. no argument. Guilty, m'lud. But consider – I was doing you an emergency favour. She wasn't on my case load. I was trying to save your arse! I was knackered, my feet were aching. I still had two more of my own calls to make when I'd finished—'

'That still doesn't alter the fact—'

'She's fifteen. Attractive. Bright. Plausible. She lies well . . . So, all right – I'm a sucker! But I'm not a bloody criminal! So unless you can go out there and do better yourself, knock it off!'

For what seemed a very long time the man in his mid-thirties and the man in his mid-twenties sat looking at each other. It was actually a matter of seconds. A long time is how it seemed. It was Chris Langley who broke the strained and angry silence.

'Now I have to say sorry,' he said. 'You're quite right, you know. On about every count. It's not the damage you've done to her. It's the damage I've done. And of course there's a chance with the mother. A chance and therefore a need to get back to her. I'll—'

'I'll do that.'

'It's not your fight. You were right about that too.'

'It is now. I did goof. No denying that.'

'Hmmn. The Confession Hour . . . I have to bottle it up for most. You're a bit of a luxury for me. Someone who can fight back.'

'Bloody had to, didn't I?'

Chris Langley smiled ruefully.

'Give it a try, then, will you?' he said.

John Graydon rose.

'Of course,' he said. 'I'll call you. One way or the other.'

Stooping, he used both hands to pick up his briefcase. He held it under one arm as he made to leave the room.

'Be in touch,' he said.

Chris Langley got his head down to his never quite routine work. He drafted a forlorn hope of an ad. for a replacement to Mrs Hughes for insertion in the local paper. He rang the nearest job centre on the same quest. He settled to write the report he must get out that day on Jonathan Ridley for forwarding to his new foster parents. That made him feel less bitterly out of sorts. Jonathan represented a quiet, unspectacular success story. Score one for the good guys. As always, as he concentrated on work, the bad vibrations criss-crossing in his skull faded to close to nothing. He reached out for his coffee.

Ugh! His initial ill-temper, his subsequent concentration had allowed him to forget it for so long it was undrinkable. Waste not want not. He drank it anyway and then decided to get himself another cup to take the taste away. He made his way to the top of the house, warmed up the pot, returned downstairs with a properly steaming cup in his hand. Waiting by his office door was Howard with a youngish girl-cum-woman.

'Er, Mr Langley, er, this is Mrs, er—'

'Miss,' the girl said quickly, 'Miss McEvoy.'

Ah yes, Jamie's sister. But the first priority was Howard. He was blushing furiously at what he obviously considered had been an enormous social gaffe. The visitor's very obvious sexuality was equally obviously a focus of severe embarrassment for him.

'How do you do, Miss McEvoy,' he was meanwhile saying. 'Won't you please go on in. Thanks very much for standing in for me, Howard.'

He smiled at the young man as he held the door open for the young woman. He was filing the incident in his mind. He must try to sort something out for Howard. The blasted tyranny of sex over these older, institutionalised and hence socially, sexually gauche boys! He stepped into the office after Jamie's sister. It was like Piccadilly Circus this morning.

'Please sit down, Miss McEvoy.'

'Thank you. Patricia, actually. Trish.'

'Ah, fine. Chris Langley.'

He had moved to behind his desk. She must be about nineteen. Where she was sitting the light from the window was full on her face and, for a few years yet, she could rest easy in her mind about so unsubtle a light source.

She wasn't beautiful, not even pretty, really. The word was elfin, possibly, as she was quite short. A very knowing elf. She had big eyes, a sharp prominent nose and wide mouth under a Peter Pan style hair cut. Not pretty but attractive. Vivacious. Attractive with a quick and urban, probably penny-wise, pound foolish, kind of having been around, of knowing the short-term score. She was wearing a navy blue trouser suit in some kind of lineny material and spending the time while he was looking at her, looking at the painting of Kingston House on his wall Elaine had done. The windows were solid blacks and the frames white. The effect was of a place you could neither see nor get out from with coffins set vertically into the walls.

'Bet he was glad to get that off his chest,' she said with a nod at the painting.

Yes, she was bright.

'It's by a girl, actually,' he said.

'Sorted her out, have you?'

He hesitated a fraction and so had to be honest.

'Not yet,' he said.

'How's Jamie?' she said. 'Behaving himself?'

'Most of the time.'

'He never was a bad lad, you know.'

'I'll believe you,' he said and smiled to underline it was his own conviction. But she misunderstood him.

'No, straight up,' she said. 'Really. Some kids you know . . . it's one bit of villainy after another. He ain't like that. Bit light-fingered, that's all.'

'If we can get him into the right school, he should be fine.'

137

'Think you will?'

'I think so. We'll know for sure next Tuesday. I'll be able to give the court a very good report on him. He's intelligent, neat – well, you know better than I. In fact I find myself wondering more and more why he did it.'

'You say did it, don't you,' she said, 'but he didn't, did he? Best it was a half-arsed effort.'

'Doesn't alter the question.'

'What question?'

'Why?'

'Easy enough, ain't it. He had his paper round. The newsagents gets sold. He loses the round. Like a fool he goes out and buys the paraffin and so on.'

'That's how he explains it.'

'Don't you believe him? I do. I mean he's not covering up, is he? Saying he didn't do it.'

'Seems such an over-reaction. Out of character.'

'It's not over-reacting if you see it as getting your own back, is it? And it's very much in character if you think of him planning it as a military operation – attack on the headquarters of the generals sort of thing.'

'Maybe.'

And maybe it was. That peasant short-term shrewdness he thought he saw in her might be absolutely on the button.

'Anyway,' he said standing up, 'you want to see him. And he'll be waiting fit to bust, I'm sure.'

'Yes. It's ever so nice arranging for him to have this day off from school like this. It's wicked having to work in a hairdressers and do a full Saturday when nearly everyone—'

'Well we can't turn it into a habit, obviously. But I explained about your mother and Sundays and the school knows it's in his best interests, the interests of his stability, not feeling left out, ignored and that, for him to spend some time with you. I'm very grateful you've come to give him a boost.'

'Oh. 'S nothing.'

'A lot of kids don't get it. They come here, their families don't want to know.'

'Yes,' said Patricia McEvoy, 'there's some rotten sods about. You really got to watch it.'

Chris Langley was smiling as she showed her out.

❖❖❖❖

Using his powerful arms on the banisters to help lever himself up, Howard had climbed unevenly up to the first floor. He found Jamie McEvoy crossing the landing on his way down. He was wearing his beret, a drab olive, military-style anorak and, surprise, surprise, that belt of his with all the badges on. Never without that. Under his pillow at night, young Donnie said.

'Your sister's here,' Howard said.

'Yeah. Saw her come.'

'How old is she?' Howard said. He managed to say it quite well, he thought.

'Why? Fancy her?'

Howard tried to fight the blushing, the empty little-boy feeling at his stomach's pit. He wasn't going to let this little sod see him go all red and have him putting it around to everyone that Howard went all funny over girls because he couldn't get one, the poor gimp.

'Seen worse,' Howard said like in a film. As he did fancy her, he couldn't really call Jamie a little sod. But that's what he seemed like saying that.

'Forget it,' Jamie was saying now. 'Got a boy-friend, ain't she? Big ugly sod. See you.'

He went rapidly, surefootedly, unthinkingly down the stairs.

The boy-friend's no rotten cripple either, Howard thought, and the endless, hopeless, gnawing ache inside him deepened into a still more terrible poignancy.

Chapter Ten

MRS WYATT, JOHN Graydon was uncharitably deciding, did not improve on closer acquaintance. Close up and at greater length, her shrewiness became quickly tamed, it was true, but the transformation beneath the sharp features, the tired, strained eyes was only to the grudging, whining, stupid outlook of one of Nature's perpetual non-copers. A bit strong, he acknowledged to himself: I ought to have more sympathy. It was the stupidity that stuck most in his throat and which, illogically perhaps, he found the hardest to forgive. It was the same in all his cases. Anyone that stupid, he would think, deserves just about everything they get.

As he sat in the Wyatts' pawky kitchenette he was having to work hard to keep his manner friendly and encouraging. A thin, sharp smell as from a flannel used and not washed for far too long came reedily and constantly into his nostrils. The sour smell of defeat and of his childhood was at the core of the smell – the gigantic defeat of those ten thousand small set-backs. And as for his sense of smell, so for his eyes. The combination of light blue kitchen cabinet on bright orange emulsioned wall shrieked that if it had its due influence Lucille Wyatt would grow up without any taste.

'Let's have something with a bit of go in it,' her mother had probably once said, 'brighten the place up a bit.'

She was ironing now, pretending to, cramming the kitchenette to its tiny limits as she went through the motions. But whatever complexity of feelings the familiar routine was supposed to cover up, disbelief was not one of them. She had taken his news of Lucy's little night-time games with a good deal of twisted matter-of-factness. Basically and speedily she had wanted to believe ill of her daughter. Despite her present conventional protestations.

'I still can't believe it,' she was repeating.

'It's true all the same,' John Graydon said.

A thought came into her foxy features. The shirt remained untouched as she set the iron upright at the end of the board.

'Why didn't you say something last night?' she said.

She had a point there. Stupid she might be. A cheap kind of instinctive craftiness was still, nevertheless, built into her.

'I should have done,' he confessed. 'I was trying to give her a break. I let her talk me out of it.'

'Oh yes,' the mother sneered with perversely confirmed satisfaction. 'Good at that she is. If talking about it got it done, she'd do real well. What with her tongue and her big wide eyes that tell you butter wouldn't melt in her mouth. And all the rest.'

She darted him a quick, knowing female look. John tried not to look put out. He had already wondered how Lucille could have inherited her bumps and grinds figure from so flat and concave a mother, but he resented the visual hint that he'd fallen for her line because his mind was on her tits. It hadn't been. She really did nothing for him.

'Yes, well, what time did she go last night?' he said.

'Must've been right after you left. Whenever that was.'

'Half past six, then.'

'If you say so. I expect so. It's her dad I feel sorry for.'

'Why's that?'

The picked up iron still hovered irritatingly over the untouched shirt. He was beginning to find it hypnotic. It set his eyes on edge.

'He's never been able to see through her,' Mrs Wyatt said. 'I could. Right from the start. Soon as she could talk. Artful! Sly! Not him, though. Never. Soft as grease with her. Always was. Right from a little kid.'

Now for the main hope.

'What about her friends?' he asked.

'Friends?'

Her daughter's friendships were not an area of life Mrs Wyatt had ever wasted much thought on.

'You see, the sooner we can find her – the better for her. The longer it goes, the more serious it becomes.'

'And I suppose I'm supposed to care!'

What do you say? What do you ever say?

'I think you should,' he said, 'yes.'

'Well, they all come and go. She never brought them round here much.'

Surprise.

'There's a girl in her class – Mandy something. And a Eunice. Awful name.'

He wrote it in his notebook all the same.

'Surnames?'

'Oooh, you got me there.'

'Any others?'

'Not as I can put names to. A baby young as mine, you know – keeps your nose to the grindstone.'

'What about boys?'

'Men, you mean! From what you've told me, I'd be the last to bloody know, wouldn't I?'

'Saturday night, Sunday . . . where did you think she was?'

'Pictures.'

'All weekend?'

'Oh, no. She was going to Jackie's.'

'Jackie's? Is that a boy or a girl?'

'Girl.'

'There you are then. That's another one.'

He wrote the name down.

'Another school friend?' he asked.

'Not now. Last I heard she was working.'

'Where?'

'I don't know. Up West. In one of those what do you call its . . . where they put on records and there's all funny lights to cover up the goings on.'

'A disco?'

'Yes. One of them.'

'Where does Jackie live? At home?'

'Couldn't say. Got a flat. Not round here, though.'

He scribbled another note. John Graydon private eye, he thought. Public conscience. O.K., sweetheart, I'm from the D.H.S.S.

'Anyone else?' he said. 'Let's just have another think.'

Still the iron had failed to descend and get on with its work.

✣✣✣✣

The recent drop of rain might never have bothered to fall as far as the grass was concerned. Brown-yellow, still, it had soaked up the quite heavy downpour as if it were no more than a cupful. It was the trees that had received the benefit. The rain had washed their leaves clean of the summer's rising dust and now, in full foliage at the centre of the year, they stretched up and sideways in the full, varied, magnificently understated splendour of an English wood. Or, as Trish McEvoy was thinking to herself, looking ever so nice and pretty. And if the grass in the little clearing where they'd stopped was going home a bit, at least it was springy and you knew for a fact that it was dry.

They had come quite a way. First a long bus ride that she had deliberately let be a bit of a magical mystery tour as far as Jamie was concerned. More important than taking him out was taking him out of himself, Mr Langley had said. But slowly. She had tried to take his advice and not force things at all but let them take their course. Jamie, as always, had stayed mainly quiet, looking at everything, making few comments. When they'd cut across the golf course he had been very impressed by the bunkers. They would make good cover, he had said.

They had walked quite a way. The firmness of the ground had made the going easy and with a nice, gentle breeze about, the sun playing hide and seek with the clouds was not so hot as to tire you quickly and make you irritable. They had gone on over the Heath, across the dried up stream and into the woods. Then the sun had sailed into a big patch of blue and grown hotter. Jamie had found a nice clearing among the trees but just as they were settling she had seen a used French letter and she'd felt the place had gone all dirty. And she didn't want to embarrass Jamie by having to explain what it was. Not that he wouldn't know by now, but if he did ask, all the same . . . She'd said she thought there was a nicer place further on and, sure enough,

143

there had been. They'd stopped there and she'd unpacked the Fine Fare carrier she'd been holding all along. Now the sun was so gorgeous she would have liked to get in some sunbathing. Working at a hairdressers she didn't get much chance. But she couldn't of course. She put the idea out of her mind. He was just the wrong in-between age.

Though she said it herself, she hadn't done a bad job on the nosh. She'd remembered that Jamie had a thing about corned-beef sandwiches and he'd gone through them like nobody's business. Now, sitting with his back against a tree – but don't ask her which sort – he was getting stuck into a conference pear. And perhaps now, while his attention was half on the juice running down his chops, was the time to start leading up to it.

'So you quite like that Donnie, then?' she picked up.

'Yeah,' he said. 'He's all right.'

'What's he in for?'

'Don't know.'

'Ain't you ever asked him?'

'If he wanted me to know, he'd tell me, wouldn't he!'

'Jamie, I never knew anyone know less about what's going on around him than you.'

'Know all I need to know.'

'Your mum – you don't ever ask about her.'

The boy's face hardened in the sunlight.

'She ever ask 'bout me?' he said.

'Always. Regular as clockwork.'

The face stayed hard. She couldn't blame him really. One lie from her was not going to put all that right just like that.

'How is she, then?' he said suddenly.

But she knew he had only made the fake effort for her sake, to be nice to her. She was gratified but there wasn't no point in it really if it was all like that.

'Let's forget it,' she said.

He shrugged and made an up-to-you face. But the reaction had pushed the hardness out of his expression. A kid his age shouldn't look that hard. A bird was whistling somewhere, low and sort of thick.

'What about Mr Langley, then – you like him?' she said.

'He's all right.'

'Just all right? What about the other kids?'

'Few yobs. Most of 'em are all right.'

'So what you're saying is that it's an all right place.'

'All right, yeah.'

Directly, pleasantly, she laughed. She had a nice laugh, he reckoned, not mickey-taking.

'Tell me something,' she was saying. 'When something's wrong or all gone rotten, what do you say then?'

He had to think about that a moment. I mean, it was hard to put it in words exactly, wasn't it?

'I'd say it weren't all right,' he said at last.

She laughed again and, seeing why, he had to have a laugh as well.

That's the first time he's done that today, she thought.

He tossed the core of his pear away. That was all right. It would rot and fertilise the ground or the ants would get it or something. She let him get away with that. But suddenly he gave this great, enormous belch.

'Jamie!' she said.

She was genuinely shocked. You could tell it had been on purpose.

'Don't!' she said. Trying to be clever, attract attention.

'Why not?' he said.

'It's piggy. Bad manners.'

'Arabs do it. At the end of every meal. Not bad manners with them. It's to let the cook know he done a good job.'

'Did,' she said automatically. She stated the obvious. 'You ain't an Arab,' she said.

He was off on one of his day-dreams before she'd finished speaking.

'Wish I was,' he said. 'On a camel. With a long rifle. Like Lawrence of Arabia. I'd fancy that.'

'More like Florence of Arabia if you were like him,' she said.

He hadn't got her joke, though, and taking it the wrong way, was hurt. You could see that instantly.

'Another pear?' she said.

'No thanks,' he said. Normally, as far as she could tell.

'All right, though, ain't they?' she said with a smile. It got him back.

'Great,' he said dead-pan.

Now or never. To give herself something else to look at she started to tidy up the bags and paper cups.

'Jamie,' she said. 'You know Jeff?'

She had to look at him because he didn't answer her. The hardness had come back into his face. There was something scared there, this time, too. She kept on looking at him.

'Well, you know I know him,' he said at last.

'I'm going to marry him,' she said. When it happened it happened quicker than she'd intended. All he did was shrug and pull that up-to-you face again. This time the hardness didn't go. It nettled her a bit.

'What's that supposed to mean?' she said.

'Means I suppose I knew it,' he said. 'Your funeral.'

Charming!

'You quite like him, don't you?' she said. She tried to make it sound as if it wasn't all too important but she could tell she hadn't fooled him. If he says 'all right' I'll scream, she thought. But he fooled her.

'Does he like me, then?' he said.

'Course!'

'Bloody best kept secret ever if he does!'

Couldn't really blame him for saying that but she couldn't let him get away with it.

'Don't talk like that, Jamie,' she said. 'It's not right! Not fair. He's shy. He don't have no brothers or sisters. He's awkward with kids. That's all it is.'

He just sat looking at her stony-faced and she could see that he wasn't going to do a single thing to make it easy for her. She might as well get to the big point while the damage was done and get it all over in more or less one go.

'Point is, you see,' she said, 'when you come home . . . I won't be there.'

No, he hadn't thought of that. You could see it in his face.

'Why not?' he said. He was realising it now. The way he'd asked that made him sound like he was half his age.

146

Like when they'd used to say he couldn't stay up to watch tele.

'I'll be living with Jeff, won't I?' she said. She still smiled, still tried to put it lightly.

'Where?' You could see his mind working. She must lead him through it, try to let him down gently.

'We're getting a flat.'

'Can't I come?'

'Won't be big enough, love.'

'Well , . . why can't he move in with us?'

'He doesn't want to.' That was a mistake.

'People get married, they want their own place,' she hurried on with. Just for a minute the doubts about Jeff she'd put right out of her mind came back to flick nastily at it. But it was so gorgeous with him. He made her make such a noise. She couldn't help herself. It was so gorgeous having him inside her. But how could you tell a kid Jamie's age all that? She tried to make some sort of best of it.

'When we get settled,' she said, 'maybe we'll work something out.'

He didn't fall for it.

'Too small,' he said. 'You just said.'

'That's for now. Maybe – a year or two's time – who knows?'

He was appalled.

'A year or two!' he said.

Well, time was different too at that age.

'Or less,' she said. It came out miserable.

He sat for a long time. The stoniness had gone from his face now but the scaredness was completely filling its place. He looked so young again. Her little brother. For a moment she thought he was going to cry right then and there like once he would've done. But he didn't.

'Been different if you'd married Barry,' he said.

Jesus Blimey O'Reily! Him!

'What!' she said before she could stop herself.

'He wouldn't've left me.'

'Barry?'

'Barry!'

147

'What the hell's he to do with it?'

To her amazement, the tears came now. They were flooding into his eyes, streaming down his cheeks. And silently. Scarily. Suddenly she was really scared. He had jumped to his feet, was tearing off into the trees. She was more slow in getting up. He was half out of sight by the time she had. She started running after him but her sandals were too open, too loose, to be any use to her. She stumbled, half tripped. By the time she had got her balance back he was completely out of sight. She could still hear him, though, as dry twigs and bushes snapped.

'Jamie! Jamie!' she called out at the top of her lungs.

Now she could hear nothing. It had gone quieter than she would have thought possible. Standing in the same spot, not going back to the picnic things, she waited a long, long time. The sun came through the trees all hot and sticky now. After a while a bird resumed its low, thick whistling. It made it all seem quieter still and reminded her how far they were from anywhere and anyone.

⚜⚜⚜

At much the same time of day but in a setting considerably less rural, a sandwich bar just off Old Compton Street, another, more determined runaway from Kingston House was fidgeting uneasily on a bar-stool. Lucille Wyatt felt nervous. On several counts. The little coffee-cup-ring-stained counter was fixed across the place's main window. You sat at it staring out into the street. People went by on the pavement just a few inches away and you felt like a bloody goldfish. Anyone could see you. The police. Someone up West playing truant from school. A bloody schools' inspector. And of course being a girl and on her own and in this area she was getting all sorts of looks from all kinds of men. She'd dressed up old so no-one would wonder why she wasn't at school but judging by the stares she kept on getting – or seemed to be getting – she'd gone and overdone it.

That was another thing worrying her. Jackie had said to get some clothes and that, something with a bit of something.

148

So she'd gone out that morning looking. She'd spent a bloody fortune. And not on the real good stuff, either. That had been a joke it cost so much. Where she'd seen it. The worst thing almost was the feeling she had at the back of her mind she'd been conned, had had to settle for something quite tatty really – ordinary. Mainly at prices you still wouldn't credit. At that rate she'd be broke day after tomorrow. Not very clever that would be. Bloody rip-off merchants! She had this feeling she didn't really know where to go. If Jackie had really wanted to help her she'd've come out with her and showed her where was best. But, being fair, you couldn't really blame her wanting to sleep in. She had, give credit, fixed her up to meet this bloke.

That was another reason to feel up-tight about. Not that she was. She felt more all runny inside. You didn't have to be twenty-one to know what his first idea was going to be. Well she could pass for twenty-one and if she came on all tough she could handle types like that . . . well, usually . . .

She glanced apprehensively around the sandwich bar again. It was very small. The big stack of rolls and sandwiches in the glass case by the coffee thingummy were making her feel all hungry. She'd have one in a minute if he didn't come. She didn't want to talk to him, though, with crumbs all over her. . . . Some poor old sod of an old boy down and out, two youngish blokes not black and talking English but foreigners all the same. Not many people in. One of the young blokes was quite good looking, really. Could be one of them Maltese, of course . . . Ah!

A man had come in. He was middle-aged and a bit on the seedy side but he could've been anything. He had a mac on and carried a folded *Standard*. Sleek straight hair and parted – a bit like her dad's. Was it him? He'd looked right through her. He'd gone straight up to the counter. Well he would, really, wouldn't he?

'Strong tea, miss,' he was saying. 'And a cheese roll.'

It was hard to put your finger on it but there was something about him reminded her of a ferret. Kind of an agent, he calls himself, Jackie had said. She didn't like to look too hard in case it wasn't him but when she went and looked away out through the window, these two other blokes were looking right in at her, grinning and all. Oh. Cripes, they were turning back, going to come in.

'Jackie's friend are you, love?'

Thank Gawd! While she was watching them he'd come over to her.

' 'S right,' she said.

He nodded, gave her a quick eye-over. Jackie had told her to leave her coat undone.

'How old?' he asked directly.

'Eighteen.'

'Oh, yeah. . . ,'

'What you want – bloody birth certificate!'

She shouldn't have said that, maybe, but he didn't seem to mind. He took a sip at his tea and pulled a face. He'd asked for it strong but even from where she sat it looked like gnats. There was lipstick on the cup. He'd turned it round to drink left-handed.

'Seems more like it's a case of what you want,' he said softly.

He had eyes that seemed sad, hard and shifty all at once.

'A job,' she said.

'What kind?'

'Needlework!'

He looked at her a moment, then took a bite out of his cheese roll. She didn't half feel starving then. She was afraid her stomach would start rumbling any second. There were bits of crust hanging on the corner of his mouth. He turned his head back to look at her and shook it. Slowly.

'Don't get on with a big mouth in any walk of life, do we?' he said.

He said it quite softly but there was something about his manner she didn't like at all.

'Well!' she answered back with, 'what am I supposed to say?'

Keep it tough. Yes. Better. He was looking at her more straight now.

'I could fix you up with a pad somewhere,' he said.

'No,' she said at once. 'Not interested!' She made her own mouth go all tight.

'Notting Hill. Good class of cargo.'

'No way!' she insisted.

'Jackie told me you was into that.'

'Told you wrong then, didn't she. Dancing, yes. Stripping, yes. But those fat creeps watching — I wouldn't let one touch me with a barge pole.'

That made him smile. A nasty, mickey-taking smile. He had nicotine-stained teeth and one missing at the side. Brought the ferret in him out stronger. Now he was thinking she was born yesterday.

About sixteen, Eddie Wiles was thinking. Green as they come. But that's all right. Mediterranean type with a bit of titivating. Bring her along slow and easy and when the rent gets a bit hard to come by and she sees what the girls on the real game are making, she'll change her little way of thinking. Need to put Lewis on her a few times so she gets to enjoy it. She's probably still dumb enough to think that on the game she can kill two birds with one stone. By the time she finds out different, she'll be into it for keeps. . . . A bit too dumb to put in Kenny's way for pushing. . . .

'. . . looking at me like that for,' she was saying.

'Just thinking, love,' he said, giving it the old soft sell, 'don't want to push you into something you don't fancy . . . what about travel?'

'Travel? Where?'

'Middle East – maybe.'

'Oh . . . well, that'd depend that, wouldn't it.'

A mistake. She was sixteen. She wouldn't want to feel completely cut off from her Mum and Dad. Always run back home from London, they thought. At first.

'Not a good number unless you've got connections,' he conceded vaguely. 'Know anything about cards?'

'Cars?'

Gordon Bennett!

'Cards,' he said pretending he was dealing. 'Playing cards.'

'Fifty-two in a pack.'

Brilliant!

'Always looking for blackjack dealers.'

'I could learn!'

'Takes time.' He pulled a discouraging face. 'There's a new dinner-dance show opens next month. I could ask, drop your name.'

'Could you?'

'No problem. There's the skin mags of course, that'd be all right, would it?'

Your Highness!

'Just posing?'

'Yeah.'

'Wouldn't mind that.'

'And, of course, film extra-ing's a nice bread and butter line. Very tight union but I reckon I can pull a string or two in the right place.'

'Could you?'

He'd played that card quite neatly even if he did say so himself. She had stars in her eyes already, visions of being discovered. Lot she knew about seven o'clock calls and third assistants with wandering hands. But strike while the iron was hot.

'Going to be your agent, then, am I?'

She didn't have the choice, now, did she? They both knew that. She nodded.

'Twenty per cent,' he said casually as he took another sip of the dishwater they had the cheek to charge 6p for. Later, he added to himself the split will be a little different. It didn't register with her, he noticed.

'But I'll need something before then, next month,' Lucille was saying. And thinking. Jackie had made it clear it was just temporary down her place. Rooms anywhere near were something shocking. And just look at the bloody tubes! For the moment a feeling of emptiness, of being lost and little, washed right through her and swirled about her stomach.

'Well I think I can help you, short-term,' he was saying. 'Pub down the Old Kent Road. Topless and that. They have a sort of amateur night. Try to get the odd girl up there doing it for a giggle. Way they work, they get a plant to go up first. You know, girl pretending its straight up for fun. Starts it off. Means a fresh face all the time. I can get you in there a couple of times.'

'Oh I done that sort of thing already!' Lucille Wyatt said.

'They pay you cash that night but they tell me how much,' he said. All right, she got the message.

'Of course,' he said, 'any local arrangement you make afterwards, that's up to you. I wouldn't want to know. All for you, that is.'

He just wouldn't believe she meant it, would he? She didn't say anything.

'One thing, though,' he was going on, 'you're not hot are you?'

Hot? She'd just said she wouldn't—

'Is Old Bill after you, I mean.'

'Oh no!' she said, understanding. ' 'Course not!'

Good, he thought. If she's on the run makes it all the harder for her to back out.

'A mate of mine, Lewis – he'll run you down this pub,' he said. 'Got a nice motor. Nice lad. Eddie, by the way – Eddie Wiles.' He grinned in a friendly fashion.

'Want to finish my cheese roll?' he said.

Chapter Eleven

THURSDAY. LUNCH TIME. Somehow they had drinks in front of them but God alone knew how. They didn't talk. They just sat there around the table avoiding the others' eyes. They were stunned. In shock. Around them 'The Crown's' busy lunch trade came and went in a series of light and bitters, shepherd's pies, ploughman's and 'swore blind to me, he'd put in a new thermostat's. A pool of despair, they were no part of it. Mourners at a funeral would have been more determinedly cheerful, have had memories to compare and argue over. Not these. They sat appalled. Max behind the bar was getting quite concerned: sitting over their drinks like 'keep death off the road' and spreading misery. He'd built up a good lunch since he took over. A group like that could ruin the atmosphere for everyone. Ah — there was one empty glass there now. If he went over and collected it maybe he could gee them up a bit.

He raised the counter flap and eased his landlord's belly out. He picked up the empty half-pint glass in front of John Graydon.

'If you're thinking of food,' he lied, 'it's going fast today.'

That at least put some sign of life in them. They all blinked, looked at each other.

'Right,' one of them said. 'Thanks.'

Pleased with himself, he moved after some more empties.

'What about it?' Graham Cunningham said. 'Anyone want something to eat?'

Of all of them he was the least knocked sideways. He had, after all, predicted how it all might go. But, his forecast having been confirmed, their own shocked gloom had largely spread itself to him.

No-one had the stomach to want to eat.

John Graydon had not been aware of sinking his half.

His glass gone, he was suddenly lost for something to do with his hands. He got to his feet.

'More drinks,' he stated rather than asked. 'Wendy?'

From his seat in the corner Chris Langley stretched out a hand holding a fiver.

'You get them, John,' he said, 'seeing's you're up and nearest. But I'll pay. I'll have a large Scotch. Malt.'

It didn't seem a time for polite arguments, conventional demurring. John nodded and took the note.

'Anyone else?' he said.

The others all said they'd have the same again. He turned to push his way through the crowd and to the bar.

Wendy Raeburn's eyes followed him for no other reason than he was in motion.

'I can't help thinking it was all my fault,' she heard herself saying.

'Nonsense!' Graham Cunningham said at once and tersely. 'Put that out of your head at once. You did absolutely everything I asked you to do. And very well. It's . . . well, it's like *War and Peace* – the system, the machine takes over and once it's in motion, God help anyone trying to stop it. We're suddenly all victims.'

We are all victims but some are more victims than others, Chris Langley thought and inwardly winced. Somewhere at the back of his mind he had managed to score a large bonus point for Cunningham that not once had he so much as hinted at an 'I told you so'.

Wendy Raeburn was grateful to the young solicitor as well. She half apprehended that in voicing a claim to be the scapegoat she was actually pleading to be assured in public that she was blameless. It lifted her that the assurance had come so briskly. And yet in an inner part of herself a sense of guilt still obstinately lodged.

It had been such a horrid room. Not a proper court room at all but something improvised during 'renovations'. The magistrates, two women, one elderly man, had sat behind sad and sorry institutional tables covered by a bit of green felt frayed at the edges. The sound of workmen knocking away at something had thudded through the walls all morning at disconcertingly infrequent and unpredictable moments and, because the cloth had not stretched down far enough, the chips out of the cheaply varnished tables' legs had been quite apparent. The dull, brutal thuds, the cheap and nasty knocked about furniture had all seemed of a piece to her and somehow blended together inseparably in her mind. She doubted now if she would ever forget them. A chipped sideboard, a mail-bag hitting a platform, and she would be back instantly inside that magistrate's court.

Graham had phoned her Wednesday morning to say he had decided to ask her to appear on behalf of the local authority after all. That afternoon and evening he had carefully rehearsed her in all the questions he would put to her and tried to anticipate on her behalf the sort of line the parents' solicitor would subsequently take with her. All the same, called to give evidence, she had found her mouth dry, her stomach knotted to the point of pain and her mind a sudden panic-stricken wall of silver nothingness. It didn't help they were all so much on top of each other. The two counsels sat at a table reaching down at right angles from the magistrates' top row and you gave evidence from one facing that. It was all so claustrophobic. The body of the court, so called, was just a few rows of cheap wooden fold-away chairs and as she'd moved forward to the witnesses' table she'd been terribly aware of the two parents in the front row, sullen and unbelievably childlike in their patent Sunday best.

Graham had led her gently into the meat of her evidence by means of a skilful build-up from easy questions to those demanding more complex answers. With the very first one her mind had cleared and her nervousness been halved. By the time he concluded, she felt she had been led to give an accurate and moving account of Dean's dependence on her. Then it had been the turn of his opposite number.

He was young too, a bit on the tubby side, not very prepossessing or even clever looking. He'd had a smooth, cultured voice slightly at odds with his swarthy, almost Arab features.

'No-one here today, Miss Raeburn,' he had said after a while, 'would question the devotion and attention with which you have tended Dean. I am sure you command the respect of all of us for the selflessness with which you appear to have won Dean's dependence. The question, however, I would put to you is this: are you expecting to have virtually sole care of Dean's upbringing indefinitely?'

She had replied no, of course not, sooner or later it was to be expected he would be placed in a good home.

'Sooner or later?'

Later, she would have thought.

'Really? How much later?'

It was impossible for her to say.

'Yes, quite. Would you, then, consider it an impossibility that another person – someone, possibly able to grant Dean more exclusive attention than yourself, if he were their sole charge – is it impossible some other person might also come to command the same affection from Dean as you seem to have secured?'

She had to say that, no, she couldn't claim it was impossible.

'And that person could be his own mother? His father?'

She had said she didn't feel qualified or, indeed, that it was proper for her to pass an opinion on that. Out of the corner of her eye she had seen Graham give a quick approving nod.

'Even though, Miss Raeburn, we have heard already here today a psychiatrist – someone who is qualified, you may perhaps think – give as her expert opinion that Dean's parents are quite capable of extending to him a full and natural loving affection.'

Then she had said it.

'As to that expert opinion,' she had said before she thought, 'I would personally consider more weight ought to be placed on the noun than on the adjective.'

The counsel had smiled. After the second it had taken to sink in, she had heard an indignant hiss from somewhere and been aware this time of two of the magistrates scribbling furious notes while the third gave her a very old-fashioned look.

She hadn't liked that counsel's smile. Nor the way in which he had announced he had no further questions and sat down. Graham had not risen to his feet to resume questioning.

The hearing had continued for another half hour or so after that. Dr Benton had strongly urged that Dean be allowed to remain at Kingston House pending a re-assessment of his behaviour in six months time. This would be in the interest of establishing some element of stability in his life. He, Dr Benton, very much doubted whether anyone else could readily replace the 'wholly good and reassuring' influence Miss Raeburn had succeeded in becoming in that life. Graham had fairly obviously played him last as his trump card.

The magistrates had announced that they would like to order a short recess while they considered amongst themselves. It had seemed longer than 'short'. For forty-five minutes, not daring to pop out for coffee in case they be called back in, they had paced and hovered in the corridor with its diagonally black and white tiled floor, its dark green emulsioned lower walls, its *eau de nil* upper, its musty pre-war smell. At intervals the thuds of the workmen had come headachingly through. Just as they were beginning to assume that lunch would intervene and extend the suspense into the afternoon they had been asked to step back into the dowdy, impersonal room. The magistrates were already in place.

Their decision had been that the 'In Care' order be revoked forthwith and that Dean be returned to the custody of his natural parents as soon as conveniently possible. A social worker, it was stipulated, must pay the household such regular visits as he or she might determine necessary and keep the local authority fully abreast of Dean's ongoing situation.

The contingent from Kingston House had listened to this decision white-faced and open-mouthed. As the Chairman had announced it, a series of even, muffled thuds had punctuated her words with crudest melodrama. Shattered, they had stumbled across the road toward the pub and, trite though it no doubt was, it had not seemed over-fanciful to hear in those thuds still resounding in their ears giant, ominous blows of Fate upon the door of Dean's uncertain future.

Or so it had seemed to Wendy. She had been close to crying then. And now as, bearing a tray of drinks with difficulty through the buzzing crowd, John Graydon made his way back to the table, she felt close to tears again. Irrespective of why or whose fault, the stark fact was that tomorrow or the day after, blinking gravely, wondering what had hit him, what was going to hit him, Dean was going to leave Kingston House for the last time. Bewildered, he would be separated from her. And she from him. Never get too attached to anyone, they had told her in her training. Easily said. All she knew now was that in some vague way her whole being was aching with a wish, impossible – or was it? – that somehow she might be adopting Dean this very week. The fantasy possessed her. Not hearing anything of what was being said around her, she sat at the table feeling she had not strength to lift a finger.

The small action of pushing to the bar and ordering more drinks, however, seemed to have injected some kind of fresh determination into John. He had returned stirred from the lethargy shock had plunged them into. He handed Chris his change.

'Well, they may have thought they've won today,' he said, 'and there's an end to it but – Chris! did you see his face at the end there? He had a look on it as mindless as a Millwall supporter who's just put the boot in! All right, Chris, all right. I know we're supposed to maintain a professional distance at all times. But I just want to say this. I hope to God it never arises, but I'm going to be as good as living in that house for the next year. And if there's the slightest sign that they're neglecting Dean – let alone ill-treating him! — I'll have their guts for garters quicker than he can say National Assistance!'

'No need for that,' Wendy Raeburn said suddenly as she erupted into speech with a savageness that surprised them all, 'We've a bloody expert opinion they're a reformed pair!'

'All right, easy,' Chris Langley said. 'Take away his emotion and John's right. This isn't the end for anybody. Least of all Dean. Life goes on; we've all got jobs to do.'

'Talking of which,' said John Graydon, 'I'm off.'

He downed the remainder of his second half.

'Lucille Wyatt,' he said to Chris. 'The ace detective continues the hunt tonight. I've eliminated a couple of local friends as possible hide-outs, I think – I'm pretty sure. If I can get ahead of my routine stuff today I think I know where I might find her this evening.'

'Where?' said Chris Langley, catching some of the younger man's recharged energy.

'Up West,' John said. 'Sort of Ladbroke Grove. Older girl-friends.'

'Because, John – if not – tomorrow I'll have to make it all official.'

John Graydon nodded his understanding to Chris and his goodbyes to the others. He made to leave. As he was on the point of being swallowed up in the crowd his progress was arrested by someone. Wendy experienced a sharp pang of something not too far from jealousy. The person was a woman. Then she was able to relax. As a burly man in a rally jacket shifted around, she was able to see it was Pat Langley. But a disturbed looking Pat Langley. Chris had seen her too. Perhaps some look had flashed secretly between them because, excusing himself, he was getting up and moving to meet her halfway.

Chris had caught a look. It did not bode well. And this was an unlooked-for meeting. Pat had not arranged to be there. Perhaps she just wanted to know how it went this morning, he tried to tell himself.

'Hello,' he said, 'what brings—'

'How did it go?' Pat said.

'Bad. They revoked the order.'

'Oh God!'

'Want a drink?' he said. 'We're holding a bit of a wake.'
She caught his arm.

'Wait a moment,' she said. 'You'd better make mine a brandy. I've got some more bad news.'

He looked at her tense, pale face and realised his intuition that her coming was for the worse had not been wrong. A sombre stain of defeat and fatigue circled her eyes and he saw suddenly how many fine wrinkles were now present in those rings. Yet, in that crowded pub and on the brink of bad news he felt his heart turn over, even as he spoke, at how beautiful she still appeared to him. .

'What?' he said.

'It's Mrs Jackson. Peter's mother,' she said. 'She died this morning.'

Now his heart plummeted down some terrible shaft.

'No!'

She was nodding, though.

'About ten. It started out as normal labour first thing this morning. All going well. After about two hours her bp sudden shot up to 200 over 120. She—'

'Why?'

'Could be a dozen reasons. Foetal distress would be one of the most likely. Johnstone gave her a third of morphia and sent for an ambulance. At the hospital Davey performed—'

'Davey? Who's Davey?'

'Consultant obstetrician. He did an emergency Caesarian. He saved the child. But she had a cardiac arrest. Resuscitation didn't work.'

He felt the pub, the whole world recede away from him. For a moment the visual swirl of animated faces, raised glasses, talk of Cortinas and sunshine streaming in through high windows across on to flocked wallpaper spun giddily around him as he alone seemed fixed and stable. Transfixed. But enough. He had a job. He made a great effort of his will and drawing his thoughts together, stilled both the circling room and the lurching of his heart.

'Davey's first rate,' Pat was saying.

'Really!'

'Yes. Really.'

'I'm sorry. Better now. What was it?'

'A little girl. She's fine.'

'And the father?'

'Not so fine. He just won't accept it. He kept saying "I won't let you say that." Said it about fifty times. They gave him some sedation, sent him home.'

Great. But he held his peace. He thought of Peter, solemn and matter of fact.

'He'll be thrilled, won't he?' he said. 'Your mum's dead, your dad's gone round the twist, but you've got a baby sister. And Dean. When one door shuts another one always closes! Jesus, what a morning!'

'And for me,' she said. 'Mrs Eames went last night as well.'

Less concerned in that brief instant for his wife than angry at the malignancy of life, he pulled a face.

'Three's a charm,' he said.

But she had steered him away from the pitfalls of self-pity. Seeing a break in the crowd by the bar he took the opportunity of ordering her brandy.

In the event, he should have made it two. They joined the others and after a few moments he decided that small-talk in the light of this new and bitter knowledge was insupportable. Better a quick death, as it were, than one that lingered. He broke the news. Graham Cunningham winced but remained, fortunately for him, a concerned and sympathetic outsider. Not Wendy Raeburn. Her face seemed to freeze as the blood left it. For perhaps thirty seconds she sat quite rigidly without speaking. Then, abruptly blurting out something quite incoherent, she had risen, was making for the Ladies. Chris watched her go and wondered if it had been for any better reason than to make life easier for himself that he had made it close to intolerable for her. No, a saving logic told him, she had to be told and better now before she gets back to the house, to Peter and to Dean. . . .

The ladies' loo was less than lovely. A single W.C., luckily not occupied. A basin and mirror. Half-tiling. All perhaps just about passably clean. Her arms extended their full length, Wendy put both hands on the basin and leaned her weight against it. The warm flooding tears went slithering down her face. At the third time of asking she had been unable to rally enough forces to fight them back. Her resistance had suddenly been paper thin, enervated, worn to nothing. She felt ridiculous and was making no sound as she wept but even as she'd groped her blind way to the loo, some deepest instinct was telling her a good cry now would be her best comforter, surest replacement of her drained inner strength. The sticky tears oozed on, a nacreous veil between her and her own reflection and already beneath their hot, messy outpouring she began to sense an inner core of calm and resignedness coolly expanding within her mind. The tears did seem to be washing away her heartsickness.

The loo door opened. Someone came in. It was Pat Langley. Wendy tried to grin at her and felt nothing but foolish as the attempt persisted for no more than a second. She brushed tears ineffectually away with the back of her hand. Pat was opening a new pack of *Disque Bleu*. She was proferring the pack.

'You don't, do you?' she said.

Wendy shook her head. Pat flipped a cigarette up and out, produced a disposable lighter from her large, practical, shoulder-bag.

'Five minutes off your life each one,' she said. 'You'd think a doctor of all people would know better.'

She lit the cigarette, inhaled.

'I've known a lot of people die,' she said without further preamble. 'Seen quite a high percentage of those deaths, come to that.'

She blew out smoke.

'A long-standing patient of mine went in the night,' she said. 'Mrs Eames. Ninety-three. Sound as a bell three weeks ago. People say at that age what's the difference? And I tell them there is no difference. Whatever the age there was a person, unique, individual, mind of their own. Now there's a body. It's worse somehow when they live so long and don't go on to make a hundred. I don't know why. Arbitrary really, isn't it. Cricket, I suppose. The Queen's never heard of them or been aware of their existence all their lives. It makes that telegram quite meaningless. When I reach a hundred, which thanks to this cancer tube I now won't, I won't bother to open mine. . . . Yet all the same, Mrs Eames. . . . Ninety-three. I don't find it nice.'

She paused, looked at Wendy. She's not quite twice my age, Wendy thought.

'I don't have to tell you,' Pat went on, 'do I? Mrs Eames died in the small hours. I took my routine surgery this morning. I've got half-dozen house calls to get in before evening surgery. One's nasty – possibly German measles in a girl who's two weeks late. I can't stop for Mrs Eames, you see. I can sign her certificate but I can't stop.'

Wendy had stopped crying. Pat reached into her bag again.

'Here,' she said. 'I've got some tissues.'

❧❧❧❧

In the television room in the corner diagonally across from the set was the Lego table. It was here that Chris Langley found Peter Jackson. He was playing busily and happily with the sprawling jumble of half-sets the home had randomly acquired. The intentness with which he was trying to extend an already fiercely lop-sided fort had prevented him from noticing that he was alone. Bill Hutton had been in two minutes earlier with excuses calculated to remove the handful of other children spending that part of the afternoon there. As Chris Langley closed the door behind him, however, it made something of a bang and the little boy looked up enquiringly.

❧❧❧❧

She'd come home by public transport tonight. It was a right bloody panic of a cliff-hanger sweating on seeing whether the bus would get her back into the centre of town in time for her to catch a tube, but, if it came to it, she'd catch a taxi rather than go through what she'd had to put up with the night before again. That Lewis might or might not be a friend of Eddie Miles, he might have a poncey sports car and a brown suit with little glittery bits in it but what he'd tried to do to her had scared the bloody life out of her, to tell the truth. In them low seats he had you just about where he wanted you. His hands had been just about everywhere at any rate. Not taking no for an answer wasn't in it. He'd thought it was all part of her come on, and ended up losing his bottle in a big way. When she'd bit him as hard as she knew how he'd punched her and half-killed her before she'd knew what had hit her. She'd only got away by screaming her head off and making him panic. He'd opened the car door and pushed her straight out on the road. Anything could have been coming even though it was late. He'd spat out the door after her, then sent the car roaring and screeching away. She'd spat up the dark road after it.

But she'd been scared, she didn't mind admitting it. She'd left Jackie's real early the next afternoon in case he came around. In the pub apart from worrying about carrying her instructions out, she'd been worried stiff he might come in and go for her. He had come in but ignored her. It wasn't until she was up on the little joke of a stage doing her bit he so much as looked at her. She'd seen him talking to Bob Purvis. Later Bob had told her she'd got to be known after two times straight so she wouldn't do no more as the nice girl out of the crowd who's had a few too many. She'd wondered if the sod had put the block on her some way.

Not that she'd be that sorry in a way. They were right there under her nose and this second time the grabbing had been something shocking. It stopped you sort of forgetting where you were and thinking it was all some kind of film. One of the bastard's hands had been so much on target it had not only hurt but it had put her right off her dancing. Made her feel dirty too. Hadn't been him, though, that Lewis. Stayed at the bar, he had, up the front. Soon as she'd got her money, little of that, and all, she'd done a bunk out the side door and walked one stop the other way to make sure he wasn't after her.

Way it turned out she'd had no problem getting a tube. They ran real late. Worse thing was the last bit. The walk. Jackie's place wasn't in what you'd call Park Lane. Looked quite cheerful, it did, in the daytime 'cause the blacks put a lot of bright colours into their places. But by night it was real run down. Real creepy. She kept thinking someone was going to jump out at her. No-one did, but every time she saw a group or someone up ahead she went and crossed the road. Her wedges banged ever so loud in the warm, dark streets and made her think of Jack the Ripper. Her heart was banging about like an old tumble-dryer and she kept her mac pulled real tight over her dress. Bit chesty that dress, Jackie had said. There weren't many cars about but every time she heard one she couldn't help turning her head in case it was that Lewis. As it happened none of them were all fancy like his but every new noise sounded like this time it was bloody him for sure.

Her shoes sounded especially loud as she turned into Jackie's street. Because it was narrow most like. No, his car wasn't parked there waiting. Blimey, if some creeping Jesus was going to jump on her he'd have no trouble coming up from one of these lots of basement steps. Home now, though, still in one piece.

She went down the area steps searching in her bag for the key Jackie had given her. Sod! She'd meant to get an extra pint of milk so's she could have some cocoa.

She turned the key in the lock and as she did so the lights snapped on inside and the door was pulled open and away from her. Gawd! He was inside waiting! Her stomach turned to icy water and her beating heart sank to its bottom. He'd do the lot to her and do her up. He was just a shadow there, a shape. Oh, Gawd! a nightmare. She was trying to run and couldn't. Oh, Gawd! As she'd turned he'd reached forward and grabbed her wrist. No getting out of that.

She started to scream, then didn't. Reaching for her the

man had come out into the light more. It wasn't him at all. It was that young bloke from the Social Whatsit.

She'd been so scared that for a moment she was glad to see him.

'Oh, Gawd Almighty!' she said with relief. She'd all but wet herself.

Then her heart sank a second time. He'd sussed her out. Found her. She was still in dead rotten trouble up to her nostrils.

'Not bleeding again!' she heard herself saying.

'That's right!' he said. 'Only different this time. Let's go.'

She tried to think as fast as she knew how.

'I got to pack!' she said. She could even let him do it, maybe, if he'd go away and not let on.

'Done it for you, haven't I.'

The sod reached down inside the little hall and came up with a duffel bag in his right hand. The left still kept a real tight hold on her wrist.

'You're hurting me,' she said. 'Let go.'

'Just to be kind,' he said. 'No.'

'I got to say goodbye to Jackie!' she said desperately.

'We're not going to traipse all over London looking for her now, are we? Not when she could be in any one of a hundred beds.'

'What you mean?'

'Oh, Lucille, love, come on! I wouldn't be surprised if you've picked up a dose just by contagion.'

'Here! She's my friend!'

'With friends like that. . . .'

'Look – you got to let me explain!'

'Sure.'

Hope jumped up inside her for a moment. She might get round him yet.

'You can explain all you want,' he said. 'Once we get in the car.'

'Bastard!' she said.

'I am actually,' he said mildly. 'How did you know that?'

While she was still blinking, not knowing whether or not

to take him seriously, he had closed the door. Not roughly, but forcibly enough to make the point, he was propelling her back up the steps. Parked across the road from the house was a Mini van she hadn't given a second glance as it went so with the area. It was his. He made her get into the passenger seat, then slung the bag in the back.

'How do you know you got all my things, then?' she suddenly had the thought of asking.

'Anything missing, you make a little list and the police'll ask after it when they have a nice long chat with your friend Jackie tomorrow.'

She was quiet for a while after that. He drove through quiet streets that all looked the same to her until, without much warning, they were crossing the Thames. She hadn't copped much money those nights in the pub. It was a fixed rate, take it or leave it, from the guv'nor. No chance to con some dirty middle-aged business man. She could still feel that hand squeezing her. And there was Lewis. He was mean. In a way she wasn't sorry. In a way she was well out of it. Well, maybe. Depends what they did to her now.

'Will he be mad, shout at me?' she said at last.

'Who?'

'That Mr Langley or whatever he's called.'

'Not with you.'

'Who with then?'

'Three guesses.'

'You!'

'He's not very keen on the likes of us letting the likes of you run off from under our noses.'

'No. Suppose not . . . Sorry.'

He actually turned to her and grinned. Quite human, really.

'No, it's all right,' he said. 'He's a good bloke. He had one go at me then left it alone. He's made a point of not dragging the police in on this just to keep your record that much cleaner. Dare say this'll go down as a voluntary return.'

'Will it?'

'If you start being honest. Remember you've still got a lot to learn.'

She thought about that for a while. They went past a Wimpey Bar with all its lights out.

'When we get back,' she began. . . .

'Yes?'

'Will you come in with me?' she said.

He must have thought she was joking at first. He started to laugh quite loudly. Then he changed it to just a smile. He turned to look at her again. He had a nice smile.

'Yes,' he said, 'of course.'

The little car went whirring on through the yellowy-dark streets and she found things didn't seem as bad.

Chapter Twelve

THE SAME STAIRS leading down. The same coffee. The same residue of fatigue behind his eyes taking its time to die. No great roar of support from the crowd as he came out of the tunnel on to the field. No standing ovation from stalls, circle and gallery. Just a curt nod from his own conscience as, another morning coming up to meet him, he once more toed the line.

He turned the handle of the door to his office and for an instant the erratic clicks and taps from inside ceased altogether. By the time he had the door wide open Robert, ever in pursuit of the cool these days, was back at his laboured conscientious hunt and peck attack upon the shell-shocked Olivetti.

'Morning again,' Chris said.

'Likewise,' Robert said. 'You're just in time, actually. What was the name of Achilles' boyfriend. You know, the one he really fancied.'

Chris was not sure he could remember.

'Hell,' he said, 'bit early in the day for *Mastermind*, isn't it?'

He squeezed past Robert and the typewriter table and round behind his desk. He put down the cup of coffee. As he did so, the name sprang out of some trap-door in his mind.

'Patroclus, wasn't it?' he said casually as if he had known from the day he was born.

'Ah yes. Patroclus. Good,' Robert said. 'You can stay now if you like.'

'Thanks a bunch,' Chris said. 'You won't be long, will you?'

'Five more minutes,' Robert said. 'Shouldn't take me longer to knock out my own *Iliad*.'

Chris tuned the tap, pause, tap, tap out. How to shape the morning. . . . If he didn't have something firmed up in his mind for the first half-hour the entire day could leak away. Well, no problem today. No problem deciding. All kinds of other problems, no doubt, with Lucille Wyatt. But at least he'd have a medical report on his desk before the day was out. In Pat's presence she was being checked over by the consultant from New Ash right that minute. In the meantime, he had to consider just what addition to his own report—

Without knocking Bill Hutton had put his head round the door.

'Sorry, Chris,' he said, 'but Mrs Grigson's on the phone. She's—'

'Who?'

'Peter Jackson's aunt. For some reason she's come through on the pay phone.'

'Oh. All right. Thanks, Bill.'

He slid back past Robert and went quickly to the phone under the stairs. Bill had left the receiver balanced across the coin box.

'Hello?' he said. 'Mrs Grigson?'

'Yes, hello,' a woman's voice said. 'Mr Langley?'

'Speaking,' he said. 'It's very good of you to call so promptly.'

'That's all right,' the voice said instantly. 'I'm calling from Peter's father's actually. There's an enormous amount of arranging to be done, as I expect you can imagine only too well, but, well Kate's gone now and Peter and the new baby – the living – have to take precedence over everything else.'

The soft voice was quite deep for a woman's. He seemed to detect hints of both decisiveness and intelligence in it. Her opening statement had not sounded pious but matter of fact commonsense.

'How is Mr Jackson?' he asked.

'Last night he was knocked completely sideways. We all were, of course. But, of course, for him – well, it was so sudden, you can imagine. He's still very subdued. But when I took him up a cup of tea this morning he said he didn't want any more pills. He said they made him feel dopey and he wanted to be able to think.'

'Well, that's encourag—'

'Mr Langley—'

'Yes?'

'I don't know, of course, how everything has to be arranged from your end, the authorities' end, as it were, but as regards Peter and his new sister, I may as well tell you right now Kenneth and I, my husband, that is, we've quite made up our minds that we'll be all to them both, and to my brother Les, what Kate would have been. We can probably sell both the houses and get something bigger up our way, Chester, and Peter already gets on a treat with my two, so I don't want any official of any sort thinking—'

'Mrs Grigson, can I interrupt you a second, please?' Chris Langley said. He had, he suddenly realised, a total confidence in the owner of that sensible, humane and unflustered voice. His day was beginning with a great surge of heartfelt relief. There were fine moments. He felt the last tiredness lift from him.

'I just want to assure you,' he was meanwhile saying, 'that nothing you could have said would more have delighted me. I've no doubt it's absolutely the best for Peter, for his dad, for everyone. Especially if Peter were to be caught up in a change of scene. The only basic question is: when would you like him back?'

No hesitation, no uncertainty.

'After the funeral, I think, don't you? If that's possible, of course.'

'Yes, of course.'

'Oh, good. That was my other reason for 'phoning, really.'

'No problem. Now – here's what I think would probably work out best. . . .'

✤✤✤

Robert was coming to the conclusion it might be well worth his trouble to learn to type properly. One finger at a time stuff like this was all very well but you couldn't possibly spend intergalactic light years of your life knocking out just one page. Not when you kept forgetting to cancel the upper case. On the other hand when you finally did get something down, it looked ten times as good as in the handwriting whose childishness he was still rather ashamed of. If he could touch-type—

There was a knock at the door.

'Come in,' he said as if he owned the place.

The door opened. It was the girl from school. Lucille Wyatt – the one with the tits who, the word was, was easy. She didn't look so switched on now. As he defensively went ultra-cool, it struck him that she hardly looked any older than himself.

'Yes?' he said.

'Oh,' she said, 'sorry. I was looking for Mr Langley.'

'He's on the phone, I think,' he said. 'In the hall.'

'Oh. I'll come back then.'

She half closed the door then opened it again. She was looking at him like he was a six nostrilled Mart.

'Here,' she said, 'you go to Corelli Road, don't you?'

It was hardly a question. He nodded.

'What's your name, then?' she said.

'Robert.'

'Robert? Don't they call you Bob?'

'No.'

'What you do, then? What are you in for?'

'Life,' he said.

'Cor! What did you do to get that?'

'Get born. He's my father.'

'Who is?'

'Mr Langley. The boss here.'

You could hardly say she was embarrassed.

'You poor sod,' she said.

'Thanks a bunch,' he said.

'Well, you know what I mean. I mean, I never thought of him as having his own lot. Family, I mean.'

'Like you don't think of dentists having toothache – you mean,' he said. She didn't notice his bit of quiet piss-taking.

'Not a lot of us, anyway,' he said. 'I'm the only one.'

'I'd like that,' she said.

'No you wouldn't,' he said, before he could not say it.

'Really?' She actually looked sorry for him. He wasn't sure he liked that. Oh, it was probably all right. As her stretched tight dress made clear her heart was in the right place.

'It's not that bad,' he said. 'I quite like it here.'

He was genuinely glad he'd said that then because halfway through it his father walked in. It was the sort of thing he could never have said to his face.

'Hello,' his father said to her, 'looking for me?'

'It can wait I suppose,' she said. Not nastily.

'No, no. Now's fine. I was just starting to look for you, actually.'

His father gave him a quick look. O.K., chief, message received and understood. He looked at his watch. Christ! He'd gone and left it late this morning. All tied up with the mechanics of the typewriter. He'd have to use the bus this morning now.

'I'm late,' he said. 'Can I leave this in the machine, though?'

'Sure,' his father said. 'I don't think it'll get used today.'

'O.K. See you. 'Bye.'

Feeling it showed some kind of willing, he nodded at the girl on the last word and left them to it.

Good, Chris thought. On two counts he had appreciated the nod. It was kind to Lucille: it included her in the scheme of everyday things. And it had been almost unforced. Eighteen more months and Robert might be chatting up his first bird with only the routine agonies. Nice kid, Robert. And, probably, Lucille.

'Sit down,' he told her.

She did so. He went behind his desk and sat down himself. He sat looking at her while, quite clearly, she gathered herself for a major effort.

'I'm sorry,' she said in a rush. 'For running away and all that.'

It was going to be a very good morning indeed, he suddenly realised. He had instantly believed she was being sincere.

'More likely to hurt you than bother us,' he said gently.

'Yes,' she said. 'I know. Now.'

'Well all can be well that ends well,' he said. 'Your dad's coming down later to talk to me. You'd better get a list made out of all the things you want.'

But, mentioning her father, he'd activated some kind of alarm system within her. She'd grown tense immediately. And pale. She looked so much nicer without all that cheap make-up.

'Does he have to know,' she was saying. 'Everything, I mean?'

'Everything?' He knew what she had meant. It might do her good to hear it spoken from her own lips.

'Well . . . you know . . . what I was doing.'

So it hadn't quite worked. Well, never mind.

'He'll know by now,' he said. 'John Graydon will have told your mother.'

'John . . .? Oh, him. The social worker.'

She smiled as if at the thought of Graydon. Remembrance of her overall position wiped out the smile in less than a second. Score one for John, though, all the same.

'You'll see him first, won't you?' She was saying. Urgently.

'Yes.'

'Explain to him, I mean!'

'I will – if you'll explain it to me.'

'You must make him understand. Please.'

'All right, as long as you make—'

'Please! It's very important. Honest, it is.'

'So why did you do it?'

A long dead-end of a pause. He could hear the answer ten seconds before it came.

'I don't know,' she said.

The classic reply. Don't know, miss. Don't know, sir. Don't know. Translation: I haven't got the intelligence or resource to express in words what I am and what I feel and what I want. Well, he would put a gentle boot in.

'Look,' he said, 'the police case is going to be that you're in Moral Danger, as they call it – that you need Care and Protection.'

'That mean court? Going to court?'

'Not necessarily. Not if all the facts are known beforehand.'

'Oh.'

'So – why did you do it? Were you bored? For kicks was it?'

'I suppose. Started out as a lark. Amateur night down the pub.'

'You're not old enough to be in a pub.'

'Not to drink, no.'

He could see the funny side of that. So could she. They both smiled.

'There's one thing,' she said.

For the first time since she'd come to Kingston House he saw her blush. She was blushing furiously.

'Yes?' he said.

'I liked the feeling. When they were all looking at me. I liked it.'

Her voice had thickened with embarrassment but at that moment he had nothing but admiration for her courage. O.K. classic arrested development. Four-year-old stage. But for her admission he could like her enormously.?

'It's a feeling a lot of people have,' he said. 'There's nothing much wrong with feeling sexy, by the way. It's when you don't you want to start worrying.'

Steady, he thought, don't go any further across that line when you're alone with her.

'What do you think your parents are going to say?' he sidestepped into. It dispelled all elements of mutual embarrassment at once.

'It's what he says,' she said. 'Her I don't care about.'

Ah.

'Never lets me help at home. Or with the baby. Don't like me, she doesn't. Jealous because I've got a bit of go in me.'

'Would you like to help at home?'

' 'Course.'

'A lot of girls don't.'

'I would.'

'Tell me about your dad, then.'

'What?'

'Whatever you want to.'

'He's a lovely man my dad is . . . trouble is – there's not enough of him to go round. Not any more it seems. He used to take me everywhere. Fishing. Walks. Darts matches.'

'Darts?'

'He's mad on it. Always has been. He gets in the papers. Said he would've liked to turn pro now they earn big money. I used to wait outside where he played. But he always used to make time . . . for me . . . time to talk, time to listen . . . know what I mean?'

She was silent a moment. He had the tact not to prompt her.

'He don't do any of that now,' she said at last.

⚜⚜⚜

For Chris Langley things were going well. For Wendy Raeburn it was proving a particularly trying morning. She now had two shadows. Peter Jackson was clinging about her skirts even more closely than Dean. It had slowed her down. The last thing she was going to be in either of their respective circumstances was brusque but, with the dead ache still in her own heart from knowing what had been imposed upon Dean by the court, she found it a treble strain being bright and matter of fact. She had whispered to Dean that they must be 'very kind' that day to Peter because he had had some news. She had hoped it might actually serve to bring Dean out. But the experiment seemed to have failed. Dean had gravely listened and had tolerated Peter's presence with no fuss. There had been no signs, though, of the little boy with the wrong parents taking any kind of initiative in helping the subdued, white-faced little boy who now only had one. It had been heavy going, heavy-hearted going, all morning long. She was glad when towards lunchtime she was finally able to park both the boys under the casually cheerful, infinitely reassuring wing of Mrs Wilson.

She would soon be back for them but in the meantime she

must do something about catching up. She still had to put clean sheets on Dean's bed for a start.

She climbed the stairs to the huge walk-in linen cupboard on the second floor landing. It was an original feature of the house that had never needed modification. The ceiling-high rows of slatted shelving were as able to swallow up the folded piles of man-made fibre sheets and pillowcases as they had once coped with Victorian flannelette. Wendy always took a momentary plasure in the clean fresh smell, the warm, dry enclosed solitariness. Now . . . they were running low on single sheets, the laundry delivery was overdue because of the work to rule, but up there on the second shelf down there should still be some of the green sort. Of course, Dean did get through them at a rate of knots.

She was stretched up on tip-toe about to reach a pair of sheets down when she heard a noise. She looked round. Howard, unusually quietly, had come into the cupboard too.

'Yes?' she said.

'Miss,' he said. More words stuck in his throat. His face was white and set. There was a totally unnatural rigidity in the intensity with which his eyes stared at her. She knew at once it was more bad news. After Dean, she thought, I don't know if I shall be able to bear it.

It was not bad news. Howard pulled the door to. Without warning he had lurched two paces and was crushing her to him. His mouth jarred into hers and with a bruising moistness his lips slewed over hers. Their teeth clashed painfully. On the rebound she managed to wrench her mouth away, turn her head sideways.

'Howard!' she gasped.

She leaned back, pushed hard at his chest. Immediately, without resistance, he staggered a step backwards. He had let go of her.

'Howard . . .' she said again.

He recoiled another step and half-leaned against a shelf. Where before his handsome face had been chalk-white it now blushed crimson. Where before it had been fixed, inflexible, it now worked in a way that seemed totally uncontrolled, involuntary. His jaw was somehow sliding sideways pulling his mouth askew. Tears were starting in his eyes. His huge hands gripped the edge of a low shelf behind him as he stared at her aghast and horrified, plainly unable to believe what he had just attempted and yet, believing it only too well, ashamed beyond belief at the effrontery, the gaucherie and the prospect of discovery.

Wendy, no longer frightened, stared at him with understanding pity. The poor, poor boy, she was thinking, trapped, as he thinks, by his limp: trapped, for certain, by the enclosed society, the prison for one of his age, of this house.

More words were strangling in his incoherent throat. He was wrenching himself away from the shelves, blundering at the door.

'Howard!' she said a third time. And with enough force of command to halt him, to turn him round.

Don't, she told herself, don't: you're off balance; the thing about Dean has thrown you; it's the most dangerously unprofessional thing you could do.

'Let me show you,' she was saying, though. Whatever they might have taught her at Goldsmiths', she had the immediate means to rescue him from the lifetime anguish of his put-down, humiliated spirit, an all but destroyed sexuality.

She had taken his head between her hands, was kissing his closed eyes very gently.

'Don't do anything,' she said. 'Try to relax.'

She put her lips to his, slowly began to kiss him. Without breaking away she reached down for his arms, drew them, unresisting, around her back.

Now, to breath, to talk, she took her mouth from his.

'You see,' she said. 'Gently. Easily. Try to kiss me back.'

She kissed him again. The tenseness had gone out of him. Instinct making him wise, his own mouth was no longer passive, no longer crudely bruising. He had, in fact, a beautifully shaped mouth, she thought, and became aware of the immense strength of his arms, his torso. She caught herself probing at his mouth with her tongue in a full lover's kiss and, a second time, drew her lips away. Careful, she told herself, you're on a knife edge. He's only four or five years younger than you.

She laid her head on his shoulder, her temple against his cheek.

'It's all a very gentle thing,' she said. 'Sssh. Just hold me. Feel what it feels like.'

Careful. But, granting him the last so necessary favour she dare offer his liberation, she must take a further risk. She reached down to his right arm and pulled it from around her waist. She slid her hand down its thickness to its wrist, its hand. Slowly she drew the hand up to her breast. Amazed at the full pounding she there discovered in herself she held it for him firm against her. She took her hand from his, left his to hold and press her.

He had not said a word so far. Staggered, of course; in an ecstasy of terrified, delighted, diminishing disbelieving surprise. Now, his hand there as in every adolescent's dream, he let out a long, thick sigh not quite a murmur.

'Ssh,' she said. 'Gently still. Just hold me.'

She could feel the weight of his other hand across her back, feel the electric strain run from his brain down to the right hand as he nerved himself, very slightly, to caress her. I'm insane, she thought abruptly: God knows where this will end. But her own arm about him, still she let him hold her. Keep your brain alive, working, thinking, she told herself: stay the right side of your brain.

His slowly exploring hand had found her nipple, was gently squeezing. In spite of herself she felt the first ageless, indescribably *frisson* flash through her to her belly. At once she reached up and took his hand away. But she must not destroy him a second time. She kept her head upon his shoulder.

'Listen, Howard,' she said. 'Go on holding me but listen. I want to make a little speech. I know this may sound ridiculous and I know this may sound cruel, but I don't want you to take this personally. It's a sort of lesson. You understand?'

She felt the head against her own nod that he did.

'I remember how I felt when I was your age,' she distancingly said. 'About boys. But it was easier for me. So I want to help you now. I wasn't angry with you earlier. I understood. But Howard. . . .'

She drew her head away and back, so that she might look him in the eye. After two beats of her heart he was not able to meet her look. She was making her point, then.

'—Howard,' she went on. 'You mustn't think this will ever happen again. Between you and me, that is. You'll have your own girl soon. Much sooner than you think, I promise. I know how cruel and long and endless the waiting can seem but it doesn't go on for ever, I swear. I promise. And now you know how to, well, how to behave. How to be gentle, easy. That's what that girl will want. But you mustn't have ideas about me. About you and me. Not at night. Not when we meet during the day. When we meet we'll just be friends like we always have been. And here, now, will be our secret. I promise you. You understand?'

'Yes,' he at last managed gutterally to say.

'You're not disappointed by what I've just said?'

He shook his head.

He was, of course. The feel of her in his arms would burn through his blood as he lay awake at night imagining with wild inaccuracy what it might have been prelude to. But it was the lesser evil, surely. She had rescued him from total vulnerability, a virginity outside of technical virginity. It was almost funny. The first girl to bend towards that handsome, almost monumental head would gain the benefit of her tuition.

She bent her own head to him and this time kissed his cheek – a sister's kiss.

'Go along, then,' she said (never say 'Run' to Howard) 'and just have a little more faith. She will come.'

She stepped back from him. He managed to look straight at her one moment and then ducking his head was extending the movement into his limping exit.

Now it was her turn to slump back against the shelves. Madness? Probably. Her knees felt weakly liquid, were positively trembling at the enormity of her action. Its implications. Chris would sack her on the spot. Give her at least the most enormous dressing down. No! In spite of the whirl of emotions and thoughts she smiled. Hardly the most apposite phrase. But that was part of it. She had endeavoured to stay scrupulously detached from the intimacies of hand and mouth. She had not quite succeeded. A fraction of her make-up, small but distinct, would have welcomed the chance to take Howard to bed. Once there the whole of her being might have gone over to the pursuit of sex with him. By means of him. Why not? She was allowed her fantasies, too. . . . Why not was because to induce calf love in him was to court destoying him far more devastatingly than even the hell of frustration had in its present power to do. And she'd probably created that false first impression of love in him already. Oh God . . . what a mess!

She reached up for the sheets again. One thing was sure. As she careered towards her twenty-third year she was unquestionably growing apace in randiness. Whenever work fatigue allowed her. She must put some kind of a bite on Ronnie. Except . . . well, he wasn't an absolute ideal, was he? She had – briefly – known better.

Oh, hell! Time was really against her now. Dean and Peter would be really disturbed she'd been away from them so long. She'd better put off doing Dean's bed until later in the day. For the moment she'd just dump the sheets down on it.

She brushed her hands back hard against her hair, tugged her blouse straight. Still distinctly weak at the knees she left the linen cupboard.

⚜⚜⚜

'Mr Wyatt, sir.'

'Ah, thank you, Howard. Come in Mr Wyatt.'

Stiffly, starchedly, in an old but no doubt his only suit, Mr Wyatt came in. Chris rose from behind his desk to greet him. At such moments he was almost glad of the pokiness of his office, the shabby dun colouring of the filing cabinets and paintwork. Unused to all kinds of official institutions, apprehensive, unsure of themselves, people like Wyatt would shuffle uncertainly round the door, cheap ties unfamiliarly tight about their necks and a look on their faces perilously close to that of a mourner at a funeral, the poorest relation at an all-the-trimmings wedding. But it was hard for anyone to stay that awed, uncertain, amid such a clutter of bulging, faintly dusty files, tired tin 'In' trays and chipped, non-matching furniture.

'Do sit down,' Chris said.

Warily, unbending, Wyatt sat down on the edge of the upright chair. He was not carrying anything and at once had the problem of finding something for his hands to do. He tried to solve it by placing them each squarely over a knee-cap with a stiff, unnatural evenness. They were big heavy hands for a man of otherwise slight build, Chris thought. And knocked about, workers' hands, the lines of old cuts scarred into their surface, the nails clipped right back, the skin ingrained with dirt beyond the power of any soap to cleanse. Swarfega hands, Chris thought.

'Cup of tea?' he asked as matily as he could manage without seeming condescending.

'No, thanks,' Wyatt said. 'I'd like to keep this short, if you don't mind. I've got to get on to work.'

'I'll be happy to write you a short letter to give your personnel manager explaining why there was no—'

'No. Thanks. Be all right,' Wyatt said. Suspicious, curiously dark complexioned, hair slicked greasily back, he shifted uneasily in his chair. Probably told them he's gone to see his doctor, Chris thought. Doesn't want word getting around. He looks just like an old-style footballer. Tommy Lawton. Well, get on with it, then.

'This must all have come of something of a shock,' he lamely said.

'I'm not sure. I'm not sure yet what it's all about.'

Truculence there and no mistake.

'But . . . your wife . . . you mean your wife hasn't passed on to you what's been happening?'

'She said this social worker or something came. Something

183

about Lucille missing school. She said she hadn't really taken it all in and you could explain it proper.'

'You don't know—'

'She said she didn't want to worry me and stop me going in on her account. Lucille's.'

'Going in?'

'To work. The wife – she's not one for talking all that much.'

Ye Gods! So he'd got to take it almost from the top. How the hell did people like this ever get themselves on holiday, organise an evening out, bring up a family! Careful, he reminded himself, you don't get paid for sitting in that kind of judgement over them.

'We'd better begin at the beginning,' he said. 'Last weekend Lucille told you she was staying with a friend of hers called Jackie. She—'

'Her mother quite likes her out of the house, you see, on account of—'

'Hang on a minute. Let's just get the facts. She told you she was going to the pictures. To one of those West End only films. In fact she ended up at this party.'

'Party? What kind of party?' Wyatt's head had come up with every kind of suspicion and potential for outrage at red alert. Barrack-room lawyer material in there somewhere, Chris had time to think.

'A noisy party,' he said. 'Someone complained. The police raided it. They picked up Lucille.'

'Lucille! Our Lucille!'

'Yes, Lucille. There were a bunch of blokes there. Car-dealers. She was doing this striptease for them.'

'What!'

The note behind Wyatt's outcry was curiously personal. The indignation could now have full play. But on his own behalf. It was as if he'd just heard his wages were being docked or the union were calling all the paint shop out again.

'I don't believe it!' he was inevitably maintaining.

Chris reached some photostat sheets out from his 'In' tray.

'I'm afraid you have to,' he said. 'I've a copy of the police report here if you'd like to read it.'

Wyatt shook his head. Belief had suddenly got to him. He looked glassy-eyed, as if he might be sick. He was a crafty fly-weight who'd just been hit by a hard-punching welter's best shot. Chris could now feel sorry for him.

'You didn't know?' he said.

Trying to clear his thinking as much as reply, it seemed, Wyatt shook his head.

'I'm sorry,' Chris said. 'It seems it wasn't the first time.'

'Who says?' The fly-weight was trying to fight back.

'She does. Several parties. It started, she says, in some pub's Amateur Night sort of thing.'

'Which pub?'

'I don't know. The police do. Does it matter?'

Chris Langley was not to know the father had automatically wondered if the pub was in his darts' league. The possible connection between his daughter's recent activities and the past evenings she had once spent waiting on the doorsteps of *The Fox* with her lemonade and packet of crisps had failed to cross his mind.

'I can't not tell you any of this,' Chris Langley said, 'because the police won't act until they're satisfied you know all the facts.'

'She's fifteen,' Wyatt said inconsequentially. 'Not sixteen for another . . . five months.'

'I know,' Chris said.

'Why, though? Why'd she do it?'

How many times had he heard that question? Always with the same rush of dawning realisation, of surprised intensity.

'I asked her that,' he said.

'What she say?'

'I don't honestly think she knows.'

'Money! She's always spending more—'

'Not really money, Mr Wyatt, in my opinion. I think it was probably a bid for attention. To be noticed.'

Wyatt let out his breath in a long hiss of cynical disgust.

'To get your attention. Win it back from her little brother, maybe. I would think that subconsciously she probably wanted to get caught. This could be the start—'

'Subconsciously! And why like that?'

'Look at it her way. What else can she do? She can't sing or paint or do the high jump. She's using such talent as she's got.'

'Talent!' Wyatt spat the word out in a way emphasising all its dirtier connotations. He managed to render it obscene. Involvement had enabled him to forget his self-consciousness but he still sat poised on the edge of the chair. Now, abruptly, he twisted sideways as if unable to confront either Chris Langley or the increasingly graphic picture his mind was painting. He swung back, lowered his head. Allowing him a moment's grace, Chris said nothing. From outside he could hear a grating, rhythmic, squeaky sound.

'Know what?' Wyatt said. 'It makes me sick. Sick to my stomach. No offence but sitting here having to talk about it with you – it makes me feel sick.'

'I can understand that,' Chris said. 'But is it so very terrible? She wants to be noticed. Needs to be, we might say. She's—'

'Needs! What she needs is—'

'She's pretty. What she did is understandable enough. Natural enough.'

'Natural! No-one's going to tell me it's bloody natural to take your clothes off, prance around in front of a lot of dirty old men!'

Wyatt's savage, personalised indignation went far to explaining everything, Chris began to feel. From outside he could still hear the persistent metallic squeak. Oh, of course – someone on the swing. The curious thing was that if you looked at Wyatt quickly he was just the sort you'd say the *Sun* ran its page three nudes for. He wasn't an old man. Late thirties. In looks he was almost the sort you might expect to keep a little bit going for himself on the side. Or, in some buried corner of the sub-conscious he did not acknowledge, fancy his daughter. He could have been one of that Saturday night audience.

'Look,' Chris Langley said. 'I honestly think it's not that serious. And there is some good news.'

Wyatt's head lifted a fraction as Chris reached for a manilla file.

'Lucille's undergone a thorough medical examination since coming here,' Chris said. 'It's possibly surprising in the circumstances and in this day and age, but she is, as it happens, still a virgin.'

Wyatt's face winced with contemplation of the implied intimacies. Yes, Chris thought, a less than healthy relationship. A part of his brain remembered that fat pig of a car dealer who'd come trying to check up. Well, let him or his boss or whoever go on sweating it out forever.

'She's not your daughter!' Wyatt said with sudden viciousness.

'That's true. I'd like to think that doesn't stop me being charitable.'

'Charitable . . . why?'

Again the truculence, a sharpness.

'Why? . . . Because kids do these things . . . in the process of learning what not to do, growing up. They don't go into the whys and wherefores. They don't look ahead – see that people'll get hurt. They—'

'What's the police case?'

I don't think I like you, Mr Wyatt, Chris thought. Careful.

'That, being under age, she's exposed to Moral Danger.'

'Will it be in the papers?'

'No. There are no reporters in Juvenile Courts.'

'She should've thought of us before she went gallivanting off.'

'Yes. She should have. But that sort of comes with being a parent, doesn't it? A lot of let downs. Some moments of great joy.'

'Hmmmn!'

'She wasn't trying to harm you. She's not malicious.'

'Not what her mother thinks!'

'That's not true. She's terrified of what you're going to say and what you'll think.'

'With bloody good reason!'

'Look, Mr Wyatt – I think she's learned her lesson. I really do.'

'. . . what happens now, then?'

'Well, pretty obviously, that's not up to me. The police'll want some form of undertaking from her that she won't do it again . . . that could, hopefully, be the end of it.'

For the first time Wyatt shifted his weight back into the chair. He seemed to have made some kind of a decision. From through the window the sound of the swing continued to make its grating presence heard.

'Another two years she'll be a tart,' Wyatt said. 'A right bloody little scrubber.'

For all his vehemence, perhaps because of it, the idea seemed to give him a certain grim satisfaction. A perverse satisfaction, maybe.

'I don't think so,' Chris said. 'But that's the danger, of course.'

'Scrubber!'

Annoyed, not wanting to show it, Chris stood up. He moved to the window. With the first glance out he had wryly to grin and bear another example of Life's never failingly abundant ability to dispense its little ironies. The performer on the swing – that swinger – just had to be Lucille. Returned full circle from the would-be sophisticated stripper she was completely a school girl again as, sending herself upward in higher and higher darts, she worked at the swing's momentum for all she was worth. The sight restored much of Chris's good humour.

'You'll want to talk to Lucille,' he said. 'She's outside. I'll just go and get her.'

He moved toward the door.

'Don't bother,' Wyatt said.

'I'm sorry?'

'I don't want to see her.'

Chris drew a deep breath. This was going to take more time and tact than he felt like expending on this type. But for Lucille's sake. . . .

'I realise it's an embarrassing moment for both of you,'

he said. 'But it'll be more so tomorrow. Harder still the day after. It really is better faced up to now, believe me. I do have some experience of this sort of thing. I'll stay with you or leave you—'

'You don't follow, do you?' Wyatt interrupted yet again with.

Chris looked at him. The man's dark eyes had turned almost obsidian with some kind of glittering malice.

'I don't want to see her at all,' he said. 'Not now. Not ever.'

'What?' Chris said.

He didn't really know why he said that. Because he was appalled, no doubt. His head was pretending to swim with shock but at its inner core all was icy-still and he knew with a dreadful, crystal-clear finality what Wyatt had decided and what he would say.

'If she's going to be a whore, she's not going on the game from my doorstep.'

'She's not going to be a whore.'

'Who says? Who says she isn't already?'

'The doctor, for one!'

'Hmmn!'

Chris looked straight into those eyes and knew he was talking to a wall of polished steel. There could be no appeal to this twisted man's made-up mind. Yet he was honour bound to try.

'Mr Wyatt,' he said. 'She's your daughter.'

'Then she should've behaved like she was.'

The unanswerable logic of the self-unmade man.

'You do it this way, Mr Wyatt, it'll be much crueller . . . a lot more punishing for all of you.'

Wyatt was nodding. Understanding had brought an unpleasantly knowing smile to a face pleased it could now look cynical.

'I was wondering that,' he said.

'Wondering what?'

'Wondering how long it would be before the threats started.'

Chris made a supremely professional effort. He did not

189

call the man a fool to his face. Or any of the other forty epithets that sprang to mind.

'I'm not threatening you,' he merely, mildly, said. 'I'm begging you. Think what you're doing. To yourself. To your wife.'

Wyatt smiled thinly.

'Think what it'll be like for her to know you've turned your back on her. You of all people.'

'Should've thought of that, then, shouldn't she? Who started it then, eh?'

His stupidity was a bullying child's, then.

'You did,' Chris said firmly.

Wyatt's mouth tightened and Chris knew if there had been a last chance it had been squeezed away by those same muscles. This was the sort of shop-floor confrontation Wyatt would think he recognised. The truth of what Chris alleged he would never recognise.

'Bollocks,' he said. 'I'm going to say it just once more. We don't want her back. We won't take her.'

So it was 'we' now.

'You're prepared to stand up and say that in court?' Chris said.

'Yes.'

'So just like that! You're giving up! Easy isn't it. At the first sign of trouble, first time something gets up your nose, you wash your hands – pass her on to somebody else to sort out.'

Wyatt had stood up.

'I'm not prepared to argue,' he said.

Prepared or able?

'There is no way that any institution on earth can give Lucille what you can give her,' Chris said. 'Could give her,' a regard for accuracy made him add.

'Pity she didn't think of that before. Think of somebody else for a change. But as I said – I'm not prepared—'

'I've heard it but I don't believe it,' Chris said.

'You care so much, you bloody look after her!'

Careful! Don't hit him. Take a breath.

'We will,' Chris said. 'We'll need her clothes.'

'You'll have them first thing tomorrow.'

'It'll cost you a packet maintaining her,' Chris said. 'She's no waif and stray now, is she?'

Wyatt had been making for the door. But that stopped him. The one thing, no doubt, which still could. Without actually making a noise he seemed to sniff. He looked meanly at Chris like a customer sure he's been swindled by a shop assistant but with no way of proving it. Then however his shoulders straightened.

'Worth it,' he said. He reached for the door handle, stopped and turned.

'Court, then,' he said. 'When is it? When'll it be? Who'll tell us?'

'You'll be told,' Chris Langley said.

He choked off his desire to add 'Assuming you can read'. Instead of speaking he moved towards the doorway. The effect was to make Wyatt retreat so that he was able to close the door and so shut out the sight of him. His earlier ration of heartfelt relief would have to last him the day through, it seemed.

The creaking from the swing had stopped at one time it seemed to him. Or perhaps in his concern and stunned concentration he had simply ceased to hear it. At any rate, it was well under way again now. Automatically, he went to the window. Lucille was now arching the pendulum of a swing up to a full horizontal with the ground. Full swing. Lucy in the sky. Oblivious, of course, to what had just passed between himself and her father, she seemed as happy as a sand boy.

Chapter Thirteen

SATURDAY. A BLACK morning. In every way. Literally. Metaphorically. Spiritually. As if in solemn acknowledgement of the occasion, leaden-coloured clouds had risen up in the night to tower heavily over Kingston House. His parents had wasted no time in reclaiming their few pounds of flesh. It was the day for Dean to go.

They had decided not to tell him until the moment was almost at hand. A swift betrayal, as it must seem, would perhaps be more merciful, less permanently harmful than one allowing time for thought. Social work, the art of the lesser evil, Wendy had sourly remembered.

Oppressed by fatigue she had in fact secured the one benefit constant round the clock availability confers and slept well that night. Except that she had woken tired and early. And instantly aware with her first thought that this was the day. She had raised herself up on one elbow and looked across the small bed-sitter that was hers to where, his battered Paddington his comforter companion in his arms, Dean still lay asleep. Even so, he was not properly relaxed. There was a tension, a fitfulness about his sleep that made a mockery of lullabies. Well, he should sleep as long as possible this morning. From tonight the bed would be gone. There would be room once more to swing a cat. She would no longer have to get ready for bed in silence and in darkness so as not to wake her tiny room-mate from his thin and far from golden slumber. She would no more have the earlier, blessed chore of telling him a bedside story, of sitting by his side until the tired, grave eyes it seemed that you might drown in, had finally stayed closed and he had drifted off.

Don't form personal attachments, the courses and the text books all alike enjoined. Impossibly. Noiselessly, so still as not to wake him, she began the day by weeping.

By perverse irony when, much later, she had roused him, his bed had been bone dry. It was the third time since his coming thither he had gone clean through the night.

Telling him had been awful beyond words. For the first time she had understood the full force of the saying about a knife turning in your guts. Chris had done the actual talking but she had, of course, had to be there. Yes, awful. Unspeakable.

Arriving, Dean had been hysterical, incontinent with fear, kicking and screaming. She would always remember the pulse of deepest satisfaction that had coursed through her when, as she held him in her arms, he had finally grown still. This time she would have given anything to have him move, to shriek, to run berserk. But as Chris had tried to explain how lucky he had suddenly become, he had just nodded once to show he understood. And started to cry. Silently, motionlessly, unblinking even, he had stood still like a particularly well-made puppet and wept. Looking all the time at her. She had tried to smile and make it seem it was because of his good luck and not because she was getting rid of him. And all the time she had wanted to rush forward, kneel before him and, enfolding him in her arms, weep her heart out as copiously as he.

Now came the worst moment of all. The moment of departure. Holding Dean's hand she had led him, unpro-testing, solemn, dry-eyed now, down the stairs, along the hall for the last time and out of the door to the top of the steps. In her other hand she had carried a duffel bag filled – but only half-filled – with his few belongings in the way of clothes, the battered Paddington, the cheap animal picture book he had silently turned the pages of time and time again. It was her own bag. The even fewer possessions of his arrival had come insecurely tied in a cardboard box. She had not been able to bear the thought that he should go forth from her keeping no better provided for.

The father had not deigned to get out of the car he had obviously wished to parade before them. He sat staring sulkily ahead out of the windscreen as John Graydon, knees bent, leaned in at the door talking earnestly and volubly.

The fat, peasant, sow-like mother had been waiting at the bottom of the steps. Seeing Dean she had let out a cry and rushed forward to meet him. Stoically, with the total courage that only children are expected by their God to give, he had let her embrace and kiss him. He had only slightly flinched.

'Here,' his mother said, 'it's real cold this morning. Let's put on the nice new anorak thing I've got for you. It's special, Dean love.'

She had made to bundle Dean back inside and Chris Langley, already on the steps, had nodded his okay across to Wendy. So she had been left to stare a moment at the cheap and nasty, rotten, horrid car.

It was old but coarsely tarted up. An Anglia, she thought, resprayed in a flashy metallic purple colour and given crude green and yellow stripes the length of its lower side. Something had been done to its back underneath. To the suspension. It made the car tilt downwards toward the front. It was a car you'd literally steer clear of.

A tinted strip ran across the windscreen's top. Their two names were picked out on it, of course. Roy and Iris. Perfect. It was all wrong, of course, her attitude, but try as she might, searching her heart, she could not find therein the smallest drop of charity towards the parents of this child she loved.

'There – that's better then.'

The mother was emerging from the hall. Dean came just behind her. Wendy's heart tilted over. The anorak, an orange-red was as cheaply garish as the car. And much too big. Dean was lost inside it. There was no need for it at all. It was not that cold. The neat, plain little grey pullover they had given him here was more than adequate to keep him warm. But the silly, flustered cow had not only zipped him into this great last-all-of-three-weeks monstrosity, she had insisted on putting the hood up. Dean's tiny wizened face was lost in it. That's why her heart had nearly stopped. His eyes stared out of it like a lemur's. It was like looking at a child drowning in blood.

She must have betrayed something of what she was thinking in her look. The mother was turning to her.

'He'll soon grow into it,' she said apologetically. 'It's hard picking them out when you've not got them there.'

When you've got no idea, Wendy thought. She smiled encouragingly.

'It's a good fault,' the mother said.

Wendy handed her the duffel bag.

'All his things,' she said. Chris had told her to keep it brief.

'His Paddington's in there,' she said. At once uncertainty glazed the stupid bitch's eyes opaque. Her forehead creased.

'His teddy bear,' Wendy said quickly. 'He likes it to go to sleep with. Helps him to get off.'

'Oh, yes.'

'He's got very fond of a bedtime story, too. I think it would be a help to him if you could manage to read – tell – him one each night.'

Another frown.

'The same one, if you like,' Wendy said. 'They like hearing what they already know.'

'Oh, yes.'

'I've put a list of things we've noticed about him lately in the very top of the bag. It's all typed out so you won't have to bother with my writing.'

'No. Oh, thank you.'

And now the moment. She would not be cheated of it but must get the emphasis exactly right. With her own courage spun from resources she had not been sure until that moment she possessed, she knelt down in front of Dean. A bright cheerful smile was on her face.

'Going home!' she said. 'Isn't it exciting! In a motor car too!'

Not trusting herself to say another word she kissed for the last time the little boy who for six weeks had been her silent, unsmiling shadow, her tender concern at the far edge of thought. He received the kiss with no reaction, no response.

'Off we go then, Dean,' his mother was tugging at his arm.

He started to follow her down the steps. Then, suddenly he had slipped out of her grip, was climbing back up the steps. Wendy's heart froze again. Now would come a repeat of the hideous, hateful screaming scene of his arrival. But no. No screams. With the deliberate gravity that was his basic characteristic and she would remember on her own death bed, he was silently offering Chris something he held in his hand. Chris was taking it.

'Thank you, Dean,' he said, with equal solemnity. 'It's very good of you to remember and very kind of you to think of me. Thank you. Have a nice journey home, now.'

With no other word the boy turned and rejoined his mother. The father made no effort to get out of the car to open doors or take the bag. Embarrassed, perhaps, by the whole thing. Or perhaps not. As Wendy inwardly shuddered, it was John Graydon who performed the simple courtesies. He slammed the door. The stupid bitch was in the front passenger seat with Dean on her lap. If anything happened—

With ostentatious acceleration the car zoomed away. She would have sworn that Dean received a whiplash there and then. God rot them! God sod them both!

There was one of those waving hands in the centre of the car's sloped backward window. She hated to seem to respond to it. Almost certainly Dean would not be able to see her from that death-trap seat. But better to betray her own fastidiousness than seem to betray him yet further in the last possible glimpse he might take of her. She waved at the fast disappearing car.

It reached the gates. Scarcely slowed as it dipped into the road and turned left out of vision. She heard it accelerating fiercely away. Between the gate-posts there was just an empty gap. It grew misty. As the tears, allowed now, pricked at her eyes, she leaned her weight against the porch's supporting column.

'Here,' someone was saying. 'His sense of completeness made him return it to me. But it's yours. You're the one who's earned it.'

Chris Langley. She looked down at his extended hand. In its open palm he was offering her a cheap, gimcracky little green plastic frog.

It was too much. She seized it and in an unseeing flood of tears finally released dashed into the house.

⚜ ⚜ ⚜

She took sobbing, heart-broken refuge in the linen cupboard. Its homely smells were comforting. After a while the racking tears had all but ceased. She was down to sniffles. She could recognise some calmer, washed quiet centre at the core of her grief. A few more moments. Then she must go and do something about putting some make-up on. This was ridiculous.

There was a knock at the door.

Oh, no! Not Howard. What a fool she'd been. What a fool to have fled here!

The door was opening. John Graydon stood there. He made no reference to the state she was in or her strange choice of sanctuary. He was grim-faced enough himself.

'Evening off tonight?' he asked.

She nodded.

'How would you feel about going out some place and getting absolutely rotten stinking pissed,' he said savagely.

She started to nod, then remembered. Damn!

'I can't,' she said. 'I've already got a date.'

'That Ronnie?'

'Yes.'

'Cancel him. You can't be in the mood.'

That was for sure. Why not? Yet some ridiculous scruple made her think again.

'I'd like to,' she said. 'Cancel him. Go with you. But . . . it's not very fair is it?'

'Sod being fair after that!'

'Look, John – next week, perhaps.'

Morosely he turned away.

'Yeah, well. We'll have to see,' he said.

⚜ ⚜ ⚜

When the day had dawned black and gloomy, David Newman had been pleased. With the weather so indifferent perhaps the Chris Langley waifs and strays brigade would cancel their specific request to come over and use the pool. If he hadn't had a little too much brandy the night of the dinner party, he wouldn't probably, have said fine, no problem, it would be all right just any time. If he hadn't wanted not to seem a rotten sport he'd have had the balls to cut the idea dead over the phone. But, well, he hadn't. . . . And toward later morning the weather had improved and there'd been a confirming phone call and he hadn't managed to squeeze in an ad hoc game of squash with Jerry because here splashing about, hollering the fences down were a dirty dozen or so of Chris' hoodlums.

Actually, now they'd turned up he was rather pleased. Good luck to them. Let them hoot and holler a bit. The noise would get right up the Sangster's toffee-noses and they'd positively bleed at every orifice seeing the unspeakable spectacle of black kids – 'well, nothing against them, David, but they do have a different smell about them, you know' – diving into the water alongside representatives of pure-bred, white-skinned, goose-fleshed English maidenhood. But his neighbours would be stymied. They would, of course, complain. Confronted, however, by the information it was all for a 'good cause', their P.R. Christian front would not permit their essential lack of charity to show. Pure-bred! Ha! Scrubbers United, more like. The sort of goose-flesh that one over there was used to, for instance, had nothing to do with feeling cold. Quite the reverse, in fact. Gee! What a superb dive! David Newman's eye was diverted from Lucille Wyatt's trimly oscillating Geneva movement by the brilliant black bow Gary had made of his body in mid-air. David sucked in his stomach muscles. The considerable schoolboy athlete largely lost in his middle-aged, middle-class, body strove jealously for a moment to compete with Gary's flat belly, thin waist and muscled ridge of shoulder. Then surrendered. Well, he had more money, a better car, than that kid was ever going to come by. Sod him. . . . His eyes flicked back to the girl. A lot of form there for a kid. And she knew it. Well they all did these days. But she'd been projecting something even as she jumped down from that wreck of a bus. When he'd told the oldish bloke who'd brought them that as owner of the pool he felt responsible for doing a little policing – just in case – the thought of her in a bikini had not been altogether absent from his mind.

The oldish bloke – Hutton, yes, that was it, easy to remember really – was trundling up and down the far side of the pool trailing the handle of an inverted broom inches in front of some frantically thrashing beginner's nose. Yes, why not? A little token chat up to go with a closer squint down her bikini top. Wasn't senior management supposed to keep abreast of teenage tendencies?

In jeans and tee-shirt he strolled towards her. And didn't she just know he was on his way! One arm behind her head on the recliner, one leg bent up, one fully stretched, she was prediscovered Marilyn to the life.

He sat down on the wall next to the recliner as she pretended to ignore him.

'You don't seem to be joining in much,' he said. 'Water too cold?'

She turned and looked at him. He'd been undressing her with his eyes all afternoon. Smarmy swine. Oh Christ! Why had her dad done that to her?

'Got the rag on, ain't I,' she shortly said.

Ah, how nice! Twenty-two carat Kensington charm school, he thought. But he couldn't think of what to say.

'I know what you're thinking,' she said.

Now he was thoroughly confused.

'Do—'

'What you want to know.'

'What?'

'What I'm in for. Well, taking and driving away,' she said belligerently

'Taking and driving? What?'

'A set of wheels. What d'you think I'm talking about? Skateboards?'

Good Lord!

'More than once?' he said.

'Umpteen. Couldn't tell you. Lost count.'

'Well . . . what did you do? With the cars, I mean.'

'Nicked 'em. Drove 'em. Dumped 'em. Nicked another to get back or came back on the thumb.'

'Just you.'

'Me and some mates. From up the Roxy.'

She must be having him on. He looked hard at her trying to make sure. Giving as good as she got, she stared right back.

'You got caught, though,' he said.

'Bloody fuzz. Eighty miles an hour on the M23, though. Pigs! I bit the thumb off one of 'em.'

'Really?'

'Right off.'

Miming, she suited the action to the word. It did look bloody convincing.

'Crashed up, I was, mind you.'

'You what?'

'You know. Bombers. Strawberry field. Green slime.'

He blinked. She tried not to grin and blow it. Smarmy money-merchant. That'd get him thinking. Fixed him proper.

'Better get changed, then,' she said abruptly.

Catlike she sat forward and rolled on up to her feet. Marilyn reborn she moved off toward the house. He watched her buttocks playing nip and tuck with each other beneath the half-obscuring blue triangle and suddenly realised he hadn't taken one good look straight down her front. Had he been monumentally sent up? He didn't know. Christ – he was getting old at that.

A shadow fell across him. He turned his head. This Hutton bloke was standing there and looking quizzically down at him.

'Don't want to believe all you hear,' he said.

David tried to imply that he hadn't for a moment.

'Thought as much,' he said. 'All lies, eh?'

'Every word. Whatever it was. Tries to be hard-boiled but soft as jelly underneath. Problems at home. Wouldn't say boo to a goose.'

With a conspiratorially man-of-the-world nod, Hutton moved back to the pool. David remained on the wall more confused than ever. It had plainly been (in every sense) a 'hands off' word to the wise. So who was telling the least lies? If she was only trying to be hard-boiled, God help the race of M.C.P.'s the day she finally succeeded. He grinned as a thought struck him: as for not saying boo to a goose, wasn't that why he'd strolled over. He grinned again. Stroll on, as you might say now.

He stood up. His good sense was restored. Hutton was quite right. The last thing he was going to do was get involved in some tacky mess with an overblown nymphet he wouldn't take a second look at in the street.

In the big bedroom that was all over wood and which, amid snorts and giggling, had been designated the place for the girls to chance, Lucille Wyatt sat on the edge of the enormous bed. She was oblivious to its size. She was sitting crying. She was still in her bikini. A towel was now around her shoulders and, head hanging down, hands gathered to her face, she was crying into one of its ends. Her shoulders heaved. Her dad! Why had he just walked out on her? What would happen now? Happen to her? Her whole stomach felt empty. Sick. She felt sick with emptiness. The worst part of the sickness, though, was not worrying about what was going to happen. It was knowing that it was really all her fault. He hadn't walked out on her. It wouldn't look like that in his book. In his book it would look like she'd walked out on him. No one else to blame. She'd brought it on herself. . . .

Jamie, too, was sitting down. His feet dangling listlessly in the water, he sat disconsolately on the edge of the pool blankly ignoring the ripples he was making. His blame was not directed inwards. Or only in one regard. He should've gone ahead and made a full escape when he had had the chance. She'd never have caught him in the woods. His one mistake was not going through with it. Or was it? An army marches on its stomach, Barry had said. There in the woods he'd had no supplies, no heavy weather gear, no cash. A good commander didn't deploy forces until he was sure he'd got a fall-back position. That's what had stopped him bolting all the way. That and the other feeling deeper still and underneath the soldiering.

Loneliness. He liked being alone, using his wits. Initiative, Barry called it. But in the woods it had suddenly gone so quiet it had made him feel lonely in a way he'd never been before. The birds had stopped calling and it had been as quiet as a grave. As lonely as his life was going to be. The bright sun showing cheerfully through all the trees just made it somehow worse. Shivery. Cow! Stupid cow! She'd never understand! There was no way he could make her understand! Barry had been kind. He had time for other people. Not just him. All sorts. The other one – she couldn't see it but he only had one thing in mind. Not even her. What he had in mind was pleasing himself on her. She'd never see it for herself, though. And he couldn't tell her. She'd say she was a grown-up and he was just a kid. He was helpless. He knew he'd never make her understand.

He had stood in the middle of the wood and thought about Barry and thought about her and about how once she left him for that Jeff there was going to be no rule that said that anything in his life was going to get better. Just as with Barry, nothing. . . . He had suddenly felt very little. Not like a cadet at all. He'd thought of fairy stories. Babes in the Wood. He'd suddenly felt all weak and tired and just wanted to curl up and go to sleep. Be covered up with leaves. Just fall asleep and not wake up. That'd show them. They'd all be sorry then.

Kershasplosh!

Someone had broken splashily up from under through the surface of the pool. Someone had grabbed his leg, was trying to pull him in. Donnie! He put his other foot on Donnie's shoulder, braced himself against the edge of the pool and shoved like one o'clock. Donnie let go and fell back and away. He went under, rose back up shaking his short hair like a dog. He trod water easily.

'Moody!' he said.

'Queeroid!' Jamie said automatically.

'Double moody! Know something? You're no fun to be with any more.'

'Never said I was!'

Donnie blinked to get more water out of his eyes. He shook his head again.

'Got to live with you, ain't I?' he said. 'You could try.'

His gran had always been saying that to his grandad.

'No law says I got to!' Jamie said.

'Moody!'

But he felt bad saying that. Bill Hutton had taken him aside and told him Jamie seemed pissed off. Down in the dumps, he'd said. It would be nice to try to be nice to him. Cheer him up. Well, it would really.

He swam the long stroke to the side, levered himself up next to Jamie. He'd half expected to get pushed back down but Jamie didn't seem to think of that.

'Blimey,' Donnie said. 'Cold when you get out.'

He nodded in the direction of the geezer who's pool it was. He had been chatting up that Lucille Wyatt like none of the rest of them could suss it out but she'd told him to get stuffed, left him. Serve the stupid soft bastard right!

'Tell him you want a shower,' he said to Jamie.

'Who?'

'Him. The owner.'

'Tell him I want a shower?'

'Yeah. Tell him you're freezing.'

'I'm not.'

'Tell him, stupid. He'll let you use the bathroom.'

'So what?'

'It's got a carpet and gold taps!'

Some of the unaffected awe in Donnie's tone of voice managed to catch part of Jamie's deeper attention. He twisted round to look at Donnie.

'Gold?' he said.

'Solid!'

'Don't believe you.'

'Bet you!' Donnie said.

'How much?'

'Your belt.'

He'd be lucky! Jamie was going to keep that all his life. Wear it at his own funeral. He'd put it in his will.

'You'll be lucky!' he said.

'Go and ask him anyhow. Go and see for yourself.'

Jamie hesitated and then got up. He might as well. Something to do. It was fair enough what Donnie had said. He had been moody lately. He had good reason to be but he might as well show willing. Never volunteer, Barry said, but always show willing when you can't get out of it.

'All right,' he said. Donnie grinned.

He went over to the owner. He was standing talking to Bill Hutton. You could tell he was rich by his hair-cut.

'Please, sir,' he said.

'You want some more?'

More what? What did he mean?

'You want some more porridge? Oliver Twist.'

'Oh,' he pretended to understand. The owner had a rich wristwatch too. It had numbers that kept changing.

'I'm cold,' Jamie said. 'Freezing!'

'Another one!'

'It's the water,' Jamie said. He pretended to shiver a bit.

'O.K. I'll believe you. Here, put this towel round your shoulders. Dry your feet on this one and then go up and have a shower.'

'Yes. Ta. Thank you.'

'That's all right. Don't make any more mess than you have to.'

'No, sir. Thanks, sir.'

'Jamie,' Bill Hutton said. 'Don't make any mess.'

'No, sir.'

He turned away.

'Thousands wouldn't,' he heard the owner say. 'But why not?'

He dried his feet with exaggerated, visible care, then, winking at Donnie in a way nobody else would see, walked across the wide, flat stones and in through the big sliding window or glass door. Perhaps they weren't as rich as all that, after all. They didn't have much in the way of carpets. Just rugs. There wasn't enough furniture to fill up all the spaces, either. And the stairs up to the upstairs were just plain wooden boards sticking out of the wall. They had no bits joining them up. You could see right through them.

On the other hand there was carpet on the landing that was really thick and springy. You'd feel yourself sinking into it even if you had your shoes on. And when he opened the bathroom door the dark brown carpet kept right on. It was all over the bathroom too, right up to the bath. The bath was another brown, not quite so dark. It did have gold taps. Gold colour, anyway. Perhaps they really were gold. He'd never seen any house with a bathroom anything like as big as this. It had a great big plant in it in a big green pot. It was bigger than the bedroom at the house that he and Donnie shared.

He didn't really want a shower but he ought to make a noise. And check up on those taps. He went over to the bath and, gingerly, turned on the nearer of the two chunky taps. No waiting. Water came out at once. There was only one spout for the water to come out. Hot or cold it came out the same one. He turned it off. The water at once stopped. No dripping. It wasn't like that at home. He turned the tap on again. Water at once. It was like electricity, it came so quick. Yeah, probably were gold, them taps. Couldn't get them off though.

The running water had made him want to pee. Bit of a problem there because there were two loos. Two loos in the same bathroom! One was sort of like a normal loo. The other was flatter and bit lower and seemed to have a different way of flushing. He'd better play safe and use the one he knew how to work. He pulled down his trunks and had a pee. Better be careful not to splash the carpet with one of the last drips.

He finished, flushed the loo. What a lot of mirrors too! A full-length one on the door of the glass cupboard. Wasn't really a cupboard – it was the shower. His hair was already wet so they wouldn't know he hadn't had one. Mirror above the basin too, of course. Mirror on the wall opposite so when you stood right here – so – you saw hundreds and hundreds of yourself – well, lots, anyway – getting smaller and smaller 'till you disappeared. Be nice if he could just jump in the mirror like in the pool and disappear himself away. It wouldn't matter exactly where. Barry might be there. Perhaps in that curvy jar with bath salts in there might be an Ali Baba sort of wizard who could show him how to do it. Ooh! There were scales down there! He must have a measure!

He jumped on the flat, fluffy-surfaced scales. They rocked a bit and steadied. With difficulty he worked it out. Seven stone, four pounds. That wasn't such a lot. Geoff Capes was seventeen. They wouldn't take you as a Regular if you were too small.

Without warning, just like in the woods, he felt the loneliness lying underneath everything else. Always there when you stopped to think, just like breathing. Always there and waiting to come out. Horrible. Shivery. It made you feel so bad you thought you must look different.

He looked at his reflection in the mirror. He did look different. He looked smaller. He looked as small as he felt. In the mirror the bathroom seemed to tower up all around him. He felt so small and sad as he looked at his own face getting smaller and smaller, the feeling was almost nice. Littler and littler. He stared at his own eyes and, staring back, daring him to break it off, they seemed to suck him down into a wicked wizard's well. He'd die down there or else go mad. It made his damp hair go all icy.

Suddenly, in a silvery, blinding flash, he had swept the wicked eyes away. He was staring at rows of jars and bottles on glass shelves. Without him knowing it was doing it, his arm had reached out to the mirror and pulled it open. It was really the front of a cabinet.

Full of things. On the bottom were big square bottles, chunky like the taps. They were full of different colour liquids mainly. Light green, browny, a pale cold blue. Pongs. Scents. After-shaves. He took one out. 'Aramis'. Yes, that was after-shave. Even without taking the top off it ponged. Barry always said that pongs like that were just for ponces. Pong ponces. He put the bottle back. What else?

Toothpaste. Elastoplast. Alka-Seltzer. Stuff in a half-squeezed-up tube called Ortho-something. Those funny ear things. Oh, more stuff on the inside of the door. Medicines. Aspirins. Paracetymol. Feo-span. Hey, what was in this little plastic phial? 'Caution: dangerous to exceed the stated dose.' Soneryl. 'Dangerous to exceed the stated dose!' Poison! Chemical warfare! Secret agents with a special hollow tooth! Kill yourself before you talked! Secret agents sometimes did that . . . . He unscrewed the cap of the phial and tipped about a dozen of the wickedly innocent pink tablets into the palm of his hand. Just like sweets, he thought.

You didn't have to be a secret agent to kill yourself. Lots of people did. When they got pissed off, felt unhappy. Lonely. Overdose, it was called. It was a way in a way of curling up and going to sleep. Not waking up. A way of getting smaller and smaller and disappearing. It didn't hurt. You just took a lot of tablets.

Carefully, one by one, he fed the tablets back into the phial. He was still holding it in his hand when he swung the door of the cabinet back shut. His face came back to stare at him all strange and serious. Lots of others of his face were staring at him and at the back of his head. It was like being hypnotised. You got sucked in and couldn't move. . . . All at once, all together, the heads had nodded at him. He nodded back.

He shoved the plastic tube down the front of his trunks. It felt a bit cold there and hard but it was well hidden there. It just looked like him. And it wouldn't be for long.

✥✥✥✥✥

The kids were a bit more of a stroppy handful that supper time than usual. Bill Hutton was almost beginning to wonder if the game of the swimming jaunt were worth the candle. Those who had been on it were cock-a-hoop making it out to be one of the seven wonders of South East London. Their stories ran the gamut from Tarzan high dives to 'Jaws'. Those who had not got to go were at outspoken pains to demonstrate their couldn't-t-caredness.

'So what?' they questioned with a loud, paper-thin show

of indifference. 'John Wayne on tele. War film. Better'n getting all wet and cold in some rotten pond.'

The onemanship had worked even down to the tinies. Seeking the accolade of a quick ticking off several of them were pulling faces, trying to help themselves to an extra bit of hamburger from their neighbours' plates. They did so with one round, cheerfully awed eye on Bill. With a gleeful, mischievous innocence that – even in the middle of telling them to cut it out, he found utterly beautiful. Don't get sentimental in your old age, he told himself. Cor! look at that little bugger there.

'Hey, Robin!' he said. 'Put that salt back at once.'

Yes, the natives were certainly restless tonight. Only Lucille at the end of one of the bigger kids' benches was not. Subdued, melancholy, she sat toying with food that a couple of nights earlier she'd wolfed. She might be better off out of a home like that, Bill tried to tell himself. But the chances were she wouldn't be. Just at an age when with a bit of commonsense guidance she might have been finding her own individuality, she ran the risk of being institutionalised. Sort of having her development as a person put into deep freeze. As he should know. Incidentally, he must have a word to Wendy, no, Pat would be better about Lucille's little penchant for vamping. If she stayed any length of time at Kingston House those little bursts of bottom wiggling were either going to start a riot or call for a free hand with the bromide in Gary and Kevin's and even Howard's tea.

'Robin!' he had suddenly to say. 'I've told you at once! Leave Cindy's plate alone.'

Having got the attention he wanted, Robin giggled with guilty happiness. He had put the salt down, though. Blimey, he was earning his money this evening. He couldn't blame Wendy he was flying virtually solo. She literally had her hands full with poor little Peter. But it was an ill wind . . . . Having Peter to deal with would help take her mind off Dean. She'd really got too involved there but . . . . what else could you ever do except get too involved. . . .

What was it upsetting him? Something was putting him on edge. What had brushed his ear as the faintest of warning

signals? John Wayne, was it? Surely not. Meaningless. . . .
With the reflex conditioned by his years of service he began
yet again to count the children. One, two, three . . . easier
now they were all settled . . . eight, nine . . . don't forget
Dean's gone, Warren's back at home for the weekend,
Debbie's had to go back into hospital . . . and, finally, Peter
Jackson. One missing. He felt the beginning of unease run
down the edges of his blood. He did the count again from
the reverse direction. John Wayne. Of course! Jamie! Steady,
though. No panic. Being as it was Jamie it could well be a
touch of your target-for-tonight games.

Casually, not changing his outward manner by an eye-
flash he strolled to the older kids' table. Luckily, diagonally
across from Lucille, Donnie was also at the end of a bench.
He was chewing at an over-filled mouth as if Mrs Wilson
was decamping that very evening.

'Easy, Donnie,' Bill said. 'Slow down a bit and you might
find it's got a taste.'

'Has, Mr Hutton,' Donnie said, his mouth still crammed.
'That's why I eat it quick. So I don't notice.'

'You won't want seconds then?'

'I'll force myself, sir. So the others won't suffer.'

All right, was Donnie. He'd be one of their plusses.

'Where's Jamie?' Bill asked as throwaway as he knew
how.

Donnie stopped chewing, looked up and around. He
doesn't know, Bill Hutton thought, hasn't even realised he's
absent.

'Don't know,' Donnie said.

'I thought I saw you with him back here after swimming,'
Bill lied.

'Oh, yeah. With him then.'

'Where's he now, then? Any idea?'

'No, sir.'

'Where were you just before supper?'

'Er . . . in the garden.'

'Jamie with you?'

'He was. But he went inside.'

'He's a chump, isn't he. He's missing his nosh.'

'I can save him some, sir, if you like.'

'No, thanks Donnie, but don't worry. I'll go and turf him out.'

More casual in appearance than he was beginning to feel, Bill Hutton rose to his feet. Wendy would have to cope for a few minutes. From the doorway he signalled to her he'd be back soon. For the untold thousandth time in his career at Kingston House he climbed the servants' stairs. The first port of call would be Jamie's room.

Chapter Fourteen

THE LANGLEY'S HAD eaten early that evening. A fry-up. Pat had announced that after a Saturday morning surgery she felt like cossetting herself. Chris and Robert had both – and genuinely – said that they could quite fancy an evening breakfast. Bacon and eggs it had been. An almost unprecedented event was in prospect for the two elder Langleys. Their second consecutive Saturday evening out. Chris had proclaimed it should be so. Lucille safely regathered in, he sensed that the ship of Kingston House might sail safely on for a few untroubled hours without his presence on the bridge. He had ordained an evening at the pictures.

'A three-way family evening,' he had said.

'Lovely!' Pat had said, all for it. 'The positiveness of my looking forward to it is terrific.'

'Do I have to?' Robert had objected as he looked up from his inevitable book.

'Certainly,' Pat had insisted. 'A family that stays together—'

'Mutually dismays together,' Robert said.

'Commonly – or something – in the case of three,' Chris had said. 'Just because you spent last night with your grandparents doesn't mean you can get out of enjoying yourself this evening.'

'Enjoying!' Robert had snorted. 'Bet you pick out some mindless James Bond bit of crap.'

'Robert! I won't have you saying words like James Bond in front of your mother!'

'Well, all right,' Robert had said, 'deal me in. But can we please go into town and see something with a bit of class?'

He fetched the paper.

'They've brought back *Annie Hall*,' he said.

'I didn't even know we'd lost her,' Pat said with a smile at Chris.

He stuck out his tongue at her.

'I'm going to go and make myself incredibly handsome,' he said.

'Film's only on for a week,' Robert had said. 'Come on, mum, *Mastermind* – while ours attempts the impossible.'

Heads bending together from either end of the slim brown plastic board, the two of them were locked in combat now.

'I didn't go to bed until half-past ten last night,' Robert said *a propos* of absolutely nothing. He was trying to stake out his second line.

'Then I'd keep quiet about it, if I were you,' Pat said. 'If your father gets to hear he'll be somewhat less than pleased.'

'Well it was his father who said that as it was Friday it was all all right.'

'And I wouldn't advise that line of argument either, young man! . . . . Finished?'

'. . . . I think. . . . Yes.'

She marked his deduction. One white peg. One black.

'That all?' Robert said. His voice betrayed he had expected better.

'Then red can't be my constant,' he said. 'Or can it?'

He was sitting deliberating this problem when, shirt tail still outside his trousers Chris came back into the room. I've actually a little tiny island in time to stop and look at my family he thought, to think. He did so. He buttoned a cuff and felt simply, profoundly happy. Pat's really 'up' this evening, he thought. She's thrown off that look of constant one-degree-under tiredness.

'What's the scene with dad's back?' he heard himself saying.

'Sssh!' Pat said.

'My God! Pardon me! I didn't realise it was Korchnoi and Karpov.'

There was a knock at the door. As he moved towards it, Pat looked up at him. There was a sudden doubting, questioning look in her eyes. Too sudden, he realised. He should be a banker.

'Only room service with the champagne,' he said.

But it was Bill Hutton.

'Hello,' Chris said, 'come on in.'

'No I won't, if you don't mind. . . .'

'What is it, Bill?'

'Very much looks as if Jamie McEvoy's upped and down a bunk.'

'Shit! You sure?'

Bill Hutton nodded.

'Sometime between getting back here from the Newman's pool and supper.'

'Damn, damn, damn! Have you looked for him? I mean he's not up to his games?'

Bill Hutton shook his head.

'Not this time, I think,' he said. 'He's left no trail. I've been right through the house.'

'Shit! . . . He went out with his sister mid-week, didn't he?'

'That's right.'

'She's on the phone?'

'There's a number. A neighbour's.'

'Can you dig it out, Bill? I'll come right down.'

Bill nodded. He gestured vaguely at the still untucked-in shirt.

'Sorry to, er, lumber you with this on a . . . er, now,' he said.

'Don't be silly, Bill. Nothing to do with you. Glad you got on to it so fast. Be right with you.'

He smiled, closed the door. He could hear Bill Hutton's footsteps retreating as he stood for a moment gathering his will. He turned and went back into the living room. Both Pat and Robert looked up.

'You hear that?' he said.

'Only the tone of voice,' Pat said. 'Sepulchral *con* expletives. I take it our evening is off?'

She was trying to be flip about it but he could see

disappointment making her look tired. Five years ago she'd had three times more resilience.

'Mine's off,' he said. 'But you two go.'

'What is it?' Pat asked.

'*Annie Hall* has gone out of the window in the guise of an absconding Jamie McEvoy.'

'Oh, hell,' Pat said. 'That could be endless.'

'Could well. You two go, though.'

'I wasn't just thinking of tonight.'

'We'll have to see.'

'Shall we, mum?' Robert said. 'Do you still want to go?'

Pat shook her head.

'I don't think so,' she said, 'if you don't mind. I can somehow feel Life's rich pattern about to get well and truly knotted. I'll make some coffee.'

Robert pulled a face. He pulled away the shield on the *Mastermind* game as token that he was giving that up for lost as well. Chris unbuttoned his cuff.

'Might as well change back and save the shirt,' he said.

'Not many more washings in it anyway,' Pat said as she got up.

'Oh . . . shit!' Robert said. 'I'd gone and got used to the idea.'

'Robert, I don't like you swearing,' Chris said irritably as he unbuttoned the other cuff.

⚜⚜⚜

Water slopped crazily about in the bath threatening to cascade over the side. Janet cackled wickedly.

'Careful!' Wendy said. 'You'll have it all over me and the floor next! Now sit down properly and bend forward so I can do your back. April – you mind your back on the hot tap now.'

'Yes, miss.'

Wendy soaped Janet's back and glanced hopefully at the bathroom door. Two five-year-olds were a handful and a half. She'd asked Lucille to help her out with the towels simply in the hope that a touch of occupational therapy would help snap her out of her depression. In fact, though, she could well do with her extra pair of hands.

Janet brought the flat palm of her hand sharply down on the soapy water's surface.

'Splatt!' she gleefully echoed.

April shrieked her approbation and made to copy her.

'Now you just stop that, both of you,' Wendy said. 'My goodness. Look at the colour of this water! It's like gravy. And you both told me you didn't need a bath!'

'It looks like that 'cause it's all come off her,' Janet said. 'I'm all white.'

'Ain't come off me,' April shot back triumphantly, 'because it don't come off me anyhow. 'S why I'm black.'

' 'S come off your feet,' Janet objected. 'Come off the bottom.'

She looked sideways and up at Wendy.

'That's what docs it,' she said with some seriousness as if it had occurred to her it might be the truth after all.

'Too many baths are bad for you,' she went on.

'Who told you that?' Wendy said. The little girl's knobbly-spined wet back was so firm and pliant.

'My sister. She heard it on her transistor. They said you should all share baths, she said.'

'That was different. That was one summer when it was very dry and there was no rain. There was a shortage of water so everyone was trying to make it go round more. Sit up and I'll sponge the soap off.'

'We're sharing a bath anyhow,' April said with that invincibility in her manner perceived fact confers.

'That's so she can finish early and have more time with her posh boyfriend.'

Chance would be a fine thing, Wendy thought. For an instant, too, she thought of Howard. Nothing had happened. Surely, she'd helped him. All that idea of cold baths was so obscenely, Victorianly, unnatural.

'Janet,' she was saying, 'you'd have ever such a job being a little gossip if I put this sponge in your mouth.'

April laughed.

'We've seen him!' she said.

'You're like a pair of spies,' Wendy laughed.

'You're not going away with him, are you?' April asked

' 'Course not. But you will be. Another ten days or so Exciting isn't it!'

As April nodded thoughtfully the door opened. A pile of towels walked in followed, as it seemed, by Lucille.

'Actually in here?' she said.

'Yes, please. That's marvellous. Put them on the chair.'

Lucille lowered the towels. She glanced at the two children in the bath. Neither her immediate unhappiness nor her habitual concern to seem cool were quite proof enough against the sight. A flicker of interest, amusement even, passed across her face. A longing even to be involved, Wendy thought she had perhaps read there.

'Don't have it in you to give me a hand, do you?' she said.

'Sure,' Lucille said. Included, she was able to be cool again.

She knelt alongside Wendy.

'You do April, if you don't mind,' Wendy said. 'I'll finish off this monster bonce.'

Janet snorted at the compliment.

'You know these two, Lucy?' Wendy said.

'Oh yes,' Lucille said. 'Hello again, you two.'

'We know her,' April said to Wendy. 'She's the Mystery Bags.'

'Who says?' Lucy said.

'Mrs Wilson.'

'Way she cooks, she should be an expert on mysteries, Lucy said.

The little girls not quite being able to catch the drift of this remark, Janet thought it advisable to turn the conversation towards a more familiar topic.

'You wet the bed?' she said.

'Not lately,' Lucy said, and Wendy admired the instinctive tact.

'I do!' Janet said.

'I don't,' April said. 'Well, sometimes I do.'

216

'There's a special word for it,' Janet said. 'You know that?'

'Yes,' Lucy said. 'I know that. I even know what the word is.'

'What?'

'Nitwit.'

For a moment the unlooked response of a word hung in the air before two solemnly uncertain, wide-eyed faces. Abruptly, April began to laugh. The spell broken, Janet joined her. Feeding off each other, they began to shriek. Their hoots rose infectiously to such a pitch that Wendy found herself laughing too. It was the best laugh she had had all day. She let the sponge slip into the bath so she could wipe her eyes. As she did, she saw that Lucille was laughing too.

⚜⚜⚜⚜⚜

There had been all kinds of kerfuffle and to-and-fro-ing getting Jamie's sister to the phone. The neighbour was plainly first cousin to Mrs Hughes. He'd obviously cut her Forsyth in half. As he listened now he could sense the inhibited note in the girl's voice. She audibly felt there was a door ajar somewhere with a large ear clapped to the gap. Almost certainly with reason. Temporarily Forsyth's ratings were slumping.

'. . . he just ran off and left me. I thought he'd gone for good. I've never seen him get that way before.'

'This was after you'd told him that you were getting married?'

Check and recheck.

'Yes.'

'That's the difference, then, isn't it?' Chris said. 'The reason.'

'I'm not sure.'

'We know he's fond of you. You'd just told him you weren't going to be home any more. It upset him. I'm not saying you are, but from his point of view it looks as though you're running out on him. He must have found that too hard to take. It looks now as if when he ran off from you

217

it was sort of a false start for now. A kind of dummy run, almost.'

'I suppose. . . . It was just as though I'd lost him then.'

Silence. He purposely said nothing. There had been blame for herself in her voice. A sixth sense told him that the pause now marked a groping towards some kind of confession. Hence, possibly, some kind of relevant information.

'. . . Mr Langley . . . I . . .' her voice tried to fumble its way around embarrassment.

'Yes?' he said.

'Well . . . I have to, you see . . . really.'

'Have to what?'

'Well . . . you know.'

Oh. He'd been slow. Doubly slow if she were eavesdropped.

'Get married?' he said.

'Yes.'

Ah well. More grist for his mill, no doubt, in five years time. One thing about his job: it might be labour intensive but it was sure as hell steady.

'I don't think that would alter things one way or the other as far as Jamie is concerned,' he said with as much kindness as he could convey: 'And at this stage I don't think there's too much need to worry. If you could just make a point of staying in and, as soon as he turns up, phoning us, I would appreciate it.'

'Yes, of course.'

'I should have some sandwiches or soup or something ready. He'll probably be starving.'

'Yes . . . yes, I'll do that. And I'll phone if he . . . as soon as he gets in.'

'Thank you very much, Miss McEvoy. If we have any more news I'll call you straight away on this number.'

'. . . Oh . . . yes. All right. Yes. Thanks. Goodbye, then.'

'Goodbye.'

He hung up. He sat thinking a moment. She was by no means a fool. Like himself she had strong doubts whether Jamie was going to show up as easily as that.

Sally wondered what game the two men were playing. They were walking through the bushes at the edge of the grass. She watched them through the window. It seemed a silly game. She liked hers better. She shook Mr Anthony up to make him move again. Mr Anthony was a creepy-crawlie. She had found him near the swings. She had put him in the little tube she'd found as well. It wasn't glass but you could see right through it so she had put him in it. She had put in some dirt and a leaf so he would feel at home and have some food. It was a good thing to put things in.

She shook the plastic phial to the full bent of her just four-year-old ability. She stopped and held it still. Mr Anthony was not moving any more. He was rolled up in a little tiny ball. He had gone bye-byes.

She yawned. With no real sense of time, she did not know that it was well past her bedtime. It was her body telling her that she was tired. And thirsty. She wanted a drinkie.

Sucking the thumb of the hand clutching her fragment of blanket comforter she left the darkening playroom. In her other hand she tightly held the phial containing the dirt and the dead ant.

⚜⚜⚜⚜

'He's a great hider,' Chris said. He shivered. The sun had set. The waning of the light was summoning a cool breeze.

'How do you know?' Robert said.

'Oh. I know. Bitter experience. You take my word for it.'

The two of them had checked the garage, the garden shed, the tumble-down greenhouse and gone thoroughly through the not very extensive shrubbery. Quite to no point.

'But why out here?' Robert wanted to know. 'There's no logic in it.'

'No logic, no. That's your department. But I thought he might be indulging in psychological warfare.'

'Oh.'

Chris wondered if Robert was miffed. Had he suggested that to be logical was to be a smarty-pants? Christ, he must stop analysing every remark down to the last syllable. It's your job, Charlie, an inner voice said.

'You're right,' he said to take the curse off it. *'Tu as raison.* Thanks for the assistance of your strong right arm.'

'Oh, it was nothing, logically speaking,' Robert said.

'How did Grandad look?'

'Pretty good, actually. He says he's cutting down on smoking.'

'Hmmn!'

'You know what time I went to bed there?'

'Don't tell me.'

'I saw—'

'And more to the point don't tell your mother.'

Father and son walked back towards the house and for a moment the boy was smiling fondly.

'I'll have to call the police in on it,' the father said. 'Damn!'

⚜⚜⚜⚜

It felt lonely without Jamie, Donnie was reckoning to himself. It was funny. Now he had their room all to himself it seemed a lot smaller. And it was hard to read his magazine. He kept expecting the door to open and that made him keep looking up. Word all over the house was Jamie had scarpered. Had to be. Half his gear was gone. Well, he wouldn't get far. Mug's game that was. You got soaked, starving, freezing. Your feet hurt. You got so tired you went to sleep on benches. Dirty men came after you. He should know. He'd found out for himself the hard way. A mug's game. Jamie'd soon be back and pretending to be sorry but glad as underneath. Unless he got hurt. Killed, even.

Donnie looked up quickly. He didn't like the thought of that. Jamie was all right. He'd talk when you felt like speaking, shut up when you felt like keeping quiet. He didn't ask questions all the time. And he'd be all right. He was tough, Jamie, smart. Him and his army tricks. . . .

Donnie went back to the three closely printed columns on Peter Barnes.

The door handle rattled as all along he'd known it would. He looked up again. It wasn't Jamie. It was Mr Langley and Bill Hutton.

'Hello, Donnie,' Mr Langley said.

' 'Lo,' Donnie said. He swung his legs round and sat on the edge of the bed. Fuzz time. They looked like they meant business.

'Like to have a little talk, Donnie,' Mr Langley said.

'I don't know anything,' Donnie said.

He said it too fast and too up-tight. He knew it and he knew that they knew it.

'Not that sort of a talk, Donnie,' Mr Langley said. 'Something a bit more man to man, I hope. We're a bit worried about Jamie and I think you might be able to help us to help him.'

'Right,' Donnie said. 'Fine.'

Hell, Chris Langley thought, I didn't get through to him. I'm off on the wrong foot.

'Anyone been bullying him? Anything like that?' he said.

Donnie shook his head. His eyes were following Bill Hutton. Bill Hutton was opening up Jamie's cupboard and going through his things. Cheek. Fucking cheek.

'Was he looking forward to going out with his sister the other day?' Mr Langley was saying.

Donnie made his face go fixed.

'Was he, Donnie?'

Better answer that.

'Reckon,' he said.

'He likes her, doesn't he?'

'Reckon.'

'I'm asking you. Does he?'

'Yeah.'

'Did he ever talk about his sister's boyfriend?'

Sod them. What business of theirs was it?'

'Come on, Donnie.'

Chris sat down opposite the boy on the room's one chair.

'Can't remember.'

Can't remember. Dunno.

Chris tried not to show his impatience. How many times, O Lord! how many? Slaves to the hollow mystique of standing together against 'them' and not grassing, the have-nots, the victims and the villains all offered up the worn token of 'Dunno' to propitiate their stupid, purblind sense of honour. And always, in the thick of your annoyance, part of your mind admired them for their loyalty.

'Donnie,' he said. 'Listen carefully. I'm not out to go for Jamie. I'm not out to throw the book at him when he comes back. But I am worried about him. If you're his friend you will be too. He could have had an accident. He could be lying somewhere hurt. People on the run do silly things. He could've got mixed up with some bad company. People who will harm him. You're old enough to know what I mean. But I'm not sure Jamie is. You know the army was the only thing he ever thought about.'

Donnie considered the man sitting opposite him. He was pretty fair most ways most of the time. It was just that his own dad had always said that when they were friendliest was when they were most out to drop you in it. His mum had said his dad always dropped his own self in it and never had no-one but himself to blame for it all. Funny how Mr Langley's mind had been running on the same lines about Jamie as his own. He'd found out what he'd found out about all that the hard way.

'He didn't like the boy-friend much,' he said.

Thank God, Chris thought. Another small victory for reason. And a giant step for Donnie.

'His haversack's gone, Mr Hutton,' Donnie said. 'Half his clothes. He had some chocolate. He had a bit of money, too.'

'How much?'

'Don't know. Not much I shouldn't think.'

'Did he give you any idea where he might possibly go off to?'

The boy shook his head.

'No, sir,' he said. 'Honest. I'd tell you if I knew.'

222

Coming in from the cold (I'm the boy who came in from the cold, he had thought to himself, I get shot in the end so I can't sit down), Robert had made a cup of tea to warm himself up. Partly for the same reason and partly because there wasn't too much of it after their 'evening breakfast', he had washed up the dinner things. Resigned to the fate of an evening in after all, and not uninfluenced by the fact she was a game up on him, he had inveigled his mother back to *Mastermind*. But for the moment, she was on the phone. Three guesses what about. He stared at the game with impatience contained but less than gracious.

'She's still on thyroid hormone and estrogens,' his mother was saying. 'No. I don't think it is . . . the purple patches are spreading. . . .'

Must be a Martian patient. Or something rather nasty.

'. . . you think? . . . Well, she's your patient.'

But it's her funeral.

'. . . . No, not very. . . . All right, John. See you in the morning. Glad you had a good holiday.'

His mother hung up. Holiday! Yes, he had heard there was such a word.

'Home sweet home,' he said as his mother came back to the problem he'd set her.

'Sorry,' she said.

'Dad loses one of his cons. and you're on the phone losing a patient.'

'First time it's rung like that for ages.'

'Great.'

'And I'm not losing a patient. I've been saving someone else's.'

'Someone back from his holidays. Crete, was it? Or just France?'

Pat flashed her son a sharp look.

'Stop yacking and let me think,' she let it rest at that.

He gave her a few moments grace. But a niggling resentment was turning in him.

'Know what Grandad says?' it made him say. 'He says we ought to have a house of our own. Separate.'

'Oh yes?'

'He doesn't think it's right us living here on top of the kids. Literally.'

Ignoring the game, Pat again looked at her son.

'And where is this fine new place he's buying for us?' she said.

'Are we so broke?'

'Yes. One reason we're broke if you recall is that your French is so bloody rotten we're saving up to send you on school exchange next term.'

He had the grace to blush.

'Sorry,' Pat said. 'Didn't mean to seem that holier than thou.'

Love Story got it all wrong, she thought. It's all about always having to say sorry.

'My fault,' Robert mumbled. 'I did rather see us all going off somewhere, though.'

'Thank you, kind sir. But a financial case of pigs might fly, this year.'

'Also, I'd got quite keen on the idea of seeing this film tonight.'

'Me too. But your father's batting average on break outs from the Big House hasn't been so hot this past week.'

She looked at Robert.

'He's too worried for me to have enjoyed it,' she said.

'He never seems that worried.'

'It's his strength. And his weakness, did he but know it. He'll end up with an ulcer yet.'

'At least he's first in the queue for the doctor. Hey – wait a minute! I've just made a connection. Dad said the kid who's gone missing was good at hiding.'

'Jamie McEvoy? Yes. He's the one fixated on the army and war games.'

'Fixated?'

'Obsessed.'

'Oh. Anyway there's the answer, isn't it?'

'To what?'

'Getting him back. You just put the word around all those immoral army recruiting offices you see all over the place and wait for him to show up trying to join up.'

'He couldn't. He's too young. He wouldn't try.'

But she was looking at her son with opened, thoughtful eyes.

'He might at that though,' she went on. 'Robert – you just might have been kissed by genius.'

'I'd have settled for Jacqueline Bisset,' he surprised himself by saying and hurried on in a vain attempt to slide the remark by before his mother noticed.

'Just my logical mind, really,' he said. 'I even know what Isaac Newton's favourite chocolates were.'

'What?'

'Toblerone. I'll prove it to you when we've saved up enough to afford a pound note.'

✠ ✠ ✠ ✠

'I'll buy you a cup of tea, Chris,' Bill had said. He had just come back from formally notifying the police of Jamie's departure.

'You're on,' Chris said.

He would rather have had a cup upstairs with his family but he wanted to make doubly sure he had blunted the faint edge of any responsibility Bill might be feeling for Jamie's running off.

They had gone down to the kitchen. Using not the big iron tea-pot but one of the small chipped china ones, Bill had done the honours.

'Let it mash a moment longer,' he said.

In pursuit of one of his very occasional cigarettes, he slapped at the pockets of his sports jacket. He took out a packet of Three Fives.

'Funny how things change with Time,' he said. 'All the go these were when I was a kid and now some say that every cigarette you get through's five minutes of your natural going up in smoke. . . . Oh well, right now that doesn't seem like too much of a bad deal.'

He lit up, inhaled smoke and blew it quickly out.

'Precious little chance he'll make a bee-line for the sister then,' he said.

Chris shook his head.

'Not on current form.'

'Nor, on past history, the mother,' Bill said.

He poured the tea, helped Chris to a cup.

'Forgotten the sugar,' he said.

He got up from the table where at random they had sat and went towards the cupboards at the end of the big empty-seeming room.

'Hello . . .' he said.

He had stooped and picked up something off the floor. He was examining it.

'What is it?' Chris asked.

'A chemist's thing,' Bill said. 'No, not a packet of three. A tube. One of the kids has filled it up with dirt and stuff. There's a dead insect in here too. Bloody little sadist. Question is what was in it originally.'

He was turning the phial round in his hand.

'Oh Christ!' he said.

'What?'

'*Mrs Newman*,' he read. '*The Tablets: to be taken as prescribed.*'

⚜⚜⚜⚜

The open line might have stretched to the bottom of the sea or out into the fathomless spaces between the stars. A faint wash of sound seemed to undulate towards him the length of an infinite cylindrical corridor. Sea-shells held against your ear. Mummy, mummy, I can hear the sea. But it was only the sound of the blood pounding in your ears. Blood, the sound of time dripping away.

He heard the 'clop' of footsteps at last returning. He had a sudden, sharply exact vision of the Newman's wood parquet flooring. He recalled David's bench-made leather shoes. There was that knock-about, grinding, bakelite sound of somebody picking up a telephone receiver from a table.

'Still there?'

Of course he was, the idiot. Even through the narrow frequency response of the phone David Newman's top person's voice still contrived to be only one suave step the right side of sufferance.

'Still here,' he contented himself with saying.

'Sorry to be so long but I think we've homed in on which one it is. Are you sitting down?'

'Just tell me.'

'You've hit on Jenny's Achilles' heel. Among other things, these days, Miss Jenny she don't sleep so good. The—'

'David, for Christ's sake! What were they?'

'All right, all right. Keep your hair on. Pinkies.'

'What?'

'Soneryl.'

Oh, Jesus. He felt his stomach lurch as his throat tightened.

'How many?'

'Jenny can't be sure. But she thinks quite a few. As she knocks them back like you and I do wine gums, I'd say you'd better figure twenty minimum. Enough for what you're thinking.'

Enough. Oh, Jesus.

'David,' he said, 'would you have any idea which kids used your bathroom—'

'You're joking, old chap. They all went ape over the shower. I could've sold tickets.'

'David, this really is an emergency. Could you please try to remember which—'

'I appreciate the emergency as much as you do, old chap. And if there's anything I can do I'll be over with bells on. But I honestly don't have the faintest idea who went upstairs and who didn't. And before you do your pieces at my expense, perhaps I can just remind you that if little fingers had been taught to keep themselves to themselves, you wouldn't have—'

'You don't think that point hasn't been well and truly lodged in my gut from the off, do you,' Chris said. 'I'm as much—'

'Sorry. But I did want to make clear—'

'Point taken and you're not to blame. Blame it all you

like on the delinquents and their inadequate mentors! Now if you'll excuse me I've a life or two to try and save!'

'Chris. I—'

But Chris Langley was snapping the phone savagely back down on to its cradle.

'Sod him!' he said.

'What were they?' Pat asked.

'Soneryl. Minimum of twenty.'

Without changing expression her face registered alarm. Inconsequentially he was thinking how, a few dented cushions out of place, books littering the floor, the ironing board up, the cheap and cheerful livability of the flat had instantly degenerated into tattiness. Sod Newman's worry about responsibility and, no doubt, law-suits.

For no reason he paced to their all purpose table. He swung around on Pat.

'It's all so bloody easy!' he said.

'What is?'

'The repeat prescription! Sleeping pills like wine gums – that's what he said. What's yours? Same again, old boy? Cheers. If it moves, give it a pill. If it doesn't give it one anyway. The magic pill. Keeps everyone happy. Fob off the patient, the hypochondriac more like, and he's happy. The doctors are happy because—'

'Doctor.'

'Huh?'

He blinked. As his feelings had come sprawling incoherently out he had all but forgotten his wife's presence. But she was stolidly confronting him.

'Doctor in the singular,' she said. 'I prescribed those pills.'

He blinked again. Of course! That's how he had met Newman again. Through Jenny going to Pat. He'd completely forgotten. He wondered if he were the more aghast at the closing up of the circle of irony or at the enormity of his insensitivity toward Pat. Yet what difference did that coincidence make? His point was no less basically true. It was better to have it out, to vent his spleen while his indignation was fired and genuine. He tried to have the courage of his convictions.

'Well that really is rich!' he continued.

'The woman has problems – she can't sleep.'

'I didn't think she had gangrene of the left earlobe! We've all got problems.'

'Hers are specific. The pills will help her.'

'Would have. They won't help the poor little—'

'Will. I shall, of course, be prescribing her some more.'

'Great. Really great. Hail to the future and a species who can't sleep without pills, can't wake without them. Pills, it'll have to make it eat. Pills to move its bowels. Pills to stop them moving! Pills to finish—'

'Chris! Stop being so juvenile. For Christ's sake!'

Normally she would have let his self-righteous anger with her profession wear itself out. It never took long for him to return to reason. But now there was not even time for that.

'When you've quite finished,' she went on as if he had, 'there are two things I would point out to you. The first—'

'Why—'

'The first is that you just said something about saving a child's life. If it's going to turn out to be a case of doing just that, there's no time for you to waste standing there doing your "My God, why have I been forsaken" bit.'

She saw him blink again. The emotion went out of his face and eyes. One more time she was able to respect the way the man she loved would master his own feelings in the performance of his endless task.

'Quite right, of course,' he said. 'Sorry. Newman was blasé to the point of being totally insufferable. But that's no excuse . . . . Let's just think a moment before we go riding furiously off in all directions. . . .'

'Can I make a suggestion?'

'Of course.'

'The tinies are the ones we should worry about first. The older ones will have an idea what they've got their hands on. A tiny will have thought they were just Smarties.'

229

'Right. You and I will do a round of their beds – check they're all breathing normally, pulse is regular. Bill can question the older ones.'

'Fine. We've got one thing going for us.'

'What's that?'

'The pills will be very bitter if chewed or sucked like sweets. It would take pretty determined and perverse taste-buds to persevere with them.'

Chris Langley smiled wanly.

'I don't know about doctors in the singular,' he said, 'but there are certainly times when it's good to have a doctor in the house.'

He moved to the door and she followed.

'Did you say there were two things,' he said. He held the door for her.

'Yes,' Pat said, 'Robert had a first rate idea on what Jamie McEvoy may have taken it into his head to try and do.'

⚜⚜⚜

The children of eleven or older had not gone to bed yet. They were mainly watching television. Bill marched into the room and without preamble, to a howled chorus of protests, switched off the set.

'What you have to go and—'

'Sorry,' he said crisply, 'but something's happened. There's no need for anyone here to be alarmed but it is serious. Kevin, Gary would you go up and ask all the over elevens who aren't here to come down. Eileen – I think we'd better ask Miss Raeburn to join us too. Kevin, make sure you ask Donnie, will you?'

'Yes, sir.'

Wendy arrived and took up a position against a wall just behind Bill.

'Might just need a mother figure,' he turned to her to say, 'I suppose all this has ruined your evening.'

It had but Wendy merely shrugged.

'Par for the course, I suppose,' she said.

She had just telephoned Ronnie to explain the crisis.

230

He'd contrived to say he understood without sounding the least bit sympathetic. No, if she had her hands full it would probably be as well if he kept right away and out from underfoot. Too many chiefs, you know. If she thought she really ought to be on hand at Kingston House, then, fine: no problem. But, if she didn't mind, he'd not come over. He'd call her Tuesday or Wednesday. O.K.?

Wendy had said O.K. She had realised while they were speaking that when she might see Ronnie next was rapidly becoming the very least of her concerns.

Donnie was the last to arrive. He squatted down on the end of the semi-circle of children facing Bill. A sense of occasion had descended upon them. Although they had been talking in low, intense voices among themselves, they had been remarkably patient. They had not beseiged Bill with a battery of 'what's happened, sir?' questions. Perhaps they were instinctively prolonging a situation they now preferred to television.

Bill took the phial out of his pocket.

'This shouldn't take too long, I hope,' he said. 'But it is important. You see this phial or tube or bottle or whatever you want to call it?'

He held it up.

'It came from the house where some of you went swimming today. Anybody know anything about it?'

Faces less curious now than faintly hostile blankly looked back at him.

'Now it's not a question of thieving,' he said. I'm sure the tube was brought back by accident. It could be a lot more serious than thieving, though, for someone. This tube had sleeping tablets in it. Strong ones. About twenty. I think you all know that if anybody takes that many tablets all at once, there's a good chance they can die. They're like poison then. There were twenty tablets in here when it left that house. There weren't any when it was found in the dining room here. We're very worried one of the young kids might have thought the pills were sweeties and swallowed the lot. If you know anything about how they've got here you must tell us.'

Bill had kept his voice steady and matter-of-fact so as to avoid any panic. I've overdone it, he thought, they just think it's a trick to get them to grass. He looked around the crescent of faces. Eyes flicked away from his with nervous resentment or truculently determined to stare him out. Nothing.

'Did I make myself quite clear,' he said. 'This really could be a matter of life or death. Someone could be dying at this moment. I promise you − no-one's going to be punished. And it's not a question of sneaking or grassing on a mate any more, is it? It's a matter of life or death.'

Nothing.

'Donnie?' Bill said. 'Lucy? You were both there. Did you see anything? Anything at all?'

Lucille Wyatt quickly shook her head. So did Donnie.

'Just don't know, sir,' he said. 'Not covering up. Just don't know.'

They're both old enough and responsible enough to have spoken up if they did know anything, Bill thought. Maybe I should tackle them one by one in isolation. Take all night though.

'Listen,' he heard himself saying, 'I want to tell you something. Something that once happened to me. It's a true story.'

He took a breath.

'One or two of you may know this already but most of you, I think, don't but I was brought up in a home like Kingston House myself.'

If he'd announced he was lawful heir to the throne of England he could hardly have created more of a silent sensation. Their hostility was gone. An astonished interest had replaced it.

'It was up north,' he said, 'where I lived when I was a kid. It wasn't such a nice place as this in my opinion. It was cold, unfriendly . . . food was rotten. But, as you can tell from looking at me, it was a long time ago. . . .'

'I had a mate. His name was Jerry. He hated the place. He hated it a lot more than I did. One day he came to me and said he was going to run away. He was making plans.

232

He'd saved up food. He was going to go over the Moors and get a job in a mill. A wool mill that is. You could get jobs when you were quite young in those days. If you could find one at all.

'I said I'd go with him. It was a good game. Making plans. Drawing maps. He'd wait for it to rain hard, he said, because that would put the dogs off his scent. He thought he was going to be hunted like a convict, you see.

'Well . . . the more I thought about it, the more I didn't really fancy doing it. I didn't really think we'd get away. And they'd told me I could perhaps start helping in the home. In the end I told Jerry I wasn't going to do it. He told me he'd only been joking anyway? Just pretending, if you know what I mean.'

He paused, looking round them again. Bloody Jackanory isn't in it, he thought. Every one of them was hanging on his every word.

'Next thing I knew,' he went on, 'we were all being called together. Just like you are now? It was pouring with rain outside. It was in the winter. They told us Jerry had done a bunk. They asked us if anyone knew anything about it.'

Bill paused and looked at them again.

'Well, I didn't say a thing, did I?' he said. 'He was my mate and you don't grass on your mates, do you? They said if anybody knew anything he should speak up because it was freezing outside and Jerry could be in trouble. I still didn't though. I could have very easily, you see, because I knew all his plans. But I didn't. I reckoned he would have trusted me not to.

'Well,' Bill said, 'they found him soon enough. Five days it took them. Only it wasn't really soon enough because they found him dead. He'd frozen to death out on the Moors. They said he'd have got very weak and then taken perhaps a day or more to die of exposure. If I'd spoken up, they would have found him in plenty of time.'

Bill swallowed.

'While I'm giving away secrets,' he said, 'I may as well tell you another one. I'm fifty-nine years old. I was thirteen

233

then. I can tell you in all truth that a day hasn't gone by in all those forty-six years when I haven't thought about Jerry and felt bad. It was my fault he died. I got things the wrong way round. I wouldn't want any of you to have that sort of feeling for the rest of your lives.'

He stopped speaking. Once more he looked around the semi-circle. Once more nothing. No hand raised. No face—

'Please, sir, I saw Sally with that tube, sir.'

Thank God!

'Sally B or Sally J, Rupert?'

'Sally B, sir.'

The round black face had contrived to look pale at the enormity of this public deed. The voice was little above a thick whisper.

'Where, Rupert? Where did you see her?'

'By the swings, sir.'

'Are you sure?'

Rupert was only just eleven. During Bill's story his saucer-eyes had been as solemnly rapt as anyone's. He nodded now.

'Yes, sir. I asked her to give it me.'

'But she wouldn't?'

'No, sir. Said it was hers.'

'Did she say how she got it?'

'No, sir.'

Bill turned to Wendy.

'She wasn't one of the swimming party,' he said. 'Better go and tell—'

'Please, sir,' Rupert said, 'there wasn't anything in the tube. It was empty. She said she wanted it to put things in.'

Bill nodded at Wendy.

'I'll be there too in just a moment,' he said as she made for the door.

'Thank you, Rupert,' he said, 'you've been very sensible and very helpful. A big help.'

Rupert flashed a quick grin of dubious pleasure at the

234

praise then dropped his head. Bill stooped and switched the television back on.

'Sorry to break into the film,' he said, 'but it was important. You carry on watching now, those of you who want to.'

Donnie had got up to leave the room. Bill was hard on his heels but as he began to nod his thanks to the boy for remembering to hold the door for him, Gary and Kevin had pushed themselves in front of him.

They exchanged a knowing glance. Gary, it seemed, had lost the toss and had to do the talking.

'Here,' he said confidently, 'that story you just told us. You made it all up, didn't you? It was just made up to con us. The old soft soap stuff, weren't it?'

Kevin returned his sideways smirk. Bill suddenly found their teenage cocksureness a little less than lovely.

'It was quite true,' he said. 'And he was my brother.'

He shouldn't have said that just to wipe smiles off two unthinking faces. It was too late now but he glanced back into the room to see who else had overheard him. Lucille Wyatt was looking at him with shocked and thoughtful eyes.

⚜⚜⚜⚜

They had had to wake Sally up. She was out like a light and a long time surfacing to anything like consciousness. Wendy, her nerves stretched crucial degrees beyond everyday commonsense, felt a wave of panic washing hysterically through her. The sleep was much too deep to be natural! If a child that size had taken twenty tablets. . . . She pushed forward to the tiny bedside to try and shake some life back into her.

'Let her take her time, Wendy,' Chris said. 'She'll be no use frightened out of her wits.'

As if at his voice the little girl's huge eyes opened an instant. They closed. Opened. When they were able to stay more steadily open than shut Chris held the phial suddenly out in front of her. She reached for it at once.

'Mine,' she said.

Chris exchanged a quick glance with Bill.

'Sally,' he said slowly, 'where did you find it, love?'

'Mine,' Sally said, 'Mr Anthony. Gone bye-byes.'

She yawned. Wendy picked her up.

'Cuddle time,' she said.

'Cuddle time,' said Sally. She put her arms round Wendy's neck.

'Sally, can you remember? I bet you can't. How did you get this little bottle?'

'Boy gave it me,' Sally said immediately.

'Which boy, Sally?'

'Soldier boy.'

Now all three adults exchanged looks.

'We search the house again,' Chris Langley said. 'This time we look into the smallest places a kid Jamie's size could possibly crawl into.'

'Sssh, Sally, go back to sleep now, ssh,' Wendy said. 'Everything's all right. Ssssh. . . .'

Chapter Fifteen

ANOTHER MONDAY. START of another working week. Life in Kingston House must move along. Once more he sat in his office staring at a cup of coffee on his desk.

Life in Kingston House was moving on. But outside in what, in moments of depression he thought of as the real world, life might have ended that past night for Jamie McEvoy. He might be curled up in a ball and dead in some niche of a bricked railway embankment. His already bloating body could be swinging just beneath the water's dirty surface on a Thames tide. He might be lying prone like Lester Chapman, face buried in the filth of an open sewer . . . . Oh come on! His thoughts were worse than morbid. They were obstructive. There was work to be done. Kingston House was as much a part of reality, the real world, as anywhere.

So he told himself. But he remained not moving, staring at the umpteen thousandth cup of coffee a little right of centre on his desk. Sunlight was hypnotically streaming down onto the completely motionless circle of dark brown liquid to find no place to reflect on to. As it grew too cold to drink he sat watching the coffee absorb the sunlight until, at last, a knock on the door roused him back to the routine.

'Come in.'

It was Lucille Wyatt. Ah yes, routine. The never-quite-the-same routine. Life at Kingston House went on.

'Sit down, Lucille. Wendy said you wanted to see me.'

'Yes, Mr Langley.'

'What was it about?'

'Well, Mr Langley . . . I was thinking. . . . Last night I got to thinking. . . .'

Hesitation. They all hesitated. He could measure out his life in hesitations as well as coffee cups.

'I was wondering if I could stay here. Permanent. Stay here and work.'

Oh dear. She'd got around to it more quickly than did most of them.

'I'm leaving school any day now, aren't I? And I mean – well with what my . . . my father's said . . . I ain't got – I don't have no place to go anywhere else. You'd have to find me somewhere else anyway, wouldn't you?'

There was truth in that.

'I don't think your father is necessarily going to have it all his own way in court,' he said.

'He can for all I care!'

That was her pain talking. But it would take time for that adolescent wound to heal. For several years now her home would be no answer for her. Even if she lived there in a cold war, her chance to find herself, evolve into some kind of genuinely fulfilled person, would be mindlessly corroded down to bitter ashes.

'So what would you do here?' he said.

'Help.'

'How. What kind of help?'

'Well . . . help. Help help, I suppose.'

'Like helping Wendy bath the little ones.'

Her face lit up.

'Yes,' she said.

He shook his head and the hope went out of her.

'But Mr Hutton said he was in a home once. There's that Howard here all the time! And Mrs Wilson says she needs someone to replace that old . . . that other woman.'

'You're too young for me to turn you into a fetcher and carrier for the rest of your life,' he said. 'Too bright. Yes. You are. Oh, certainly, we can badly do with another pair of hands round here. Several. But it would be a waste of you.'

'But I'd like it!'

He sighed.

'You know,' he said. 'I've seen quite a lot of girls like you. More than you'd think. There's always a moment when they come and see me and say what you've just said. Word for word.'

Stubbornness alone made her stick to her guns.

'Don't see why that makes it wrong for me,' she said. 'In any case, I'm soon going to be free to do it, aren't I? Available.'

He reached down and behind him to a pile of thick manilla files stacked less than tidily on the floor.

'Listen,' he said. 'These are case histories. The sort of thing, sort of people, you'd be dealing with. All the time. Every moment of your waking day.'

He riffled through a file.

'Melvin,' he read. 'Five-and-a-half. Jamaican. Illegitimate. Mother rejected him. Placed with foster parents. He half tore their home apart. Would do things like defecate – crap – in wardrobes. They've given him the bullet. He's now a candidate for Special Education.

'Modlin. Sixteen. Your age. Both parents mental. Both in institutions. She has a heart condition. She's not expected to live past twenty.'

Lucille blinked.

'Willie,' Chris went on. 'Twelve. Irish. Mother living with another man. He attempted suicide. Refused to go home from hospital afterwards. We took him into care. The mother appealed against the Care Order. She attacked the social worker involved. A case of eight stitches.

'Faith. Nine. Very small for her age. Battered time and time again by her parents. Doesn't realise they're not married . . . at least not to each other. . . .'

He stared hard at Lucille as, crestfallen, she looked at him.

'Now,' he said, 'be honest. How would you set about helping children like that? Some older than you.'

'I . . . I'd be kind,' she managed at last.

She had said it simply and meant it. She was really a very nice girl. Her basic decency had made the hair on the back of his neck stand up. But it was too simple. He must not get unprofessionally sentimental.

'Kindness just isn't enough,' he said. 'That sounds hard

239

but it's true. It isn't all jolly times giving nice little girls a bath as if you were playing with dolls. When you're being run ragged, day after day, minute after minute, kindness runs out. You'd be surprised how soon. You need something to back it up and keep you going. Training!'

He quite deliberately had shot the last word at her.

'Well . . . couldn't I get some?' she said slowly. 'I mean' like where do you go?'

'University,' he brusquely said.

'Oh,' she said.

That, as he intended, had been the body blow. Her face at once betrayed she recognised he'd spoken of another world. It had not suited his present purpose to tell her that of staff working in homes such as Kingston House, only one in five were qualified.

'Oh,' she said again.

But he had misjudged her. She had not quite been knocked out. She still had a token resistance left.

'What about learning on the job?' she said. 'Boy down our road's a mechanic. He did a sandwich course, they call it, at Woolwich—'

'Have you just taken you 'O' levels?' he cut her short with.

'No. C.S.E.'s.'

'Going to be any good?'

She just shook her head.

'You see,' he said. 'Polytechnics and so on won't take you just because you want to go. They expect some qualifications, don't they? To show willing. And that isn't so unreasonable.'

'But I didn't know!'

They all say that, he thought. Sooner or later they all say that.

'It's not bloody fair!' Frustration had made her indignant, passionate.

'If you won't help me, then no-one's going to!' she said.

True, probably. Certainly. It came to him that, con sciously or not, she was aware that she had stumbled up to perhaps the major cross-roads of her life and it was the knowledge that this was literally what she was pleading for – her life – that fed her passion.

'Suppose I stay on at school,' she said suddenly. 'I mean, you could talk to him. Bugger all he'd care now. I mean I'd take it seriously this time!'

His head came up. He had realised that she might have saved herself.

'Would you be prepared to do that?' he said.

'Of course! Now I know—'

'I've a better idea,' he said. 'Between your father and the exam results you seem to think you've managed, staying on at school won't be the easiest thing in the world to arrange, I fancy. But there are places where you could take some 'O' levels as a part-time and outside student. If or when you got them you'd be able to go on to 'A' levels and so on.'

He realised she was literally holding her breath. He stopped speaking until she had exhaled, breathed in again.

'We're talking about a long, long time,' he said, 'but—'

'Oh; I wouldn't mind that!' she exclaimed.

'Yes, you would. Sooner or later. We all mind things that seem to be going on for ever. The important thing is to be able to make yourself keep on when part of you just wants to curl up and go to sleep.'

He had a sudden vision of Jamie McEvoy stretched out pathetically thin on a mortuary slab.

'But it's not easy,' he said. 'It's hard. Very hard.'

'If I could have a chance, I could try. I never have tried properly about anything, I know. But I can see now it would be terrible not to have tried about something once.'

And he believed she meant that too.

'I can talk to your headmistress,' he said. 'I know her well, of course, because my own son goes there too.'

'Yes, I met—'

'And because of my job I do know various education people in the district. . . .'

He sat there a moment trying to put the possibilities into some kind of working pattern. Without intending to he was all but torturing her.

'. . . what would . . . how would it work?' she said.

'What we might be able to do is give you a job here. You could live here, help Mrs Wilson, help Wendy Raeburn and so on. And we could release you a couple of days a week to do some 'O' levels somewhere as an outside student.'

Her face had become so ecstatic that he felt embarrassed at the closeness he seemed to have achieved to playing God.

'I'll have to check on your exact status as a school-leaver,' he said to take her down again. 'And I warn you – you'll get paid next to nothing.'

'Oh, that wouldn't—'

'No new clothes every month. None of the latest gear. And the other stuff – the stripping routine. The slightest suggestion of that or anything stupid with the older boys here and, well, you'll have blown it.'

It was the most he had ever seen her smile.

'Don't look like I'll have the time,' she said.

⚜⚜⚜

The Army Careers Information Office at the top end of Blackheath Village was conducting a blitz on the cadet front. Deployed across the bottom of the window display was a complex arrangement of Airfix tanks and personnel carriers supported by several score of the same manufacturer's infantry. They seemed bent on advancing not only to take the papier-mâché high ground to the left of the window but also to reinforce the proposition that life with the Professionals was just an extension of good, clean, simple, schoolboy fun. It was all fun, the window implied, in the South East London Army Cadet Force. You could wear these brightly coloured hard hats. You could run around calling up your mates on this only just totally obsolete wireless transceiver. Until you read the small print, the window seemed to promise you that, once with SELACF, you could drive tanks, pilot helicopters, fire bazookas. Not given as he is to reading or comprehending small print it was a display well calculated to capture the imagination of the averagely raised British youngster.

The papier-mâché hills were to the left as you pressed your nose against the window and looked in from outside.

That's what the lad on the pavement was doing as, yawning, Sergeant Thomas Nicholson looked up from the racing pages of 'The Mirror'. St Petersburg ought to trot up against that lot, he was thinking, won't be worth doing though. . . .

There was an intensity about the expression on the face of the boy outside that interrupted the form of his habitual early morning speculations. Well, the shop, as he always thought of it, was the world's deadliest bore.

'Careful how you look, Stan,' he said, 'but by the look on that kid outside's boat I'd say we were about to start the week with yer actual cadet enrolment.'

Sergeant Stanley Edwards came casually out of the tiny inner office where he was in the process of brewing up. He was a younger man than Nicholson. The glance he gave in the direction of the window as he crossed to the desk seemed no more than cursory.

'You just could be right at that, my son,' he said. 'But the question I ask myself is what's a kid that age doing hanging around here at this time of a going-to-school day. He's never left, has he? Does answer the description we got too, such as it was.'

'Well, you took it down, didn't you?' Nicholson said. 'I never really looked at it.'

And we bloody well know why too, don't we, Edwards thought, glancing down at the newspaper.

'Reckon it's him?' Nicholson said.

'I think so. If he comes in get him talking. I'll have a listen from the back. If it seems it is I'll get the nick on the other blower.'

'You could be right at—'

'Watch it! Here he comes.'

He raised his voice as, the boy nervously approaching the desk, he himself strolled casually away.

'We could go all the way to the Royal Tournament this year,' he improvised.

The boy meanwhile had reached Nicholson. The Sergeant looked up as if taking in his presence properly for the first time and smiled.

'You're bright and early today,' he said. 'What can we do for you?'

'I want to sign up,' Jamie McEvoy said.

'Cadets?'

'No. Regulars. 42nd Commandos.'

'Ah! Nothing but the best, eh? Well, we like people who know their own minds. How old are you, then?'

'Seventeen.'

Like I'm Princess Anne and Colonel of the Regiment, Sergeant Nicholson thought. Something of the mental reaction must have shown in his coarse fat face.

'Next birthday,' the boy was blushingly blurting out by way of qualification.

Looked like Stan was right. Nicholson pretended to believe the little bugger.

'I see. Oh, well, fine. No problem there,' he said. 'First thing we have to do is clear some of the old paperwork out the way. Go in for a bit of the old form-bashing, if you follow me. Name, rank and serial number sort of stuff.'

He raised his voice a touch as he heard the clink of the phone in the inner office being lifted.

'Takes a bit of a while, I'm afraid,' he said, 'but once we've got it all down, we've got you for good.'

'Now – first of all your name.'

Chapter Sixteen

THE POLICE STATION was small and old in a brick-built Victorian way. If you were not a member of the force, there was nowhere private to talk in. The cramped reception area seemed too near the open street door and the comings and goings of the desk sergeant for comfort. Anyone might come in and hear you just when you least wanted them to. . . .

Patricia McEvoy and Chris Langley stood facing each other halfway down the short corridor that led to the interview rooms. The corridor seemed tired and bored as if its scuffed green walls had seen it all so many times before it really didn't want to know any more, thanks all the same. Its air seemed stale and second-hand, the light thick and faded. It was like being under oily water. The building's like the police themselves, Chris thought, it can no longer enjoy the luxury of feelings. Like I ought to be, he added to himself.

Opposite him, pert, defensive in a mild, matter-of-fact way, Jamie's sister was shrugging.

'I say things like "I blame myself" to myself,' she was saying, 'but I'm honestly not sure that's true. . . . I just told him – I'm damned if I understand him.'

'It takes a while,' Chris said. 'Particularly inside families.'

She darted him a quick Cockney smile.

'It takes for bloody ever,' she said.

'He's just told me he's "sorry",' Chris said. 'I chose to think he means that.'

Once again Patricia McEvoy shrugged her boyish shoulders.

'Sorry,' she said, '—I'm not sure I know what that word means any more. If it means anything. . . . He tried to burn down a shop. He says he's "sorry". He says nothing else of any account about it but, he's sorry. Then it's the police, the courts, the home . . . each time he tells me "he's sorry"'

Now he does a bunk off that gets nowhere. Once again they're coming round and getting onto me and I feel such a fool and like it's me done something and I get to thinking where's it going to stop. . . . "Sorry" doesn't really mean anything any more, does it?'

She grimaced ruefully.

'Especially when it's another day's wages down the drain,' she said.

You couldn't say her point of view was that unreasonable, Chris thought.

'He's just had a little bit more to say for himself than that,' he said. 'In between mouthfuls.'

'He must have been starving, poor little bugger.'

'He said he tried to join the Army because of "Barry". Who's Barry?'

'Barry! It's all Barry all of a sudden.'

'You know him then?'

'Oh, yes! Jamie was on about him with me before you got here. If Barry this . . . if Barry that. . . . This wouldn't have happened if. . . . That wouldn't—'

'Who is he, though?'

'A two-year-dead soldier, that's who. Those Irish sods got him in Belfast.'

Ah. Army games. The belt of many badges. And the eyes tightly shut before Armagh news bulletin.

'Was he your boyfriend?'

'Him! Christ, no.'

'Well how did Jamie know him?'

'Well . . . I did let him take me out a couple of times. But he was very . . . indrawn, if you know what I mean. But he still used to come round our place and talk all hours to Jamie. Quite useful as a baby-sitter, really.'

'What did they talk about?'

'All the old soldier chat.'

Remembering, she put her dark head back against the sombre wall.

'Armalite rifles,' she went on, '. . . no-go areas . . . the Ardoyne . . . Provisionals. All that. As far as Barry was

246

concerned by then I could've stood there starkers and he wouldn't so much as bloody noticed.'

So. An old wound there, Chris thought. The girl, not much older than the older 'children' at Kingston House was fumbling in the chunky leather handbag hanging from her shoulder.

'I don't care what it says on that wall,' she said. 'They can come and nick me for all I care. I'm dying for a fag and that's all about it.'

He shook his head as she offered him one first and she lit up a Silk Cut.

'This Barry was probably the first person who ever took the time to talk to Jamie properly,' Chris probed with.

He saw resentment climb into her face but she had enough honesty not to deny her own guilt.

'Could be,' she said.

'Why didn't Jamie tell us this?' he wondered.

'You tell me.'

'Had he known Barry long – before he took you out?'

'Don't think so. Not to talk to. He must have seen him around, I suppose.'

'Oh, Barry lived locally.'

'Yeah. His mum and dad had a shop. Right round the corner. They moved, of course, after he bought it.'

He had a sudden, totally clear perception of the whole situation. It was, in a sense, absurdly simple.

'The parents' shop – it was a newsagents.'

He didn't even make it a question.

'Well, of course,' she said, 'the one he tried to burn down.'

He shut his eyes a moment as if in acknowledgement of his own blindness. What a black comedy of missed perceptions! What a near tragedy of garbled communication. Non-communication. Messages received and not understood. Three simple questions of Jamie a few weeks back and the whole performance of the running away, the stolen pills, would never have occurred. And a boy's in-turning grief could have been ministered to. His troubled, confused mind healed. Three simple questions. He hadn't put them to him. He hadn't sat down and talked, circled around, until he'd known which ones were the three that counted. It was no excuse that, day to day, Bill Hutton had always been closer to the boy. The old story that there hadn't been sufficient time – sufficient time to put two and two together – was no excuse.

'Thank you,' he said to the sister. 'I think that makes things a good bit clearer to me.'

'I thought you knew,' she said.

'No. I didn't. I should have but I didn't.'

But all right. It had been late coming. Later than necessary. But it had come in the end. Humiliatingly obvious as it seemed now, it was a huge step forward. They could surely put Jamie back on less agonised lines now. They were valid excuses – the perpetual lack of time, of funds, of qualified personnel. Better late than never could still be a positive enough philosophy to give you strength to keep on.

'I think what I've just been able to piece together in my mind may make all the difference as regards Jamie,' he said. 'I think we might finally be able to sort him out. I think we can probably keep this current escapade from involving him in any court proceedings, too.'

She was dragging on her cigarette with a nervousness that seemed out of keeping with the upswing in his own feelings.

'Well,' she said, 'something else I've just been and told him that ought to cheer him up. Me and Jeff – remember. I'm not going to marry him now.'

Was she edgy because, the supreme sacrifice made, she was as bitter as anything?

'Oh . . . I'm sorry to hear that,' he ventured, 'if it's on—'

'No need to be,' she said shortly. 'My idea. Jeff – he's all right short-term, you might say, if you know what I mean. I decided he's not the type you marry for good, though . . . even if he has knocked you up.'

She blew out smoke as she looked at Chris. It was a gesture so totally derived from bad Hollywood he found himself pitying her.

'You forget sometimes, don't you,' she said, 'how bright kids can be? Some things they can see real clear.'

Again a nervous drag. More smoke. He made himself say nothing to ensure she spoke again.

'Dare say,' she said, 'if you can straighten Jamie out a bit and make me believe it. And fix it with Old Bill. . . . Dare say I could have him back. Keep a better eye on him, maybe.'

He smiled his gladness.

'Dare say we can do all that,' he said.

⚜ ⚜ ⚜

He had unfolded and refolded the letter so many times that it had come apart into four quarters. The ink had got rubbed away and faded to next to nothing. Letters right on the folds had been frayed away altogether. But it didn't matter. He knew it by heart. He would always know it by heart. As long as he lived he would remember it.

He wondered at the bottom of his heart if that was true. Perhaps it was asking a lot. As long as he lived? Yes, he would! He owed it to Barry. He'd do it each day like homework. As high up in the VW bus' front passenger seat he stared out at the stream of thick High Street traffic, the crowds of shoppers bumping into each other along the pavements, the old girl holding them up as she waddled across the zebra crossing, he set himself his first test.

No. It was all right. He could do it without trying.

'. . . then every four months we get a five day pass' he was remembering, 'R and R they call it; Rest and Recuperation.'

Yes, it was all coming easy. In his mind he could see where each word was on the page.

'Back to Blighty. Should give us a chance to have some chats. What else is news? Lots of patrols, lots of rain, little else to report. . . . Glad you like the—'

'Why didn't you say that newsagent's had been where Barry lived.'

Mr Langley interrupting him. Almost as if he'd known what he'd been thinking. And he didn't know quite what to say. It was hard to put into words how he'd wanted to keep

249

Barry dead all to himself even more than Barry alive. What they'd had had been something just between the two of them. Barry had said so. When the rotten bastards had killed him it'd been up to him to keep things just like Barry would've wanted them. That was part of it. But you couldn't say that. He looked straight ahead out of the high up window and shrugged.

When he does that, Chris Langley thought, he's the spit and image of his sister. Better try him with something more direct.

'What happened to the pills?' he asked.

'Threw them away,' Jamie said tersely. 'No use for nothing, were they?'

Ye Gods! The heart wrenching to a stop. The ice in the stomach. The prayers to a God you didn't believe in but prayed to anyway. The questionings. The almost ceaseless searching. For them. For the body. And now this anti-climax.

'Bet you tried one first.'

He might as well tell Mr Langley the truth there. Not much point not.

'Wasn't half bitter,' he said.

It had been. It had scared him half to death. Made him realise what dying might be like. Getting all doubled up and stiff. Rotting like maggot's meat. You wouldn't really end up meeting Barry somewhere else.

'Tell me about Barry, Jamie.'

'He was a Marine Commando.'

He'd said it without thinking. It had just come out.

'Forty-Second Commandos,' he said.

As he'd said it, he might as well get it quite right. They were going faster now and the trees whizzing by were making him feel giddy.

'What was he like?'

'He was all right.'

'Like an all right brother?'

'Yes. I used to pretend he was. It was him got me my paper round. . . . I heard it on the wireless. No one ever told me, you know. Not them. I just heard it. 'Another service-

250

man has been shot dead in South Armagh. Marine Barry Clark of the. . . ." '

Chris stole a sideways glance from the road. The boy's voice had thickened. The cords to his locked throat were tautly visible as, his head held high, he stared grimly ahead.

'. . . Barry . . .' he said.

Chris aimed to force a crisis.

'It must have been a hard way to find out,' he said.

His remark hung unanswered as the bus whirred tinily on.

'He was shot on a Sunday,' Jamie said out of nowhere. 'I got a letter from him on the Tuesday. Nobody remembers him now.'

'You do, Jamie.'

'Yes. I do.'

And with that, after two years, something cracked. The cenotaph that Jamie had so stolidly built up split asunder. The dam was breached. The pent up tears of those two years came flooding forth in a paroxysm of silent, unchecked weeping. Chris said nothing. Nothing needed to be said. What was suddenly very necessary was to swervingly correct their abrupt collision course for a parked Fiat station wagon as, equally dumbly, Jamie slid like an animal across the bus's old bench seat to bury his face against Chris's side. Touch, tear-blinded animal touch, was all he needed now and the steering wheel corrected, Chris freed his left arm to put it encirclingly around the boy. They were on to a stretch of by-pass now. The road ahead was straight. Now that the tears had come, Chris began to hope, Jamie's route into the future might be broader, less twisted too. He let the boy cry on.

'They never talked about him,' he sniffled out at last directly into Chris's rib cage. 'His own mum and dad. They never said a word.'

Chris drew a deep breath.

'That doesn't mean too much,' he risked.

The boy's tear-streaked face came wanly up. For a moment, perhaps from his surprise, the tears had ceased to flow.

'What do you mean?' he said suspiciously.

Chris rescued his left arm.

'I think you're probably being unfair to them,' he said.

'How?'

'Sometimes things are too painful to talk about. People don't talk much about them because it hurts. He was their only son, wasn't he? They did move away. They didn't say anything or talk about it but I think they moved away because they couldn't bear to go on living there any more.'

He drew another deep breath then played his ace.

'I mean, Jamie,' he said, 'you didn't talk about it either, did you?'

Astonished, the boy lifted his slumped body upright. He had never had that simple thought and it stunned him now. Oh God what a near tragedy of a farce, of unperceived obviousness, he thought again: adults and children stumbling lunatically around each other blindfolded by grief. But a happy resolution possibly in sight. Jamie's red eyes were wide-open now as, the idea of two parents stricken by an untold sorrow still dumbfounding him, he was rescued from the tyranny of his own point of view. He had cried once. He would cry more times. But henceforth the tears would be for a shared grief and, Chris knew, a grief shared carries seeds of healing in those tears.

That knowledge allowed him to relax a moment and then, as he turned the corner into Albany Road his hands, as of their own volition, were tightening on the wheel again. The better to help him concentrate on a new crisis. It was incredible. He had thought for a second, several seconds, the man was joking. There was a line in Longfellow about someone whom something disaster followed fast, followed faster. He had suddenly felt that that was him. Poe it was, not Longfellow. The sergeant had almost said the same thing.

He had finished his chat with Jamie's sister. Doors of sorts had finally seemed to be opening for the boy. Together they had taken the few paces to the interview room to collect him. He had actually had the door open, had had the satisfaction of seeing Jamie look up from the wolfing down of what turned out to have been his second plate of bangers and mash and, reassured, smile. At that moment he had heard footsteps in the corridor and glancing back seen the Desk Sergeant hastening towards them. Patricia McEvoy had instantly cupped her half-finished cigarette in her curled palm and held it down behind her back. He had had time to be amused and touched by that. The action had been performed so smoothly he knew that as a schoolgirl she must have done it on dozens of occasions when the Deputy Head had suddenly appeared around the far corner of the bicycle sheds.

The sergeant had coughed once and sniffed rather loudly to show he wasn't fooled but, experienced as he was, said nothing. About that. Instead, he had nodded at the door.

'Might be as well to shut the door a second, Mr Langley,' he had said.

Chris had done that on an immediate reflex and still not lost his sense of optimism. But the Sergeant had been shaking his head.

'Never rains but it pours sometimes, does it, Mr Langley,' he had said.

'What is it?'

'Forewarned's forearmed. Thought I might mark your card. Just had a complaint over the phone. The mother's coming in shortly to make it formal.'

'Complaint? About—'

'Seems she's claiming one of the older boys from Kingston House assaulted her daughter yesterday evening. One who limps.'

Chapter Seventeen

VERY OCCASIONALLY AND in his absence, Wendy Raeburn would make use of Chris Langley's office. It gave her the chance of being alone with herself for twenty minutes and in that time she could usually take care of the mercifully small amount of paperwork — laundry lists, breakages, the odd report on a child — that came her way. It was not often, however, she found herself hemmed in by the filing cabinets alone in there, pen poised over the cheap desk with its cracking varnish. When there was a knock and, before she could reply, John Graydon's head appeared around the door, she knew at once he had come looking for her especially. She did not find the thought so totally displeasing.

'Chris, you've changed — and from where I stand a lot for the better,' he said.

'I'm very pleased for your sake that you should be having such a conventionally healthy reaction,' she said as she put down the pen. 'You'll lose out on the Personal Columns but by and large things will run much smoother for you.'

As once before with a twist-jump he had athletically sat himself on top of the grey filing cabinet. His plain, low-heeled boots were as immaculate as usual. There was a sheen to his semi-long hair that announced he had washed it that morning. She found she was glad of the interruption.

'What made you decide to apply for the post of Warden in a Care Centre?' she said, playing up to her apparent position of authority.

He grinned broadly. It stretched wide his moustache in a rather nice way, she thought.

'The money,' he said. 'The fabulous personal fortune I could thereby be certain of amassing.'

'Plus London weighting.'

'I think that's rather more than my basic, actually,' he

254

said. 'No, couple of reasons I looked in. I was just passing, as they say, and, er, well, the two—'

'Fancy a cup of coffee?'

'Downstairs?'

'Yes.'

'In just a moment, I'd love one. But two things first while we're alone. First I thought I'd give you a quick unofficial report on how Dean's got through his first few days with . . . them.'

Oh. She felt a tiny, trusting hand clutch at her heart and shiny boots were suddenly of the smallest importance.

'Er . . . well, it could be worse,' John was continuing. 'Not much perhaps, but there's no suggestion of violence. I've been in there every other day to make bloody sure they get the message that there better not be. All the other problems are still there – the bed-wetting, worse if anything as far as I can judge, the almost total passivity. Fortunately from a short-term point of view the most impressive bit of furniture in the house is a God knows how many inches across television and he spends hour after unblinking hour with his little eye-balls glued to that. God alone knows what it's doing to the part of his mind that hasn't already been scarred for life but at least it keeps him out from under their feet.'

'Well . . . I suppose . . . if it helps him blend with the furniture and they get used to him being around. . . . Can they afford the tele?'

'Fair amount of money around. Surprising amount, even. He's working as a van roundsman for a meat-pie, sausage outfit. I should think the fiddles are legion. And talking of furniture – you should see it! All Lewisham High Street carpets and Capital Radio warehouse bargain buys!'

He thought for a moment.

'Still,' he went on, 'that's what it usually is, isn't it. We mustn't get superior. . . . Only if people had nicer things around them, they'd be nicer too, wouldn't they. If things are cheap, well, life is. Right?'

She wasn't sure about that.

'So it's not all . . . gloom, regarding Dean?' she said.

He crossed his right leg over his left, swung his boots in a slight arc.

'I think we might just start to be guardedly optimistic,' he said. 'Very early days yet, of course, but if we can get him the right schooling next year, it may be a case of while there's life there's hope.'

Like her he had realised the darker implication of his last remark and was hurrying on.

'Anyway,' he said, 'item number two. Our date next Saturday. It is confirmed, I take it.'

It was not a question. Neither was it arrogant.

'You must have forgotten,' she said. 'You're picking me up at seven.'

It took him by pleasant surprise.

'I am?' he said. 'Oh, right. I am. A meal, though? Pictures? Or—'

'Why don't we just see how the mood strikes us Saturday?' she said.

'Fine!' he smiled. 'In fact – great!'

He jumped down from the cabinet.

She realised that for no reason – for every reason, perhaps – she felt happy. Just that – simply happy.

'And now,' John was saying, 'there being only shop and small talk left which Mrs Wilson is welcome to drop eaves on, how about that coffee?'

She was actually in the process of getting up when the door suddenly opened and a frowning Chris Langley strode in. He had managed two preoccupied paces into the room before their presence registered upon him.

'Jamie!' she exclaimed. 'Something bad has happened.'

His face softened. The worry momentarily passed out of it.

'Jamie's fine,' he said. 'I've just brought him back. At this moment he's down with Mrs Wilson enjoying what I think is his third square meal of the day. And more to the point and better, more by luck than judgement, I've stumbled across what is obviously the root of his problem. And I do mean obvious. It's a classic example of how things, important things, get lost in our everyday wash.'

'What—'

'I'll tell you later. Right now there's something else. You won't. . . . Wendy, let's change places. I think I need the moral support of being formally behind my desk.'

Shufflingly they did as he had requested. He sat down.

'It's good finding you both here,' he said. 'Part of me is still in shock. If there'd been a day's gap in between I think I could have taken it in my stride. But the timing, the coincidence was so unbelievable. I was picking up Jamie. Everything was clicking into place. I'd got some really good vibrations from the sister. I was on the point of leaving. This policeman comes up to me and tells me a complaint has just started to come in. One of our boys has apparently assaulted a girl in Sandy Lane Park.'

Wendy felt a rod of ice pierce rigidly down from her throat into her stomach. She sensed what was coming and it was like a dark bullet already fired and unavoidably aimed at her. Guilt flushed sickly through her. She had pointed the rifle and pulled the trigger herself.

'Assault!' John Graydon had exclaimed. 'You mean rape?'

'No, thank God. But bad enough. Apparently he struck her. Half knocked her head off.'

'Who did?'

'I say "boys" but that's less than accurate. The "boy" in question is—'

'Howard,' Wendy said.

Surprised out of his state of half-stunned shock Chris Langley looked up sharply.

'How did you know that?' he said.

Wendy swallowed as she gathered herself. The bullet, arriving, had proved to be a dark stone. It had shattered the bright shining windowpane of her happiness in a splintering second. Then, mysteriously, it had replaced her heart.

'There's something I have to tell you,' she said. 'A confession. Something I should have told you before. It's quite a major confession, actually. A few—'

She became aware of movement behind her. She turned sideways. John Graydon was moving to the door. It was a movement requiring an exit line.

'It doesn't sound as though, being non-staff, so to speak,' he said, 'I'm really necessary—'

'No!' Wendy said with a shrill suddenness that took her by surprise. She seemed not to have complete control over her voice. It was taking its fluttering from her pulse.

'In view of what we were just talking about, John,' she said, 'I think it might be a good idea if you stayed. Just for a moment anyway.'

She looked at her superior behind the desk.

'If it's all right with you,' she said.

Chris Langley looked from her to John and back again. He seemed bemused. The way she had put it really left him very little option.

'All right,' he said. 'What the hell is it that—'

'A few days ago,' Wendy said, 'I was in the big airing cupboard upstairs. Howard came in. He . . . he made a grab at me.'

She saw the lines about Chris Langley's mouth tighten.

'And you never told me?' he said intently.

'Wait – there's more. Worse. He tried to kiss me but he'd really no sooner touched me than he'd sprung back as if I were on fire. Only he was. He was blushing beetroot red.'

She could feel that she was now. Her voice had levelled out at a flat, slightly hesitant monotone.

'He just stood there. He couldn't speak. Couldn't go away. Couldn't come forward again.'

Picturing it again made her voice break with an urgent pity.

'He was so ashamed! So . . . so humiliated! I . . . I felt sorry for him. I couldn't let him go away like that.'

She steadied herself. Chris was looking at her like an expressionless Grand Inquisitor.

'I went up to him. I let him put his arms around me. I let him kiss me. I tried to show him how to kiss me properly. He had no idea you see.'

She'd said it. Her mouth felt as dry as chalk and yet she was swallowing. And Chris was letting his breath out in a long sustained hiss.

He followed it with a long sustained silence.

'I—' Wendy began.

'Yes,' Chris Langley simultaneously said. 'I think it would be as well, John, if you were to leave us now.'

She had half forgotten. She turned sideways again. John Graydon was looking at her with his head a little on one side and a sadly, wondering, reproachful expression on his face. Now he was edging toward the door. He opened it, paused and looked at her.

'About seven, then,' he said softly. 'I'll have the car.'

He went out. She was left alone with Chris. He continued to look at her. And look at her. In the midst of her complete embarrassment she was abruptly able to realise that he could look quite old. He looked careworn. With good reason, God knows, she thought.

'So,' he said at last, 'you felt sorry for a sexually deprived youth and despite everything your training ever taught you decided then and there to become an instant sexual therapist!'

That was too much.

'There was no . . . no unbuttoning,' she said. 'No—'

'Known as prick-teasing I believe! Ye Gods!'

'I told him it was never going to happen again. He must put any idea of that right out of his mind. I—'

'Ha!'

'I told him that one day he'd have a girl of his own and he'd—'

'So he immediately goes out to practise what you've been preaching! Demonstrating!'

'For Christ's sake, Chris. He's not a youth. He's a young man. A cripple. A sexual cripple. He's in an agony of shame and embarrassment and, well, physical desire because of the gap between his sex urges and his, er, social graces and, er, *savoir faire* and *savoir* pretty well everything else and, well, what was I supposed to do? Go and tell him to take a cold shower? Tell him to see a priest? A G.P.? His house-master. Tell him to go and see you?'

Chris was staring at her as if he had not heard a word.

'What you were supposed to do,' he said glacially, 'would have been evident to anyone with an ounce of professional-

259

ism. You should have admonished him as pleasantly but unmistakably as possible and, in every sense, made sure you kept him at arm's-length.'

'Chris, you don't understand! He was humiliated beyond words! I couldn't send him away and make it ten times worse for him. Destroy him with women – as a man – perhaps, forever. I couldn't.'

'You could have and you should have.'

'You weren't there! You don't know how he—'

'Of course I know! I'm a man, too, aren't I? I was his age. I went through all that, give or take. Do you seriously think—'

'You were never a cripple!'

That seemed to bring him up short for a moment.

'All right,' he said eventually and more moderately, 'it's true Howard has a doubly bad deal and the age he's currently at is the one where he's going to feel it more painfully than at any other time in his life. But, God damn it, that is a fact of his life and there's nothing we can do about it but privately blame his Maker. The immediate fact seems to be that your short-term instant remedy has precipitated a crisis potentially far more damaging to him than the humiliation you stupidly thought you'd save him from.'

'I—'

'The things you were taught in your training, you know – about personal involvement and so on – they're arbitrary, you know. There's a damn good rhyme and reason for them! They work. However imperfect they often seem, they work better—'

He broke off. A further thought had struck him.

'I suppose you are prepared to assure me that your conduct in all of this – what you physically did – was motivated by a wish to quote help him unquote that was purely disinterested?'

She hadn't thought he'd actually ask that question. But he had. She realised she'd been dreading it all along. She could feel her face flinching as, determined to be as truthful as her confusion allowed, she drew herself upright.

'The moment I found myself wondering that – wondering if I'd crossed over some line myself – was the moment I told him that was enough and that we had to stop,' she said.

She was positively frightened by the reaction to her words. Chris Langley seemed to explode on to his feet. His chair crashed back and would have toppled over had it not smashed into the radiator right behind. He was glaring at her unblinkingly but she had never seen such a flux of emotion working across his face. Abruptly he had wheeled about and his back to her was staring out of the window. He remained like that a long time. When finally he turned again he had resolved his feelings into one emotion. It was controlled now but it was still anger.

'I think you'd better go now,' he said quietly. 'We'll talk about this later when I know exactly what I want to say to you.'

'Yes,' she said. She turned at once and went to the door. She had almost said 'Yes, sir,' she realised, and with that thought the idea which had been gathering in her mind behind her misery seemed to become an essential. She must resign. She opened the door and went out.

⚜⚜⚜

He sat there knowing he was listening for it and making no attempt to disguise the fact from himself. He could hear all the other late morning Kingston House sounds but only unconsciously. They added up to silence. Still nothing. Then there it was: that unmistakable lurch of uneven sound that was rhythmically so unsatisfying it set your nerves on edge from the wish to do something about putting it right. Howard was coming downstairs.

Chris Langley moved from the window out of which he had been unseeingly staring for the past, waiting, seven minutes and took his seat at the desk again. He took a deep breath. The whole of his will-power must be concentrated on being as matter-of-fact with Howard as possible. Wendy was quite right. The boy's entire psyche could be wrecked by his wretchedly pathetic, his over-postponed attempt to break out of the sexless prison life had fashioned for him.

261

The thing was to play it as low-profile as the facts could possibly allow. Quite the reverse of with Wendy. The tactic there had had to be to go in hard. She had the guts to take it and the intelligence to see that her foolishness was close enough to the limit of the inexcusable to warrant how he'd treated her. He'd had to take that line in fairness to herself. Such foolishness must never be allowed to come from her again. The vital thing had been to make no bones about it at once and, putting the fear of some kind of God into her, absolutely cauterise any lingering romantic notions of tea and sympathy she might still harbour.

The dragging shuffle, the dot and miss one had reached the level of the hallway at the bottom of the stairs now. Chris swallowed. He hoped he hadn't gone over the top with Wendy. He was kidding himself if he tried to pretend his anger had all been calculated, all been tactically controlled. The gross enormity of what she'd done had got well under his nails. Sitting at this desk now he was uncomfortably aware that – what? – three per cent, say, of his reaction had been fueled by jealousy. He had all but told Wendy. Of course he knew how Howard felt. Wendy contrived to combine prettiness with a clear-cut air of sexiness. By no means always one and the same thing. And she was so nice with it. All right – part of his reaction to her bombshell had sprung straight from the fact that he too had whiled away the odd five minutes wondering what it might be like to make love to her. And he had a wife he loved whom he could climb the stairs to any time he liked and sleep next to. Or with. Howard had what he had always had – a cold, institutional bed. One he could never be sure, even at his age, he would not wet.

The shuffling ceased. There was a knock at the door.

'Come in,' he said.

The door opened. Howard came in. Chris tried to calculate the smile he gave after his look up to a nicety. Enough to take the chill off the temperature: not enough to encourage familiarity or camouflage the summons to his presence had been for official reasons. Quite clearly, Howard was already nervously on edge.

262

'Sit down, Howard,' Chris said. Howard did so. He is good looking, Chris thought, positively handsome with that weight of head. And shoulder. I certainly wouldn't want to stop one from him.

There was no virtue in protracting the misery or insulting Howard's intelligence by stalking the subject through an obviously artificial thicket of small talk.

'I hear you got into a spot of bother in the Park yesterday, Howard,' he said. 'You want to tell me about it?'

Howard straightened in the chair and seemed to freeze. He stared straight at Chris with his mouth open in fly-catching horror. Slowly at first, then with unbelievable speed he blushed. The window he faced mercilessly allowed him no disguising of the fact his fresh complexion had turned something close to a pillar-box red. Beetroot, Wendy had called it. He still sat staring, quite unmoving. Then, in a flash, as if ducking a punch, he had jerked his head down, was bent forward holding his face in his hands. For a few moments, not without embarrassment, Chris thought that he was weeping. But the shoulders were steady and not heaving. There was no sound. He realised the boy, the young man, quite literally could not face him. Or perhaps face his memories. His shame, as it would seem. What would be the colloquial way of putting it? Ah yes: the very thought of it made me go hot and cold all over.

'Just tell me about it in your own words, Howard,' he said.

The young man slowly lifted his head. White outlines of his fingers were printed on the crimson of his cheeks. For a time as he still couldn't speak, the red area seemed to bleed into the white.

'How did you find out?' he at long last said.

'Never mind right now. Just tell me the way it all seemed to happen to you.'

Howard gathered himself.

'I went up the park,' he said. 'I don't know why. To get out, I suppose. . . . No, I do know why. To see girls. . . . You don't get to meet them here, do you? Not if you're me. I mean they come in, older ones, sometimes. But they don't

263

stay like I do. . . . I mean you have daydreams, don't you? You dream, you hope that you'll be somewhere and – out walking, say, and this girl will come up to you and start talking – because she likes you, you know.'

'Yes, I know,' Chris said quietly. 'They never quite have a face, do they, the girls you think of like that. You can never quite imagine what they look like? And the girls you know so you know what they look like, can hardly ever imagine doing the things you're thinking of.'

He had been wondering if in allowing Howard to be the exception that proved the rule and stay long-term at Kingston House, they had cruelly wronged him. But it would surely have been the same for him anywhere. At least, as he could read from Howard's quick, startled look, his interruption had rightly been interpreted as a confession. Howard had been made to realise that his problem was not his alone. It was one Chris had had before him. Chris flattered himself Howard might not have found too many examples of such tact in places outside the Home.

'So,' he said, 'you went to the park. . . .'

'Yes. It was quite nice while the sun was out. There were these three girls sitting on a bench. The sort that's just a plank, like. They were about as old as me. Bit younger, maybe. It's hard to tell with girls. The path went right by them . . . I felt . . . embarrassed walking by them but . . . I didn't want to seem chicken. Seem like I wasn't cool . . . I just kept walking. One of them was . . . pretty.

'When I got level with them I wasn't looking at them but one of them, the pretty one, called out and asked me if I had the time. They all laughed and I knew why, what she really meant, I mean, but I pretended not to and I looked at my watch and told her. She'd talked to me, see. Then I saw she had a watch on too and I thought perhaps she'd said that because she wanted to talk to me anyway.'

He stopped, looked down at his knees. The colour that came into his face now was that of a remembered anger.

'I'd gone a bit closer to them,' he said. 'The same one said would I like to sit down and rest.'

His colour deepened.

'I didn't like that,' he said. 'Because . . . you know why. If it had been a bloke I thought was taking the mick, I'd have told him to get stuffed. . . . But this was different. I still thought she was maybe taking the mick but she was a girl. I tried to make out like she wasn't to myself. . . . I said I'd like to sit down. She told one of the other girls to get up and let me. . . . Then she said something about they were going to be late for something to get rid of them. That got us left alone.

'We talked a bit. About records. About films. But I hadn't seen hardly any films. . . .'

His voice trailed away as he sought a moment in which to gather his remaining reserves of courage. His huge right fist was squirming in the cup the left hand made about it. His bravery remained constant.

'She put her hand on my leg,' he said. 'High up. She told me to put her arm round me. She – she kissed me.'

He swallowed noisily.

'She said I could, you know, have a feel . . . I did . . . I couldn't believe it . . . it was like what I'd thought about happening but never really ever thought ever could . . . then, I saw the other two coming back. I could see them coming towards us a long way away across the grass. One of them was fat. I wanted to say something to mine. To make sure I'd see her again. All of a sudden I couldn't think of anything to say. It felt good sitting with my arm round her. Made me feel I'd broken through, like, got into the game. I felt quite a big man. Proud. Her waist was ever so small. But I couldn't think of anything to say. I didn't want her to turn me down, you see, if I asked her anything direct. I reckoned she must have lots of boyfriends. I could see these other two getting nearer all the time. . . . In the end when they were real close I asked her anyway. I just asked her if she'd see me next Saturday.'

Now his hands were quite still. The knuckles on the open one were quite white and there was a massive tension in the still-life thrust of fist into braced palm.

'And?' Chris breathed.

'She said "yes" . . . I couldn't believe it. I'd really broken through . . . but then she said there was one thing. . . .'

'Yes?'

'She said there was only one thing she wanted to do on Saturdays. . . .'

Chris saw it coming. Howard gulped, ducked his head.

'Go dancing,' he said. His voice had threatened to break but, supremely, he had held it together.

'The little bitch,' Chris said to help him.

'. . . I . . . I thought she might have forgotten. But the others had nearly got there and she called out to them "Hey, guess what! Saturday night the gimp's taking me down the Lyceum." And they all started laughing.'

'So you hit her.'

Howard shook his head.

'No,' he said, 'I just stood up. I hated her. I knew she'd been having me on all along. But I just felt like crying, if you really want to know. I'd never felt so lonely. Then she said something else.'

He stopped again. His eyes blinked. His head jerked in small, staccato bobbing movements.

'Howard – what did she say?'

He shook his head.

'Howard. I need to know.'

'She said "Good riddance". She said she could tell from the way I'd been with her I . . . I . . . I wouldn't be no better in bed than I would dancing. . . .'

This time the voice did crack and break completely. This time, the face buried in the huge hands again, the shoulders did heave in rhythm with the weeping. Chris got up quickly from behind the desk and came around it. For a brief instant he rested his hand on Howard's shoulder, then slipped a handkerchief between the hands. Having grasped it, they were obliged to start using it. Chris waited a moment longer. The story was as neat a little cameo study in sadism as he'd come across for a long time. He believed every word of it. No liar could ever have exposed his nerve ends so rawly. Not at Howard's age.

'That was when you hit her?' he eventually said.

266

Howard nodded.

'A lot of times?'

Howard shook his head.

'No,' he said. 'Once.'

'You didn't blow your stack? Go berserk?'

'No! Once!'

'You hit her hard?'

'Yes. Pretty hard. Quite hard.'

'You punched her?'

'No. I hit her with my hand. Across the face. The back of my hand.'

'Did it knock her off the bench?'

'No. . . . It made her nose bleed, though.'

'So, you hit her just once quite hard with the back of your hand?'

'Yes.'

'You could have hit her the same way a lot harder?'

'Yes.'

Chris snorted his relief.

'I'd say myself you let her off pretty lightly,' he said.

Howard twisted himself around to look over his shoulder at Chris.

'You're – you're not angry?' he said.

'Not angry, no. Bitterly sorry it happened that's all. Oh – you were in the wrong to hit her. I hardly blame you. But I'd have thought still more of you if you could have held yourself together just a moment longer and walked away without doing that. You got half-way down to her level, doing that.'

He moved back to his chair.

'You know,' he said, 'there are very few girls who would have done that to you. There are very few who aren't really very nice. If it's any consolation – I know it isn't now but it will be – you weeded out the lousy one first time out. On the law of averages it'll never happen to you like that again.'

The cheap, nasty little prick-teasing opportunist, he was thinking.

Howard repeated his original question.

'How did you know about it?' he said.

'I happened to see you,' Chris lied. He did it with the casual smoothness that the combination of a good education and a position of some authority confers on certain people when lying is required.

'It must have been just afterwards. It was only from the distance but I had a hunch something like that had happened. I'm not trying to be nosey, you understand. In fact I appreciate – I very much admire – the frankness with which you've told me everything. It can't have been easy. Personal things like this never are. . . . No, it's just that if something more serious had taken place – something that could affect your future, well, it's my responsibility.'

'I've been scared stiff ever since she'd go and tell someone and it'd all come out that way,' Howard said, 'and it would all end up stopping my starting on the sandwich course next September.'

Chris could imagine. All perspective knocked for six there would have been a literally sleepless night.

'No. No,' he said. 'Not much danger of that.'

He had kept his options open but there wouldn't be. He'd guarantee it. He'd head this one off at the pass even if it cost him a week without sleep bringing the right pressure to bear on the wrong people. And he would not bring up the incident with Wendy, either. What Howard had gone through at the hands of that little bitch might be, in one regard, a blessing in disguise. It would possibly act as an unlooked for, unfortunate but highly adequate corrective. If it did not over-correct. He attempted the impossible task of fine-tuning.

'You know, Howard,' he said, 'when you get out on your course you'll find that what you're naturally looking for – some romance, a nice girl – it'll all come bit by bit. No pun intended. To start with, we're all on a hiding to nothing. We go up to someone we think we'd like holding our hearts open to and just praying they're not going to drive a knife right through it. You have to have faith. Be brave. You've just shown me you've got the right kind of courage it takes.

'As for sex itself – well it's a lot like riding a bicycle.

Awkward and painful while you're learning. Fine once you've got the knack of it and know how – just so long as you don't get over-confident and fall off.'

He winked to confirm the joke. Howard felt free to smile.

⚜⚜⚜⚜

If it were done, when 'tis done, then 'twere well it were done quickly. No time like the present. The sooner you do a thing, sooner it's over. Putting something off don't make it go away.

Wendy had tried to make an alloy of a dozen tags and meaningless old saws to steel herself into doing what she knew that she must do but which, she knew also, would cause her a sorrow so immediately acute that it could linger on her soul as a dark bruise for years to come.

But to strike while the iron is hot requires an iron. Chris Langley was not in his office. Nor anywhere that she could find in the building. The delay began to work on her. As it failed to happen, the encounter she had thought she could get through with a surface, matter-of-fact brusqueness grew more daunting in the still unachieved prospect. But she had started out. She must finish it if she could. The die once cast, she'd feel better. Flustered, a little out of breath she finally found herself doing what all of the staff at Kingston House tried to keep to a minimum – climbing the stairs to the Langley's flat.

She knocked on the baize door. Even before her knuckles made contact she had that sense you get sometimes that no-one is in. No steps came. Damn. She'd have to live with her resignation gesture a while longer. One more knock for luck, then. She raised her arm and, as if she had been working a charm with the gesture, the door opened. Robert stood there.

'Oh,' she said. 'Hello. Is your fath – is Chris in?'

'No,' he said. 'He had to go out.'

'Oh. Did he say when he—'

'He should be back quite soon, I think. He said something about having to go and see the police. Do you want to come in and wait? I was just making a cup of tea, actually.'

She was parched, actually, what with her uptightness and her searching around. She really felt like one. But she'd better get back down and keep an eye on things.

'Thanks,' she said, 'but I'd better get back down and keep an eye on things.'

'Oh come on,' he said. 'Bill's down there, isn't he? Five minutes won't hurt. I'm bored out of my skull if you really want to know. Mum's out too.'

She looked at his unformed, wise face held at a slightly oblique angle to her gaze with a studied lack of concern that did not quite convince. Yes, he was bored. The chances were, since he was thirteen, she might just escape charges of trying to compromise him.

'All right,' she said. 'If it's quick. Five minutes won't hurt, I suppose. Thanks.'

He stood aside to let her into the cluttered, much lived in main room. Scattered cushions, books, isolated cups revealed that ordered housework took a distinctly low priority in the flat's daily comings and goings. A Penguin was open on the table. *War and Peace*.

'Who's reading this?' Wendy asked.

'I am. Come in the kitchen while I make it.'

'You are!' She was highly surprised. 'I've never got around to it,' she said. 'How do you like it?'

'It's all right. Very good, in fact. Worse thing about it is the print, actually. So small and grey.'

'Well, there's a lot to squeeze in, I suppose.'

They went into the too-small kitchen which did not look like something out of *Good Housekeeping*. Robert started to make the tea.

'So you're bored,' Wendy said. 'I suppose it must get a bit lonely here in a funny sort of way.'

He shrugged.

'A bit,' he said. 'Sometimes.'

'Well, it's not quite a normal home, is it?'

'A bloody sight more normal than they have to put up with down there – however much you may try to pretend otherwise.'

She saw him dart her a quick, anxious look. She knew he was worried that he'd offended her.

'No denying that,' she said quickly. 'I mean no-one's a bit worried about taking five minutes off from keeping an eye on you.'

'Right,' he said. 'Most of the other kids at school don't know how the other half live. Not really. I'm lucky, you see, that way. Here. One cup of tea coming up.'

He poured it out. It came out very weak.

'Pretty weak,' he said, 'I should've let it stand longer. Shall I—'

'I like it weak,' she said.

He grinned his disbelief at her.

'I'll believe you,' he said. 'Thousands wouldn't. I'll have that one.'

'Robert!' she said. 'You're just like your father.'

'Well I could do worse, couldn't I?' he said.

He looked at her.

'I mean he tries, doesn't he?' he said. 'We may not have a TR 7 or a swimming pool in the garden but at least he's not all fat and an estate agent or some sort of dead from the neck up commuter. Sugar?'

'No thanks.'

'Wish he wouldn't be so sort of off-beat noble, sometimes,' Robert said, 'if you know what I mean. Makes it hard for me to know what I want to do and all that.'

He grinned.

'Anarchist's a good bet,' he said. 'Push drugs. Nick mum's prescription forms, a spot of forgery and bang, I'm in business. Here, talking of swimming pools, how about sponsoring me for our school swim?'

'So that's why you asked me in.'

'Right. Diabolical plan. So much a length, whatever you like, times as many lengths as I can swim in half an hour. I've got the form here.'

She looked him hard in the eye. His round schoolboy face had gone suspiciously dead-pan angelic.

'I've got a feeling that when it comes to swimming you're a bit useful,' she said. 'And how big's the pool?'

He laughed out loud.

'If I'm like dad,' he said, 'you're a dead ringer for mum sometimes. I suppose that's why dad reckons you so much. He says you're the best housemother he's had since the legendary Mrs Ames. It's a standard pool but I am quite good so what about 1p a length? Can't do much damage, can it? It's for Multiple Sclerosis.'

'All right,' Wendy said. '1p.'

As she signed the form she had to make a considered effort to stop her hand shaking. For a short while, talking to Robert, her mind had actually been diverted from the single, overriding preoccupation that, to the exclusion of everything else, had been cruelly dominating her churning thoughts. She had behaved quite irresponsibly. It might have been on impulse but she had put Howard at grave emotional risk; caused him untold mental damage, perhaps. There was no putting it right but, by resigning she could at least atone to Chris. She could go back home and have a good, long, hard think about her future. She had made that decision and, in a way, it had helped. It had been the first paper-thin layer of scar tissue over the wound.

Now the fresh tissue had been ruptured. With the effect of a jolt of delicious agony the length of her nervous system, his son had off-handedly indicated she possessed – or had possessed – Chris Langley's esteem. It . . . it made it suddenly all seem a bit different. Was she just possibly over-reacting? Acting like a schoolgirl or something out of a woman's magazine all over again? Was there something gushy, soft, about resigning. . .?

She looked away from Robert and out of the window over the sink. The day was getting on. The low sun was behind a thick range of clouds. Everywhere else they were grey but where they concealed the sun they were turned into the sombre pink-purple of a bruise. Very romantic. She tried to assess whether it were virtuous or self-indulgent to spend a long future constantly fingering and refingering such a bruise on her own soul when it had arguably been self-inflicted.

'Who was Mrs Ames?' she heard herself say. 'She may be a legend to you but I don't think I've ever heard of her.'

'I don't really know,' Robert said. 'Before my time. But she's the one dad swears he learnt all he knows from.'

'All?' Wendy said, 'I doubt that. Drunk it anyway, you see.' She put down her empty cup.

'Another?'

'Thanks. I'd better get back.'

'Didn't like it then, did you!'

'Terrible. Never had such a lousy cup. Or such an expensive one, either.'

'Come again. Any time.'

'Thanks. I will. No, don't move. I'll let myself out.'

She picked her way across the living room and opened the door. Halfway up the stairs was Chris Langley. She felt herself tense and saw him fractionally check his upward stride.

'Oh,' she began. 'I was—'

'It's going to be all right with Howard,' he said at once. 'Regarding the law. I had a long talk with him. He was much more sinned against than sinning. He had the rotten luck to fall into the clutches of a right little madam. I've had a talk with both the police and—'

He broke off to turn and see what was causing the scrambling up rush of noise upon the lower stairs. The answer was immediate. Two steps at a time, John Graydon came bounding into view.

'Sorry about the low-profile on decorum,' he panted, 'but I've got to be over the Fairlight estate in ten minutes ago. The thing is. . . .'

He stopped, looked suddenly embarrassed. His eyes flicked their focus from Chris to Wendy and back again to Chris.

'Thing is,' he repeated, 'I know it was all going on a bit this morning but, well, as I'd heard a bit, well, you know, I wondered if I could help in any way. It sort of rang a faint bell somewhere. So, I went down the nick and had an off the record word with Len Hadleigh down there and he told me what Howard was supposed to have done. Who'd charged

273

him. Well, thing is – this girl, this Denise Potter, saving your reverence, Wendy, she's just about the biggest punch in town. Denise Roundheels, more like. She's already on probation for an—'

He stopped. Chris had been nodding for some time.

'I've been doing exactly the same thing,' he said. 'In fact it's obviously been a classic duplication of effort.'

Even as she began to breath more easily Wendy could notice that sheer fatigue seemed to be keeping any note of jubilation out of Chris' voice.

'I went round to the girl's home,' he was saying. 'I had a word with her mother. They've dropped the charge.'

Thank God, Wendy thought.

'Blimey, you've done more than I've managed, then,' John said. 'But that's why I came. Great. Good, then. . . . Here – why d'you think they were set on making such a thing out of it?'

'There's no indignation quite so righteous as that of a villain who thinks he's got the law on his side at last,' Chris said. 'It took quite a while, believe me. I told them the charge would be contested all the way up the line and the police were considering bringing a charge against the girl for soliciting.'

'Are they?'

'No.'

John leaned back against the wall and let out his breath.

'Crafty sod,' he said. 'So all's more or less well that ends well.'

'Setting aside the trifling question of Howard's well-being,' Chris said with a hard look at Wendy, 'yes.'

He shifted the angle of his head slightly.

'Was there something you wanted to see me about, Wendy?' he said.

The moment she knew he knew exactly what had been on her mind all day and when she'd climbed the steps. She could feel John looking at her as intently as Chris. But all right, she could tell a white lie as well as the next man.

'No,' she said, 'I've just been signing on the dotted line

for Robert. He's inveigled me into sponsoring him on his Cross Channel swim.'

There was a space of two of her heartbeats before Chris curtly nodded. He continued to look at her.

'It's been what we might call a cautionary tale,' he said. 'A lesson to more than one of us, I hope. As far as you're concerned, Wendy, I trust you'll do something about adjusting your attitude. We'll get along better around here without any female Don Quixote's, thank you very much.'

A touch of hardness seemed to leave his face.

'And while you're at it, you'd better do something about adjusting your hem and bra-lines. If they give me trouble at my age, God knows what they're doing for John here.'

Chapter Eighteen

IT WAS A LONG time since she could remember feeling so warm and relaxed. So comfortable. Perhaps she had never felt quite so totally, so easily, content before. She lay with her head angled across John's chest and felt its steady rise and fall. It was steady now. Earlier she had felt his pulse beating with a possessed wildness. Yet even then there had been no sense of strain. With no sense of panic or of competition they had fallen perfectly into step with each other in their love-making.

She stared across the tiny bed-sitter. It was an attic-room − a servant's once in the days when the big house facing the heath had boasted such. It was pretty crummy in a way. Small. Anonymous. John had said he was looking for something better. He had said the daytime view was glorious but as she'd drawn the curtain upon the darkness outside, she had had to take his word for that. Within, the only touch of character had been John's surprisingly expensive looking hi-fi system.

And the sloping ceiling. Towards the end of the room the ceiling of the one-time attic followed the line of the pitched roof. It imparted that hint of artist's garret, of escape to a left bank of life, to romantic poverty. She scrunched up still tighter against John's lean, bare flank and looked up at the sloping ceiling with her top, right eye. It was near to midnight but for some reason Rod Stewart's *Sunshine on my Shoulder* was running dreamily through her mind. Romantic. That word again. She must beware of it. But she had a feeling that she was going to remember the way that ceiling dipped down to meet the peeling wallpaper top for a long, long time to come.

Her right arm was diagonally across John's body. His right arm was underneath and round her. Gently, abstract-edly almost, it seemed, he was stroking her waist with the outside of his thumb. She felt sleepy but not like sleeping. She sighed with pleasure.

'John,' she said, 'I didn't say before. It was . . . nice of you to take the thought to go to all that trouble on my behalf – running around to see how bad things were against Howard.'

For a breathless moment he squeezed her crushingly right into him.

'Perhaps I thought you were worth doing it for,' he said. 'Perhaps I even thought that if—'

The phone he had had to have especially installed shrilled its interruption to his joke. She felt the exasperation run through his body.

'Has to be trouble,' he said. 'At this hour. Hang on.'

With difficulty he drew his arm out from underneath her. He swung himself out of the narrow bed and loped across to the phone.

'Hello?' he said. 'Yes?'

Wendy slid herself sideways face-downwards into the centre of the bed. Where John had been lying it was deliciously warm against the whole length of her body.

'Right,' he was saying. 'Yes.'

There was something very flat, very subdued in his voice.

'Twenty minutes. At the outside,' he said.

He put down the phone. He turned to look at her.

'That was Chris,' he said in the same tone of voice. 'He said he had some bad news.'

What on earth?

'What?' she said.

'He said it was something he'd rather talk about face to face.'

✛✛✛

Once more the cramped office was over-full. Bill Hutton, a faded brown tartan dressing gown over his pyjamas, was wedged into a corner by the door. John was lounging against the brown filing cabinet. Wendy was in the mockery of a visitor's chair. Unusually for this location and an indication, almost certainly, of the seriousness of the occa-

277

sion, Pat Langley was present too. She was leaning against the wall on the other side of the doorway from Bill. That meant she was directly facing her husband.

Chris was sitting on the radiator behind his desk. The big, curtainless window was immediately behind him.

'It's bad news,' he said simply. 'The worst possible. Dean is dead.'

Wendy felt an electric surge of anguish rush through her. The room reeled giddily about her but she was rooted. She was transfixed by the nails driven through her heart and through her throat. There had been a 'clump' of some kind. She realised that straightening up with shock, John Graydon had pushed completely shut a just left open drawer in the filing cabinet. She realised he had gone utterly white. It must have been his breath she had heard hissing out. Unless it had been her own.

Chris had paused but, so stunned were they, no-one had so much as cried out one word.

'I heard about two hours ago,' he went on. 'From the police. It's all that we feared. The wife has made a full statement. Pat knows about it already. The rest of you had better all take a grip on yourselves. It's a terrible story.

'The wife says that up until tonight neither she nor her husband laid a finger on Dean. However . . . all along—'

'Oh no!' Wendy cried out. 'He wasn't beat—'

'I'm afraid so, Wendy,' Chris Langley said. 'If you'd rather not hear the details, I'm sure Pat will—'

'No,' she gulped. 'No. Sorry. I'd rather stay. I'll be all right.'

It was part of her job to be whether or not her blood had turned to water.

'But – yesterday . . . I was there,' John Graydon said. 'He was fine. He was . . . alive.'

Pat Langley stiffened. He hasn't quite let it sink in yet, she thought. Better watch out for when it has.

'This evening there was a flash point, it seems,' Chris said. 'All along, ever since Dean went back home, they'd been upset by his bed-wetting. It was messy, a drag, all the rest of it. No reason for it, they'd think. No excuse.'

His voice became tighter.

'This evening his father got a bright idea. An instant cure. He'd give the boy a lesson that would put a stop to wetting the bed for good and all. He got a beer mug. In front of Dean he filled it up with his own urine. Then he gave it to Dean and told him to drink it.'

'No!'

'Yes, Wendy. The wife was there too. She says Dean understood what he was supposed to do. He took the glass and then without saying anything threw it down over his father's trousers and shoes. The father apparently just went berserk. He punched Dean once and knocked him down. Out, too, the wife thinks. She says he never made a sound. Then he bent down, picked Dean up and just threw him across the room. As hard as he could. They've got one of those low, flat stereo things, it seems. Dean's head went right onto the corner of it. Multiple skull fracture.'

As if in some macabre way the sound of that unspeakable impact of bone on wood had been stored up on tape by a malign Fate and now played back to them, a violent detonation of noise crashed savagely in upon Wendy's fixed, horror-stricken, clear-picturing imagination. She whipped her head round. John Graydon had smashed a full-force body-blow of a punch into the side of the filing cabinet. His eyes were staring. He seemed quite oblivious to what he must have inflicted on his hand.

'I'll kill him,' he croaked hoarsely. 'I'll kill him. The swine! I'll kill the swine of a bastard. I don't care—'

'You'll do no such thing, lad,' a voice rapped out. It was Bill Hutton. Wendy had forgotten he was there.

'I will. I swear. I'll seek—'

'You won't and you know it!' Bill said. 'You'll shut up this minute, stop that line of thought at once and get on with doing your job!'

'What job? Seeing old ladies get their pension books sent to them? Seeing kids—'

'You'll control yourself now,' Chris Langley said, 'so that when you appear in the witness box to testify against Holder your statement carries the maximum weight and force. You won't in any way have undermined your own professional status, nor lost any of the passion you have now. You'll just have it under control. Pressurised.'

He had spoken less loudly than Bill Hutton. Softly even. But his voice had cut through John Graydon's outburst. And the frantic look had gone out of his eyes. With reason, Pat thought. There had been a quality of menace in her husband's tone which she had never heard before. It had made her shiver. She knew he had dedicated himself in the past two hours to seeing that, however inadequate a balancing any retribution must be, justice of a sort would be done.

John had turned toward the filing cabinet. He had put both arms on its top and hung his head down between them. The right hand was already visibly swollen. She must check it for the almost certain break before he left tonight.

'All right,' John Graydon's muffled voice now said, 'I'm sorry. Of course you're right. I can't descend to their level or it never ends. It's just. . . .'

'I know,' Chris Langley said. 'I know.'

'How did it finish, Chris?' Bill Hutton said.

'A neighbour heard the . . . the thud. She came and knocked on the door. They—'

'Mrs Crowhurst,' John muttered. 'I'd asked her to keep her ears open for any ill-treatment. God! Ill-treatment, I said! I didn't say bloody murder!'

'Come on, John. It doesn't help.'

'It won't help Dean, no!'

Chris ignored that.

'The husband, Holder, wouldn't let her in. But the wife had called for an ambulance. Dean was dead when it arrived. There was no way it could look like anything other than what it was. The ambulance crew called the police.'

Wendy heard a sound of crying. It was not her. It was John. He had folded his arms on the top of the filing cabinet and buried his head in them. His shoulders were shaking. Nobody spoke. Pat Langley walked over to him and looked at the hand he had smashed into the metal of the cabinet. He let her without otherwise moving.

'I was there last night. He was alive,' he said.

Silently, softly, to herself, Wendy had begun to cry. She had remembered something. She had taken her handbag with her to the restaurant that night. She had had it with her at John's place. Naturally she had brought it on with her now. It must have happened while we were eating, she thought. While we were making love he was already dead. She looked down at the handbag that was at her feet. In it was a keepsake, a souvenir, a good luck charm. A cheap, nasty, gimcrack toy. A tiny green frog.

'Holder's already been charged with manslaughter,' Chris said. 'They're holding him down there.'

John Graydon straightened up. He turned round. He was under some measure of control again. Or rather, indignation was beginning to get the upper hand of grief again.

'So what will that all boil down to?' he said. 'Five years probation? A two year suspended sentence? I—'

'John. There's—'

'I'll tell you this for nothing – at the end of the day, after all the trials, all the inevitable bloody enquiries, it won't be us who come out of it smelling like a rose. Those fat, unthinking magistrates who decided it was in Dean's "best interests" for him to go home and be murdered, that self-important, bloody woman of a psychiatrist who said it was O.K., that smooth hireling mouthpiece of a two-faced solicitor who was, of course, just presenting a brief to the best of his ability and to its own best bloody advantage – none of them are going to miss a bloody beat in going on to do the same damned thing next month or next year. Tomorrow. Their bloody professional bodies, the bleeding Law Society, the BMA and whatever'll close ranks so fast it'll make the Trooping of the Colour look like bloody Playschool.'

'He could be right there, Chris,' Bill Hutton said.

'Of course I'm right! It'll be me, the social worker on

the case, who ends up the villain of the piece. Me and Kingston House.'

'John, don't get hysterical,' Chris said sharply. 'How can that be given the line we took at the hearing?'

'They're organised professionally. We're not. The devil has all the best P.R. these days. They'll find a way of twisting, just you mark—'

'Do we have to talk about things like that now?' Wendy heard herself saying. 'Please. Dean's dead.'

'Yes. You're right, Wendy,' Chris said.

'And we know what happened, don't we? We know we all tried so hard. That has to count for something, doesn't it, however little?'

'Yes. I'm sorry, Wendy,' John Graydon said.

'I think it might be an idea if we all went up to the flat and had a warm drink or two,' Chris said. 'Cocoa, brandy – whatever you want. O.K. Pat?'

'Of course. Except that it'll have to be whisky.'

'All right. I'd just like to say this, though, formally before we do. I promise all of you just as I've already promised myself – when the case of Dean Holder's death is brought into court, I'll make every effort to see that man receives the sentencing he deserves. I want him to have all the years he needs for an idea of the enormity he's perpetrated to dawn on him. Right now he feels only sorry for himself. In ten year's time, perhaps, he may just feel sorry for Dean.'

'I doubt it,' John said.

'We have to hope he will. There's no other place to go. . . . And another thing. I'll do everything possible in my power, within my influence to see the trial, the sentence have as big a deterrent effect as possible.'

'They won't, though, will they?' This time it was Wendy. 'Not on people like that. People like that don't think. They just . . . they're like animals. Worse.'

She began to cry again.

'Nothing you do will bring back Dean,' she struggled to say. 'And – I said what we tried must count for something but – who's to know? John's right too. The terrible thing is – there'll be more Deans. Other little children will—'

'Yes, of course there'll be more Deans!'

Chris Langley had slapped his open hand down flat upon his desk. That he could suddenly be angry in such circumstances so amazed her that she forgot to continue crying.

'Some will always fall through the net. Yes – there are going to be more poor, innocent, defenceless children who, one way or another are killed or destroyed. But there will be hundreds more Jamies and Lucilles and Ruperts and every name you like to think of that one way or another get lifted up and taken care of. The important thing is that the net should be there. And people holding it stretched out. People continually repairing it. Or why live at all? Any of us? If we don't care – someone – on behalf of everyone, well, you're left with Hitler in the end. Someone has to do it all and we're the ones who're here. No one else. What we do does count, Wendy. And that's why—'

Making all but Chris jump, the phone had rung. In that small room at that late hour its noise seemed enormous. Chris picked it up.

'Yes?'

With one hand he pulled a desk drawer open, took out a pad. John had taken a ballpoint out of his denim jacket and was leaning across to offer it to him. It seemed to be a woman's voice on the other end.

'Go ahead,' Chris said.

He jotted down a name, a couple of squiggly notes.

'O.K.,' he said. 'Got it – oh, don't hang up. As you're up, would you mind putting the kettle on. Ta.'

He hung up.

'That was Robert,' he said, 'relaying a message that came through upstairs. From the Duty Officer at Fairchild Lane. They've got a new one for us, it seems. A bit special, it seems. She's white, fourteen and apparently from a very good – that is to say "lousy rich" – family. She's well-spoken and very nicely behaved. When she's sober. She happens also to be an alcoholic. A patrol car found her in the gutter earlier this evening passed out in her own vomit. Her parents are both out.'

283

He looked at Wendy.

'Your department, Wendy,' he said. 'You've just about got time to grab that drink and do something about making yourself look human again before she gets here. That is if you care to.'

Wendy gulped as she nodded. At the back of her numbed mind was the memory, part of history now, that a few days ago she had been looking for Chris so as to resign.

'In the circumstances, it had better be coffee,' she said. 'Not Scotch.'

Chris nodded a brisk approval. He stood up. They began to go.

'Oh, John,' Chris said. They turned toward him again. He had remembered something.

'It's trite,' he said, ' cliché. It's no help or consolation to the dead but, you see, in the most trite way, we've just had proof of it. Life does go on. It does need to go on. It's trite. But it's not meaningless.'

John Graydon swallowed.

'Yes,' he said thickly. 'I know.'

'Truly?'

'Yes.'

'Then I'll tell you something. When I first heard about Dean I sat down and cried too. Ask Pat if you don't believe me.'

Pat Langley did not bother to nod.

'Come on,' she said, 'Robert needs his beauty sleep even if none of us do. And you, young man – you need an elastic bandage on that hand.'

Bill Hutton held the door open for her. They filed out of the office. Chris had locked the open cabinet and was the last to leave. He turned out the light. He bent to lock the door. The others had begun filing up the stairs but Pat waited for him. She was looking at him as he straightened and put the key ring back in his pocket and she thought that this was the man she loved and that she loved him because he could take great weights from other people and, suppressing his own griefs, his own anger, ignoring his own endless fatigue, bear those weights on his own shoulders.

He was human, very human, but by repeated acts of willpower that she chose to regard as heroic, he possessed that sort of strength to endure which could outlast all tragedy. Even such a tragedy as Dean's. Because of this man, her husband, it would be as he said. Life at Kingston House would continue when, in just a few hours now, the morning came again.

Also Available from Magnum Books

OSCAR SAUL
The Dark Side of Love

A beautiful young rich girl runs away from the wealthy parents who do not understand her. Totally adrift, lost on the streets of the city, she allows herself to be taken home by Denny, a blind newspaper seller. Grasping at any security, she knows that at least he cannot recognize and betray her.

But Denny knows who she is and plans to extract money from her parents for her safe return, a return which, for her own secret reasons, she must postpone as long as possible. What neither had bargained for was the deep, strong current of feeling which was to develop between them . . .

CHARLOTTE VALE ALLEN
Running Away

Isabel Gary is forty years old, beautiful, glamorous, talented – every woman's dream figure.

But Isabel is tormented . . . by the memory of the beloved husband who had died so tragically young . . . by the heartache of a rebellious teenage daughter who seems determined to destroy herself . . . by the growing demands of a lover who appears less and less ideal . . . by the mounting pressures of a challenging job that thrusts her into a TV world of sudden success and cut-throat competition . . . and by the magnetism of a man whom she fears to love lest her hopes be betrayed yet again . . .

WILLIAM MURRAY

The Mouth of the Wolf

A swift night-time grab on the streets of Rome signals the start of the kidnapping of young Livingstone Snow, Jr., the grandson of an American multi-millionaire. But Armand Snow refuses to pay the ten million dollars demanded in exchange for his grandson's safe return. Instead he dispatches his tough trouble-shooter, Horatio Blake – with instructions to free the boy, but on no account to pay the ransom demanded. Blake discovers there is more in this case than meets the eye and uncovers numerous intrigues as he pieces together the real truth behind the kidnapping. But Blake too is losing his perspective on events, distracted by his increasing involvement with Livingston Snow Jr.'s beautiful mother Lisa . . .

BOB RANDALL

The Fan

A dazzlingly suspenseful shocker of love, hate and fear, THE FAN unfolds its horrifying story by letting the reader in on the private correspondence of a famous movie star. Little did glamorous Sally Ross imagine that amongst the pile of letters dealt with by her tough secretary Belle there were many from one who signed himself Douglas Breen, the Fan. Nor did Belle realize that behind the calm, polite phrases of the Fan's letters lurked the crazed mind of a psychopath – a deadly killer for whom overwhelming love could turn overnight into violence and terrifying hate.

More top fiction available from Magnum Books

These and other Magnum Books are available at your bookshop or newsagent. In case of difficulties orders may be sent to:

Magnum Books
Cash Sales Department
P.O. Box 11
Falmouth
Cornwall TR10 10GEN

Please send cheque or postal order, no currency, for purchase price quoted and allow the following for postage and packing:

U.K.   19p for the first book plus 9p per copy for each additional book ordered, to a maximum of 73p.

B.F.P.O.   19p for the first book plus 9p per copy for the next 6 books, thereafter 3p per book.
& Eire

Overseas   20p for the first book and 10p per copy for each additional book.
Customers

While every effort is made to keep prices low, it is sometimes necessary to increase prices at short notice. Magnum Books reserve the right to show new retail prices on covers which may differ from those previously advertised in the text or elsewhere.